# DEADROADS

# DEADROADS

## A Novel of Supernatural Suspense

# ROBIN RIOPELLE

NIGHT SHADE BOOKS
NEW YORK

Night Shade books may be purchased in bulk at special
discounts for sales promotion, corporate gifts, fund-
raising, or educational purposes. Special editions can
also be created to specifications. For details, contact the
Special Sales Department, Night Shade Books, 307 West
36th Street, 11th Floor, New York, NY 10018 or
info@skyhorsepublishing.com.

Night Shade Books™ is a trademark of Skyhorse
Publishing, Inc.®, a Delaware corporation.

Visit our website at www.nightshadebooks.com.

10 9 8 7 6 5 4 3 2 1

Library of Congress Cataloging-in-Publication Data is
available on file.

ISBN: 978-1-59780-513-1

Printed in the United States of America

6824

For Aaron, Genny and Charlie
Storytellers all

*Le soir des noces à la veillée*
*Trois hommes noirs sont arrivés*
*Trois hommes noirs sont arrivés*
*Ont demandé la mariée*
*"La mariée n'est pas ici*
*Voulez-vous donc vous mettre à table"*
*"Nous n'voulons ni boire ni manger*
*Mais nous voulons fort bien danser"*
*À peine eurent-ils dansé trois pas*
*La mariée fut enlevée*
*La mariée fut enlevée*
*Sans que l'on puisse l'en empêcher*

*Le lendemain dans son jardin*
*Le beau galant qui s'y promène*
*Le beau galant voit arriver*
*Le Diable en forme de cavalier*
*"Oh! Dis-moi donc mon cher galant*
*Tes belles noces d'hier au soir"*
*"Mes belles noces d'hier au soir*
*Ma mariée fut enlevée"*
*"Mets donc ton pied des sur le mien*
*Je t'y ferai voir Marie ta mie*
*Je t'y mènerai, je t'y ramènerai*
*Sans aucun mal je t'y ferai"*

*Quand il fut rendu aux Enfers*
*Il aperçoit Marie sa mie*
*"Marie ma mie, j'suis-tu la cause*
*Qu'aujourd'hui si tu es ici?"*
*"Oh! Non! Oh! Non, mon cher galant*
*Ce n'est pas toi qui en es la cause*
*C'est les trois méchants frères que j'ai*
*Qui ont fait jurer de pas m'marier"*

*"L'anneau d'or que j'ai dans le doigt*
*Je t'en supplie de m'le laisser"*
*"Si tu n'y enlèves pas cet anneau-là*
*Je m'en vais t'y trancher le cou"*
*"Je n'en avais que pour trois mois*
*Trois mois et puis quelques semaines*
*Maintenant que ma bague est ôtée*
*J'en ai pour l'éternité"*

Les trois hommes noirs
*traditional*

# LUTIE, BEFORE
## Louisiana, 1992

Lutie didn't know for sure if she could catch a ghost, but she felt better about her chances with Baz at her side. Not that she was going to tell him, of course.

She'd been planning this the whole summer, requiring only two things to happen simultaneously: her father had to go away for a few days, and then someone else had to do something stupid, like choke on a chicken bone or walk into oncoming traffic.

On the seventh day of August her father left the house with a change of clothes in a bag, Sol tied to his side like a little raft. Two days later their closest neighbor, Old Robichaux, obliged with the stupidity.

When it came to ghosts, Baz scarcely paid attention, couldn't tell they were around even when they were sitting right beside him, but Lutie had an idea about music, and so she asked him anyway. All he did was complain about the heat and the fact that she was making him come out into it. He hadn't said no, though. He never said no, not to her.

Her t-shirt was a hand-me-down from Sol through Baz to her, and had been washed to a faint parchment gray, thin enough to read a newspaper through. Lutie wiped heat-sticky hands against it and thought maybe she was melting, dripping away bit by bit, not unlike the corpse in the crypt, or the land itself, disappearing into salt water beyond the levees.

Some not-so-recent hurricane had stirred up the cemetery, made a mess of the place. Lutie didn't know which storm, their names all sounded like big-city dancers. Marble boxes lay scattered about, a giant's birthday party gone wrong, some spun spell that changed the presents and the guests to stone, even the angels.

1

One looked down on her, calm chill face impossible to sex, its wings casting a sheltering shadow as though that might cool her, but Lutie didn't think angels cared much about shade or heat, or mosquitoes or any of those other things that bothered humans here on Earth. Papa had said as much. Her father hardly ever talked about angels, didn't talk about much, really, but the old domino players had told her that Aurie Sarrazin knew all there was to know about angels and devils and everything in between.

The statue's shade was a happy accident, Lutie understood, geography and astronomy come together, not anything more than that. *Better if dem angels don't make notice of you, ma pousinette,* Papa had whispered to her with a whiskery kiss after he'd overheard Maman at prayer, asking for angels to watch over her.

Baz squirmed beside her, scratching an itch along his spine on the corner of a broken marker. His shoulder blades stuck out like he'd been starved, which was crazy, because Baz ate like a big dog with worms. That's what Maman said, anyway, and she was the one who portioned out the food. At this year's Cochon de Lait Festival, Lutie had seen her brother eat three boudin sausages in the space of time it would take most people to wash their hands.

Lutie was sure Baz wouldn't tell Maman about this, but that didn't mean that he wouldn't scare the ghosts away and call her stupid and a baby. Older brothers, even goofy ones like Baz, were made of certain stuff.

*What, you like dem?* he'd have said. *You like dem ghosts, T-Lu? You wann'em round, you? For what?*

Baz didn't care at all that he couldn't see ghosts, always said it was enough for him that Papa could, like he was glad Papa was around to put food on the table, or Maman was there to make it. The talent had skipped over him, which seemed to be A-OK by Baz, even if it gave Sol one more thing to lord over him. Everyone said that Sol was gonna be traiteur after Papa when he got trained up enough. Which left baby Lutie and she saw everything: angels, devils, and ghosts. Her father's daughter, for all he noticed.

In the bright noon sun of high summer, the ever-present swamp water stank like peanut oil shimmering in a hot pan, just down from the cemetery, across the road, right by the house. Too hot even for water moccasins. Maybe too hot for ghosts. There weren't many ghosts in most graveyards, because her father knew how to send the dead on the proper road home before it got to being about ghosts.

But Papa had gone to the Atchafalaya Basin, whistling in vexation because he didn't like being away, would be gone for a week at least, he'd said. Papa didn't like leaving Maman alone for that long, but the fishing money was good and Sol was old enough to help this season. Maman had been angry; she'd started talking to herself. Lutie knew Maman wasn't really talking to herself because her mother had a secret, didn't she? Maman hid it from Papa, and Sol hadn't noticed and Baz couldn't see.

Maman had a pet ghost and if she had one, then Lutie could have one too.

As a general rule, Papa didn't leave his territory, but you worked when you could get it because taking care of the sick, laying down paths for the dead—being the local traiteur—paid nothing. Maman made some coin with her cards and tealeaves, but if there was real money-work to be had, that's what Papa did, especially with three kids to feed. Besides, no one was needing his services in their own neighborhood, not even a cough.

So Papa was away hauling up shrimp when Old Robichaux kicked the bucket—Baz's words, not Maman's. Maman didn't put things that way, but she'd seemed interested in the death herself, waiting. Watching.

You sure didn't hang onto a body in this heat. You boxed it, and fast.

In the bright washed-out noon, sky the same color as real lemonade, Lutie spotted Old Robichaux's ghost, faint as a sinner's hope. The ghost sat across from the stone angel, feet dangling from its own resting place, skinny old-man's ass perched on the edge of the new cinderblock crypt. He'd died not thirty feet away, on the highway. The ambulance had taken him to the morgue, then brought him back here. Waste of gas, Baz had noted.

Robichaux's ghost looked a little confused, but that was nothing new; he'd been plenty confused two days ago when he'd walked in front of one of those minivans going too fast on its way north. Death apparently hadn't made Robichaux any sharper, and Lutie was saddened for it. She'd been hoping that dying made you smarter. Maman always said it did.

Beside her, Baz shifted, moved like he was gonna bust out of his skin, start walking down the raised highway, just away, onto the next thing. Not so much annoyed as bored.

"Baz," Lutie said under her breath. "Baz." It was hard to get his attention when he had ants in his pants.

Bright greenblue eyes on her, unshorn hair matted to his forehead in the heat, white vest clinging damply to him. He smelled of goat. A smile. "Quoi?" Slow and long like he had a caramel melting in his mouth, sweet. Not bothered by his sister. Not bothered by the heat, by summer vacation winding down into its last weeks, school so far away it might as well be happening in the next century.

"Sing me a song," she said, twisting a strand of hair fine and light as cornsilk around her finger, but keeping her eyes on the ghost, cause you sure didn't know what those guys would do when you looked away.

"A song?" Baz repeated, tilting his head, brows rising, teeth gleaming briefly. "C'est trop chaud for singing." Lutie knew it was all show. Might as well tell a fish not to swim.

"Is not, Baz."

"Okay, Mademoiselle Je-sais-tout." He took a breath, one hand coming up, pinching his nose. He didn't look at her, his eyes were on the angel, Lutie realized.

Baz never did a single thing quietly, but especially not music. Their mother might hear him from her kitchen window, even way over here across the road, but it was a happy sound, nothing to worry anyone. Jaunty, an old song, one that Maman sometimes sang, which meant it was from way up north, in Canada, where she said it never got hot like this. Lutie knew the words, all of them. About being Acadian, losing your home, being put on a ship, destination unknown.

No time like now: her father was gone, Baz was singing, and Robichaux's ghost happily swayed back and forth to the tune, waiting for a new owner like a dog at the pound. Lutie laid one hand on the ground, open and fingers splayed, like she'd seen Papa do. She closed her eyes. A bead of sweat splatted on the back of her hand. *Concentrate. Call Robichaux over, bring him in.* Bringing a ghost in was the opposite of what Aurie did. Her father sent them away, slid them off the leash with a gentle command.

The old man's ghost came slowly to its feet, bones shaking beneath sloppy clothes, lines solidifying. To Lutie, Robichaux's ghost seemed like the man always had, creepy and addled, and she could see clear through it to the moss-shagged cypress behind.

Baz, unaware of the ghost next to them, laughed through the chorus, tapped his heels against the dry ground, keeping rhythm, goose-fleshed. He didn't pay attention to things like a sudden waft of ghostcold, was too into his song. Papa had given Baz a second-hand fiddle a few months ago, and Lutie could tell her brother wanted it now, just to scratch out the tune. A fine singer, had been for as long as Lutie could remember, good enough now that people talked about it, and he'd be just as talented as a fiddler, no dumbass couyon needed to tell Lutie that.

The ghost's face drooped, and Lutie could see how the bones of the left side were broken, smashed across the hood of an out-of-state vehicle in a hurry to get to town. Robichaux smiled and it was wrong. It occurred to Lutie that she should be scared. She hadn't much liked the old man in life, and nothing had really changed about that. *This guy's gonna make a good pet?*

For a moment, Lutie thought she saw something else move beyond Robichaux, but it was only the wind picking up again, shifting moss in the trees. Then it wasn't, it was a shimmer, soft as milkweed silk drifting in the breeze, there if you didn't look at it, gone if you did.

Another ghost, and now Lutie *was* scared, because Papa said only the newly dead and the angry dead stuck around and Robichaux was the only recent death she knew of. Which meant this ghost was the other kind and she was only seven years old and that was far too little to deal with an angry ghost.

It didn't seem angry, though, this other ghost, which had the form of a woman, Lutie could now see, a black woman with long hair in plaits, a dress that looked old-fashioned, but might not be. The two ghosts came closer, but not for her. Not because of her.

Baz kept singing, one hand slapping against his bare thigh in rhythm with his heels, nothing better to do than sing for the sheer joy of it on a day like this in the shade of an angel. She might be able to catch one ghost, but not two. Maybe if Baz shut up, they'd go away. Lutie tried to hush him, but stopping Baz from singing was a whole lot harder than getting him to sing in the first place.

The sun came out from behind a wisp of cloud and the whole cemetery lit up, bathed them in it, bleached out their features so that Lutie thought they might be scorched, might be reduced to ash. Baz's eyes were closed and he sang on, one song after the other.

By the time Maman found them, there were more than seven ghosts gathered around. Lutie had no idea where they'd come from, because their father was a better-than-average traiteur, and there were no stray ghosts anywhere near his house. Aside from Robichaux, these ghosts weren't from around here, and she'd never seen so many in one place. Her guess about music—about Baz—had been a good one.

Maman halted the singing with a sharp word. She was a woman who saw ghosts on the sunniest of days. There was no hiding what they'd done. What Lutie had done; Baz was oblivious. Maman stared around and raised her hand, words under her breath. The ghosts fled, melted into the earth, evaporated like a bead of sweat in the wind. Not *gone* gone, how their father did it, but away, out of sight. The sun returned behind its cloud and the day darkened, an out-of-control fire snuffed under a blanket.

"Basile Sarrazin," Mireille warned, low. "Qu'est-ce qui se passe?"

Baz scrambled to his bare feet, brows knotting in confusion, swiping dried cemetery grass from the seat of his threadbare cut-offs.

"Nuthin'," he explained, teeth gleaming against skin so tanned he looked like that smiling cat in the book Sol had read to her. Baz would try charm with Maman first, Lutie knew. "Je chante, c'est tout." Innocent, but older than Lutie, and a boy; when it rained, Baz got wet first.

Mireille's brows rose, and she crossed her arms beneath the dark sweat patch staining the yoke of her shirt. "Luetta? Dites-moi." And her green eyes glided to Lutie, who flushed.

No point in lying.

"Je veux un fantôme, M'man." She paused, knowing the power of what she said. *I want a ghost, Maman.* The next words part pride, part anger. "Comme toi."

*Just like you.*

Maman didn't talk about her ghost with Papa, never mentioned it. Her ghost was so difficult to see, even for Lutie. She thought that maybe Papa couldn't see Maman's pet, and that maybe Maman hid it on purpose. Laying ghosts to rest was more than Papa's job, it was his calling. So Lutie had some idea what her words might start, a small one.

Mireille's anger came first, or was the first thing Lutie recognized. If it was just Lutie who knew about the pet ghost, that was one thing. But Baz was there to hear what Lutie said. Baz would tell Papa all about the hidden ghost, no doubt about it. Maman grabbed Lutie's upper arm in a grip like death itself and she dragged Lutie from the cemetery, told Baz to get to the room he shared with Sol and stay there until their father came home and she didn't care if that meant days.

Maman had other plans for Lutie, and she was not sent into solitary confinement like her brother.

Mireille was ice to Aurie's fire, always out of step in this slow southern climate, heavy with unshed rains and frogsong and heat. She said, disparagingly, that where she came from the word 'traiteur' meant a caterer, not some kind of fancy faith healer, some social worker for spirits. Mireille hated it here, and Lutie knew it.

Aurie would deal with Old Robichaux, would deal with the others, too, Maman said. *Mais, we don't stick around for it*, she added.

By the time she'd gathered what Maman said she must—clothes, a doll, one storybook—the sunlight was slanting from the west, cutting across the kitchen table. It winked from where Maman had placed her wedding ring on a chipped saucer like a treat left out for some stray cat.

Maman turned over the Pontiac's engine, naked fingers clutching the wheel like a lifeline. They were leaving Baz in the upstairs bedroom. They were leaving, period.

# ONE

## NOT OSBORNE

S ol Sarrazin stood apart from the local North Platte cops, stolen ID tag clipped to his parka, trying to blend in. Hard to get a good look at the mangled corpse without appearing too interested, though. In and out, that's what he was here to do, just check out the body, no point in making conversation. No point in standing out, and he didn't, everything about him medium sized and standard issue, except maybe the expression on his face, which he kept lowered to the frozen ground.

A quick look, that was all he needed.

The wind was traveling fast, rushed right over the Great Plains, howling past the railcars in the switching yard as though its sole purpose was to flash-freeze the body on the ground, reduce it to so much frozen meat. Already stiff—cold or rigor mortis, that would be for the forensics team to figure out—what had once been a man was now surrounded by pooled blood misshapen as neglected cherry popsicles in the back of a freezer.

Sol knew he didn't look much like the guy on his railroad police ID tag, but nobody was really paying attention to him, least of all the cops. Ignoring their low talk —new regulations for overtime, wasn't this turning out to be a bitch—he swirled the coffee in his Styrofoam cup, hoping to leech some warmth from it, because his leather gloves were too thin for Nebraska when the wind was up. He pulled his knit cap down low over his dark brows, knowing that he looked enough like a railroad cop for a cursory glance.

Lifting his eyes to make a brief survey of the gray and rust-colored railcars in the bleak morning light, he saw nothing out of the ordinary, if you didn't count the body at his feet. He wondered who this guy had been to get on the wrong side of a train. He half-hoped it was just a drifter or a suicide, but there had been too many deaths at this yard in too short a time for anything as simple as that.

Last week, it had been a different body here at Bailey Yard: an older guy, blue eyes staring at nothing, dead inside a parked freight car, head smashed in. Biggest goddamn railyard in the world, bound to get some deaths, especially in winter. Drifters froze to death all the time, had cargo shift on them, mistimed a jump. Nothing to put in the papers, not unless the bodies started to pile up. Not unless the dead guy was a retired teacher who had no reason to be in the yard. Not unless it was the second strange death in December. The first body had been an accountant, newly moved to the North Platte area and he'd had no business in the yard, either.

This one today, the third, had been an average-sized Caucasian man, thrift store wardrobe, middle-aged probably, hard to tell. Less than twenty bucks in his front pocket, no sign of ID or keys. Not much left of the head, smashed like a suburban pumpkin left out too long after Halloween. Sort of body you had to scoop off the tracks using a shovel and pan. The temperature would help with that, he had cause to know, would make things more solid, all the bits and pieces, all the stuff that usually slid around on a warm day, that made picking up a body more like chasing jelly across a table with a spoon. He watched the forensics team throw a sheet, poor dumbass had left a nasty corpse, the kind of thing no one wanted to look at for long. One of the yard switchers had lost his breakfast, much to the amusement of the cops.

"Hey!" A short local cop, gray hair in disarray—*should have a hat, idiot*—shouted across the tracks over the sound of the trains. They hadn't shut down the yard, of course, too much coming in and going out here, running east to west, to Chicago and the Great Lakes on the one hand, California and the Pacific on the other. "Hey, you, there! Wanna lend me a hand? What's your name?"

Sol sauntered over, took a quick glug of his tepid coffee. Hell, he was used to cold coffee. Maybe railroad cops got to finish coffee while it was still hot, but he sure as hell never had the chance. Always some emergency. "Osborne," he said, though it was printed on his tag, easy to read unless you were blind. Or an asshole. Sol suspected this guy was both, which suited him just fine. "What do you need?"

"Well, Osborne," dripping with condescension, "I could use a light," while he fished out a deck of smokes from his pocket.

Sol tilted his head, a half-smile touching his chapped lips. Too early for this shit, really. He'd been up for more than twenty-four hours already, the last three on the road, getting here. North Platte was a long drive from Denver. It had taken him a few minutes to steal a tag, as well. He shrugged with one shoulder, dipping his head in a way he knew most people took to be deferential. "Sorry. Those things'll kill you."

The cop swore, jammed the cigarette in the corner of his mouth, unlit. "You're new? Haven't seen you around before."

Sol didn't answer, moved him off with flattery instead. "Thank God you're here. You city cops must see this kind of stuff all the time. What do you think happened here?"

The cop grimaced, gestured to the body as though Sol hadn't noticed it. "No wallet this time. Maybe a mugging gone wrong? Missed the bills in the pocket, useless fucks. Gotta be connected to the others." He peered at Sol, who looked away, hoped he looked cold and bored. "You're a railroad cop. What does this look like to you?"

Sol wondered what the cop would do if he told him what was on his mind. Over the years, he'd seen a lot of dead bodies. Most were pretty run-of-the-mill. But some were what he'd call the oddly dead. People dying out of place, dying in terror. A different look in their eyes, not the mild surprise of most corpses. The oddly dead were killed by ghosts, bitter spirits bent on revenge. But today's body? No eyes to look surprised or terrified or anything, not much of a head to speak of, either.

Sol shrugged. "The other two, last week? They were murdered, hit on the head with a blunt object. This one, he was hit by a train. Probably a rail rider screwing up a jump." Sol paused. "Not the same thing as the others." Improbably, he was disappointed.

"Well, aren't you an informed sonofabitch? You think this is an accident? Why the fuck am I here, then?"

This wasn't the sort of question you answered, so Sol shrugged again. Let the cop do his thing, if he could. It wasn't something he was going to interfere with. Let him run this any old way he liked. Sol crumpled his empty cup, shoved it in the deep pocket of his parka, hunched over his shoulders, drew himself in, became the kind of guy that could escape notice if that's what he wanted.

One last look, just to make sure. He was here for the same reason as the cops: too many deaths to be mere coincidence. It just happened that he was looking for ghosts, not living murderers. Returning to the body, now wrapped like the world's shittiest present, Sol inserted himself between two suits from the Tower, bent down and flipped the sheet back, revealing a mangled hand. Bruised and swollen almost beyond recognition, two fingers missing, scattered, squashed or eaten by crows. A wonder no one had spotted the body before now; this guy had been dead for at least twenty-four hours. Sol had been keeping tabs on North Platte emergency calls for the last week; his regular work took him in and out of Denver hospitals, where access to such information was easy. The first report of a body had come at 4:30 that morning, just as he was finishing his shift. He'd driven fast.

He didn't touch anything. *In and out*, he reminded himself. An accident was the obvious explanation, the easy one. But nothing was easy, not with Sol, not for him, because he then noticed something he'd missed before: the mangled hand was curled upwards, almost in appeal, the blackened forefinger crooked, the thumb folded under, the remaining fingers like the bulbous roots of some tuberous plant pulled unresisting from the soil.

*There might be a ghost working this part of the tracks, but this isn't a ghost's work, not this one.*

The hand's gesture was not random, not how rigor mortis usually set things. Fingers in a pattern, one he recognized. He could almost see the motion that went with it, had to stop his own cold hand from making it in response.

Hit by a train, yes, but no accident.

Sol straightened. He had seen enough and knew that he should back off now before the cops starting asking him questions. He took orders for five coffees and walked slowly over to the Tower in the distance. The gravel crunched and shifted under his boots, and Sol worried the lighter in his pocket, thinking about which of the many possible warding gestures the dead man's hand had been making, given the missing fingers. He didn't know enough about the prevention of evil, only half-remembered fairy tales and late-night swamp stories. The gesture hadn't warded against whatever had killed this guy, of course, but that wasn't the point.

The point was that there'd been something to ward against.

A day dead, at least. Making a ward. Knowing how to make a ward. How many people knew how to do that? Too late to round up this guy's ghost, probably long gone, anyway. Bien shit, around this yard, ghosts were the problem in the first place, weren't they?

He walked right past the white railroad police Bronco parked outside the Tower, unclipping the police tag as he approached workers who might recognize the name or the blurry photo. There was a shift change going on, plenty of people around, coming and going, so he slipped out the yard via the tourist store where they sold Guinness Book of World Records books open to the Bailey Yard entry. He smiled at the girl behind the counter.

"Did you catch up to the morning tour?" she asked, absently straightening her name badge, drawing his eyes down.

"Yeah, I caught up with them, me," he returned. He put Osborne's ID tag on the counter. "Found this on the tracks. One of your guys musta dropped it." He smiled slowly. "This is some place you got here, Katie."

She was young enough to blush. "You come back anytime."

"I will, chère." Sol paused for a moment, suddenly tired beyond belief. With a farewell grin, he slowly took the steps to the parking lot, let gravity help him out.

His truck was an elderly Jeep Wagoneer, one black door still sporting the wood panel, rust and peeling paint held together with gray bondo. After he climbed up and in, he swiped off his cap and lit a cigarette from the deck on the dashboard. The engine turned over with a roar, and Sol waited for it to warm up, thinking about what excuse he'd offer Robbie this time.

She had waited up for him, which didn't help anything, because Sol had been gone for the better part of two days, and that meant she was tired as well as pissed off.

Out the Wagoneer, one hand on the gate, and the dog started up, baying piteously, recognizing the sound of the slammed door, maybe. *Sold out by the dog. Merci beaucoup, Renard.* Sol wasn't across the threshold, wasn't even up the steps, before the front door opened and Robbie was there, worn housecoat over flannel pajama bottoms and one of his old t-shirts, arms crossed, hair uncombed and long down her back. Christ, he was tired, but he did love a woman in flannel.

Maybe she'd forgotten how he felt about flannel, but he doubted it. The dog burst out the door, a blur of white and tan and black. Robbie paused, maybe a little unsure of his crooked grin.

"Beausoleil," his full name, which she stretched out into bo-so-laaaaaay, and he knew he was in deep shit. "What was it this time?"

"You're gonna catch your death of cold, Roberta Mack," he returned, held his arms away from his body as though to tell her he was unarmed. He came up the snow-drifted walk, each step crunching. The snow had started as he'd crossed the border into Colorado, the foothills dusted with powder, not golden and glowing, not at this time of year.

Robbie cocked her head, gun-hammer sharp. "Your shift ended at five. It's now past friggin' lunchtime, Sol. You don't call. You don't tell me your plans. Where the hell have you been?"

She didn't usually provide him with a laundry list. Sol bent one knee and Renard licked his face with the same enthusiasm he'd have shown a dropped pork chop. "North Platte," he said wearily, knowing the reaction. He'd been a couple of times over the last while, once for each railyard death. He hadn't told her that part of it; it occurred to him that she probably thought he had a woman in Nebraska.

Robbie gestured with one hand: You're insane, I give up, Go screw yourself. All of the above. She turned into the clapboard house and slammed the door. The beagle's head jerked around, spotting a jay in the neighbor's scrubby pine, and Renard abandoned Sol with a running ruff of sheer pleasure.

A moment, the dog gone through the open gate, and Sol stood alone on the icy cement walk. He sighed, rubbed a hand across his head, dusting off snow, drawing black hair into little tufts. Another call from the pound, doubtlessly. With slow, deliberate steps, he mounted the stairs, and knew his luck wasn't quite out, because Robbie had only closed the door, she hadn't locked it.

\* \* \*

The shift went by fast. Ten hours on four hours sleep ought to have been torture, but it was busy as hell, the usual Friday night gong show. An ALS call for chest pain, an OD/psych, one fall at a nursing home, another in a bar, an MVA, another psych, this one at dawn, after the snow had stopped falling. Along East Colfax every other person thought they were Elvis at four in the morning, at least it seemed that way to Sol.

The hospital was jumping, and they had to wait around after the tavern fall, check in with the Denver cops. More paperwork, but it wasn't Sol's turn, so he didn't much care about the wait. He preferred hanging with his patient to pushing a pen, even if it meant having the same conversation five times over with Elvis, something about being cheated out of overtime pay and some guy standing way too close at the bus stop.

While his partner was taking a leak and they were waiting for dispatch to clear them for leaving, Sol used the phone at Admitting to call the police station in North Platte. Sol gave his partner's name and ID number, knowing it would check out on their system, and the cop would already know from call display that he was phoning from Denver Health. Besides, he thought, juggling the phone while taking another sip of coffee, it was amazing what they'd tell you when you worked in EMS.

No identification on the body, not yet, no leads. What's your interest, son?

He cleared his throat and lied, said they'd had a similar death in the Denver Yard not two months ago and he wondered if there was a connection. Better than telling the cop that a rogue ghost was killing people along the tracks, Sol supposed. He was then told, in so many words, to get the hell off the phone, they could handle their own cases, thank you very much. Except the cop didn't say thank you.

Sol flipped his partner for the last of the shift's paperwork, lost, and sat in the medic's room, smelling someone else's microwaved meal while he turned a leaking ballpoint pen in his fingers. His stomach growled, causing laughter among the morning shift—you hungry, Sarrazin? Get that girl to feed you, you look like you need it. He showered, changed, his body not yet ready to rest, days off looming like Christmas.

A raw bacon-streaked dawn spread across the plains and lit the Front Range all pink, a special show for the morning commute. He drove the

Wagoneer slowly back to the suburb of Aurora, past the crumbling Chuck E. Cheese and the half-vacant strip malls, turned down Robbie's street. It had been the address on his driver's license for the past two years and he still thought of it as Robbie's street, not his. He sat in the truck after he turned off the ignition, not sure he was tired enough to sleep.

Renard had returned, or been returned, and slobbered Sol with indiscriminate love as soon as he was through the door. Sol pushed him back down, heading for the kitchen. Robbie would be at the salon by now, so he didn't bother to take off his heavy parka or his boots. He wrenched open the fridge, got a beer, and continued to the dim workshop out back. Might as well keep busy until he got too tired to see; the motorbike Baz had left in pieces last visit to Denver wasn't going to put itself back together. That had been four months ago. Sol had no idea when Baz would roll through town again, and he was fed up seeing the machine strewn across the work table like old roadkill. *Might as well get it done.*

His heart thudded uncertainly—*I should rest*—but he snapped on the heater anyway, blew into his hands. The workshop had been the back porch once, and had been converted to a mudroom long before Robbie had taken up the lease. It wasn't insulated, made for a cold work place. The light was bad, too, just one small window high up, so he turned on the clamp lamp above the table, drank the beer slowly as he planned his attack.

The dog was relegated to the kitchen, whines and scratches be damned. Sol wasn't wanting company. The world was too damn noisy most of the time. He finished the beer, set down the empty next to his tools, ran fingers over them, so cold to the touch they almost burned. He picked up a socket wrench, flipped its weight experimentally in his hand.

"You always fixed things for him," came from the corner, in the shadows behind the makeshift shelving unit scavenged from the hospital. Cans of used paint, boxes of obsolete electrical wires, the summer tires for the Wagoneer. Voice so known it was almost like talking to yourself.

Sol dropped the wrench and it clattered to the workbench. "Christ," he hissed. "Dammit, Dad, why don't you call first?"

The shadow moved behind the shelves and Sol turned half away, anger boiling up like a shaken bottle of Coke. He bit the inside of his mouth, hard. How long had it been? A year, more than a year. He couldn't remember, had maybe blocked it out.

"You don't pick up, you," Aurie said. "And machines..." He trailed off and Sol heard the shrug.

Sol wanted another beer, but then he'd have to invite the man in, and that wasn't in the cards. In the kitchen, he heard Renard growl, paw the door. He kicked the wood lightly, annoyed, exhaled sharply through his nose. "What do you want?"

Doors and locks meant nothing to Aurèle Sarrazin, so Sol didn't have to ask how he'd gotten in. Aurie moved on catfeet, always had, so Sol had to look to see where he was. Still in shadow. The room was so cold Sol could see his own breath, which was coming fast.

"These suburbs, they all look the same, gars. I got turned around. I passed alotta time getting here. Some cold cold, this town. Never been such a great a place, here." And it would have been so easy to stop him, then, with a word, with a gesture. With a comment thrown like a circus performer's knife. Sol held his breath instead, willing calm.

"I like it just fine," he replied, crossing his arms.

The shadow shrugged again—if you say so. "You like your *girl* just fine, you mean. Not this place." Aurie laughed, dark and amused. "J'ai besoin de ton aide, mon gars. I gotta job—"

Sol had heard enough. "I have a job. I don't want your job. I don't want your kind of job."

Aurie sighed, and Sol knew that sound too. "You already got my job, toi. What, you think I don't see you this morning at the railyard? Non, reste calme. This isn't a job comme ça."

He had been at the railyard? Full of damn surprises, him. But Aurie rarely ventured anything, and he wasn't coming out from behind the shelving. Sol grew quiet, waiting. "Quoi? Qu'est-ce qui se passe?"

"You gotta take care of your brother."

"Look who's talking." That was too fast, wasn't what he'd wanted to say, and it happened every time with this man. There was a reason Sol didn't pick up the phone.

Aurie wasn't moving, and Sol took a step toward the shelves, only to feel cold that seeped right into his bones. He pulled up, understanding. Not understanding.

"He's special, him." Flat, a statement of known fact.

"I know that," Sol murmured, rote.

"I don't think you do," Aurie refuted, edge of anger. "You don't see it. Eyes too full of numbers and cities. Too full of medicine." Like it was a dirty word and maybe to Aurie it was.

The shadow did not move again, and Sol could barely make out his father's outline against the dark, the whiff of cold so deep it froze the hairs inside his nostrils. His father took a breath, coughed against his hand, and as the hand came up, it caught lamplight maybe, or dissolved in it, and Sol couldn't breathe.

The hand was swollen past recognition. Fingers were missing, and Sol struggled to say something, but that would make it real and he wasn't quite ready for that.

"You be sure they don't make no monkey business with Baz, 'cause they'll try." Aurie became very still, as though he was waiting, as though he sensed Sol was catching up. Treating Sol like a man. Giving him his due. Sol already had his father's job, after all.

"Who? What happened? Where have you been?" Sol asked, ignoring his father's request, suddenly numb, wondering where the words were coming from. "Where—"

Aurie's form shook, shimmered, and Sol didn't want to see any more clearly than he already did. "You know where I am, Beausoleil." It was bright outside, but it didn't penetrate the workshop, not much, just enough to dazzle Sol's eyes in a soft gray light, make forms and outlines blur. That's what he told himself. "It's hard, bein' all the way here." A chuckle again. "And you shouldn't be talkin' to me anyways. No good comes from talkin' to ghosts."

It was too dark to see him properly and Sol didn't want to anyway. He remembered what the body had looked like at Bailey Yard, and that was enough. Though it was probably hard, Aurie held still, gave Sol some time. Only the sound of Sol's uneven breath interrupted the workshop's quiet. Both men were good at waiting, at silence. *More than a year,* Sol thought, *closer to two.*

"Who did this?" he finally asked, because that's what he had been trying to figure out since he'd heard about the suspicious deaths at Bailey Yard, and it must have been the same with Aurie when he'd heard, too. They looked at a newspaper with the same eyes: 'Weird deaths' was all either of them needed to read. *He's been to the rail yard; he was there and something was expecting him.* The strange deaths were enough to warrant suspicion from guys like Aurie Sarrazin. *From guys like me.*

"It wasn't no ghost," Aurie coughed, soft and wet. "Not for me, anyway. Those other stiffs, yeah, you know that. You passed by, cher. Mais, for me? One of the dirty p'tit guys. You know." And Sol, in theory, did. A devil, a small dirty thing, evil, different from a ghost. "It wanted me dead. I don't do any favor for it. Pisses those guys off, not gettin' what they want. They're so easy to piss off. Remember that. Puis, you don't do any negotiating. D'accord?"

After a moment, Sol nodded. He wiped his eyes, which were full. "I know." He knew what the job was, too, of course; he hadn't really wanted it, what his father did, what his father had done, but it was his. "Papa?" he whispered, but his father's ghost was gone.

# TWO

## THREE TAPS

Baz hoped whoever was trying to get hold of him would give up soon, because it occurred to him—Marianne moving on him like a circus seal—that his phone had a really stupid ring tone. The bayou tune made him feel like he was thirteen years old, sneaking into his first gig with his fiddle tucked under his arm, and that wasn't the impression he was going for when it came to the ladies. And, *c'mon, whoever you are*, he wasn't going to pick it up anytime soon, because Marianne was sliding around now, nails raking his abdomen in a way that was going to make him, make him go—make him—and there it was again. He couldn't even remember which joker had programmed it, some Zydeco riff that wasn't his style, but that everybody thought was. The Ragin' Cajun, screw you very much. A joke, that's what they'd called it, the other guys in the band.

Swamp music called up heat and mosquitoes and catching wind with an outboard motor, all sorts of things he barely remembered. Here it was, damn near winter, just off the plane from Cancun and the Christmas decorations were up all over Colorado Springs. He and Marianne had been gone that long. Lost track of time, nothing weird about that.

The bedroom was bigger than most bars he played and she made some noise, her, but he didn't mind that so much. The best thing about ladies

19

Marianne's age, Baz had found, was not so much that they knew tricks he didn't, it was more that they weren't afraid of using them.

The sun disappeared fast in this part of the country, dropped behind the Front Range like a lost sock behind a sofa, but the soft orange light lasted. After quite a stretch of sheer physical pleasure, Baz finally felt like he might need something to eat, and so he rolled out of bed in the last golden light of the day, body lit like he was on stage. *Always.* Open suitcases on the floor, and he thought that maybe most of his clothes were dirty, and a shower wouldn't be out of the question either. He eyed the surf shorts and flowered shirts as he passed. Too Mexican, all of them, foreign somehow. Relics of a vacation past.

He wondered where he'd left his jeans and plaid shirts and camo jacket, seemed to recall that Marianne had sent them to be cleaned before they'd left. Weird to think that they were somewhere in this airplane hangar-sized house, encased in thin plastic like the contents of body bags.

He felt her eyes on him from the bed, and so he turned to give her a good look. Smiled, because this was all okay, really, and he could give her that, it cost him not a thing. This wasn't permanent and they both knew it, which was part of the dance. Baz leaned one elbow against the huge opening to the ensuite—he thought that's what they called it, one of this house's seven bathrooms—and stretched, giving her the tableau she wanted, the one she'd remember later, the one she'd tell her friends about.

"Mmmmn," Marianne breathed from the bed, inching onto her elbows and not bothering to pull up the sheet. "Damn, I knew you shouldn't have worn those shorts."

He looked down and saw that the Mexican sun had striped him straight across the middle. She'd advocated for him to tan naked on the private beach. She had a point; he was brown as walnut wood, mostly, where he wasn't white as a graveyard angel. He scratched his head, hair in need of a cut, fingers brushing over a three-day growth of beard, not really caring.

His phone rang again and he met her eyes, a little chagrined. All he needed was an accordion and a 'gator, for God's sake.

"A month down south, no calls and now this?" Marianne asked. "You should pick up. Sounds like someone needs you."

Baz shrugged, sauntered back to the huge bed, bigger than some rooms he'd had as a kid. "Doubt it, ma cocotte." He leaned across the expanse of Egyptian cotton, stretched Marianne's arms above her head where her fingers clutched the wrought iron headboard. "No one needs me," he teased, slow with smile. He ran his tanned hands down a body that hours of yoga classes and daily runs had made sharp and sinewy. Bending his head down, his tongue drew a line from her breasts to her belly button and beyond. "It can wait," he murmured into the only soft bit of her.

"Talk French to me," she said on a taken breath, and Baz sighed, shook his head.

"Don't remember enough," he said indistinctly.

"You remember enough," she replied and that was true.

Later, when evening had fallen over Colorado Springs, the city lit up like a parade, Baz lounged in the sitting room next to the kitchen, still wet from the shower, wearing Marianne's husband's bathrobe. He couldn't figure out how to turn on the TV, let alone the stereo. He put his feet up on what she called an ottoman, and ate a bowl of Cheerios with table cream. The cleaning staff had made sure that groceries were waiting for their return. It was like Disneyland or something.

Marianne was still in the shower and he remembered that her husband was back in town tomorrow afternoon because remembering such schedules was really in his own best interest. He knew that he'd been an excitement, a brush with danger for Marianne, a tale to spin, grounds for divorce, payback, who knew, and that was okay, was fine. No illusions one way or another, but now he needed to get his things, figure out where he was going next. He was between bands at the moment, his fiddle was somewhere around here, been a while since he'd touched it. It wouldn't be hard, picking up where he'd left off, it never was. Make a few phone calls, see what—*damn*.

An indication of how long he'd been gone and how little he'd thought about it, that it took him a good five minutes to find his phone. It was in the suitcase, underneath a pair of cheap flip flops. Baz scanned the call log, could barely remember how to negotiate the interface. Four missed calls today, all from his brother's number. *That can't be good*, he thought, pressing the call return button. He tried to remember when he'd last talked to Sol and came up empty.

It rang twice.

"Hey, Robbie," he tried, staring out the bedroom's huge plate glass window, recessed halogen lights reflecting from the hardware he wore in his ears, nose, through his eyebrow, distracting from the snow outside, big Santa flakes, city twinkling beyond.

She sounded a bit pissed off, that wide flat voice of hers. He could almost see her brows drawn together over her freckled nose. "Baz, is that you?"

"You don't have to make it sound like a disease, Robbie."

"He's been trying to reach you all evening. Are you still in Chicago? I'm sorry, I should let you, but he's…" She regrouped and Baz didn't know what the hell she was talking about.

"He's gone to work?" Baz guessed. Sol was always working, it seemed to Baz.

"No." Emphatic, and the dog was barking and Baz could tell she was walking through their house, something about the quality of the call, her sudden breathlessness. "No, he's here, he's just gone, hang on, let me put on my boots." A pause, and Baz sat down on a chair, not wanting to look at his sun-browned face floating above a winter landscape.

He heard muffled voices, Robbie's matter-of-fact mumbles and his brother's more fluid cadences, swearing in two different languages. Baz rubbed his temple. This wasn't good, Sol swearing. In the next room, the shower shut off, an abrupt cessation of white noise, and Baz dropped his voice. This was a life apart, this wasn't Mexico and fucking on an acreage mattress.

"Sol?" he asked uncertainly, hearing slow breathing on the other line. "Ça va?"

"Hey, man." Low and boozy, from a frozen place like someone had opened a door to the outside. "Hé, cher." In the background, Baz could still hear Robbie. She was telling Sol he should come inside. Sol didn't seem inclined to come inside, and Robbie's voice receded like Sol was pushing her back through the door. The dog's barks subsided and Sol was back. "Where you been?"

"Around, you know," Baz said. "I was out of the country. Down south, near Cancun."

Sol laughed. "Down south." Like it was a joke between them. "Where you now?"

Shit. Baz held his breath, quietly closed the door to the bathroom, wondered how long it would take him to get his things together, because this was pointing in only one direction. "Not far, Colorado Springs."

A pause. He could hear Sol smoking, maybe taking a swig of something. "That's good." A dry, humorless chuckle. "C'est bon, ça."

Oh, man, he didn't want to ask, but you always had to with Sol. He made you. "What's up? What's going on?"

Another break, and *please*, Sol wasn't going to make him ask again, was he?

"When's last time you seen Dad?"

What? He had to think. "Did you guys have a fight? You know you shouldn't get into it with him. I thought you weren't talking to him anyway."

"When you seen him last?" Insistent, tongue sliding on—rum. That would be it, that was the poison on the menu tonight, Sol's weapon of choice when he needed to get lost.

"I dunno. Last month, maybe? Before I went to Cancun, around my birthday. I was hanging with him in—" Where had that been? Some place with good clubs, big city. "Minneapolis. Up there."

Another swallow. "Up there, hey."

"Sol?" This was just great. Baz had returned a drunk call. "Sol?"

"He's gone, Baz. He's dead."

"You don't know that." It came out automatically, a repudiation. "Christ, you don't even talk to him. How can he be dead?"

The line was snowfall silent, and once again Baz heard Robbie's voice, coaxing and cajoling Sol, softer than he'd ever heard her before. That was the thing that made it real, otherwise it was just his brother, drunk and making shit up. The void of the non-shower loomed big, and then Marianne opened the door and Baz found himself staring at her and not able to do much else. He must have looked helpless, or struck or something else that made people look after him, a bird dropped by a sudden stop of window, because the older woman took the phone from his loose grip and talked to Robbie for a few minutes, making arrangements, making plans, as Baz slowly circled the room, hand drifting over his solar plexus like it hurt. Like something hurt.

Baz chose the music, and Sol let him because that filled all the hours of not talking. Baz sang along, as he always did, gorgeous, tuneful voice that Sol only allowed in the moving car, because that was the rule.

North Platte was only marginally improved by the layer of snow blurring the gray and yellow brick buildings, but the glare was blinding and Sol's sunglasses could only mask so much of it. It didn't help at all, either, that Baz had lost his license last year, which meant Sol had spent close to four hours behind the wheel this morning. With a hangover. He couldn't lie to himself, though: a robust hangover was nothing compared to what churned underneath. The thudding headache, his queasy roiling stomach, all of it was just a convenient excuse to say not much of anything during the drive.

Sol sent Baz alone into the County Coroner's Office, mute retaliation for his failure to drive, said that if he went in with Baz, he'd get recognized. By who? Baz asked, but Sol had already spotted a coffee shop across the street from the office and was out the door. Deep down, Sol knew if he started talking he wouldn't be able to stop, so it was better to just shut up, even if Baz had a million questions.

*Don't ask to see the body*, he felt like saying, wanting to keep Baz from the worst of it, but how else was there going to be an identification? Hell, Sol hadn't recognized his father's body when he'd been lying dead at his feet. First thing that morning, they'd put together a list of Aurie Sarrazin's scars, the prison tattoo on his right forearm. Things that even a violent death would have a hard time erasing.

An hour and two trips to the coffee shop passed before Baz slid back into the Wagoneer, way too pale for someone who'd just come back from Mexico. Sol bit back a comment about Baz's ridiculous new haircut. Robbie had done it last night, or early this morning, sometime after Sol had passed out in any case, because Sol would not have allowed it.

That morning, just as the sun came up, Sol had staggered into the living room to discover Baz asleep on the couch with a half-hearted and disheveled mohawk, the kind you immediately tried to grow out. Baz's eye had cracked open, and he'd been instantly awake and hungry, eating anything that wasn't nailed down even as Sol rejected anything solid, Baz's eyes wild and blue and glittering. Grin sharp enough to make Lucifer wary, lightly joking at Sol's wretched expense, setting Robbie at ease. Baz was good at that, Sol knew.

# DEADROADS

Sol couldn't remember if he'd been awake when Baz had arrived.

The coffee was hot, and he eyed his brother through the steam. Baz's ears were painfully red. He'd have to invest in a hat, but knowing Baz, it would probably be one of those stupid ones with earflaps and rabbit fur. It was like hanging out with a traveling freak show. "So?" Sol asked after a long minute.

Baz scowled, expression serious, and Sol was immediately sorry for his one syllable conversation. "Yeah," Baz said too quickly, pinching his nose, head down. Sol stared at the bright street, and despite the glare, took off his sunglasses and tossed them on the dash. Baz's head came up, following the sound. "Yeah, so it's him all right," Baz told him, voice even. "They found his truck. ID in the glove."

"Hey," Sol started. *Please*, he thought, not knowing what he was hoping for. "So you didn't—they didn't actually make you look at—" He recalled the smashed body, and how crows had picked at it, their father's blood frozen in the gravel. Sol was used to such sights; Baz was not.

Baz stared at him, eyes glowing. "Did he…did he come to you? Is he stuck?"

Sol grimaced. "Ouais," he admitted slowly into his coffee, not knowing how to say more.

"So," Baz said with a flick of his fingers outwards. A supplication of sorts. "You're gonna fix that, yeah?"

"That's why we're here," he said, knowing that Baz needed to hear that almost as much as he needed to say it. "He made it all the way to damn Aurora but he died here, Baz. That's some trip for a ghost. No way he found his way to…" He waved his hand vaguely. To wherever ghosts go when they're at rest, he didn't say. The coffee was cooling rapidly and Sol took in a good mouthful, swished it around his mouth like Listerine.

"Why was he in North Platte? Why were *you* here?" Baz had been asking variations of these questions since this morning, since they'd pulled out of Robbie's earshot. Part of the reason for the soundtrack, all the way, so Sol wouldn't have to answer. "What did he say to you?"

Sol rubbed a hand across his face, in need of a shave. Maybe he'd grow a beard again, except a beard made everyone say he looked like he came from the bayou, which meant he looked like his father and he wasn't sure he was ready for that. "He said that you're a goddamn menace behind the wheel and that I shouldn't let you get a stupid-ass haircut, that's what."

"He didn't say that," Baz protested without heat.

"You have the forms? Are they releasing his body to the funeral home?"

Baz allowed himself to be steered from his original question and handed over a sheaf of papers. "Yeah. I told them to go ahead and cremate." He grew quiet again and Sol looked up from the paper—all standard forms, ruled a train accident, but at least they'd associated a name with the body. That seemed right.

"What?" Sol prodded after a minute of silence.

Baz scanned the street. "We don't have to stay in this goddamn place, do we?"

Sol started the truck. "We have to stay here. I'll go down to the tracks tonight." He paused, resisting the urge to involve Baz. But didn't Baz have the right to be there, when it was his own father? Screw that, didn't Baz have an obligation? Why did it always fall to Sol to clean things up? *You always fixed things for him.* There was no fixing this, though. "It matters more where he died, not where his remains are. I gotta go there, where he died. It don't matter about his body." Only to the living, anyway.

"He'll be there?" Still, after all these years, the wonder. Baz had a way of looking pleasantly surprised, no matter the subject.

Sol spared him a glance. "Yeah, he'll be there." He checked his blind spot before pulling the Wagoneer into non-existent traffic. "You could come. If you want." Never mind what *he* wanted, because when had that mattered? Baz looked stunned, then perplexed, then scared, and when he said 'sure', Sol couldn't name what slid into place.

Baz wasn't going to ask, because he already knew the answer. It would be the same answer Aurie had given him his whole life—*well, no, not your whole life, Basile, you didn't first ask until you were nine years old, you didn't need an answer until then.*

No. That would be the answer.

True, Sol wasn't Aurie, but sometimes that was easy to forget. Sol had the same way of not saying what was on his mind, just letting you guess, usually wrong. Every once in a while, Sol would look at a spot behind Baz, fix on it and go still, just like their father did. It made you feel like they weren't quite right in the head, and Baz knew he wasn't the only one who noticed. There'd been that spate of school psychologists wanting to test Sol, once, before Aurie had moved them to Denver.

So Baz wasn't going to bring up Mom, or Lutie, not when the answer was a foregone 'no'. *Lutie has a right to know her father's dead.* That had been almost his first thought after Marianne had hung up the phone in Colorado Springs. He'd worried it, worried the phrasing of his question, all the way to Denver, sitting on an inter-city bus that reeked of urine and potato chips. Worried it as he paid for the cab to Robbie's place from the wad of bills Marianne had forced into his hand as he left—*you stay safe, okay, baby?*—and lost all will to voice it when Robbie answered his knock, that dumb dog running around his legs and barking like he was the meat fairy making a delivery.

He wouldn't have gotten a straight answer from Sol last night, anyway, none that Baz would have been able to hold him to in the morning. The best Baz could do was to keep Robbie calm, because Sol was the center of her universe even when their father hadn't unexpectedly died and Sol wasn't stone drunk. Baz had asked for a haircut, but only after they'd put Sol to bed and finished the bottle of rum; the haircut was an easy target for his brother's ridicule, took Sol's mind off the dark places.

None of it meant Baz had worked up the nerve to ask about Lutie. He couldn't even begin to think of asking about their mother. Sol didn't talk about her, not ever.

North Platte was big enough to support a number of identical chain motels, generic as suburban paint. Sol selected one seemingly at random, discerned beige from beige, could have closed his eyes and pointed for all it mattered. They both slept away the late afternoon—musician hours, Baz had joked. Paramedic hours, Sol replied, not joking. They rose with the moon. People'll think we're vampires, Baz said. No such thing, Sol answered back, taking the first shower and leaving Baz alone to think about what he knew was real and what was fairy tale in their screwed-up world.

Sol had good wire-cutters in the back of the Wagoneer, along with a first aid kit better than those found in most ambulances. They parked on a secluded side road running parallel to the main tracks and Sol cut a hole in the fence. He'd already warned Baz to be careful, that the trains moved fast and they didn't brake for musicians with stupid haircuts. Company security patrolled the area at all hours, looking for railriders and other trespassers, and those jerks wouldn't think twice about hauling their trespassing asses down to the station, or inflicting a beating.

Baz followed his brother at a discreet distance, hands deep in his pockets, ears almost numb but not quite enough. The night was moon-bright and the snow turned it to near day. Easy to see the parked rail-cars, the switching tracks, the crossbuck signs. Baz had the feeling that Sol wasn't even looking at the same things he was, because he occasionally cocked his head to one side, all in black, just a smudge against the gray gravel, snow swept away by the wind. He walked hunched over, alert, like he was listening to something Baz couldn't hear.

It didn't creep Baz out, not anymore. It's just what they did, his dad and Sol. Dad had done a whole lot more than just see ghosts, of course. Baz was less sure of Sol's calling, but despite his brother's lights-and-siren job and settled home life, this kind of traiteur work didn't wiggle its way out of your blood. At least, that's what Baz thought. Finally, Sol crossed the tracks, motioned with a jerk of his chin for Baz to follow, and stepped down into a hollow between the fence and rail. Sol slowed, then stopped.

Baz, at his shoulder, could see nothing other than the dim smear of fenceline, the splotched gray of gravel and snow. He was shivering, so cold now that he could barely breathe; his lungs ached with it. It hadn't been this cold by the truck, and that's when Baz knew. No matter how many times he'd been in similar circumstances, waiting for ghosts to arrive, he felt exposed, *visible*. This was unnatural, in the most basic sense of the word. His breath came out in an unsteady stream. "Sol?" he asked, not really knowing what he was asking.

Beside him, half a head shorter, more sturdily built and safely solid, Sol didn't move, not even as he said, "Shh." It was gentle, though, a reassurance.

Baz waited, and he wasn't good at that, fidgeted, played with the coins in his pocket, turning them over like good luck charms. After a moment, Sol took one step forward, hesitated, and then bent down to a crouch. He took the glove off his right hand and dropped it to the gravel before spreading his fingers wide and settling his hand among the rocks. Baz had seen their father do this any number of times, and watched as Sol dipped his head as though trying to remember something important.

Sol's head came up with a snap, and from his crouched position said, "Ta gueule, Dad. You don't have the right to say that."

Great. They were going to fight. From beyond the grave, they were going to go at it.

"Is he here?" Baz asked his brother, more to get in the middle than anything else, to remind Sol why they'd come. His brother slowly rose, and by the moonlight, he was pale, dark eyes and dark chin. Baz remembered their father saying that you didn't get into conversations with ghosts, you just sent them on their way, because they were messed up, weren't like you anymore.

Apparently, Sol hadn't taken this lesson to heart. "This isn't your show. He's here if I say so." Not talking to Baz, obviously. Talking about him instead.

This was by far the weirdest conversation Baz had ever listened in on: his older brother arguing with his dead father's ghost about whether or not Baz should be present when the ghost was laid to rest. He could almost hear his Dad's soft burr. He tried to match his stare to Sol's, tried to will himself into the conversation. "Hé, Papa," he said quietly, and heard the quick inhalation Sol took beside him. "You should get some rest, Dad. You deserve it."

One ear to Baz, Sol turned away at these words, perhaps to hear the spirit's response. It was still and quiet, and if their father's ghost said something to Baz, he couldn't hear it, not at all. His breath was white in the winter air, and eddies whirled within it as though something moved through, close enough to touch, and Baz stepped back, startled.

A few feet away, Sol stumbled, caught himself, straightened, his hands balling into fists at his side. "Leave him alone." Two steps towards Baz, Sol's eyes rimmed white, looking at what Baz could not see. "Non, Papa. Je lui dis pas. No way."

"Tell me what?" Baz asked, confused. He'd seen ghosts move things, and he thought that his father's ghost had just shoved Sol, hard. It had sometimes gotten physical between these two. Why would death change anything?

The newly dead, and the angry ones, those ghosts were the easiest to find, Baz knew, and Aurèle Sarrazin was both.

Sol's eyes were focused on a spot just to Baz's left and Baz looked. "He wants you to sing." Sol shook his head. "The bastard wants a song."

Baz swallowed. Crazy damn ghosts, because his whole life, Aurie had told Baz 'ta gueule', shut up, no singing. Play the fiddle if you have to, but no damn singing, except maybe in the car, but nowhere else. And now, now when it was so damn late in the day, when things had already crossed over, or were crossing, *now* the man wanted a song?

"What," Baz whispered, cold and truly scared. "What should I do?"

A spasm crossed Sol's face, anger maybe or something deeper—*loss*—and he wiped one hand across the landscape as though erasing something. "Comment est-ce que tu peux demander ça?" he asked thin air. "What right do you have, to ask that?" Not talking to Baz, not with that voice.

More in French that Baz didn't understand; Sol had been older when they'd left Louisiana, and had more of Maman's time, more of Papa's. More of everything, both good and bad.

It was a last request from his father and it was the one thing Aurie and Baz had always shared, maybe the only way in which they were alike: a love of music. So Baz called up what he knew, what he remembered. An old song that his mother had sung. He didn't know all the words, or didn't remember them. "J'ai passé devant ta porte," he sang, remembering, and then worrying it was their mother's song, and that maybe it would further infuriate Aurie's ghost. Still, it was what had come.

Beside him, he saw Sol stiffen, turn toward him, mouth open a little. Horrified that Baz was doing it, was doing as their father had requested.

Despite his father's encouragement in other musical directions, Baz knew he could sing. Aurie hadn't told him to shut up because he couldn't hold a tune. As much a part of him as anything else, his voice was true, especially on a cold night, prairie wind the only accompaniment, that and his brother's uneasy sigh.

"Assez," Baz heard his brother say under his breath then, at volume: "C'est assez!"

Baz stopped, because Sol didn't yell often and not like that. He wondered, briefly, if his father's ghost was cowed. Probably not.

Into this silence, Baz whispered what his brother had shouted: "That's enough." Nothing moved. "Both of you." He turned to Sol, who was not looking at him, was not moving in the slightest. Baz knew that bandages were best taken off at speed, but he was reluctant to tell Sol what to do. There wasn't much precedence. "Send him on his way," he begged, softly. "Please."

Baz realized that Sol's eyes were full, were brimming in the cold, cold night. In spite of this, or maybe because of it, Sol wouldn't look at him. Sol shook his head, his stare on something—someone—Baz couldn't see. "I can't," Sol said and Baz had to reach for the words they were so soft.

Baz reached out with one hand, drew Sol into a tight embrace, whispered into his ear. "You have to. There's no one else." Then, laughing. "Vraiment? You want him dropping by your place all the time?" Baz had already said his goodbyes at the morgue, he realized. His father was gone. This was just a ghost his brother was seeing. Easy to believe that, just slightly-cracked Sol seeing things that weren't there.

Sol pulled away, one hand, the bare one, wiping his face. "You don't understand." And he looked over the empty tracks, eyes hollow in the night. "There's so many."

Baz swallowed, looked in spite of himself. So many? "You only have to get rid of the one."

"The one?" Sol repeated, chuckling without warmth. Then he shrugged with one shoulder, bent down again, looked out into the emptiness that was not, not to him. "D'accord," he agreed quietly.

He stretched out his hand, buried it in the frozen gravel, and said some words so low that Baz didn't even know which language he was speaking. After a few minutes, still like this, Sol brought his hand up to his chest, unzipped his parka, and pushed his hand under his sweater and his shirt, hand against heart for a moment only, then to his lips, a word muttered, then to the ground again. He glanced up, and his eyes were swimming, reflecting light, and he tapped the ground with his fingertips, three times in closure.

He stayed like that for a long time.

Finally, Baz bent down beside him, drew him up, but Sol came up quickly then, pushed Baz to the side, and said more words, one word, actually, and Baz recognized it: *Dégagez!* What his mother had said among the crypts, fifteen years ago, the day she had left them. *Maybe she was talking to me,* Baz thought. *Go away.*

Sol stood shaking for a few moments, and Baz didn't know what he was seeing, what he was watching, but he could guess: ghosts, fleeing from him, because he could send them on their way and the confused ones were scared of Sol, and the angry ones simply hated him.

* * *

They went back to the motel, but the room was too small, and Sol knew he'd go nuts if he stayed there with Baz's quizzical brows and his thoughtful words and more thoughtful silences. He said he was going for a walk but Baz wouldn't let him go alone and that was almost the same as him saying that Sol was a child that needed looking after.

They crossed the street to a bar instead, a cheap kind of place where the light came from brewery neon and plastic faux-Tiffany pool table lamps. Baz stood out like a peacock in a henhouse. In a way, Sol wished one of the burly railworkers slouched over the beery tables would start a fight, make some comment about the pierced eyebrow, or nose, or ears. Even about the mauvais haircut.

As always, Baz grinned through everything, and had the bartender joking within seconds. Sol sat back on a bench, ordered a Beam while Baz babbled innocuously to a complete stranger on the other side of the room.

There had to have been at least ten or twelve ghosts tonight. At least. Old, new. Pissed off, most of them. All there because Baz was singing, and Aurie had wanted Sol to see that, damn him. The song had been a lesson, for Sol's edification. Reminding Sol of what Baz could do, as if Sol could ever forget.

*You look out for him.* Aurie's ghost had repeated itself, smile sitting sad on a grizzled face, head not so fucked up by the train accident this appearance, thank God. Listening to Baz sing, to his beautiful voice, transported, at peace. Then said, last words to his son, *What are you doing, gars, having a conversation with a goddamn ghost? What the hell did I teach you?*

In the end, as Sol had opened a pathway shining in the night, tear-blinded, he recognized the longing in his father's eyes, listening to Baz. Not wanting to go anywhere. Mangled body coming together at last, straightening and unfolding and *becoming* and Sol thought that maybe that was what had been hardest, seeing his father as he should have been—whole and happy, before Mireille had left, before exile, before incarceration.

*Shouldn't that make me feel better?* But it all came down to what had never been, and what was and what was left, which was fuck-all.

Sol had another bourbon, a double, making a bee-line toward oblivion. Baz was still yabbering at the bar, a couple of girls there now with their witless boyfriends. Better that kind of attention. Better than all those ghosts, transfixed by his brother's voice, from the first fucking note. Sol rubbed his face with one hand, felt the walls like a vise, wanted the open road keenly as a drug, as a woman. Wanted the thrill of being in the cab of the ambulance with life or death in the headlights. Wanted to feel alive.

Instead of this.

He should have been more alert, more *aware*, but after the performance down by the tracks, Baz was shaky inside and needed the warmth of company, the bub of low chat, interest in the eyes of others. He needed to be seen by living things and Sol didn't count. It was only a couple of minutes, and then it was an hour, and then he realized that it wasn't a night for leaving Sol alone, that it was already too late.

From across the room, Baz heard Sol's voice raised in discord, flinging abuse with all the abandon of an inmate at a monkey house, the object of his tirade a man roughly twice his size. Baz eased away from his new friends, walked over, sat with Sol, laid one hand on his sleeve. Sol jerked his arm away, and wouldn't meet Baz's eyes. "This trou d'cul," he started, and Baz smiled, turned to the bigger man, who glowered in return, recognizing the word 'asshole' in any language. Not as much liquor as Sol, Baz guessed. Still able to hit edit. "He can 'brasse mon cul."

"He's had a rough night," Baz explained to the stranger. "He doesn't mean—"

"I fucking mean every fucking word," Sol complained and Baz hated the sound of alcohol, wearing away his brother's more reasonable lines.

"You don't," Baz replied firmly. "And we got a long drive tomorrow, and—"

"Coque-toi," Sol said, and stood.

As arguments went, it wasn't exactly a coherent one, but at least Sol seemed to be heading out. Or not. Walking a straight line that would have done a roadblock cop proud, Sol sauntered over to the bar, leaving Baz and the big guy.

"You a fag?" the big guy asked. Okay, maybe as much liquor as Sol.

Baz decided that he wasn't going to answer that and instead followed Sol to the bar, where he already had a tumbler full of what Baz guessed was bourbon. Either that or rum, but rum was usually drunk straight from the bottle. A glass seemed to be Sol's sole concession to civility.

"Laisse-moi tranquille," Sol straight-armed him before Baz had a chance to say anything.

"This one," holding up a finger and gesturing to the glass, "and then we're out of here."

"Pique-toi."

Baz didn't say anything in return, but Sol drank the bourbon in one slow steady gulp like salvation might be found at the bottom. He spun the glass on the counter, dropped some bills beside it. "Encore," gesturing with the same fingers that had sealed their father's ghost to its road, and Baz snatched back the money.

"Non, Beausoleil."

"Oh, man, you guys are Cajun, right?" one of the guys Baz had been talking to earlier asked, his girlfriend eyeing Baz with unconcealed interest, distracting him for the one second that mattered. "Our dog was a rescue pet that we adopted after Hurricane Ka—"

And Sol's left-handed undercut moved so quickly, Baz couldn't have stopped it, eyes couldn't even track it. Baz barely understood what had happened, even as the guy dropped to the ground, dazed, and Sol advanced a step. This, Baz could deal with, and he pushed between them, shoved Sol back a foot, kept his hand on his brother's shoulder.

"I'm not a fucking Cajun, you fucking tout-emmerdé." Sol's voice caught but Baz had a fistful of his sweater and pulled him out the door, Sol blank and unresisting.

Baz understood this, knew what had to happen next. Without saying anything, Sol retrieved a half-bottle of dark rum from the back of the Wagoneer, uncapped it, took a long swig, wiped his mouth with his sleeve as Baz opened the motel door.

He lasted another fifteen minutes before crashing. Baz watched, not really watching, eyes on the grainy television screen, as Sol downed the rest of the bottle, not stopping for anything now, goal in sight. After a couple of minutes, Baz cautioned a look, but Sol's eyes were closed and the empty bottle was on the bedside table beside a truly objectionable lamp.

Baz snapped off the television, tossed the bottle in the garbage can in the bathroom, rolled Sol to his side and draped him with a blanket. A touring musician knew how to put a passed-out person to bed safely. *I know how to keep Sol safe.* But he didn't know how to do that, not really. Baz touched his brother's head with tentative fingers, hair sticking out in all directions. Baz had been waiting for this, for Sol to apply the only anesthetic he knew, the same one Aurie had used to great effect. That's what Sol had been working towards.

Baz was working toward something a little different. This was his chance to get out, to follow the thread of a question he wasn't going to ask. Sol didn't move as Baz retrieved the truck keys from the front pocket of his jeans. *Just as well*, Baz thought, but didn't mean it. Part of him wanted Sol to wake up, to stop him. *This is crazy.*

The snow meant he didn't drive fast. He told himself that was the reason—the police would show a lot of interest in his driving record if they caught up with him, and no insurance would cover the damage Sol would do to Baz if he dented the truck. Sol's truck rumbled slowly along the white street alongside the tracks, to the place where they'd been earlier that night.

He pulled his brother's cap over his head, deliberate in everything now, killing minutes, extending the gap between decision made and decision enacted. Finally, he took a deep breath, shut off the engine, left the keys dangling in the ignition, ready for his return. Without further deliberation, he got out, ducked through the broken fence and kept to the shadows, breath steaming from him, its own kind of apparition.

His mother had used ghosts for her own purposes, that much Baz understood. She had told fortunes, divined the future. Aurie had told him about it, anger in his eyes, explaining why she'd gone and why they weren't going to talk about it. *You don't use them, gars. You let them go.* Not that Aurie had been particularly good at letting anything go, but Baz understood the principle. The thing was, that meant ghosts were useful, useful for otherwise hidden information, and Baz didn't think his mother was evil, not like Aurie had insinuated.

He had no idea how the calling of ghosts worked, but he had to try. Their father was gone; Sol had seen to that. But his brother had also said that there were many more ghosts down by the tracks, and the ghosts had come when he sang. They didn't talk about that, neither brother nor father, why Baz was only allowed to sing in the car. Nobody talked about anything of importance. Baz didn't want to remember, couldn't remember much, and couldn't rely on what he did remember. An August day, down south, long ago. *Sing me a song*, his sister had begged. An August day, housed in him like a bat high in a rafter, invisible until it lifted to flight.

*It's too hot for singing,* he had complained. But: *Anything you want, Mademoiselle Je-sais-tout.* And Baz knew what had happened next, that day and in the days that had followed.

*All my fault.*

The sound of metal moving on metal came to him from across the tracks, the smell of cold, of iron. He sang, self-conscious at first, tentative. *It might not work, I might be doing this all wrong.* So cold—was it colder than before? His heart tripped high in his chest. Only the one song, though, before he halted, hunkered down like he'd seen Sol do, one hand on the ground. Screw it, it was like trying to fix an engine blindfolded. "Okay," Baz whispered, teeth clattering in the night. "Where the hell are you guys?"

Only the wind, and the far call of engine and train whistle.

Another song, and he was definitely unnerved, because they might be all around him, and he couldn't see a damn thing. The moon was behind clouds now, and the yard was all line and smudge and blur. "Hey, c'mon. I need a favor."

He felt open, felt seen, felt cold fingers run across his hand. He startled, drew his hand back from the ground, shaking. Wind maybe. Or not. *I don't want to remember,* he thought, briefly. *I don't want this.*

Then, beside him, behind him, beyond the chain link at his back, gravel shifted, skirled. Baz held still, wouldn't see anything, even if he looked. Maybe all this was predicated on not-looking, who knew? Maybe this was his way with spirits, different from Sol's.

As long as it wasn't one of the railroad bulls, coming to check out what Baz was doing in the yards. The gravel crunched again, sound of lifeless bleak density shifting in the night. Then, a jagged breath, a cancerous intake of air over scar tissue and through blood frothing in the lungs. Baz held very still, hand back out against the ground, fingers aching with cold.

"A favor?" The question rattled from behind. Not a rattle. A chuckle.

Baz licked his lips, quickly, half-hoping it was a cop, telling himself that it was a cop. "Yeah, no biggie. I just—"

"You want to know where she is."

No cop.

Despite himself, Baz looked. He couldn't see anything at first. And then, behind the chain link, metal holding it back, somehow, like that might matter, a dark haze as insubstantial as smoke. Still on his haunches, Baz pivoted on the balls of his feet, faced it, though that was the wrong word. There was no face, there was nothing.

There was something. *Don't look at it. Oh God, please don't look at it.*

A memory boiled under the surface, this voice, this feeling of being watched, of being *seen*, and Baz's breath came short and fast, heart hammering, hair on his arms raising, everything in him begging for flight.

"Are you a ghost?" Because this didn't feel like a ghost, and he'd never seen a ghost in his life. His voice, warmed up by the singing, sounded pathetic, thin as though the music had leeched all life from him.

The thing just chuckled again, shifted. "I don't answer questions." And it drifted down track, away from Baz.

No time to second guess what this was, ghost or not, because he hadn't come here just to drive opportunity away. "Wait!" and the black smudge stalled. Baz straightened, tried to steady his voice. "Yeah, that's what I need."

The sound of amusement came again, covered by a rough cough, like the air didn't suit it. "Fait attention. Needing is dangerous, Basile Sarrazin."

Baz's heart banged like a pinball in his chest, and he put his hand to his mouth, blew on it, covering up his shaking. Fucking perceptive for a ghost, if that's what this was. Something from the swamp, stirred up here on the dry prairie by his need, a childhood nightmare made real. "Still."

The thing came closer, but didn't seep through the fence, seemed contained and Baz hoped it was. "Long time no see, bougre. You got real tall, didn't you?" it asked. What the hell? Did it *know* him? Baz's stomach curdled, turned in on itself, and he tried to concentrate on the here and now, even though memory tugged hard.

"Do you know me?"

"I don't answer questions, like I said."

Baz sucked air. He'd been told. "I don't need to know where she is. I'm just…curious." Such a lie and he wondered if it could tell. "Just want to know if she's okay."

The thing laughed again. "That so? What are you offering me?"

"Hey," Baz complained, eyebrows inching up. "I already gave you two songs."

Only the wind again, and Baz couldn't see it, and he wondered if he'd said the wrong thing. Finally though, like the wind had shifted it, the black smudge appeared again on the periphery, down track a little way. As Baz watched, it solidified slightly, crabbed along. It didn't move like smoke, it darted, backtracked, zigged unnaturally. Despite the keen freezing air, Baz broke out into a sweat.

"Your songs?" Like he'd served up dog shit.

"Fine. What do you want then?"

"I'm doin' you a favor, boy," it said, but it kept its distance. "Being nice."

Baz knew that it wasn't and he found he didn't care. "Nice?" Baz repeated, buying time. "What do you want?" Made him ask twice, and Baz hated that.

"Want, or need?" the thing said, playing, past chiding him about his questions. "No biggie," it repeated without any trace of humor. "We can settle up later." And it shambled away, and Baz let out an involuntary sound of protest like something was being taken from him, wrenched out, a hot dark hand on his chest.

The creature stopped, and Baz heard the chuckle again. "In your pocket, child." It dissipated between one moment and the next, maybe between blinks, and Baz shook where he stood, hot and frozen beyond measure.

Dreading it, head so light he thought he might blow away or fall down, Baz reached into his coat pocket with a chilled hand, fingers bone white, bloodless, trembling. He withdrew what he found there: a scrap of paper, a ripped corner of unidentifiable newsprint. Letters and numbers scrawled with a malfunctioning ball point pen. An address. His own handwriting. An answer and a promise made in the night, and Baz wondered what he'd be made to pay for this gift.

# THREE

## THE VISITOR

The construction worker lay on his back amid stacked lumber and reels of cable and he wasn't moving at all, a piece of rebar protruding from his left side at an angle that would make anyone wince, pointing out the direction of God, perhaps. Sol checked himself from looking up, but just barely. *Shoulda said a Hail Mary, buddy*, he thought. The loose piece of scrap iron had likely punctured something significant, but there was no way Sol could tell what just yet.

The worker's airway was clear, his breathing shallow but steady. His eyes weren't open, however, and Sol checked the packing already in place; less bleeding than you'd think. Hadn't hit an artery. All good, for the moment.

There was the matter of the drop, but Sol didn't have time to worry about that. Emergency medicine meant assessing the situation and then focusing concentration to only what was at hand, and in this case it was a very narrow ledge indeed, a slab of cantilevered concrete about the width of mid-sized car, no railing, nothing but air and wind. Sol opened the ALS bag he'd brought up to what he estimated was around the twenty-third floor of the condominium under construction. He'd need more gauze and bandages—moving the patient in any direction was going to mean blood, maybe lots of it. He rooted around in the bag, found the extra gauze.

At that point, he did glance down the giddy height, but that was only to ascertain how many vehicles were on-scene, nothing more. Two engines, three ladders, an X-car. A goddamn party. No news vans, thank God, always a relief as far as Sol was concerned. Probably most reporters had taken the day off, a Friday sandwiched between Christmas Day and the weekend. *Only keeners like me and Mr. Rebar on the job today.* Sol wondered if the construction worker was avoiding home, too.

"We can bring him down with that," he said to his partner Wayne as he gestured upwards to the white construction crane, cross-arm barely visible from their angle, strung with Christmas lights. From this close proximity Sol could see the wind whipping the cables around, lines tangled, held in place with plastic ties.

"Man, you had your Wheaties this morning," Wayne observed, eyebrows shooting up, gaze direct. It was a question: you, or me?

"Cakewalk. I'll do it." Even as he said it, Sol factored in the wind: it would be one hell of a bumpy ride. One hell of cold ride, too. He could barely feel his fingers in the thin blue gloves. At least the construction site was close to the trauma center at Denver Health, because this rescue wasn't going to be pretty or neat. One of the firefighters radioed instructions while Sol stabilized the patient's neck in a collar and put the extra packing around the wound.

"Hey. Hey! What's your name?" Sol asked the construction worker, even though he knew the man's name was Marty—one of the guys down below had said it: Marty's up there, and he's bad, man. "Hey," he rubbed the man's sternum with his knuckle.

Marty's eyes opened, and he stared at Sol, tried to focus. "That's good, Marty," Sol continued, dropping his voice low. "I'm Sol, I'm a paramedic. We're gonna get you down from here, don't worry." Wayne was still getting details from the firefighter; at least they didn't need to cut the rebar, it was just a scrap piece, no longer than twelve inches, which was long enough, and the Fire Department's EMT-first responders had done a good job stabilizing the wound before Sol and Wayne had rolled up. Sol listened to Marty's chest, but the wind was high and that was all he could hear, no suck of a punctured lung. Just a matter of not jostling that bar and keeping the BP steady as possible.

Sol looked up and saw where Marty must have fallen from—a gap in what was going to be the ceiling fifteen feet above on the next level. Marty was damn lucky he hadn't fallen just a couple of feet to the west, because then he'd have gone down twenty-three stories and at that point, Sol wouldn't have been worrying about stabilizing Marty for much of anything.

The day was clear and cold and the mountains were so sharp they almost drew blood from the sky. But thinking about mountains was widening the scope of concentration, and wasn't useful at all. With a groan of metal against metal, the crane lurched into motion, swinging round, startling Sol, like spotting a hunting bird circling overhead, a primitive reaction to danger. He started an IV for Marty, put in something for the pain, and met Marty's eyes, which were following Sol's every move—good. Alert was good. He retrieved a harness from another bag and belted up, adjusted the buckles and bindings, kept his eye on the crane. Satisfied, he knelt beside his patient again, checked his vitals one last time.

"Am I going to die?" Marty asked, and Sol noticed red froth at the corner of his lips. Sol listened again to Marty's lungs, this time heard that one was good, and one was not. He checked the wound under the packing, knew he'd need to do something about it, because that piece of bar had hit lung, collapsing it. The wound looked too low though, the angle impossible.

Broken rib piercing the lung? No time to wonder; Sol called out to Wayne for the bag. Seconds later, a 12 gauge needle was in Marty's chest, the trapped pocket of air decompressing with a hiss, quick turn of the valve and Marty took a stuttering breath, color back. Sol repacked, asked Wayne for an occlusive bandage, and sealed up the wound, leaving a flutter valve.

Marty's question, though. "If you can ask me that, I'd say no." Calm, with a smile. He laid one gloved hand on the man's chest, fingers splayed wide. Wayne and a firefighter were behind, near the drop, getting the stokes basket ready. They all wore helmets and heavy gauge gloves, neither of which would matter if they fell off that edge. "Let's move it, mesdemoiselles," Sol called out.

Without warning, Sol felt pressure against his hand, like something was rising from Marty's chest, something pushing upwards. "Not on my watch," he muttered, meeting Marty's wandering stare. "You stay in there," he said quietly. "Stay put. You don't need to go no place." Anyone listening would think he was crazy, but the wind was up and Wayne and two firefighters appeared to be in a life or death struggle with that basket, attaching it to the crane's hook, steadying it with one hand. Sol concentrated for the moment it would take, keeping things together for just a little while longer, his hand acting as a latch to Marty's soul, refusing to budge.

Marty's lips moved silently, but he kept his eyes on Sol the whole time. Sol nodded to him. "You hang in there, we're going to go for a little ride."

On the count of three, they carefully lifted Marty into the basket, the rebar sticking up incongruously, horrifying. "Don't look," Sol advised, clipping his safety harness to the ring above the basket and double-checking all the fastenings. It was a long way down, but he'd spent a few summers working construction, so he didn't think about it, just nodded to Wayne. "See you downstairs," he said, keeping one hand on Marty's chest as the crane started to take up slack.

"I'll keep the car running." Then Wayne was on the radio again, checking in with the captain down on the ground, and Sol was suddenly grateful, because Wayne might tell the worst and dirtiest jokes Sol had ever heard in his life, might be a walking invitation to a sexual harassment suit, but he was a rock when things went sideways.

Wayne tapped the hook one last time, gave the order and Sol felt himself lifting, sudden weightlessness, a sway, harness cutting into him. Sky and city and mountains turned a slow disorienting circle. Wind-tears froze on his lashes. He grabbed one of the ropes attached to the basket with one hand, and looked to Marty, whose blue eyes were reflecting sky and not much else.

*Shitshitshit.*

Sol, now dangling off the side of the building, tore off one latex glove and put his bare hand onto Marty's chest, into the rip that they'd cut through his vest and shirt and undershirt. Hand to chest, skin to skin. The pressure welling against his fingers was enormous, without heat or cold, so big it was like a whale breaching the ocean's surface.

"No," Sol said, firm as the earth, solid, spinning in the wind and the air, a hundred feet in the sky. Flying. "No," looking Marty in the eyes. "Écoute-moi, Marty. You stay right here, this isn't anything a doctor can't fix. We'll get you down to the ground, into the rig. Wayne drives like every day's the Indy, five minutes to the hospital. Don't you get all morbid on me—" and the pressure lessened. Sol checked Marty's vitals, which were better, his color was better, the eyes blinked and focused.

"Am I gonna die?" Marty asked again as Sol peered over his shoulder, could make out the faces waiting for them on the ground. He glanced back at Marty, shook his head.

"Not this time," he answered.

\* \* \*

Marty's paperwork was hellacious, mostly because it was a workplace accident, which always brought out the lawyers. Every T was crossed, every I dotted. Sol put up with Wayne's running monologue about a stripper he'd once dated while they ate a very late lunch in Denver Health's cafeteria.

Up until Marty, the shift had been pretty boring, as daytime shifts sometimes were. Now it looked like snow was in the forecast after a surprisingly un-white Christmas, and Sol knew that sale-shoppers rushing home plus snowstorm was sure to equal vehicular disaster.

"I tell ya, Sarrazin," Wayne went on, oblivious to Sol's concentration. "The suction that girl could bring to bear—"

Sol held up a hand. Wayne, to his credit, stopped. "Who was the attending?" Sol asked, knowing full well but wanting Wayne to shut the hell up.

Wayne rolled his eyes, told him, and then got up to help himself to another coffee. "Next year, you and Robbie should come with us to Vegas. Cheryl always has a blast and if you fly Christmas Day, it's a steal. I mean, gambling all night Christmas Eve? It's like...like..."

Sol glanced up. "Nothing says 'Come let us adore Him' like a straight flush."

Wayne's smile widened. "Exactly!"

The idea of Robbie spending Christmas Day in Vegas was virtually inconceivable; she always insisted on going to her sister's and spoiling the nieces and nephews while Renard ran amuck. This year, while they'd been seated for turkey, the dog had eaten an entire gingerbread house left unguarded on a coffeetable, crawled under a bed, and thrown up extravagantly. Sol had heard all about it this morning when she'd come through the door, Renard following sheepishly behind. Sol was glad work provided some excuse for missing this sort of bonne spectacle.

Sol read over the last of the report, signed it, and then stood. "I'm gonna check on Marty, see if he's out of surgery yet." Wayne shrugged magnanimously: whatever you say, partner.

Marty was still in the OR, but seemed to be doing well. His wife was in the waiting room and as soon as she spotted Sol and Wayne, she burst into tears, wrapped herself around Wayne's massive frame, and cried on his uniform. Sol drank from the fountain and tried to make himself invisible, which wasn't difficult with Wayne around. Mrs. Marty told them that she had always *known* her husband was going to die on the job, she'd had his chart done.

Sol assumed that Wayne would say something totally inappropriate, given five additional minutes.

Then he realized he could use a few minutes. He gestured to Wayne over the wife's shoulder, rotated one finger in the air, then splayed all of them wide: take off in five. Marty wasn't dead, wasn't even dying thanks to them. Wayne would probably point that out real soon to the missus because Wayne didn't have a lot of time for superstition.

Down the corridor in Admitting, Sol sweet-talked one of the counter clerks, asked if he could use her computer to check the latest weather warnings, and waited until she was busy with a desk request before tabbing the browser window and entering a new address in the field. He keyed in an EMS search site, and using the login already associated with the terminal, entered the Nebraska system, then made a specific inquiry for Lincoln County.

It had been almost ten days since the last death, after all, and Sol had been keeping an eye on this part of the rail line, just to see if anything else was happening. Ten days and counting; the whole thing felt like a time bomb.

Sol looked up, had to close his eyes briefly before continuing. Ten days since his *father's* death, not some anonymous body by the tracks. He swallowed. The last time he'd seen his father in the flesh, he'd been just another stiff, mangled beyond recognition, fingers curled in a ward, and his own son, who had learned all he knew about death and ghosts from those hands, had not known them. That death had been the last one for this particular ghost working the lines in and out of North Platte. Although, technically, it was more than ten days, because Aurie's ghost had said it had been killed by something different than the ghost both father and son were hunting. If Sol could believe his father's ghost, Aurie's killer wasn't a spirit at all. It was something baser, more lethal. *Hated.* Les petits mauvais, les diables.

Not something that Sol had ever thought to contend with, a devil. Not something he knew much about.

The computer's little hourglass circled around, waiting for the site to cough up the data. Not a lot of people had been the subject of EMS responses in Lincoln County over the last ten days, so it didn't take much effort to scroll through the entries. Then: December 24, two DOAs eight miles west of North Platte down the line at Hershey. Possible murder-suicide, nature of injury blunt trauma to the head. *Like with the others in Bailey Yard*, Sol thought, knowing it was a stretch. This nice couple hadn't died in a rail-car, weren't accountants or retired teachers inexplicably trying to catch a ride at the tracks and getting murdered by a ghost for their troubles. This couple had died in their house. He checked an online map: the house was right by the tracks.

Identity, Paul Hurst and his wife Aileen. Sol wrote this down on a piece of paper, along with the names of the investigating officers and the dead couple's home address, and folded it into his jacket pocket. He exited the site, erased the history, and got to his feet as the clerk gave the visitor at the counter directions to the outpatient clinics.

Sol called thanks over his shoulder, wondering when he'd get a chance to go back to Nebraska, given that he was working a double shift tomorrow. He wondered why he was really going. *Bon Dieu, don't I have ghosts in Denver? Why go looking for them, even asshole ghosts?* But he knew how many had come when Baz had sung, and he felt a sudden chill, a swoop of dread, like he'd forgotten something enormously important. Ghosts were one thing, devils another, and there was Baz, right in the middle. *Take care of him, gars.* Dammit. Their father had been killed while hunting a ghost, but he'd been killed by a devil. Were ghost and devil linked?

And that's why he had to go back.

Still the tail end of a shift to go, thank God, otherwise he'd just worry this like a bone, might give in and call, make sure Baz was okay. He returned to the rig, parked out front under the Speer Street entrance, and saw that Wayne was already sitting in the passenger seat, a satisfied smile on his round face. Sol tapped the window, and Wayne rolled down obligingly.

"You don't like that kind of shit, do you?" Wayne asked as Sol held his hand out for the keys. The temperature was dropping, the sky was the color of dryer lint. "The thank yous and the hugs. Sweet baby Jesus, it's the best damn part of the job. That and the thank-you pussy."

Sol opened the back, jumped in to stow the cleaned and resupplied ALS kit. He secured the compartment, then returned to the cab, where he took the driver's seat. Wayne had managed to grab two cans of Coke for them, and since there were no calls from dispatch, they sat for a moment, considering the landscape: low buff and brick-colored buildings, the park just to the north, trees fine and fuzzy as an old lady's hair.

Sol took the soda without comment, and considered Wayne's question. "The thanks are just, you know. Not necessary."

"Aw, you're such an uptight bastard." Wayne slurped loudly. "That's what Robbie tells me anyway."

"Mais, not when we're in bed, she don't," Sol returned, laughing softly. Robbie had once commented, after a particularly out-of-control staff BBQ, that bear repellent would work well on Wayne.

Wayne shook his head in disbelief. "That guy was circling the drain, man. I mean, seriously, Marty was a cocktail weenie on a toothpick. He's all pre-code-y, and you're swinging like Tarzan out there. I'm down the elevator, get to the bottom thinking no point in hurrying, because you're coming down with a stiff, and then. Dude's alive." Wayne stared in frank admiration. "Fucking amazing."

"Bon," Sol said, nodding. "That's why I do it. So I can see your little face light up like that." He grimaced. "Not for thank-you sex. Jesus."

The next call, whenever it happened, would probably take them to end of shift, so they lingered in the bay for longer than usual, taking a break. The construction site rescue had been one of those textbook ones that you read about, the kind that would have made the evening news if someone had been there with a camera, and both of them knew it. Not an everyday call, that one. Most calls involved confused old folks, vomiting drunks, infants with ear infections. Might as well savor the big shiny ones.

But Sol had already moved on from Marty's rescue, had returned to the tracks, which led to Baz. If his brother had tried to call on Christmas Day, Sol had been working and no one had been home to answer: Sol had forgotten to turn on the answering machine, maybe on purpose but he wasn't sure. In any case, there wasn't any way of saying 'screw you' to Baz without calling him directly.

Which Sol wasn't quite ready to do, on account of how they'd left things.

Sol had woken up in the shitty North Platte motel room, the keys to the Wagoneer on the bedside table, holding down a note. *Going to Minneapolis to get Dad's stuff. You can pick up the ashes this afternoon. I'll be in touch—or call me. Keep my stuff, okay? I'll be back in a few weeks. Thanks! Baz.*

He'd used an exclamation point, spazzy idiot. Sol had stayed in that bed for most of the day, only getting up to shower, shave, and drive over to the funeral home, where a suitably dour matron had given him a cardboard box of ashes. He didn't have any idea what to do with them, where the proper place to return them was. *Last seen beside the tracks. Adieu, Papa.*

He knew where, was lying to himself. Down south, that's where you re-turned someone like Aurie Sarrazin. That's where he belonged, always had, his river-blood running with salt, had been exiled to these white northern roads. People like Aurie belonged at the edge of the continent, where the land gave up, lost its battle with water. Where things shifted and changed and were unmappable, roads raised like veins, only to be washed away by the sorrow that was Gulf weather. Routes lost, land, history, soul—all temporary things.

Half his co-workers had volunteered after Katrina, and despite his father's stated wishes to the contrary, Sol had gone too. Had wanted to be a hero, do what his father couldn't, what his father had forbidden. Sol had come back within days, had been sent back, actually, had taken leave for weeks afterwards, another casualty of what that place had become.

He was never going to Louisiana again, not for any reason. And he hadn't spoken to his father since, save a handful of times, all at Baz's behest.

So Aurie was just going to have to make do in this landlocked place, where the land married sky, not salt water. What did ashes matter, in any case? After putting the cardboard box on the floor of the front passenger seat, Sol had crawled back into bed, slept straight through and returned to Denver the next morning, put what was left of his father on a shelf in the back workshop, next to Baz's half-constructed bike. He had picked up an extra shift an hour later, and had not looked back.

Of course, he'd told no one at work, nor used his father's death as an excuse for taking off a few extra days, especially with it so close to Christmas. In fact, he'd taken more shifts as the weather worsened in the week leading up to Christmas—a memorable skidding plane at the airport providing ample overtime even without the usual mayhem. Christmas was always the best time to pick up shifts: lots to do and no one wanting to do it. Robbie had been busy too, people needing their hair done around Christmas, though a new haircut meant squat by the time Sol saw anyone. It was true: no one in the back of an ambulance cared about clean underwear. Or hairstyles.

They'd almost finished their drinks when the snow started. It didn't take long for the light to fade, the temperature to drop, and for the calls to come in. Dispatch: MVA, ten minutes out. Sol started the engine, Code 10—lights and siren—and they were wheels up.

The Grindery had slumped into bored neglect some time in the mid-80s, judging by the vintage plastic letters that spelled out 'Todays Soup: gardan veg'. The diner could have been in any small town anywhere in Canada, but it certainly wasn't in downtown Toronto, and that's all that really mattered to Lutie. She stared at the plastic wrapped pastries stacked on the counter beside a 'We Support the Troops' coin donation box and wondered if she was hungry enough to experiment with botulism. God alone knew how long those buttertarts had been embalmed.

There was almost always a double-double to be had at the base Canex, but she'd had enough of army culture to last a lifetime, and coming up here for Christmas break when her family's last posting had been at CFB Kingston added insult to injury. Kingston, at least, knew coffee from coffee.

Lutie chewed her pen, compiling a mental list of pros and cons about the city of Brandon, Manitoba versus Kingston, Ontario. Plenty of cons, damn few pros. Take travel times: Kingston was two hours from her home base at the University of Toronto. Brandon, or more precisely, CFB Shilo, was two days straight west, if you didn't need sleep. The weather hadn't exactly cooperated, either, even though Lutie had good snow tires. The Trans-Canada highway had been closed just west of Winnipeg because of white-outs and she'd had to overnight at a crappy motel.

*I should have flown*, she thought. Flying though, that meant tickets and arranged schedules and being trapped on a military base without wheels, and that was how Lutie had spent the last ten years of her life. Not a chance, thank you very much.

She'd driven into downtown Brandon because she couldn't stand her mother fussing over her anymore; since Christmas Eve, when she'd arrived typically late, her mother had made sure everything was the way Lutie preferred it. Her own room, with familiar pillow cases. First choice of television offerings. And yesterday, she'd been given far too many presents, an overflowing stocking, and the turkey was browned to perfection. Dad had given her the drumstick before remembering that she'd been eating vegetarian for close to a year.

This morning, citing Boxing Day sales as her excuse, she'd eaten a peanut butter sandwich on the fly and fled. Dad had sat back in the worn leather La-Z-Boy that he'd had since before forever, smiling at her in a way that said he understood her fidgeting. He had been in uniform, had been working non-stop. Troops had just come back from Afghanistan; meaning that the chaplain's services were required more than ever. A weird reversal of common sense: coming home was often harder than leaving.

The irony was not lost on Lutie.

She glanced up from her novel, hoped that the practice of leaving a paying customer alone for hours on end applied here as much as it did in big city coffee shops, and checked the clock on the wall. Maybe another hour, and then she'd have to get going. She should probably grab something to eat, though. In deference to Lutie's eating habits, Mum was making lasagna for dinner and Lutie hadn't had the heart to tell her that her vegetarian version sucked.

Finally, she slipped the novel and a notebook into the day pack she carried around like it was part of a uniform, and smiled obligingly at the woman behind the counter, who also nosed a book, chicken soup for somebody's soul.

Outside, the thermometer had dipped way below freezing, and with the wind kicking up from the northeast, it was bitter. When they'd lived in Edmonton, there had been chinooks, but there was no such winter relief here. Her car, a dependable Japanese model that was as non-descript as the landscape, complained and didn't want to start immediately. She was careful not to flood it with her efforts, but also considered how having car trouble might be turned to advantage: No car, no way home, no lasagna, no stilted conversation.

But then her dad would have to pick her up and that would make her feel guilty, because he'd do it so willingly. They were so damn normal, all of them. In contrast.

She pulled the car from the curb, edged down a road lacy with cold-cracked pavement, and headed north. It didn't take any time at all to be in the country, flat sheets of white, grass poking through, dotted tracks of coyote or dog or some other animal running across fields and over fences, tracing paths to destinations unknown. The landscape was solid, permanent, didn't change much. Despite the snow, the view would be pretty much the same in summer, just different colors, leaves on the far trees. Changes were slow, not easily parsed. In some ways, the prairies were better than a lot of places in that regard, where change came so fast, so frequently.

It wasn't a long drive, not long enough by far, so she took it slow, hardly any traffic at all, just white in the headlights as the sun fell behind her, starting its slow descent to the west. Nightfall would take forever around here, like the sun was just as reluctant to go home as she was.

Home. Strange word. Toronto had been home now for a year and a half, first in a college dorm, and now with roommates in a shared house off Queen West. Every minute of every day there was stuff going on, and when there was lots going on, things didn't stick out as much, just became wallpaper, which was fine by Lutie. White noise was good, things blended in, because otherwise, you noticed the weird shit.

Like that. Take that, for example.

She'd seen the ghost on her way into town and it was still there, no great surprise. She might not have noticed it this time in the fading light and the white on gray on white, but she realized she was looking for it. Just a guy, looked like it had lost its way, feedlot ball cap jammed on its head, wearing a plaid work shirt. The ghost looked at her as she slowed, pointed to something behind it, then back to her. Gray on white on gray—that was blood on its face, sad lost look in its eyes, in its very stance. It stood beside a makeshift cross jammed into the snowy verge, decayed flowers coated in snow and ice.

There was no traffic behind her, none in front, either, so Lutie slowed to a crawl, unrolled her window. She didn't get too close, kept her hand on the stick and her foot hovered above the accelerator. This was the kind of behavior her doctor told her not to indulge, but hell, she had time to kill, didn't she?

"Hey," she said to the ghost. "Are you lost?"

It looked surprised that she'd stopped; no one had probably stopped in a long time.

"You should get going, eh?" She gestured along the thin road. "It's cold out here. You should go home."

Again, that word. The ghost nodded to her, then lifted one arm. Behind it, Lutie could see the line of trees planted as a windbreak marking a far fence-line. "I don't know…" it said, and Lutie knew she shouldn't have stopped, that this was a sucker's move. The medication was for exactly this—so she didn't see shit like this, didn't talk to apparitions made of thin air. But the medications also meant she didn't *feel*, which was worse by far. Lutie regularly flushed the meds down the toilet and said she didn't.

"Sure you do. Don't even think about it. Just do it."

The ghost farmer scratched his head and staggered a little, like he was a couple sheets to the wind. "Just like that?"

"Just like that." She started to roll up the window, hadn't really come to a full halt, had just slowed—*I just slowed down, Mum, I'm not really stopping, I'm not really hearing voices, or seeing ghosts*—and kept it open a crack, just to have some fresh air, just so she didn't lose it. *I can ignore them.* It would be better to ignore them.

When she looked in her rearview mirror, she couldn't see the ghost anymore, just the sun slanting down. She'd drive by tomorrow, see if it was still—*No, you won't. You won't get caught up in this. It's not there, none of it.*

CFB Shilo was an open base, so she nodded to the guard at the gate, but didn't slow down—*I suppose he's not there, either, eh Lutie?*—and circled the maze of residential crescent streets until she found the one with the right name, a row of houses curving for no reason on the flat, flat land, pale blue aluminum siding blending into the early evening snow shadows. At least in cities like Halifax they had had the right idea: paint the hell out of the houses, make the place a little brighter. Here, though, the houses were on heavy meds, functional at best, as boring and unnoticeable as her car, as her clothes, as her presence in a classroom, at the back, not joining in the discussion, quiet not because she was shy, quiet because that meant she could get by and she had nothing to say to idiots, anyway.

There was a price to pay when you were noticed.

She pulled into a driveway, hoped it was the right house, because they all looked the same, then noticed her family's SUV parked two doors down. She backed up and re-parked in the right driveway. Stupid CFB subdivisions.

All the lights were on like there was a party, like electricity was free, like the planet wasn't going to hell in a handbasket, and Lutie knew what she'd find when she walked in—Bree bitching about having to set the dining table, Mum with everything under control, Marshall playing a computer game up in his room, the Major sitting at the kitchen table, newspaper spread out before him, everyone just waiting for her to be back, and it felt stifling.

God, she loved them, but it was a lot to handle, how much they loved her back. She sat in the car for a minute, preparing herself for it, telling herself to just take it, not to question it, just smile back. Take it easy.

*When have I ever been easy?* she thought, finally opening the car door, locking it out of habit when nobody was likely to steal what she had.

She went in the front because it was closest and she hadn't actually lived in this house, didn't know which way you were supposed to come in. It was unlocked of course, because her dad believed that you should keep your door open when you were in his position; the gesture was symbolic, as gestures often were, and Major Jim McGregor believed in the symbolic almost as much as he believed in salvation.

The light and heat and smell of cooking were all-encompassing, and she could hear the blare of Marshall's new favorite metal band thumping upstairs, the low throb of the Major's voice in the kitchen, as easy and smooth as peanut butter in August. Then the peal of her mum's laughter, and there was a nervous edge to it that caught Lutie by surprise. Karen McGregor didn't have a nervous bone in her body, ran a tight ship. The Major had his own arena down at the chapel; the homefront was Karen's.

And she was nervous.

Lutie had time to register this, then Karen's voice came down the hallway, reeking of the east coast in its wide open As and Rs: "Are you home, Lutie?" Then her mother appeared in the foyer, where Lutie was knocking the snow from her city boots, dropping her mittens on the stairs.

Karen smiled brightly, warm amber eyes gleaming in the dim hall light, wiping her hands on a tea towel. "Safe drive? Brandon's not much, eh?" She flicked a strand of auburn hair past her shoulder, gold winking from her hand.

Lutie startled slightly, alarmed at the sudden attention. "You're not kidding. What—"

"You have a visitor. Come into the kitchen."

A visitor? A *visitor*? Then caught the subject of the sentence—the visitor was hers. She padded in front of her mum in socked feet, pushed up the sleeves of her sweater, wondered that Karen was following her, not leading her. *Maybe she thinks I'll take off,* Lutie thought, too off-guard to find it funny.

Who would this be? Some soldier she'd gone to high school with, coming by the new chaplain's place? A university friend—but none of them were from Manitoba, none of them would just drop in.

There was no door between the hallway and the kitchen, and so she could hear the Major clearly. "Most of the guys come back okay, but you can imagine, one minute dodging IEDs on Afghan roads and then," snap of his fingers, "shopping at the neighborhood Loblaws, it's—" and he halted as she came into the kitchen, eyes to her immediately, telling her to *take it easy,* she knew that look, even as his voice was even and soft and steady.

*I'm no good at taking it easy, you know that.*

Beside him at the table, a cup of coffee in his hand, a young man followed the Major's gaze. He didn't look like he'd just come back on an AF transport, didn't look Army-issue at all: short caramel brown hair in an understated punk cut, a pin through his eyebrow, tall as he stood in one fluid motion, dark brows coming up over tropical eyes, long-lashed and blinking. Dressed like he didn't mean it. Ridiculously good-looking, had seen the sun sometime recently, which meant he wasn't from around here.

He licked his lips like everyone expected him to say something. "Hey, Lutie." Followed by an uncertain smile, eyes serious as they could be in a face plainly made for laughing. He looked like something was trying to get out of him—words, emotion, a joke.

*Ants in his pants.*

One hand came up like he was going to move towards her, then he jammed both of them into his jean pockets, looked to the Major first, then to Karen, but neither said a word.

"Yeah?" Lutie said slowly, drawing it out.

"It's me," the young guy said, a little half smile on his face, like he was talking to a cat in an alleyway. Like a smile would matter. "Baz."

# FOUR

## SALT BLOOD

Why drivers in Colorado, where it snowed every damn year, still got surprised by the first dusting and forgot all common sense was beyond Sol. Slow down; allow more time for braking; get snow tires. Assume when it's raining and the temperature drops thirty degrees within hours there will be ice, especially on windy stretches like bridges and overpasses.

People were seasonally-challenged: those first serious snowfalls, all hell broke loose.

The afternoon was so dark it might as well be night, and icy snow covered the overpass where a five car pile-up had closed the road in both directions, snarling traffic so badly everyone was going to miss their turkey leftovers. Sol drove along the shoulder, fast as was safe under the circumstances. A flower delivery truck was at the center of it all, petals and blossoms strewn across the wreckage like a NASCAR wedding gone terribly wrong.

Three rigs were already on the scene, and more Fire Department personnel than Sol could easily count in the snow-speckled dark. One crew already had a casualty on a stretcher; an older woman wept in a firefighter's embrace on the concrete median divider.

Sol took his bearings: flower truck man, check, over there with a FD

54

blanket on his shoulders, talking loudly in Spanish to anyone who would listen.

A Volvo, barely dented, least of anyone's worries, and there, the businessman that belonged to it, talking on a cell phone. The businessman looked pissed, was tearing someone's head off and shitting down their throat. Maybe he was a lawyer. Probably wouldn't appreciate a paramedic asking to check his blood pressure. In any case, Sol could tell what it was from here, no cuff needed.

An SUV, long scrape along its side—its driver was the one being hauled away on the stretcher.

A serious country truck, the cowboy inside it now outside, talking with a police officer, holding a bandage to his head as a paramedic tried to get a word in edgewise.

Further away, a body was on the ground, a first-responder from the FD crouched close by, working it. They were beside a tiny import car, totaled, like a hard-shelled beetle crushed beneath a boot. Wayne met Sol's inquiring eye; no one seemed to be in charge. Wayne gestured directions: I'll check out the flower delivery guy, you see if the firefighter on the pavement needs help. Sol snapped on gloves, heaved the ALS bag with him. He crossed the median strip, running in the blowing snow but as he neared, he could see right away there was nothing to be done.

As he hurried, a movement snagged his glance, hard to see, white on white among the scattered petals blowing across the roadway, snow and confetti. A blur—form of a woman, terrified, gesturing back and forth, frantic. Sol could see right through the ghost, it was barely there at all.

He glanced into the wrecked car, smashed glass scattering light across the ice. A deflated airbag draped the mangled steering column. In the backseat, a child's booster seat sat empty as a question mark. The firefighter looked up, face white. Beneath his hands the woman hadn't stirred, eyes wide to the falling night. Not a scratch on her face, surprisingly, but the damage was massive: her heart, her lungs, her ribcage, all pulp. The firefighter shook his head and without much emotion, gave his assessment, "Injuries incompatible with life."

Sol wasn't even going to run a strip; this woman was definitely dead. He didn't need her ghost yelling at him to know that. The ME and investigators were doubtlessly on their way, so Sol sent the FD first-responder back to deal with the cuts and scrapes. Sol considered the dead woman for a moment, then looked to see if her ghost was still hanging around, wondered if it would be on its way shortly, no help needed.

But no, the ghost was still there, on the edge of the lights the FD had set up, yelling and yelling, though Sol couldn't hear it above the sirens and noise.

Wayne was busy—his Spanish was pretty good, and he was getting an earful—so Sol walked slowly toward the ghost, kept an eye out for another EMT or fire crew or police that might call it in if they spotted Sarrazin talking to himself.

"What is it?" he asked when he got closer, knowing he shouldn't. *You don't talk to them, gars.* Lesson number one. But the ghost, hovering near, staring at its body with an expression of dawning understanding, wasn't confused, wasn't even really surprised.

It was frantic.

When Sol came closer, the ghost calmed but didn't speak, then seemed to remember something, turned, pointed to an area across the road, a planted landscaping effort, now populated by sparse grass and generic frost-burned juniper. The ghost's mouth moved: *Please.* Then, with nothing more than that, it vanished, winked out, was gone. Had found the road home on its own.

Sol blinked snowflakes from his eyelashes; the wind was blowing whatever snow was falling, caused what had already settled to eddy and flow on the pavement, a white tide moving across the road like a sidewinder. Standing, the ALS bag slung across his shoulder, his mind didn't work quite as fast as his instincts: he started running to the bushes, knowing what he would find.

Glass and flowers had been sprayed this far, easily. Part of a tire, peeled into strips like a huge blackened banana, marked the trajectory of the crash. A police officer was just starting to assay the scene, marking on a clipboard, and he looked up quickly as Sol rushed past him. Coming up on the landscaping, Sol jumped over the nearest bush and saw a small crumpled figure, legs and arms akimbo, clad in pink, nestled among the dried grasses and snow, thrown nearly thirty feet from her mother's car.

Damn it, damn it, why didn't people wear seatbelts, but Sol knew that all it took was a dropped juice box, a new Christmas toy just that small distance too far, and most kids this age—what, maybe four, five?—could press the release button, come unbelted at just the wrong time, just when a florist's van took a corner too fast for balding all-season radials.

This kid, this little girl, had gone through the windshield or a popped door, hurtling past her mother in the instant of her death, and had now landed here, arms all splayed as though she was trying to find her balance.

Sol swung his stethoscope from his neck: she was breathing unsteadily—he called out for the cop to alert the other EMTs that they had a ped trauma over here, bring a backboard and a stretcher, get ready to load and ride. Soon there was intense action, five different pairs of hands, a board, clear airway, that was good, bleeding from a scalp laceration, somewhere else, too, for her snowsuit was sodden with blood, but without destabilizing the spine, Sol didn't know how far he'd be able to examine her. Basic triage, though: if he didn't find the cause, she could bleed out before anyone had the chance to worry about her back.

Using his shears, he cut away the snowsuit, saw a penetrating wound along her back, nine inches of raw jagged opening. Field dressings, pressure, gentle on the back. Priority one.

Time was of the essence, and for all the frantic action of the medics, things slowed to individual moments: the flutter of heartbeat, erratic. The listless loll of her arm as they got her onto the board, strapped her down unresisting. Sol rode in the back, and Wayne drove far too fast for the road, but Sol didn't really care as long as the ride was steady.

"Hi there, ma poussinette," he said quietly, hardly able to hear himself above the siren and the rhythmic clatter of equipment rattling. She didn't move, didn't open her eyes, though her pupils responded to light, which was enough for Sol. "Hey, p'tite chère, your mom showed me where you were. She wants you to make it, okay? She's looking out for you." All the while he kept one hand on her, right on her sternum above the strap, could feel her struggle to breathe.

"Wayne!" he yelled through to the cab. "What's the ETA?"

"We're here!" Wayne shouted back, and the rig lurched to the right as Wayne swung into the ER bay, the back doors opening to a whole team of white coats. Sol jumped to the ground, dragging the stretcher with him, swinging down the carriage and locking it in place, calling out her vitals to the doctors and nurses, one hand on her chest, medically unnecessary, but he couldn't help it. He pepper-sprayed the team with his assessment, numbers and jargon fluent as any rapper on a roll. They wheeled her through the automatic doors, disappearing down a corridor, one nurse leaving them at the door of the trauma unit and coming back more slowly to get additional information from Sol and Wayne.

Sol's whole body was shivering, electric with spent adrenalin. Turning from the nurse for a moment, he ignored the busy waiting area—bound to be a back-up in the chairs, people showing up with stuff that they had ignored Christmas Day—and put both hands on his hips, walking a slow circle. He needed to regroup. The staff mostly knew him, allowed a moment.

"You should get cleaned up," the nurse said, staring at him. Marisol, if Sol remembered correctly, and he followed her gaze. His hands, he realized, his open coat, shirt, all were soaked with blood. Marisol held a clipboard, pen in hand, dark eyes serious. "Do you know her name? Anything?"

Sol couldn't speak, could barely understand her words.

Wayne, thankfully, had ridden with Sol for the last three years on and off; it was generally up to him to do the talking. "The cops'll get that for you," he said.

Marisol persisted. "Did she say anything en route?" Directly to Sol.

Who blinked, then shook his head. "No," he caught his breath. He didn't know what Marisol was talking about. Then, "She came from the import car, the crushed one." He looked to Wayne helplessly.

"Mother's paws up," Wayne explained. "Maybe the cops can get Dad here."

"You get clean," Marisol advised again, maybe thinking of those waiting out in the chairs, not wanting to horrify them. "There's donuts over there, help yourself. You can hang out here if you like."

Sol didn't feel like a donut, he wanted a smoke, so after he went to a sink in the staff washroom, he stepped outside into the snowy night, watched it come down, knew that he was going to stick around for a while, see if she made it. Wayne joined him for a bit, then went to the rig to get the end-of-shift paperwork started. The back of the rig, Sol knew, would be a catastrophic mess. He should get started on that, pick up a little.

He lit another cigarette instead.

Ice shards pelted down now, almost hail, dry and stinging. His bare fingers, clean and exposed, were frozen. He finished his cigarette, ground it out with his heel, rubbed his eyelids with his fingertips. *It's okay*, he told himself, *really, it's okay.*

Then the little girl walked out through the double doors, looked around like she was lost, hair blonde and long and curly like a doll's. Sol swallowed, tried to make peace with what turned inside him, what battered against his ribcage, at war with his salt blood. He had saved Marty today and you couldn't win them all. He knew that. "Hé, chouette," he called to her. Not her. Her ghost. "Sweetheart." And the girl looked at him, confused.

Sol bent down to a crouch, his breath crystallizing in the air, ice pellets unperturbed by the little girl's apparition, passing right through it. The ghost was in the snowsuit still, and Sol was strangely comforted by that: *At least she's not cold*, he thought. Not a 'she', an it, but he couldn't think of her like that, not yet.

He smiled, met the ghost's eyes. With his right hand, he found the ground, touched it for one moment, as though declaring his intention. Then he shoved his hand under his parka, through the opening of his shirt, right to his chest against his heart. *My aim is true.* Withdrawing his hand, he brought his fingers to his lips, blew on them like he had a seedy dandelion head there, scattering his intent to the night, opening the way. "Go find your mom, mon p'tit chou. She isn't far."

The ghost gave him a small smile, maybe to reassure him: Yes, I understand. Then it was gone, just like that. Sol tapped the ground lightly, three times, sealing it off, barely a ritual. Life was too fast and too heartless for trivial things like ritual, like ceremony. See need, deal with need. Do it in the most expedient fashion possible.

Still, there was grace in this, and against his cynical nature, he knew it.

He stood too fast, before his blood and heart could keep up with gravity, and the night swirled around him. It had been a long day, after all. Wearily, he went inside the hospital so he could be given news he already knew. So he could carry that weight and give it to Wayne. They would wait for the police, help piece together the sequence of events. He would do the paperwork. He would clean the rig, because he wasn't going to leave her blood for anyone else. Hours to go before either of them would find bed.

This was a terrible, terrible mistake. Funny how Baz only realized it now. This very instant, matter of fact.

After all, he'd had the whole trip up to re-think this stupid, idiotic idea. The succession of truck stop rides from North Platte to Minneapolis, then the bus north across the border, change in Winnipeg for Brandon, followed by the shuttle service to CFB Shilo, all of it made with rising excitement, a kid's countdown to Santa. Christmas Day stalled at the Brandon Super 8, not wanting to arrive in the middle of presents and turkey, whatever normal people did on that day. No matter the amount of time he'd been given, had taken, he still hadn't thought it all the way through. Find Lutie, that had been the goal, and now it seemed that just making contact wasn't the point at all. *I am such a goddamn idiot.*

And there she was, eyes just the same color as his, as their mother's had been, fair as summer grass, like her, so much like her. Looking at him as though he'd just strangled a kitten in her kitchen.

Surrounded by these nice people, so concerned for her, for *him*, and Baz thought for one wild minute he might actually have a breakdown at the table. He kept his hands in his pockets, wishing for a pit to open up and swallow him whole.

She hadn't said a thing.

"Lutie?" the man—Major McGregor, her foster father—prompted. "Sit down, both of you." Baz caught the look exchanged between the woman—Karen, introduced as Lutie's mother—and the Major: this was going downhill fast, was heading for out-of-bounds.

Tears clawed at Baz's throat, an early warning signal. He'd come here to tell her that her father was dead and why the hell did he think that would be *welcome* news?

"Baz," Lutie repeated, dumbstruck.

"Lutie, sit." Karen dragged out a chair, and Lutie looked at it. Finally, she took the seat, which meant Baz could sit too.

They stared at each other across the newspaper-strewn kitchen table. Lutie was of course older than Baz had prepared himself for, if indeed he'd spent any time preparing for anything on the long ride north. But she was also younger, protected. Sheltered. Jesus wept, why had he come?

"Why," Lutie started, then stopped, unsure. "Why are you here?" Like she was reading his mind. But, no, wasn't that the question anyone would ask?

The Major was a profoundly nice man. Baz had decided that more or less instantly, from the moment the man had opened the door on Sapper Avenue, backlit like Jesus coming down from the cross. The Major placed one hand on Lutie's, covering it like a winter blanket. "He's got news, Lutie."

"How long's he been here?" Lutie demanded, not meeting Baz's eyes.

Baz had told them, before he'd had his coat off, who he was and what he'd come to tell their daughter. They'd still let him in, given him a cup of tea, sat him down in the kitchen thick with the smell of cooking dinner. A couple of sentences before he'd figured out they were her foster parents, not enough time to wonder where his mother was. "He just got here, fifteen minutes maybe."

"You let him in? You knew who he was and you…" On par with shooting babies, apparently. She turned her attention to Baz. "What do you want?" Which was different from 'why are you here?'

Baz licked his lips, laughed on an exhale, nervous now that it was here. It had seemed so simple, such a great, easy plan: come up here, bring her back into the family, restring the beads of a broken necklace. "I, ah." He swallowed. "It's Dad. He died. Week before last. A train accident."

Lutie blinked, then shrugged, but it looked like it hurt her to do it. Behind her shoulder, where she wouldn't notice, Baz saw Karen take a step forward, then check herself. "So? What do you want me to…" It might have occurred to her right then how she sounded, Baz thought. Not made of stone. "She's dead too." Lutie looked at the Major, then at Karen, who now leaned against the warm stove, arms crossed as though she didn't trust herself to keep still. "You told him, right?" Back to Baz. "You know that."

Maybe being hit by lightning felt like this. Cold, followed by hot, a giddy light-headedness that immediately preceded a weightless fall, a void. He remained speechless, and in the silence he heard the breath Karen took.

"He just got here, Lutie." There was warning in it: Be nice.

Baz froze, was frozen. Like he'd been robbed of his voice, of his ability to think. He just *felt*, that's all he could do.

Lutie was sturdily made, like their father, like Sol, all of them made for balancing in uncertain terrain, knowing where their feet were. Went through life as though they were taking a stand. Baz knew he didn't have that, recognized that his center of gravity was up near his heart, that he moved like a kite on a string. He'd been wrong to come, to interfere. Maybe Sol had the right idea, shutting all this away.

Baz watched his sister's lips thin, grim humor lighting her eyes, honey hair pulled back in a ponytail, long high-bridged nose pointed directly at him. He steeled himself, mostly because he felt her do the same thing: hurt to say it, hurt to hear it.

"She lay down in a bathtub and cut her own throat with a carving knife. I was nine. *Nine.* We were alone in some crappy New Brunswick town, and she checked out. No one ever came, no father ever contacted anyone, asking where the hell I'd gone. So," and she caught herself, not on tears, but on a rising tide of anger, he could see it in her flushed pale face, "so don't you come here expecting me to feel anything." Lutie stood suddenly, the chair scraping back on the linoleum. "Get out of my house. Get—"

Two voices, both sharp with parental authority: "Lutie!" Baz noticed two younger kids in the hallway—teenagers, curious. He didn't know what to do, how to stop any of this. He'd lit the match, and the fuse was on slow burn, and he had no other role to play, other than to watch the whole thing explode.

"I shouldn't have come," Baz stuttered, rising, wondering where Karen had put his coat, needing to be out the door. There was dynamite, after all. "I'm sorry. I shouldn't—"

All color drained from Lutie's face, and she ran, pushing past the kids in the hallway, pounding up the stairs. A door slammed, distant and final.

Baz looked into the Major's eyes, blue as a bad bruise, steady. So different than Aurie's, which had danced, rhythm of blood. Better, this steadiness, Baz knew. It had been needed, by all of them, though only Lutie had gotten it. But Baz didn't know how much a steady hand would matter, coming so late. He kept his gaze there, even as everything else swam.

The Major didn't try to comfort. He seemed to be waiting for whatever was inside Baz to come out. Karen shooed the teens downstairs, and a television's rude blare followed. She stayed, the post to which the Major's line was tied; he, the lifesaver out at sea. And Baz? Drowning perhaps, tide running high in hurricane season, all known roads washed away. The moment held past breaking, through breaking, and Baz finally wiped his eyes with the heels of his hands.

"I'll give you a ride into town," the Major said quietly. "How about that?"

Wordlessly, Baz nodded, and Karen handed him a tissue without comment and went to get his coat from the hall closet.

The cold air helped, Baz found, pulling the fur-lined hat over his ears, stepping out into the snow. He thanked Karen, a stammer of useless apology stuttered to the night air, then hauled up into the black SUV. The Major threw his wallet on the dashboard, checked the rearview mirror behind him. It was a clear night, no snow, so cold it hurt to breathe. Baz inhaled unsteadily, concentrated on the house in the headlights as they reversed out the driveway.

"She's prickly," the Major started. "You know that."

Baz huffed an astonished laugh. "No, actually. I don't."

The Major put the truck into gear and gently advanced down the icy road. "You will. She's just surprised, and she doesn't like surprises much. Likes things just so."

Baz took off the hat he'd bought in Minneapolis and worried it on his lap. "I'm sorry."

"I know that." The houses were so similar as to be disorienting and Lutie's foster father drove blessedly slow, taking his time.

"I don't know what I expected."

"Most people don't, not until after it all goes south." The Major glanced at Baz, then back at the road. "We can try this again."

Baz laughed low and it rattled in his throat, stuck. "I think it's pretty clear—"

"Pretty clear you surprised her, that's all." They slowed at the gate and the soldier stationed there waved them through, grin on his face. A well-liked man, Baz thought of the Major. "You didn't know about what happened with your mother, did you?"

God, there was that. On top of everything else. He shook his head, not trusting his voice.

"Lutie came to us shortly after, a kid needing a foster home. Marshall and Bree were babies practically. We didn't know how long it was going to be for. I was stationed at CFB Gagetown. Lutie," and Baz heard the smile, the love, "Lutie's English was all over the place back then, don't know what francophones were doing in such an anglo area. We all learned from each other. The Children's Aid people, they looked for you guys. But the records were spotty, and no one in Terrebonne Parish knew where you'd gone…"

He left it hanging, waiting for Baz to fill in the enormous blank.

Baz cleared his throat and obliged. "We left Louisiana right around then, no work, still recovering from Hurricane Andrew, I think, part of it anyway. We went to Texas for a while, and then north. Dad moved us a lot. After… after Mom left with Lutie. He was," and it felt like a betrayal to say it, and so Baz didn't. "Dad didn't look for her, it was like she was dead. He always spoke about her like she was dead. I don't know what he wanted for Lutie, what he was hoping for. I stopped asking, because he never answered. He didn't have much education, not in the school sense, and he could never get decent work. It was like he was a foreigner, never fit in anywhere we were. We were… really poor. We didn't have much."

The countryside wound past them like an ocean, thin line of pavement a dark ribbon among the waves.

"Sounds like a hard way to grow up," the Major finally said and Baz was aware that he was good at this, that this was the man's job for God's sake—being wise and calm. Getting people to talk. After what had just happened at the house, Baz didn't care. In fact it was good he was here with someone whose main point in life was to listen.

"Then Dad was in prison for a few years, got into some kind of argument at a party; a woman died and they blamed him." Baz kept his gaze out the window, because it was safe. They went past a roadside shrine, a cross, plastic flowers, then gone. A marked death. The Major was leaving him room. "He didn't do it. Wasn't really his style, violence. One good thing about him."

"How old were you then?" Gentle, probing questions, maybe to check him out, make sure he wasn't a raving lunatic. Protecting Lutie first, and Baz should remember that.

"Thirteen, or thereabouts. We were in Colorado by then, in Denver."

"So, foster care for you, too?"

There had been no relatives to call, Baz remembered. "No, we caught a break. We were renting rooms from a social worker. She convinced the courts that it would be better for me if she supervised Sol, who was seventeen then, or just about. So we stayed there, in her house, until Sol turned eighteen and could legally take care of me. Little bit of luck, for once."

"And he's your brother, the oldest one?"

Baz looked around in surprise, and the Major shrugged a little. "Lutie doesn't talk about any of this. I didn't even know your names, only that there'd been older brothers, and a father down in the States."

The Major might be protecting Lutie, and Baz couldn't hold that against him. But with those words, he felt a huge wave come over him: Grief. Pride. "He was a good man, our dad. He might not have always been thinking clear, but he loved us. And Sol—" It was important, and Baz needed to say it, needed for this man, this gatekeeper, to hear it. "Sol took it on, even though he was just a kid himself. So—"

"Okay, okay," the Major said, unruffled. "I can't imagine how hard that must of been. For all of you." Emphasis on the 'all'.

It was okay, in this moving confessional booth, to talk. Baz forced his shoulders down, purposefully relaxed his clenched jaw. "It was. But there was good stuff, too. Dad was in for five years, and after he got out, the two of us went on the road, spent half our time touring around the Midwest. Sol stuck around Denver." He wasn't going to get into *that*, though. "Dad was a really great musician, that's how he made his money, so we always had that."

The Major looked over briefly. "Well, that seems to have skipped over Lutie," he said with a smile.

Baz was grateful to have the opportunity to smile back. "It's how I make a living, too, usually." He shrugged. "I play fiddle, tour around a bit. You know."

"Cajun? Or Zydeco?" the Major asked.

Baz laughed outright. "Hell, no. Neither. More what you'd call roots, I guess. The old country guys, but updated. Mostly around Chicago, Minneapolis, down to Nashville sometimes."

Baz had already told them that he was staying at the Super 8 and the Major remembered this, of course, wasn't the kind of guy to forget much, something that Baz liked because it meant he didn't have to worry himself with details. They stopped in the parking lot near the covered entrance, and Baz sat quietly, turning his plaid and rabbit fur hat over in his hands. Finally, he pulled the handle, not able to bear sitting there any more.

"Does your brother know you're here?" the Major asked, insightful eyes under dark brows; he'd waited until Baz had opened the door so the dome light was on. So he'd be able to see his answer, which he did. They shared the admission in silence. "You're all alone. Okay. Tell you what. Give me your number and I'll call in the morning. We can sort this out. You didn't come all this way just to have our door slam in your face."

Baz nodded, not trusting himself to speak, though he stood at the door longer than was necessary. "Sure." He gave the Major his number, which he wrote down on the back of a parking pass.

As he wrote, the Major said, "You'll be okay?", like it was inconsequential. The voice was pitch-perfect: concerned, but allowing that Baz was a man who could take care of himself. Careful, that's what this pastor was.

"Yeah." Baz paused, nodded again and Major McGregor looked up with a reassuring smile, put the number on the dash along with his wallet. "Merci beaucoup, padre." Baz made to shut the door, a weight in his chest.

"You know," the Major stalled him. "We would have taken you all, if we'd known."

Baz found the smile, just where it always was, ready. "We had a dad. But thanks." If the Major offered money, Baz thought he'd have to leave town tonight.

The chaplain seemed to sense this, and said goodnight, but nothing more. Baz watched the tail lights leave the lot, and then pulled the hat onto his head, cold.

He should have phoned, but wasn't that the story of his life? No cell phone for a reason, so he wouldn't have to make excuses. Wasn't silence better than lies?

Better than the truth, for sure: *Hi sweetheart, sorry I'm late, but I had to show the ghost of a little girl the way to her dead mother. Knew you'd understand.*

That was one way to ruin a perfectly good relationship. Another, Sol argued with himself as he tried to be as quiet as he could coming up the un-shoveled steps, would be to tell Robbie nothing and let her assume he was an uncommunicative jerk, which he probably was. Plans for a quiet entrance were destroyed by the yapping of the damned dog, and Sol cursed under his breath. Robbie had gotten the puppy because Sol worked so many unpredictable shifts, to keep her company, for protection.

To screw Sol up when he tried to sneak in late.

He'd gone for a couple of beers with Wayne after they'd filed their reports, after they'd sat with the father for a few minutes—Wayne had handled that, because for all his crassness, the big man was much better with living people than Sol was—and Sol had resisted plunging headfirst into a bottle, for once. Like Sol, Wayne worked in Denver but lived in Aurora, and had insisted on The Boneyard, which wasn't the kind of place where you wanted to get completely pissed, not that and keep your wallet or your teeth.

Once inside the house, Renard stopped barking, tail thumping against Sol's leg, and was rewarded with a rough stroke to the head and a Milk-Bone from the cupboard as Sol helped himself to cold leftover spaghetti straight from the fridge. He didn't heat it up; the microwave's beep was loud and a hot meal was not what he deserved at this late hour, anyway.

After a minute of eating standing up, leaning against the counter by the sink, looking out the window into the snow-spackled darkness, Sol put down the bowl. He didn't turn. "I'm sorry," he said. The words came out hoarse, and he didn't recognize his own voice.

Robbie sighed, padded over to the sink on bare feet, put both arms around him, resting her head in the hollow between his shoulder blades.

"Come to bed," she said finally, words muffled against his back.

Sol took a breath to make an excuse, and suddenly felt all his clenched forward motion dissipate. He was more than merely tired; he was without reserve, bottom of the tank. Turning, he bent to kiss her, and she accepted it without question. There might be recriminations tomorrow, but Sol couldn't think beyond the next minute.

They stood entangled for some time, Sol taking what Robbie offered, hands on her face, her hair, down her shoulders and back, slipping off her robe, hiking up the big t-shirt she wore to bed when Sol wasn't coming home. All extraneous, unnecessary things were left on the floor, and Sol carried her to the bedroom, where he took strength and comfort from her in equal measure.

# FIVE

## TEN LETTERS

Lutie knew the Major would call her brother, because Baz hadn't seemed like a deranged psychopath, and that's the only thing that would have truly prevented her father from allowing him access. Her foster parents were so damn reasonable, that was the problem, and they saw no reason whatsoever to deny Basile Sarrazin. Probably thought it would do her some kind of good, given her past.

She thought she was doing a decent job at suggesting she didn't want contact, though. Through the closed door, she'd refused dinner, then refused a conversation later in the evening. The room was small, the smallest of the four bedrooms, and her mother had set up her sewing machine and craft table in the corner. The guest room, when all was said and done, like a line had been drawn in the middle: one side, craft central; this side, the last vestiges of Lutie's childhood—stuffed animals, a CD player, an old iPod and some cheaply framed certificates for academic excellence.

Bree knocked and was let in, but the minute she said that Baz was cute, Lutie threw her out. She'd brought a couple of carrot muffins, though, and those held Lutie's hunger at bay.

Sleep was hard, when it came. Full of dreams, nightmares almost.

Cypress shaggy with moss, and heat, so out of place in this cold, desolate land, and water. Movement in the water, sinuous sideways movement. Snake. Night heat sonorous with frog. Not knowing where to put your foot, sinking up to her ankle, then her knee, and she woke with a start, sweaty in the electric heat of the over-hot room.

In the morning, Karen was waiting for her in the kitchen, armed with coffee. She looked like she was doing the crossword. Lutie knew better and pulled up a chair. The Major was already out, and Bree was still sleeping.

"Ten-letter word for a sympathetic feeling," Karen said, making no pretense of looking at the half-completed grid. The Major always skipped the puzzle page, but her mother was made of trickier stuff.

Lutie swallowed a comeback that involved profanity. She was too old for that, too careful. Instead, she busied herself getting milk from the fridge.

"Dad's dropping Marshall off at the rink, but he said he was going to give your brother a call." Her brother Baz, not Marshall. Deliberate, not dodging anything. God, these people she'd ended up with.

"Let him," Lutie murmured, sipping the coffee. "Knock yourselves out." She returned to the table. Avoidance got you nowhere in this family.

"Luetta," Karen said softly. "He came all this way."

"If he's looking for puppies and rainbows, he's gonna be disappointed."

Her foster mother's eyes crinkled at the corner, and Lutie knew she'd been thinking exactly the same thing. "He's not the one to blame, if it's blame you're looking to hand out. He was just a kid, too."

Lutie laughed, low. "You always had a thing for the motherless kids."

"Evidently." She got up, rinsed her mug in the sink. "Listen, you don't have to do anything, Lutie. The ball's in your court. I'm just saying that he's lost his dad, and he's reaching out. We have no control of the timing of these things. You want to look back on this and feel like you did the right thing. A little bit of *compassion* could go a long way." She emphasized the word. Ten letters.

Lutie nodded. "I know."

The phone rang and Karen answered; Lutie could tell by the tone of her mother's voice that it was the Major. A soft, golden warmth, and Lutie knew what was required: she needed to step up. Knew that she would step up. *Because that's how I've been raised. We don't leave people behind, and we're there when we're needed.* Instead of compassion, she felt a kind of proud resistance.

Also ten letters.

Karen gave her the phone so the Major could tell her himself. They didn't pass the buck in her house, either. "Lutie," her foster dad said. "How'd you sleep?" There was laughter in his voice.

"Not bad," she returned.

Something in her voice caused him to pause. "All right, then. I'm meeting Baz in a few minutes and I'm planning on inviting him to service tomorrow. We're having him over for lunch after." Not asking her, telling her his plans, and letting her decide how she wanted to play her part.

Lutie took a deep breath. What, was she going to go back to Toronto, just allow this interloper to hang out with her family? Like leaving the house with the back door open. "Sure. Tell him that I—" Dammit. "Give me his number and I'll tell him myself."

"That's my girl," and he meant every word and for the first time, Lutie thought she might cry.

The bar was so generic as to be almost a stage set, and Baz had the weird feeling that people were watching, had bought tickets for the big Saturday-night show. Lutie spotted him immediately, came over stiff-legged, a puffy down coat so white it smarted same as a slap. She moved like she was mad, and the only reason Baz knew this was because he'd had a fair bit of experience with pissed-off women. She shed the coat over the back of the chair, the faux fur trim dangling like a dead animal she'd brought in from the traplines.

Baz had just sat down himself; he glanced up at her and smiled, recognizing the nervous hammer in his chest. "Hey." He turned around the plastic menu stand in the middle of the table. "What's good?"

Lutie raised dark brows, slanted, defining. A beautiful face, in its way, similar to their mother's, what he remembered of her. He only had one photo, and in it his mother had looked tired and angry.

She shrugged like she was indifferent, but Baz knew indifference was impossible. "Probably nothing. It's a pub."

This bar had been her suggestion: grab something to eat for dinner, have a beer. Someplace neutral, she might have said, someplace that wasn't her kitchen table.

He ordered wings; she had the nachos. A beer came; she had a soft drink.

He opened his mouth to apologize, but she was already talking, almost like she didn't want to hear anything he had to say. "You don't see him, do you?"

Baz closed his mouth, quickly. "Pardon?"

As though he'd just failed a pop quiz, his sister shrugged slightly, eyes glancing to the side, staring at nothing. "Never mind." Eyes back to him, intent. "How'd you find me? I don't go by Sarrazin."

Actually, he'd prepared for this question, because he couldn't really tell her the whole truth without explaining about ghosts and railways and whatever that thing had been that had given him her address. "I hired a private detective." Which was kind of the truth.

"Really?" and she meant, 'it was so important?', but she didn't say that. Baz could still tell, though. Her voice warmed up. She wouldn't mean for him to hear that, but he did.

"Your last name's Cyr," and he pronounced it correctly; it had been their mother's name after all. "I figured that out."

This time, she smiled back, took a sip of her drink. "You're a musician, the Major says," and he liked how she was being careful with him, calling her foster father the Major, like anything else might hurt him: father, Dad. He didn't think it would, but just the fact that she'd thought of it was a sign. He could hope, anyway.

Baz nodded. "So was Dad." He smiled again, shifted. "My Dad, your father. Aurie. Fuck it." It was possible to overthink these things.

Lutie's eyes narrowed. The food came, and Baz had never been less hungry in his life. The wings were coated a toxic orange, reeked of vinegar and he wrinkled his nose at the smell, picked up one anyway.

Something in his gesture made Lutie laugh. "You know, I don't remember much about Louisiana, but Maman always said you ate like you had worms. Those are the two things I remember about you—that you could eat like a pig. And that you could sing." She stopped there, and they stared at each other and Baz didn't know where to start.

He shrugged, tried to appear modest. "I don't sing so much anymore. I play the fiddle, mostly." He sucked one finger clean of BBQ sauce, going for an air of nonchalance, but couldn't manage it. "What else?" he asked, because his own memories of back then, of the swamp and the bayous, were not much more than hers, he suspected. Baz had been given the one photo; Aurie had taken everything else, her clothes, her cookbooks, their marriage certificate, left them in the house, and burned the whole thing down, signifying his intention to never return. Baz remembered that, could call up the chemical smoke, the petals of blackened paper, oil seeping in rainbows across the salt marsh.

"Not much," she said.

"Me neither." He picked at the celery sticks and baby carrots, swirled them in the blue cheese dip. "Sol remembers more."

The nachos didn't look much better, were smothered in pale orange sauce, not cheese, bits of dried parsley scattered like birdseed. Baz had played his fair share of gigs in places like this, and avoided the food whenever possible. "Want some?" she asked, pushing the plate towards him, noticing his stare, maybe.

He shook his head. She wasn't asking about Sol, or their father. Concentrating on him, not wanting to know more than that. It was enough. Baby steps, he cautioned himself.

"Tu parles?" he asked, wondering if that might get her going. "Un peu?"

She shook her head. "Nah. We moved around too much. The McGregors don't speak—"

"What was she like?" Baz hadn't even known that question was in him, that it was coming. He was as taken aback as she was.

One moment, thinking seriously about his earlier language question, the next, eyes blinking in surprise, and he knew—dammit, he knew—that she didn't like surprises.

"What do you think?" Lutie threw back. "She was nuts. Crazy."

"I don't remember her like that," Baz murmured. Wrong, God, he'd gotten it wrong again. And was about to make things worse. "Strict, maybe. Proud."

"A cold distant bitch." The words seemed to be hurting her, because she flinched. "Probably should have been on Thorazine, talked to herself all the time, dragged me out with her day and night. Never made it to school, only ate when someone took pity on us. Moved all the time."

*Why didn't Aurie try to find you?* Baz almost asked, then thought better. She didn't know the answer to that question, didn't know about ghosts and black things in the night with lungs like rusted out mufflers.

"You were lucky, you got out," Lutie continued, and there was the anger, right there.

Baz chuckled a little, but sadly, and he hoped that she understood, or remembered, that you just had to laugh sometimes. "Mais, chère, she was the one that left, no?" He swallowed, then kept going, quickly, because he knew every word cut her. "Alors, je suis désolé, mais—neither of us got out, T-Lu." Abruptly, he thought of Aurie, coming home dead drunk, sobbing. And the expression on Sol's face by the rails a week ago, tapping his fingers against the ground in farewell.

Of his mother, how he imagined her from the one photo, so fair she was like sun on snow—of his mother floating in a tub filled with blood, golden hair a halo.

Neither of them. *None of us.*

She only wanted the one drink, and that was probably enough, Baz decided. They split the bill, and she dropped him off at the motel. He said he'd take the shuttle bus out the next morning, no need to pick him up. As he had with her foster father the night before, he watched her pull away, and had no idea what he was hoping to accomplish.

Sunday morning found Sol in Hershey, Nebraska, still running on the caffeine consumed during a double shift, a full twenty-four hours since his last sleep had ended. The Hursts had lived in the small town, ten miles west of Bailey Yard along the old Lincoln Highway. The faded gray road followed the tracks westwards, away from and between the low conver-gence of the North and South Platte Rivers, a crotch of mud and grass, lack of water counter to Sol's experience and one of the many reasons he liked Nebraska. Land won here, not water.

The couple had lived in a little clapboard house built at the turn of the last century and re-painted in heritage colors to match other up-and-comers in the neighborhood. Mrs. Hurst had evidently taken a lot of care, had read magazines about antiques and decorating, probably had watched home and garden channels, had learned how to trap tole paper scenes behind glass, how to scrapbook.

The lock was nothing for Sol's fast hands, but he checked once over his shoulder; neighbors were probably nosy around here, doubly so when the house was a crime scene. Not hearing anything above the clack of the nearby tracks, an endless line of boxcars and tankers, grain hoppers and piggyback trailers, Sol lifted the police tape with one finger and crouched under, shutting the door behind him. Better to be quick, because he would have a hard time explaining his presence here, with or without a

Denver County EMS ID tag. The house was immaculate, except for the bloodstained couch and the scent of iron.

No unearthly cold, no lingering spirits here. Everything as it should be.

Maybe this had been just as the police had described it: a murder-suicide, Paul Hurst offing the missus, misery brushed over with Benjamin Moore paint. But. He crossed his arms, shook his head. Two people, heads cracked open with a blunt object, maybe a brick, maybe a club—it had bothered him when he'd first scanned the report in Denver, and it bothered him here in the couple's living room. Sol had cleaned up plenty of suicides and not one of them had involved the victim hitting themselves on the head with a blunt object.

He went upstairs, glanced at the boxes scattered around, half unpacked. Still packed. Online records had indicated that they'd moved here two years prior, but the place looked as though they'd just arrived. No sign of the Christmas just past, no tree, no decorations other than a few cards on the mantel. Sol went into the bedroom, queen-sized bed unmade, curtains drawn. Books everywhere, stacked against the wall, in bookshelves, on the desk beside the computer. He looked at the desk more closely—a drawing of a boat, a blueprint, a sailing manual. On one bedside: *Around the Caribbean by Sail*; *Voyage of the Kon Tiki*; *Photographing the Tropics*. He went back out into the hallway, stared at the boxes again. Not unpacking, he thought. Packing up. They were going on a trip. Sure Christmas was stressful, but why commit suicide when you had a trip coming up?

He found an open diner on Hershey's main street, where he bought time on a computer with internet access, thought about the Hursts, how perfect their lives seemed. Things, he knew, were rarely perfect. Sol made a few phone calls from the payphone at the back of the diner, dug around a bit before he pieced together the information he needed: the Hursts had bought a sailboat with two friends who lived in Miami; they were getting ready to leave on a once-in-a-lifetime trip to the Caribbean. They were the nicest couple ever, can't believe that Paul wanted to kill Aileen.

Perfect couple, perfect house. He ordered lunch, the blue plate special, something with a pork chop. The couple did seem damn nice. Maybe it was something to do with the house's location? Right across the street from the tracks, after all. The other deaths had occurred in the yards proper, in and around railcars, not in a house. Same general MO, though, just a slightly different location.

Sol realized that he had never searched for deaths in houses, only railyard-related deaths. *I need to widen the search.* A furrow creased Sol's forehead and the blue plate came. He bought more internet time.

Half an hour later, he'd plotted suspicious deaths on a map, noting the dates. *This ghost is moving west.* Were the Hursts the most recent deaths? If he kept checking west, would he find anything more? A few more key-strokes and he turned up another murder, this time in Ogallala, less than an hour west of where he sat. Only the day before yesterday. Except the police weren't calling it a murder, had already ruled it accidental, a guy dead in his garden which happened to abut the tracks. Someone who had fallen off his porch and landed headfirst on an unspecified blunt object.

Aurie had taught Sol a couple of things, and one of which was how to second-guess a newsclipping: Local man dies tragically in his yard. The railway went right through the backyard. According to the news story, the victim's house had been left wide open the night he died, and a neighbor said she'd seen him running out the front door. Not suicidal, the article went on, the man was a respected lawyer about to embark on a trek to Nepal the next day, had everything to live for. No mention of what the blunt object was. No mention of why he'd run out of the house.

He was onto something, Sol felt it. How many more between Ogallala and Bailey Yard?

A couple of phone calls, and a number of online community newspa-pers yielded more results. Three suspicious death clusters, a total of seven people with heads cracked open, blunt force, no weapon found. One a murder, one called murder-suicide like the Hursts, and the third ruled accidental, another railway mishap. According to the town directories, all these people lived along the rail line that stretched from Bailey Yard through to Ogallala and points further west. According to friends and families, all of them had been planning trips or moves.

It didn't matter that the victims were lawyers or accountants, librarians or teachers. If you were about to leave it all behind, if you were thinking of putting your feet on the road and seeing where it took you, then this ghost was going to find you.

Sol pushed away his plate, the grease congealed, mashed potatoes a shade of vague gray, same viscosity as spackling paste. He needed to find out who this ghost had been when it had been alive, how it had died. Where it had died. *West of here,* he thought.

If he pushed it, he could drive to Ogallala, investigate the deaths there, stay overnight and talk to people when offices opened Monday morning. He could make it back to Denver in time for his evening shift. He looked at his watch, sighed. Just enough daylight left to do this, because the ghost wasn't stopping, wasn't even slowing down.

He still had no idea about how or if a devil figured in this, he only knew ghosts, knew how they operated. It would have to be enough.

He settled with the waitress and gassed up the Wagoneer. The lawyer's death in Ogallala was recent, day before yesterday, and if it was a ghost hunting drifters and those looking to catch out, Sol knew where to start.

Cold scoured the sky blue, shiny as a pot in the sink worked over with steel wool. Into this sky, the chapel's spire quested heavenward, and Lutie wondered if this was a good sign, as if the spire was a not-so-secret signal, alerting angels to their presence.

Mireille had been devout, had said rosaries, repented for sins unnamable and manifold, always hovering on the edge of churches and temples, never braving the doors. Her deviations were perhaps too unforgivable for easy entry. Mireille's approach to religion had been wholly different than the McGregors'. Hers had been about guilt, not love.

Baz met them at the church door, dressed cleanly but not much more than that. Plain black button-up shirt, jeans, a scruffy khaki-colored canvas coat, he wasn't out of place in a prairie army base, not by much. In the brutal light of a flatland winter's morning, his eyes glittered like bus shelter glass broken by a vandal, and he grinned as they came up the swept walk, was formally introduced to Marshall and Bree as the Major led them in. The Major was not giving any sermon this morning, was leading no readings. He'd made alternative arrangements, wanting to simply be with his family, this the first Sunday after Christmas, with God's light illuminating their lives in all their complex and strange rhythms.

Lutie stopped Baz as they entered, one hand on the sleeve of his pearl-button shirt, and he pulled up, eyebrows climbing incrementally. "When was the last time you were in church?" she asked.

He shrugged. "A friend's wedding. Maybe."

"How religious are you?"

His hand waggled, equivocating. "Not very. Raised Catholic, to a point. Why?"

Unfair, what she was going to ask. She caught her foster father's eye, and he drew close enough to hear. "Well, you know what would be great? If you'd sing something. Wouldn't that be great?" She looked at the Major, who wasn't committing. "He's an amazing singer, Dad. You should hear him." She paused, didn't know if she was inviting mayhem, but she had to know. She wasn't crazy. "It's one of things I remember."

Her brother's expression was guarded and it didn't suit him; she could see the swallow he took. Him, a professional musician and she could swear he was nervous. He doesn't sing so much anymore, he'd said. There must be a reason for that. The Major stared hard at Baz. Not much got past him.

"We'd be delighted," the Major said, offering both a way in and way out.

Baz didn't take his eyes off Lutie. "Vraiment?" he asked, chewing the inside of his mouth. "Really? You want this?"

She nodded. *I'm not crazy. I remember what I remember.*

It was arranged quickly—a guitar instead of a piano, the other musician a soldier just back from Afghanistan. Song ideas were bandied about: Baz came up with "When the Man Comes Around" or maybe "Ring of Fire", and Lutie knew for sure then that he'd not seen much of a church's interior. In the end they decided on the one that everyone could agree on—of course he knew "Amazing Grace", who didn't. The young gunner, a corporal, was originally from Baie Comeau, and Baz said he'd alternate verses in French and English, if that was okay. The guitarist smiled widely—yes, that would be okay.

Lutie saw the joy this gave and wondered if it would be all right, asking this, because the thought of Baz singing filled her with a certain dread. She'd picked that awful bar last night because it had been the site of a manslaughter in the summer, and she'd guessed right about there being a ghost hanging around. It had hovered in the corners, checking patrons out, and Baz hadn't noticed at all.

Maybe she was crazy, after all, just like her mother. Maybe ghosts were something beyond her, beyond the ability of medicine and talk therapy to fix. *We'll see about that.*

Inside the church, the late morning light was far from muted; it reflected from the burnished oak beams and pews, from modern stained glass cut and layered to form suns and stars and bursts of light. It was always hard to see ghosts in bright light, Lutie knew, so she tried to peer in the corners where shadows lingered, but she saw nothing. Maybe this was not a place for ghosts, this home of light. She'd never seen a ghost inside a church, but that didn't mean anything, she didn't think.

Beside her, Baz sat straight-backed, nervous, eyes darting across the crowded room. Some of the troops were home, a reason to be thankful, a reason to ask for forgiveness. One of the inter-denominational reverends gave a sermon about finding grace, but Lutie didn't pay attention to it; she was staring into shadows and hoping she didn't look too weird. She was good at it, disguising the tendency to look weird, had to be.

On her other side, the Major rose, leaned over her to Baz, "If you want to sing, now's the time," he said, honorable refusal still possible. Baz flicked a glance to Lutie and she knew he didn't want to do it, that he was doing it solely because she'd asked. Really? his eyebrows asked. Is this what she wanted?

Yes, because she'd felt unhinged and different for as long as she could remember and here was the one thing that might provide proof. He could give that to her, at least.

So Baz went to the front, waved away a microphone because he wouldn't need one, Lutie remembered, that you didn't need to amplify a voice like his in a quiet church. He bent for a moment to the corporal, said something and the young gunner grinned wide, delighted, and Lutie remembered this, too, that Baz made people smile. A trick, or a talent? Had time to think: *gift*, then she had no time to consider the many talents or sins that Baz made manifest, because he was singing, starting in French. The crowd hushed, and then stilled, the words lifting around them, drawing eyes up to the light-filled apse where winter's harsh glare was re-made into sanctuary.

Peace. A harbor from the flood, a blessing, a kiss from above.

Lutie did not let herself be drawn into that, no matter how the song—

the voice—begged her for it. She had not been misremembering anything: her brother could *sing*. And there, when she turned and looked
back through the double-wide entry into the lobby, a fleeting figure, gray
against the gloom where the light did not quite reach.

A ghost. Up against the space between the staircase and the cloakroom,
leaning forward, and expression of rapt transport on its thin face, listening
as though its heart might break. As Baz switched into English for the next
verse, the Major dropped his head down, watching Lutie. She shifted in her
seat, stared forward. Unafraid of the high notes, Baz embraced them, and
not for a minute did Lutie imagine he couldn't hit anything he was aiming
for. She looked to the first story windows, northern exposure, hard against
the community center, not much light even at noon. Through the amber
pane, a pale face, watery, young. Yearning for what was happening inside.

Maybe a church's holy ground did make a difference; the ghosts could
not come too near.

Baz let the guitarist have a gentle solo, smiled at him as he took up the
next verse, again in French. Behind her, Lutie heard a sniffle, someone
crying. It was bound to have this sort of effect, given where and when they
were. She thought it was probably a good thing, the sort of release that
made someone feel better afterwards.

And then, at the top of the apse, where the stained glass came to a peak
above the altar, a cloud must have moved away from obscuring the sun,
because a beam of light lit Baz like he was under a spotlight at a concert,
and the congregation murmured, but that didn't stop Baz from singing. In
fact, Lutie could almost say the light came from Baz, or was reflected by
him, and it made her heart stop for one breathless moment.

Then Baz finished, and the guitar's last chords lofted into the silent
chapel as the sun's light dulled and faded behind another wandering cloud
outside. Lutie counted five ghosts, here in the middle of blank Manitoba
prairie, hovering by the staircase, at the windows, near the doorways.
Those were just the ones she could see. Bending down, Baz put one hand
on the gunner's shoulder, thanking him with a wide smile and the gunner
seemed dazed, eyes blue and glowing even from the fourth row, where
Lutie watched carefully.

Baz didn't seem to take any notice of the ghosts, which even now lingered, perhaps expecting more, hoping for more, in any case. To her sur-

prise, the Major took her hand, something that he rarely did nowadays, and turned it over in his broader one. Her family stood to let Baz back in the row, and as he passed, the Major shook Baz's hand and Lutie knew that her life was changing, and that these changes were irrevocable.

Turning to him, one hand still in her foster father's, Lutie raised her chin so she could look her brother in the eye.

"Is it what you wanted?" Baz asked, troubled, but not angry. A little scared, maybe knowing what he'd done, and guessing what she'd seen as a result.

Which meant it was all true, and this was the gift that Baz could give to her today.

Lutie remembered it like a scene from a movie, colors saturated: a cemetery and Baz, so hot they could have fried an egg on any one of those crypts. Singing, wanting him to sing, because it brought them to her and kept them there. He couldn't see the ghosts, she'd known it then and knew it now, but they could see him, hear him. There was only one reason to gather ghosts and lull them into a dream state: so you could catch one.

Mireille had had hers, tucked inside, only let out when her mother had loosened the bindings that kept it there. A kept ghost was enormously helpful in telling the fortunes of others, the very best of the psychics and fortunetellers always had one, but Lutie knew it was dangerous, her mother had told her that repeatedly. It was why they had left Papa and the boys, because Aurie wouldn't have approved. To him, ghosts were something to be shunned, to get rid of, he didn't see their use.

It was either him, or my ghost, Mireille had offered as explanation. Having your own ghost must be damn fine, to choose as she had. *Aurèle, he would have gotten rid of it, would have left me. Would have left us.*

Well, he was dead, wasn't he? And Lutie wasn't sure she could catch a ghost, but she'd feel better about doing it with Baz at her side. She wasn't crazy, or if she was, her whole family was crazy right along with her. Baz had sought her out; she had been found. Compromise—*I let you in, you let me in.*

And compromise was another of those ten-letter words.

# SIX

## PHONE HOME

Corrugated iron, loaded garbage bags, mangled grocery carts, a tatty boxspring set on end. A group of ragged men with wild eyes, off meds, about as calm and collected as feral cats. These weren't the kind of tramps who asked for handouts, they were the kind that found them. On the outskirts of Ogallala, where a shantyville occupied the dip under the highway bridge, the tracks running close and inexorable as God, a small group of displaced men, of misplaced men, made a kind of home.

Aside from his short haircut and morning shower, Sol knew he wasn't so different from them. An army surplus parka and denim covered him; boots once good now near the end of their usefulness kept his feet reasonably warm. Mostly, though, they shared an expression in their eyes: *Don't fence me in.*

He approached the small fire, things used as fuel that most people wouldn't think of as fuel: abandoned furniture, found wood from crates and pallets. Cooking and eating things most people wouldn't consider food, either.

He'd brought a pouch of tobacco, which he handed over wordlessly, and was offered a cup of coffee that he didn't refuse. He'd had worse, and recently. They made small talk for a bit, smoking. Drinking. Staring out at the horizon, at the fire, at their feet, anywhere but at each other.

"You guys have any trouble lately?" Sol asked after hearing about rail traffic and other realities, one guy going off about religion and another about his ex, the bitch. "Aside from God and women?"

Two drifters deigned to talk to him in a manner that approached organized. A skinny black-and-tan dog nosed around, licked the older tramp's fingers. The tramp had introduced himself as Claude, his friend Tomson. The dog was Sparky.

Claude rolled a cigarette in hands that might have been a hundred years old, fingers the color of old cinders, a thousand campfires, roast sausages almost burned beyond edible. "You're not one of those assholes from social services, are you?"

Sol laughed, low and in his throat. "Do I *look* like I'm with social services?"

Claude considered him. Finally, he shook his head and Tomson—a slightly younger man with a beard to rival any Civil War general's—laughed loudly. "Hell, no."

Sol kept his silence, wondering if Claude would circle back to the question.

After a moment, he did. "Nah, the cops don't bother us much. It's the damn ministry that really pisses me off." And that started them off about church ladies and soup kitchens and how sleeping under a roof was just about the same as being incarcerated and all of them went on at length about that.

Sol commiserated, joined in, rolled his own smokes. *Dad wouldn't recognize me.* He shook his head. *Maybe he would.*

"You still ride some?" he asked, pointing with his nose to the nearby tracks.

Claude chuckled, rubbed Sparky behind the ear, smoke trailing from his nostrils like some kind of dragon. "Nah, not for years. They just barrel on through now, barely even slowing down for crossings. And the yards around here. The bulls have radios and the crews, well, they're too scared to help us out, usually."

Tomson rolled another cigarette, fingerless gloves unraveled like moss hanging from a plantation tree, a fire hazard, the mechanics of lighting the damp smoke without setting his hands on fire a distraction to Sol. Once lit, almost no difference between the muddy brown of the knit glove and the sepia fingertips, Tomson smacked his lips, revealed stumpy gray teeth. "Bailey's always a good bet; Ogallala yard's fine, too, if you're scouting around. The bulls are the bulls, eh, they check, and you take a beating, but mostly you get where you're goin'."

They talked about riding for a bit, about keeping warm on open boxcars, about avoiding the tankers filled with toxic crap. About how to ride between the car and the wheels, about shifting cargo killing people they knew. About the inclines once you hit California, about the valleys so green they hurt your eyes, about smelling salt on the air like the answer to a prayer.

Tomson sucked the cigarette right down to the end, squished it in his fingers, then put it in a hinged tin that he kept in one of his outer pockets.

"The bulls just think us guys are lazy. They don't get it. Not at all," and Tomson spat to the side.

"What don't they get?" Sol asked finally, throwing the dregs of the coffee into the bushes beside the track, wiping the handle-less cup out with his gloves and handing it back to Claude with a nod of thanks.

"Don't get it at all," Tomson repeated, then eyed Sol again as though he'd just appeared.

But Sol did get it. He did understand. "The cops, people in houses. They think you're just out here, sucking off society, right? Maybe it wasn't a choice so much, at first. But you don't go back." Something shifted inside him as he said it, and he didn't know if it was something sliding out of his grasp, or something coming home to roost. Tomson nodded, however, so then Sol finally asked if they'd seen anything weird lately, anything that was beyond normal. Something in his manner or his look, Sol didn't know which, maybe the fact he could roll his own and spoke with the soft cadences of the swamp, but Claude blinked rheumy eyes and muttered. Tomson was the one who spoke up.

"Always damn weird shit around here," but he wouldn't look at Sol. "You should ask DJ, up near Brule. Right, Claude?"

Claude wasn't saying anything, and Sol noticed his hands were shaking. Sparky came and circled to a rest at his feet.

Tomson rubbed a spot on his knee, over and over. "Bad stuff happened in Brule, or just west of there. Some bad stuff."

Sol had a fair bit of patience; he could wait out Claude's fear. "What's the story, Claude?" he asked, pronouncing the name just right, and that brought the man's eyes into focus, probably had a parent who had spoken French, Sol thought. Sol passed him a rolled cigarette, lit one of his own with the ember end of a fire stick.

Claude shook his head. "I'm a peaceful man, son. So's Tomson here. We don't hurt no one. But you ask DJ if he's seen anything, he's down that way." He halted, wandering hands shaking. "DJ's too young, he wasn't around back then, but used to be…" His voice trailed away, lost like smoke on the wind. Then, he shuddered. "Used to be harder, back in the day. We don't talk about it, us old-timers."

Tomson took out a label-less can, punctured it and set it on the flames, balanced on a piece of broken cinderblock. Sol was glad for the fire, because it was getting damn cold, Arctic wind coming straight off the prairie, no mitigating foothills to temper it.

Claude continued. "Don't know why they picked fire, those assholes. That's a nasty way to go. You don't light a man's home on fire. They blamed us. Check my record, spent time inside. But it weren't our fault. Well, weren't my fault." He shifted, uncomfortable. "All of 'em are dead now, anyway. The guys that did it."

Tomson shifted on his crate. "All of 'em?" Unsure.

Claude spat to the side. "Yeah. Old Leaky died down in Mexico right around Halloween, not two months ago. Cancer finally caught up with him. Died in a bed." Like that was a crime in and of itself. "Blame him, I say. Weren't my fault."

Sol gave his cigarette stub to Tomson, patted Sparky, who had looked up at the motion. "It wasn't your fault," he agreed, wondering if Claude would tell him more, or if he'd have to look elsewhere. "Before my time, and before DJ's time, too. When was that?" The light was starting to fail, and the temperature dropped some more.

Claude shook his head. "Thirty, thirty-five years ago. Worked in Bailey Yard, the big asshole, but lived up there." He jerked his thumb to the west, closed his eyes. "We don't talk about it."

Sol let it lie for a few minutes, didn't push. If he pushed, Claude would never tell him. Thirty years was a long time, and it was yesterday. "The weird shit you guys been seeing, it had to do with that fire." A statement for them to agree with, or ignore.

"You're from down south, ain't ya?" Claude changed the subject.

Sol persevered. "Mais, hard to disguise, that."

"So you know weird shit."

"I do."

"There's something been killing folks along here, mostly us tramps. Never see it, never hear it, but there's a lot of busted heads. That's how Lewis used to do it, way long ago. That bull's paying back, but all those who deserve it are already dead." Claude poked the fire with a stick. "You make it up to

Brule, you look for DJ. He weren't around then, but he's closest to where it happened. He might know more."

Two names now: DJ and Lewis. That was something. The whole trip was worth it, just for that. A railroad cop named Lewis, dead for thirty or more years. A possible witness or informant, DJ.

Claude didn't precisely excuse himself, but he got up then, bent double to get into his shack, and Sol eyed Tomson, who shrugged. "Thanks for the smoke, man. You gotta home to go to, you should get there."

Sol thought about that as he walked back to the Wagoneer, considered the idea of home as he drove back to his Ogallala motel room, where he stared at the telephone like it might bark at him. He was a goddamn master at fucking relationships up, he knew that. But there were a few things he did well and this was one of them, following a ghost trail, putting things to rest that had no business upsetting the peace. Too bad none of that extended to his own personal life.

*Mais, you can't have everything.*

He had something to go on, now. Lewis. The former Bailey Yard bull had died somewhere near Brule, burned alive in his house by a bunch of vagrants. The last of his murderers had died in October, right around when the spate of rail deaths had started. An asshole ghost bent on vengeance haunting the tracks between where he'd worked and where he'd died.

The only thing Sol didn't know was how a devil fit into it.

Outside the motel room, Sol smoked a last cigarette, considered the moon hanging in the bowl of prairie sky, begging to be followed. He couldn't stop thinking about the nearby tracks, could hear a train even now, the clang of the warning at the crossing, thought about trains going slow enough that you could run alongside them, jump for an iron bar, swing up and into an empty car, just get the hell out town and catch out.

The lunch had lasted at least seventeen hours and Baz thought that Armageddon might have come and gone in the time it took to receive all the thanks after the service, to walk back to the McGregors' house on Sapper Avenue, and listen to the young gunner, Corporal Fortier, tell him one more time what it meant to have heard that song today. Inviting Corporal Fortier to lunch had been Lutie's idea, surprisingly, and Baz wondered if Lutie had a crush on him.

Only for a moment, though, because Baz had the immediate sense that Lutie was playing this whole lunch event like an orchestra—she had the gunner there to keep Baz talking in broken French, keep him pleasantly distracted while she minnowed between parents and foster siblings, a little word here, a chat there. An additional outsider cut the tension, everyone on good behavior.

In the kitchen, while the Major talked to Marshall about recent trades and standings and Fortier listened in, offering his considered assessment of the World Junior team, and Karen and Bree gently argued about how much cocoa to add for hot chocolate, Lutie brushed up against Baz, who didn't know the first thing about hockey, and asked, quietly, "So where do you go from here?"

He didn't know if he understood the question, and then he thought he did. A private conversation, right in the middle of everything, an easy way to get out if the talk got too weird or personal. She was a smart one, this sister. "Minneapolis. Dad kept some things there. I should collect them. I'll phone Sol, see if he's got a few days off. He might help."

Or might not, it was hard to tell with him especially in matters concerning their father. Jesus, Baz thought, not for the first time, how was he going to tell Sol about any of this?

Lutie passed him a plate of sandwiches, and he took one, handed it to Fortier. "I could give you a drive. I have to get back to Toronto for the second week of January."

Just like that. He noticed Lutie wasn't telling her parents about this plan.

The sun was setting when Lutie said she'd drop Baz back at the motel, and Karen gave them a solid smile. *This is going to be okay,* Baz thought. Maybe he'd ended up doing the right thing after all.

Baz flipped through her radio stations on the way back until Lutie told him to leave it, so he did.

"You were great, you know that," she said, about halfway to town.

Baz, looking out the window, glanced back at her. The sun sliced diagonally in their eyes, and he'd pulled down the visor to block it. Her white coat was blinding, even compared to the snow. He shrugged. "I don't sing much."

"You should," she replied, keeping her eyes on the road.

Baz laughed. "Dad gave me a fiddle so I'd stop singing."

"He was wrong," and she slowed the car. Baz wondered if she was going to stop, then realized that they were at the place where a roadside cross poked up through the thin covering of windswept snow, faded flowers sagging under ice.

She stared through the passenger window and Baz knew that stare, had grown up with it. "You pass by this place," he interrupted softly, not following her gaze. "You keep going, chère, there's nothing good here for you."

It was freezing in the car, ghostcold, and Baz knew he was right. But she had put the car into park on the empty highway and now her gaze searched him out, sunlight sloping into her eyes. "You don't see them." But it was a question.

Slowly, he shook his head. "I don't." It was dangerous, talking about this with a stranger, forbidden. Even with her, maybe especially with her. "Can we keep going?"

"Here's the deal," Lutie said, eyes tracking movement that Baz couldn't see, and his hair rose along his arm inside his coat. Dad had known how to keep safe in this kind of situation, and Sol knew too, in his own contrary and bull-headed way.

He didn't know about Lutie, though. Dragged around by a crazy mother who could not only see ghosts, but who had kept one surely as a Rottweiler on a chain. A mother who had left her sons for reasons Baz had never understood. Mireille had taken Lutie with her, though, had done that deliberately. Again, for reasons that Baz couldn't fathom and maybe he didn't want to know.

Lutie licked her lips, and Baz felt every year lost between them like steps down to a dark basement. "I'll drive you to Minneapolis. You tell me more about this," and she waved her hand vaguely to whatever was outside, which-ever ghost was associated with that cross and this cold. "You *help* me with this."

It was Sol she needed, not him. Baz wasn't going to be able to keep these two realities separate. Sol was going to kill him.

He cleared his throat, and she eased the car out of park and into drive. A long moment of silence followed, and Baz watched his sister as she checked the rearview mirror several times until they rounded a long slow corner and that stretch of highway was lost in the gloom.

Sol made good time for a country road, the eight miles between his Ogallala motel room and the tiny village of Brule. He followed the South Platte River, a runnel of standing water too wet to plant, too dry to fish. On its way to nowhere. Signs for country auctions and abandoned farm houses, people leaving all over, this was the sort of place you passed through, that you wanted to see in your rearview mirror.

A hundred and fifty years of European occupation hadn't made much of a dent: the road was as empty as the sky. Nothing came through here except the trains. Nowadays, traffic took the interstate, not the tiny strand of the old 30 highway, a filament of cracked asphalt sporadic as Morse code. Running between the two—the dying river and the crumbling highway—bright open sky, thin dry earth, blocky black cattle destined for the dinner plate, and iron rails. These were the constants, cardinal points in this limbo.

The village came up fast: one minute sky and faded brown grass, the next, civilization. To the south side stood the tall silos of the granary, and to the north, a huddle of old wood frame houses and post-war pre-fabs overseen by a faded blue water tower, rolling beige hills beyond void of vegetation like God couldn't be bothered. Landing in Brule, Nebraska was like stepping back fifty years. More.

He drove through the village before he realized that's all there was to it. He pulled the Wagoneer in a U-turn, slowed down on the return pass. DJ could be anywhere along the tracks, could be holed up in any abandoned house or vehicle, would take some time to locate. It was close to noon already; he had maybe an hour before he'd have to turn around and head back to Denver. It was a double shift, too, if he remembered correctly, time off traded like glass beads for land. Double shift for a weekend and this was what he'd done with it, spent it talking to tramps, sleeping badly at the Ogallala Super 8, spending a fruitless hour at the local library. Nothing left but to try to find DJ. The things he chose to do off the clock, because Brule was a flyspeck, a nothing, literally two churches and the water tower.

There, by the empty grain silos and the track, he made out a sign: coffee. *Please dear God, let it be open.* He turned into the hard dirt parking lot. It was a tiny place, an old caboose with a barrel for a garbage bin outside, competing signs executed in burned wood advertising The Coffee Caboose Museum, souvenirs, and a meeting place for the Platte River Historical Society.

"Perfect," Sol sighed. One-stop information shopping at its best, research combined with caffeine.

The guy behind the counter was tall and young, blond as a Viking, looked as though he ate a dozen eggs for breakfast every morning. As Sol came in, the boy put down the book he'd been reading, looked up expectantly, pink face just past the ravages of teen acne. There was a moment's silence, and then the kid, dressed in a red Nebraska Husker sweatshirt, motioned with his hand: take your freakin' pick of tables, his bland features seemed to suggest, it's a morgue in here.

Sol slid in to the counter, scouted for a newspaper, found none. He ordered coffee immediately and was handed a menu. The kid leaned against the counter, not even pretending to give Sol room to decide.

"The steak and eggs are a good bet. The muffins just came out of the freezer this morning. I can microwave you a bowl of mac and cheese, but we're out of most everything else."

Sol set the menu down. "Steak and eggs, then," he said. The kid didn't ask him how he liked his steak, instead moved into the servery area and Sol heard the slam of a fridge and the beep of a microwave. Sol wondered how awful the rest of the menu was for this to be the best bet. He looked over at the dog-eared book lying face down on the counter. Hesse's *Siddhartha*. Of course. The kid was the right age for it.

Surprisingly, the steak wasn't tough, and Sol ate methodically, the timing of the next meal always in question, his line of work. As he ate, the farmer's kid in the college football sweater came back out, ignored the book, inquired about the steak, and introduced himself as Bart.

"You from here, Bart," Sol asked around the eggs. Scrambled, no choice when it came to a microwave.

Bart nodded, happy to be engaged. "From Paxton, just east of here. Born and raised."

Sol gestured to the sweatshirt with his knife. Bart seemed to understand. "Finishing up a graduate degree in history."

Bart laughed at whatever expression Sol had on his face. Sol had been hoping for an old-timer, but maybe this budding historian would do. "You part of the historical society, too?"

Bart was still pink, looked as though someone had held him down and scrubbed him with a potato brush. He ducked his head, eased onto the stool by the cash register. "Nah, I think you have to be over seventy for that. They let me type up the minutes."

"No shit," Sol said. "So, what kind of history does a town like Brule have?"

Bart shrugged. "Homesteaders. Indians. You know. The regular prairie stuff." He leaned in. "I'm more of a Germanic studies type." He gestured to the book. "Still, you can't really avoid it, here."

"Railroad history?" Sol led, using a piece of toast to mop up the steak juice.

Bart choked a sigh. "Well, yeah." Like Sol was stupid. Sol held the stare. He wasn't stupid. He wasn't making small talk. He didn't have enough time to be charming, enough energy. Charm wasn't what was needed anyhow.

"I'm looking into railroad history around here," he said firmly.

"Writing an article?" Bart sounded dubious.

"Maybe." Sol folded his cutlery across his plate. "If there's anything interesting to report. This place," his eyes slid out the narrow window where nothing but gray fencing and the abandoned silos signaled civilization, "anything interesting ever happen here?"

Bart reddened some more, crossed his arms. Education was not the only thing that separated them. Not a farmer's kid, Sol revised his original assessment. A railroad executive's, maybe. Finally, Bart shrugged. "Not much. During the Depression, there used to be a squatter's village here."

"Any drifters still around?"

"Rail riders?" Bart's eyebrows shot up. "There were a few in the summer, I think. Had a little camp to west, between here and the old Megeath crossing. But now there's only DJ."

Sol waited expectantly.

Bart sighed, maybe annoyed. "DJ's been here a few months. He's not going anywhere. He's settled right in. Are you writing an article about rail riders? Because you'd be better off at Bailey Yard for that sort of thing."

Sol gave the kid a break, sighed. "I've been there already. I talked to the guys in Ogallala, down by the tracks. Those tramps are all scared. There's been some trouble, a couple of deaths."

"Ah, I shoulda known it. You reporters are all the same." His blue eyes flashed a little. "Like vultures."

Sol held up both hands. "It bleeds, it leads." As a paramedic, he knew all about reporters and blood. "Blame the editors, man. I'm just looking for the story."

They were quiet for a moment. Sol was aware he didn't look much like a reporter, but Bart didn't seem to notice, or care. "Listen," Bart finally said.

"The guys who work for the railroad get pretty jumpy about any deaths. Honest, there hasn't been anything like that around here. I'd have heard about it."

Not as far as Brule, then. The ghost was working its way to where it had died—if the ghost was indeed that of Lewis—and Sol wondered if Bart had heard about the most recent murder in Ogallala, the Nepal-bound lawyer. Probably not, especially as the police had ruled it a suicide. Sol sighed. He only had time for direct shots and this kid would probably spill whatever he knew anyway. "The guys living by the tracks in Ogallala, they told me about some guy called Lewis. A railway cop, a bull. Might have died around here in the 70s?"

Bart shrugged. "Before I was born." But he was thinking about it, Sol could tell. The kid licked his lips, thoughtful. "Was there a fire?"

Bingo. Sol tilted his head. "I don't know. You tell me."

Bart looked around the caboose, cluttered with the detritus of prairie history—hand tools pinned to the walls, a yoke, yellowed certificates behind scratched glass. "Yeah. Jack Lewis lived up by the Megeath crossing, I think, if we're talking about the same person. You should ask one of the old guys."

"Who do I call?" Sol asked, crumpling the paper napkin onto the plate.

Bart wasn't playing that game; he seemed suddenly protective. Sol had gotten the kid's back up. Great. "I'll ask around. Check with me in a few days." He paused, judgment in the blue eyes. "Don't leave it longer, though. I'm back to school next week, and this place'll be closed up until May."

Reluctantly, Sol told the kid his name, said he'd check back later on in the week. He glanced at his watch. No time to look up-rail for DJ, not that and make it back in time for his shift. Sticking around the extra night to check out the Ogallala library and Brule had been a complete waste of time; he'd have been better off going home and continuing his search from there.

He paid with cash, tried to give Bart an accommodating smile, but it came out wrong and Sol wondered if the kid would really ask around on his behalf. Bart gave him the number of the phone on the wall that seemed to serve both the coffee shop and the historical society. There's no answering machine, Bart told him, so just keep trying.

*It's coming here*, Sol realized as he pulled away from Brule, heading directly to the interstate, no time for railroad-hugging backroads any more. *That ghost is coming in this direction and God help anyone in its way.*

He wondered if he'd had a phone with him, if he would have called home. Just pick up on impulse and wiggle out of his shift, make an excuse to Robbie, simply stay here and gnaw this bone. And he wondered, as he sometimes did, if not having a phone was his way of staying in touch, instead of its opposite. It meant he always came home, because he had to.

That night, Baz could put it off no longer. He'd been out of contact over Christmas and even though Sol wasn't exactly freaking Santa when it came to seasonal festivities, there were limits to how long Baz could maintain radio silence, considering the last time he'd seen his brother, Sol had been unconscious in a motel room. Baz didn't know if Sol would be worried about him, it was hard to tell sometimes what would worry Sol, but Baz knew Robbie would be concerned.

He wasn't wrong in that; Robbie sounded relieved beyond measure when she heard his voice, asked him how his Christmas was, if he was going to be playing somewhere close by for New Years.

Baz wasn't sure he could lie to his brother, which was part of the reason he hadn't phoned. Then Robbie told him that Sol wasn't there, hadn't checked in with her for almost three whole days, not since he'd gone to work on Saturday morning, pulling a double. And when Robbie asked Baz where the hell *he'd* been for the last two weeks, Baz *knew* he wouldn't have been able to lie to Sol, so it was just as well that his brother wasn't home.

Better for Baz, anyway.

Robbie's voice sounded both tight and worn, fed up and a little giddy. "You know," she said, after he'd explained that he was heading for Minneapolis, "you Sarrazin guys should form your own club, call it Assholes Anonymous."

"I know, Robbie, we're not exactly reliable material."

"Well, you, you're a musician, no surprise," he heard dishes clattering in the background, "and your dad was like a friggin' ninja when it came to dropping in and out whenever it pleased him." Running water. The house would be spotless, Baz knew, household chores one of the few things in Robbie's control. "But Sol? I never thought he was like you two." The water stopped and Baz braced himself. "But you know? Saturday, he tells me not to wait up. I'm pretty sure he's gone back to Nebraska. Is he seeing someone else, Baz? Some cowgirl rodeo starlet? You'd tell me, right? I deserve to know."

Baz, phone in hand, pacing the small motel room, window to bathroom door, back again, sighed. "Robbie, sweetheart, that is one thing you don't have to worry about." And Baz knew it to be true. "He's crazy about you. He's

92

just not good at showing it, you know that. And nobody else would put up him, anyway. He's just—" *Worried that you'll think he's mental if he tells you about what he sees. About what he can do.*

"He's just a secretive asshole who saves all the heroics for work." There was silence on both ends, because Baz couldn't agree without being a traitor, and couldn't deny without being a liar. The dog barked and then whined, then barked again—Robbie must have thrown him something. "I got him a phone for Christmas."

God, she was persistent, Baz would give her that. "And?"

"And, it's sitting here on the kitchen table, just where he left it."

"Well, at least he didn't lose it. Or break it."

"Yeah, well, it's the last phone I'm giving him."

"I'll talk to him," Baz offered, knowing it was foolhardy in the extreme, given what else he had to say to Sol: Listen, Sol. Maman, she killed herself, I've found our sister, she could really use your help in the ghosts-are-making-me-nuts department, and by the way, could you please use the phone your girlfriend got you for Christmas?

"If you can find him," Robbie grumbled over the clatter of cutlery.

Baz wondered if Sol would be at the same motel in North Platte. Something up in Nebraska was worrying Sol, that was evident, something that had caught their father's attention, too. Maybe the same something that had killed their father. Which meant that it had to do with a mean ghost, a dangerous one. You could tell when Sol was worked up about something that was dead, but not necessarily when he was concerned about a living, breathing person. One of Sol's faults, Baz knew.

Robbie sighed when Baz didn't answer her. "He's working tonight. He never misses a shift, so I'd try to get hold of him through the health center."

"Yeah, I'll do that," Baz agreed wincing. "I've got news for him. He'll be interested." And that was one way of putting it.

# SEVEN

## PLAY BY EAR

If Lutie didn't think the Sarrazins were all hopelessly nuts by now, Baz was fairly certain she would shortly. They'd left CFB Shilo at dawn, and now it was three in the afternoon, New Year's Eve; they'd made damn fine time to be in Minneapolis so early.

Evidence of the Sarrazin hard-scrabble lifestyle was rampant: Baz had no car, no license and no apparent job. He had no education to speak of. Their father, also of no fixed address, had just been killed in a train yard, and hadn't been able to hold down anything approaching regular employment since being released from prison for manslaughter six years prior. The most stable member of the family was currently incommunicado, hunting ghosts in rural Nebraska and she didn't want to meet him anyway.

Baz could tell, for example, that his sister was appalled at the wretchedly maintained turn-of-the-century house—Jean-Guy Landry wasn't exactly a meticulous guy, a shortcoming exacerbated by an apparent desire to collect scrap metal in various forms. This, Lutie's face said exquisitely, is where my father lived?

Baz hunched over in his coat, hands deep in the pockets, leaning against the peeling door frame as he raised a knuckle to knock. "Dad only stayed here when he was in town. Otherwise, he'd kinda—" and he shrugged, unable to explain.

"Kinda what?" Lutie asked, and Baz was saved from answering by Landry pulling open the door, holding a borderline psychotic mastiff by a studded collar. Lutie, in her pristine white down coat, jumped back about a foot.

"Hé, man, ça va?" Landry said, and Baz was momentarily distracted by the gun tucked into Landry's waistband. The man was also missing his front teeth and eyed Lutie with undisguised interest.

"Jean-Guy," Baz said, taking off his hat.

"What the hell kinda haircut is that? Goddamn, Aurie shoulda taught you better. For a beau goss, you are some weird-lookin'." Landry pulled the dog back, slobber lashing his thigh. "Who's this?"

Baz raised a shoulder, unwilling to draw Lutie close to this life, suddenly questioning the upside of this visit. "This is Luetta," Baz said. "You heard what happened, I guess. With Aurie and the train."

Landry nodded. "I heard, and I'm sorry about that. Sol takin' care of it? Makin' sure everything's in order? He should." Being careful with his words, of course, if with this one thing only.

"I dunno," Baz answered truthfully. "He don't tell me much."

They were let in, but Baz didn't take off his coat and saw that Lutie was following suit. Besides, the house was scarcely warm, smelled of old newspaper and dog. As he passed by Landry, he dropped his voice. "Can you save the gun, cher? She's Canadian. You're gonna scare her." They were offered something to drink, but Baz turned it down for both of them.

"I thought I'd get Aurie's things out of your way, if that's okay."

Landry scratched under his cap. "Go right ahead. You know the room. You need a box or something?"

Baz said yes, and a box was procured, one that had held some industrial sized paper towels according to the print on the side. Baz knew their father wouldn't have much worth carting away; the box was probably more than big enough.

Landry said he needed to feed the dog, and as Baz turned to go up the stairs, the old Cajun pulled out the gun dramatically, and made a show of putting it in a drawer where it 'would be safe'. *Well, that'll set Lutie's mind at ease.* Baz lost no time shoving Lutie up the stairs, seeing all this with an outsider's eye and knowing that it didn't even approach normal.

"So, you stay here when you're in town?" she asked, the question floating up into the dim stairwell.

Baz laughed. "Sweet mother of God, no. I got better places to crash than this."

At the top of the stairs, Baz rattled the knob of the first door to the left, found it open, and went in, knowing this was as much of a home as his father had kept since leaving Louisiana: a single mattress bed, neatly made, a clutter of what could only be defined loosely as junk on top of a dresser, and a closetful of workshirts. In the corner, a worn fiddle in its case, known and loved since Baz was a baby. *Thank God*, he thought.

Aside from the fiddle, which was the real reason Baz had bothered to come, none of the stuff was really worth taking, but Baz thought his brother would probably like one or two of the shirts—the two men were of a size—and perhaps some of the other things on the dresser that Baz couldn't identify. He thought they might be some sort of medicine bags, and Sol would likely throw them out, calling them bayou poisons, but he might not.

Lutie stood in the corner, watching with big eyes, and Baz smiled at her, tried to ease her mind. Generally speaking, he was good at that. He had expertly negotiated the rough waters of the McGregor household—the Major had been dubious about Lutie's change of route back to Toronto, but Karen had put her hand on the Major's shoulder and he'd touched her fingers with his and that had been that.

"It's not much, I know." He examined some jeans, but thought that Sol would have better taste, or at least Robbie would. Robbie would wonder about these wretched things, would probably throw them in the trash when Sol turned his back.

"No," Lutie said quietly, hand drifting over the piles of paper in the corner—old magazines and newspapers. "No, it's okay."

Landry had already said that he'd sell Aurie's truck, sitting in the North Platte police impound lot. It wasn't worth much anyway and Baz told him to keep the money, that it would at least cover the back rent. There was no bank account, no credit cards. Aurie did everything by cash and barter, always had. If he had an off-shore account in the Grand Caymans, his children would never know about it.

They were going to drive through the night, leave Minneapolis and spend New Years on the road. Lutie would drop Baz off in Des Moines, Iowa, from where she would head east; a little out of her way, but not by much. Baz had said that he'd go west after that, no need to worry about him. He'd already fielded a phone call from the guitarist of a band he'd played with last year, wondering if he'd like to join them on a western tour, starting with a gig tonight in Rochester. Baz had asked the vintage of the tour van, was told mid-80s, and declined. He wasn't that desperate, not yet. Hell, he could even phone up that Minneapolitan alt-country trio that had scouted him in September and see if they needed—there was a box under the bed.

Baz grabbed it with one hand and hauled it out; it was light, thin cardboard, had contained Nikes at some point. Baz looked up at Lutie, crouched on the floor beside him.

"What do you think?" she asked.

Baz shrugged. "Aucune idée," he replied. He opened the lid. There, inside, was the wallet that the police hadn't been able to find down by the tracks. It had over a thousand dollars in small bills inside it, and a number of fake IDs. None of this was entirely unusual; if Aurie had worked a construction job lately, he would have had a cash payout, and the IDs were part of avoiding taxes and police checks, Baz knew.

He held the wallet out to Lutie, who shook her head: too personal maybe, too close. Baz set it on the threadbare carpet between them, examined the remaining box contents: a book holding down a square of paper; a matchbox.

The matchbox fit easily in Baz's hand and he only hesitated a moment before opening it. God alone knew what his father might keep inside: a dried finger, a baby's caul, a priest's toenail clippings. Instead, Baz found a small square of folded white cotton. With Lutie's eyes on him, he unfolded it on the palm of his left hand, revealing a small circle of thin pale gold. A woman's wedding band, and Baz felt his breath stick in his chest at an odd angle, jagged like it cut.

"She left it," Lutie said after a moment, but she didn't look at him. "She must have left it when we…"

Baz remembered. He remembered way too much.

He held it out to her, but Lutie shook her head, so he wrapped the ring, put it back into its box, and slid it shut. He held the box for a moment longer, wondered what they should do with it. They didn't have to make a decision, not yet, and Sol should be part of any of it. Which meant telling

Sol. Baz would cross that bridge when he came to it. Gently, he set the matchbox beside the book, felt shaky.

The book came from the Houma Public Library, according to the stamp on the inside cover, years overdue; it was in French and it seemed to be poetry. Baz flipped through it, looking for anything tucked inside the pages, but there was nothing.

Not poetry, he realized, reading the title. Song lyrics.

Along many of the margins, in Aurie's tight scrawl, were notes in pencil and in pen, in English and in French. Notations, difficult to figure out: Works well, only when needed, celle-là est bonne, ce n'est pas utile. It reminded Baz of a recipe book, edited and tested and commented upon. He shook his head.

Aurèle Sarrazin had been an odd guy, something that Baz had always admired. Aurie had disliked all kinds of authority, from the courts to their home-room teachers. The truth was that Aurie hadn't socialized all that much, and usually only with Louisiana ex-pats, scattered like seeds across the Midwest, guys like Jean-Guy. Baz and Sol had agreed about not having a funeral, but for different reasons: Baz suspected no one would come, and Sol, the opposite. He'd said that he didn't want to see any of 'Aurie's coonass friends'.

Lutie picked up the piece of paper, which turned out to be a photo. She stared at it, and Baz wasn't sure, but he thought maybe for the first time since he'd met her less than a week ago, she might cry. He didn't try to take the photo, he simply crabbed round behind her, looked over her shoulder.

It must have been taken in the early 80s, although at first he thought maybe the photo was of Sol and someone else, some pretty girl with severe brows disappearing into a fringe of honey-blonde hair, eyes dark-lashed and enormous. It looked to be a summer day some place with windswept trees and land sloping away to far ocean. There was action in the background—a striped tent, an old van with its side door up—a casse-croûte advertising Pogos, frites and poutine.

It wasn't Sol, of course, it was Aurie, so young and unworn that Baz had to blink twice in rapid succession to make sense of it. Dark hair worn longer than Sol did, same scruffy beard and sardonic smile, suggestion of dimples lost somewhere in the beard. A faded red t-shirt advertising a

Terrebonne excavation company. His tanned and muscular arm around the blonde, dark dancing eyes directed at her and only her.

Mireille looked directly at the camera, and whoever the photographer had been couldn't make her smile. She had a lanyard around her neck, and a tag of some sort. She could have been eighteen or maybe twenty, but not much more than that.

"Is that—" Lutie asked, finger tapping Aurie's face.

"Yeah, that's Dad," Baz said softly. "I haven't seen this photo before. I have another one of M'man, from when I was a kid, before we left Louisiana. I didn't know about this one."

"It was taken in New Brunswick, I think. Look—" and she pointed out the lanyard, the writing on it. "Some festival, I guess." She turned it over. On the back, in faded ballpoint blue, was written 'Caraquet N.-B. 1980'. It wasn't his father's almost illegible hand, it was flowing, slanted to the right.

Baz held one side of the photo and Lutie the other and Baz wondered if their father had ever thought that they would be here one day, looking at this image, together. He doubted it.

"Funny," Lutie whispered. "Maman didn't talk about him at all, or you guys. She cried a lot, though, when she thought I was asleep." She looked up and tears had spilled silently down her cheeks. "You know she had a ghost, right? You know that."

Baz nodded, once, dry throat. Lutie didn't remember, maybe, that she'd been the one to reveal that to him, years and years ago.

"She got mad at that ghost, sometimes. Said that she had given it all up for nothing."

"Did the ghost answer back?" It wasn't an idle question.

Slowly, Lutie shook her head. "Not that I ever heard."

"Aurie," and it felt so strange to call him that in this room while he still held the man's wallet curved to fit the body, the weight of his clothes in a box beside him, "Aurie said she was evil."

Lutie was staring at the photo again. "Is that the look of someone who thinks his wife is evil?" she asked, holding the photo closer to her brother, and it was true.

Midnight found Sol standing over a body outside Kitty's on East Colfax, pondering the effectiveness of 'We Never Close!' as an advertising come-on.

The dead guy at his feet was certainly taking a break from Kitty's twenty-four-hour party. Lividity had set in, someone's New Year's Eve gone horrifically wrong, ghost long gone, stoked to the max with barbiturates mixed with alcohol, if Sol didn't miss his guess. Nothing for them to do here.

Tonight he was partnered with Dan, a mild-mannered kind of guy who always pressed his white shirts and never got flustered, no matter how cooked the call got. Sol had once seen Dan—middle aged, with two kids in college—recite turkey-basting instructions to his youngest daughter over the phone while administering anti-seizure meds to a freaking out junkie in the middle of a housing project's public commons.

While Dan finished the paperwork, Sol loitered to the side of Kitty's bar, sizing up the Fillmore Auditorium across the street, wondering when the show was going to let out and how to deal with the crowd of people that were sure to be interested in the dead body on the pavement. That would be a police problem, Sol assured himself, still going through the mental exercise to keep boredom at bay.

"Happy New Years," Dan surprised him, passing Sol a cup of coffee hastily obtained from inside Kitty's. Sol saluted him with the white paper cup. "You got a resolution?"

Sol shrugged. "Don't mix business with pleasure," he muttered. "You?"

It was astonishingly cold tonight, too cold for snow, and windy, a bad combination. They'd been collecting frostbitten drunks up and down the Colfax strip all night. The appearance of an overdose was a bit of a reprieve. Dreary and constant, Sol would call tonight's work.

"I'm gonna drop ten pounds, Darlene tells me."

Sol grinned into his coffee. He'd barely made it in time for tonight's shift, had slept away the day after working a double the day before. Since returning from Brule, he and Robbie had missed each other completely: the salon was busy during the day, and he was pulling night shifts. Nothing was coming together properly.

Though he'd looked, he hadn't found anything online—nothing fitting Brule, Lewis, fire. Hell, he'd even tried to find out if someone named Old Leaky had died in a Mexican hospital over the last few months. He'd tried phoning Bart at the Coffee Caboose Museum, but hadn't gotten through. The kid hadn't been lying about the lack of an answering machine. Not enough hours in the day to go back. Not enough time, not enough sleep.

# DEADROADS

The phone had wakened him from a dead sleep at two that afternoon. Robbie, phoning from work, inviting him to come with her to a party, not pleading, but close to it. There was no way he could have found a replacement, not on New Year's Eve and not at that late hour. He hadn't been at his courteous best with her, groggy and already running late. He'd parked the truck in the employee garage along Bannock, grabbed a uniform from his locker, received his assignment and met Dan at the rig, ready to do his check. That had been eight hours ago, and it had been non-stop, pick-up-drop-off since.

Sol sighed, looked with irritation at the police milling over the body, waiting for the ME to show up. "You ready to give these guys your report, Dan? Let's get out of here."

"Boy, Sarrazin, what's your hurry? You should work on that resolution of yours."

Sol zipped his jacket all the way to the top, harder to coordinate because of his gloves. "Mais, I'd rather be in the rig than freezing my ass off out here."

Dan shook his head and walked over to the police sergeant, handed him the top copy of his paperwork, and they were back in the orange and white unit, ready to go. Sol called in their availability to dispatch and was told that nothing was hot yet. They drank their coffee while Dan outlined his diet plans, which seemed to involve a whole lot of bran, as far as Sol could determine.

Four messages had been waiting for him when he'd arrived at work—one from Baz and three from Wayne, trying to get him to come to his party so that he could monitor people for alcohol poisoning. The calls from Wayne he'd ignored, wondering when the guy was going to get his ass fired, and the call from Baz he'd returned right away, only to get an out of area message.

Dispatch blurted on the line: the next call was to a townhouse complex in Westminster East and Sol was glad Dan was originally from New Mexico, because chances were this was going to be an emergency conducted in Spanish. They went in lights and siren, Sol speeding just enough, response time under ten minutes, which was how the policy wonks at admin liked it.

The middle-aged woman was in cardiac arrest, first few minutes counted, and Sol looked for the Fire Department's first response team's truck pulled up to the brick townhouses, let Dan take the ALS bag, run the call. Sol took the second bag with the defibrillator, and followed Dan into a wind tunnel between two decrepit brick buildings, bits of tinsel and broken lights all that remained of Christmas hanging tattered around the entranceway.

He almost missed the sign as they went in, but had to double check the address against what dispatch had sent, because stuff like this got messed up all the time, especially in housing developments with all the pedestrian access routes. Right address, and underneath the number, hand-drawn in shaky black marker on Corplast: Madama Lopez, Maestra en Ciencias Occultas! Lectura de las cartas y Palma de la Mano. A crude drawing of a hand appeared underneath.

Down the semi-enclosed corridor, Sol could hear Dan calling to the firefighter-EMTs, then talking to someone else in Spanish, and the lights from their two rigs were flashing red and blue against the brick. It was desperately cold and Sol couldn't move.

*Another sign—Madame LeBlanc, La meilleure sorcière de la Nouvelle-Orléans! Crazy old bitch doesn't speak a word of English. No one in the immediate vicinity speaks French, no one but the kid from the Denver unit, and the water is rising, pouring up through the sewer system; they wade in green-brown floodwaters up to their chests to get to the apartment building. They enter from the third floor. Everything smells of death, he's almost used to it. The temperature is soaring in the high nineties. He's been up for more than thirty-six hours straight, has a fever of 103, and couldn't say when he's last eaten, or had a drink of water.*

*Shit.*

Sol took a deep breath, swallowed down the sudden swim of spit in his mouth. The wind whistled in from the mountains, cut through the corridor linking the street to the courtyard, and he could hear Dan calling him, voice clear and unhurried, like he had all the time in the world, which he did not.

Without pausing to properly collect himself, Sol plunged into the dark passage, toward a light-filled doorway at a T-junction, several tall firefighters towering against a frame of light. Further in, down the hallway, Dan was on the ground with an older heavy-set woman. Her face was gray, and Sol crouched on the opposite side, unzipped his bag, let Dan do the talking.

Dan ran a strip and there was reason to hurry, because there was hope. Sol leaned back, told Dan he'd go get the stretcher and Dan nodded tersely. As Sol stood, he took bearing of where he was: a small room hung with embroidered curtains and lit with candles, though many of those were extinguished now, the EMTs with bags of equipment stacked against walls thoroughly papered with symbols and old woodcuts depicting Cinco de Mayo-type death heads in various stages of festivities.

He turned and noticed a black-clad woman, mid-forties maybe, standing aloof in the corner, a shawl draped over her shoulders, dark gray-streaked hair pulled back into a severe braid. She hovered for a moment, then shivered, and was overlaid, like she'd stood in front of a movie projection in a theater. Sol saw a ghost, a tall man, taller than her—a head above the fortuneteller, must be the fortuneteller—and the ghost was screaming.

Sol backed up two paces, and bumped into a firefighter behind him. The ghost disappeared and Sol saw the fortuneteller—Madama Lopez, evidently—make a gesture with her fingers, in what he thought must be a sealing ward, to lock an uppity ghost in place. Her dark eyes flashed in the recesses of deep-set sockets, and her gaze swept up to meet Sol's. It was more than enough to share a fractured, fraught moment of recognition. He'd seen her captive ghost; she knew that he was the sort who could see such things. She recognized the danger he represented.

He took another step back, apprehending a specific and sudden potential for harm, then ducked his head, darted back into the cold corridor, heading for the rig to get the stretcher. On top of everything else, a patient was busy fighting for her life in there, and he had to do something about that, first and foremost. The heart attack had been Madama Lopez's client, perhaps, there to get her fortune read, ghost silently at the ready to help extract useful information not privy to most souls.

He sucked in the dark night air, knew that he'd hyperventilate if he didn't calm down. His father had taught him to tell no one about what he could see, that no one outside their scattered community knew anything about this. Furthermore, the only ones that tended to know anything about ghosts only knew about them because they were seeking to exploit them, and their ghosts were some méchant trou d'cul. *Stay the hell away from a fortuneteller's ghost, Beausoleil, because they're crazy fuckers, they'll rip you apart, gars.*

Sol had learned that the hard way, and wasn't inclined to test those floodwaters again.

Still.

He unlocked the back of the rig, pulled out the stretcher and slammed the door behind him, trundling wheels across pavement bumpy with frozen runnels of dark ice. His hands were frozen on the metal bars.

Might come to nothing, going back in there, live and let live. What was he going to do, anyway? Free her ghost in the middle of a call? With a roomful of firefighters watching? There had been what had happened in New Orleans, he still had that to live down, there was no need to add to it.

Not in public anyway.

And this woman, this patient with the failing heart who had wanted to know the future on this night that was all about burying the past and ushering in the new, deserved his undivided attention. He made a promise to himself: *Just leave it alone, Sarrazin, no need to go borrowing trouble, no need to put every damn ghost you come across to bed. Not your damn job. Let it be.*

It was hard to ignore the ghost's screams, though. Even though he couldn't see the ghost, and decided to not even look at Madama Lopez, Sol could still hear it, begging for release, over and over again. Sol spoke enough Spanish to understand: *Let me go! Make her let me go! I'll kill you, I'll kill you all!* Over and over, so loud Sol wondered that everyone didn't hear it.

Luckily, Dan had everything under control, as usual. The patient was now lucid, and they transferred her from floor to stretcher in one heave, Sol anxious to be out of that room, but not happy about turning his back to the Madama, who had not—as far as he could tell without looking at her—moved.

Sol was driving and was glad of that, because anyone else behind the wheel couldn't have gotten him out of there fast enough.

They spent the early part of New Year's Eve driving south into Iowa, Baz humming along to some country station he'd found, keeping time with his fingers drumming on his thigh.

"You know," he said suddenly, and Lutie jumped a little, already accustomed to his constant car singing, but not to his actual voice in conversation. Hurtling down the highway at sixty miles per hour, they didn't seem in any danger of attracting ghosts with song. "We should go to Chicago. There's this great bar there, it'll be jumping tonight but I know most of the doormen and we could—"

"Baz," she said, smiling, because that's what he made you do. "Baz. We're nowhere near Chicago. It won't be jumping at noon tomorrow, which is when we'd get there. It'll be closed." Not to mention that he wasn't heading in that direction, he was heading in the opposite direction.

He stirred himself from his slouch, unperturbed. "It's still a great bar." He reached into her back seat, all legs and arms in the small import car, threatening to dislodge the stickshift, then he was back, the fiddle case on his lap.

He opened it up, ran his hands up the loosened strings. He took the instrument out, found the bow and rosin, put the case down by his feet. It could have been a rare and exquisite form of torture, but Baz started to tune the thing. In his hands, somehow, the tuning sounded curious, a quest for finding form out of chaos, and he plucked and tightened while some Nashville blonde warbled about Jesus. Finally, he seemed satisfied and Lutie stole a look at him.

He was beaming at the instrument, fingers running down the strings, over the worn veneer, dark in the highway light. Perhaps sensing her attention, Baz smiled deeply, snapped off the radio, brought the fiddle to his shoulder, scratched out a short run. "Hey, you must remember this one," and launched into a lilting lullaby.

Lutie did remember it, like a half-formed dream, a dream of a dream. There had been words to this, but they were lost to her. Maybe to Baz as well. He stopped after a few bars, looked out into the highway lines, dotted and straight.

She didn't want to interrupt his reverie, but it seemed unfair, suddenly, why she'd done this, why she'd agreed to Baz's scattershot plan and driven him south. It was so easy to like Baz. *Angels smile on him*, and shuddered as she thought it.

"Baz, you don't believe it, what your dad said about M'man." She made it a statement, like that would make it true.

Experimentally, Baz plucked a few notes, then drew the bow across the strings like a shiver. "You were the one who said she was a cold-hearted bitch," he pointed out, but with a burble of laughter.

"But she wasn't evil," she continued, not getting drawn into Baz's hilarity. "It's what some people can do, like how Aurie could hunt down ghosts. Maman—she took care of her ghost, kept it close. It helped her, sure, but she protected it, too. It wasn't all bad."

There were no highway lights along this stretch, and Lutie was depending on the moon, which was obscured by cloud. She could hear the intake of breath Baz took. "I don't know anything about it, poussinette." The silence was only marked by the whir of the heater's fan. Baz sniffed. "But I don't remember Maman being evil." He paused, and he might have smiled, for all Lutie could tell. "And I don't remember her being a cold-hearted bitch, either."

To which Lutie said nothing. Their father hadn't known about the ghost when they'd all lived together, Lutie remembered that much. Maman's little secret. Neither their father nor Sol had seen it. Lutie had. Lutie had known. Hot day, hanging heavy as wet laundry on the line, nothing stirring in the cemetery, not even birdsong. Then singing, Baz singing, and she had known: *Je veux un fantôme comme toi, M'man.*

Her mother's pet ghost had been that of a young woman, hair like cobwebs, dressed in a winter coat. It had been the first winter coat Lutie had ever seen. From the north, then, not a Louisiana ghost, not dressed like that. *What's your ghost called, M'man?*

*You don't name them, T-Lu. They aren't like us.*

A couple of miles later, and a number of short tunes on the fiddle, and Lutie noticed that they were coming up to the outskirts of Des Moines. It was almost midnight, new year, new life, things on the horizon she hadn't considered even a week ago. She'd never made a resolution in her life before, thought them silly and a waste of time, but she made one now.

"I'm like her, Baz," she said between the chorus and the verse of Baz's song, interrupting something vaguely celtic. Baz was singing softly above the tune, posing the question 'When will we be married?' He let the song still.

"Quoi?" he asked, soft. "What do you mean?"

"I'm like her. I see ghosts. And for as long as I can remember, Baz, I've known that I could catch one, same as her. I could."

"Mais, what would be the point, chère?"

That was the hard part. To explain in a way that made any sense, when he did not have to live with what she did, couldn't even see what she did. "To keep the others away," she said finally. "So I don't go crazy." No more meds. No more strange ghosts in strange places. Just the one and it would be hers.

Baz leaned back into the seat, plucked out a cheery little maritime melody that Lutie was fairly sure she'd heard before. She gave him a bit of room, because she'd learned at least as much from the Major as she ever had from her mother.

"So, what do you want me to do?"

She kept her eyes on the road, heard the softest of feather runs up and down a scale choked close on the neck, could imagine the hard calluses on his fingertips from wrenching music out of nothing but tension, vibration and air. "I want you to help me, Baz. I'll take you all the way back to Denver if you like, but I can't catch a ghost without you." Then, she clarified, because her parents, all of them, had taught her to be honest. "I don't want to do this alone."

Another tune, this one sounding like it came straight from the swamps, filled with heat and dark things, and it was all about loss and loss and loss. Into this song of longing, Baz said, very quietly, "Okay."

Don't fix other people's problems. That was Sol's second New Year's resolution. Then he'd become distracted, the fortune-seeker's cardiac arrest needing a fast run with no room for error. He made the resolution in good faith but it only took forty-five minutes to break it.

Because he had seen the fortuneteller's ghost, had *heard* the ghost, and that made it his problem. There *was* no one else. Everyone's problems— falls on ice, missed medications, overdoses, car crashes—they eventually made it to him. Same with this. Once he knew about it, it was his. Ignorance was the only excuse and he didn't have it, not now.

*See? I'm not breaking any resolution.*

They'd cleaned and re-stocked the rig and Dan was writing up the last run, which meant—at four-thirty in the morning of the first day of the year—Sol was off-shift until four that evening. Mind made up, already plotting out the route back to Madama Lopez's townhouse off Pecos, Sol stopped at the payphone outside the lockers, and called Robbie.

He didn't care that it was too early, or too late, or if he woke her up. Or he did care, but it wasn't enough to stop him from dialing. He didn't really want to talk, but he wanted to hear her voice something awful.

It rang and rang, going to the voicemail after five, and Sol leaned against the wall and closed his eyes, listened to Robbie tell him that she wasn't able to answer, but to leave a message.

"Hey," he said, then cleared his throat. "Hey. I'm running late, and…"

Kept his eyes closed, mustered some truth. "I love you." There was more to say, of course. "Hope you had a good night. I'll see you soon as I can, chère." It wasn't much, he realized, it wasn't nearly enough and it was much too late, but it's what he had.

At least he didn't have that damn drive to North Platte this time. No, this time there was a murderous ghost right close by, and no he wasn't going to let it be, he wasn't going to ignore its pleas for release. Not so much for the ghost—it wasn't human, after all—but the Madama looked stretched thin, and their cardiac patient might have had a real MI for perfectly natural reasons, or she might not, but with these kind of crazed, furious ghosts, it was only a matter of time before everything went to shit.

The sun was coming up as he headed north, the Front Range painted pink with reflected light, ceiling high. He wondered why he wasn't more nervous. After all, he'd only tried this once before, and memorably fucked it up. He hoped to even the odds this time; he told himself he knew what he was doing, had learned from the last time, wasn't screwed up by heat and fever and flood, was going in cold and intact. In the back of the Wagoneer he had everything he needed, which was simply salt, a lot of it. Not much else was required, unless you counted balls. And talent. He hoped he had enough of both.

Luck. That was important, too.

All of that, plus a little bit of knowledge gleaned from a father whose definition of 'explanation' was 'watch this', and Sol had only seen him exorcise a fortuneteller's ghost once, and that once had resulted in significant jail time.

For all intents and purposes, Sol knew, he was playing it by ear.

# SOL, BEFORE

The house looked like it might walk away, feet in the swamp, head in the air. Already the mosquitoes were out in force, but Sol was nearly immune to them. He imagined his skin tough as a reptile's, darkened from long days, from sun and sun and sun.

The shallow-bottomed boat kissed the dock, and at his father's signal, Sol cut the outboard engine and jumped onto the prow with one foot, the other already heading for the uneven dock, prickly nylon rope no match for his summer-rough hands. He secured the rope between boat and cleat, loop and loop, magic figure eight, symbol of eternity.

Maman was taking her time coming down to the dock to greet them. She must have heard them coming: not much was moving on the bayou on such a lazy August evening, and they'd been gone for more than a week. His father was already taking the duffle bag from atop the Styrofoam cooler, which brimmed with shrimp and oyster, partial payment from the grateful Chaisson family for working their boats. For laying their grandfather to rest.

Sol was strong enough to take the cooler himself, and he met his father's dark eyes, sparkling with the satisfaction of a successful excursion—money in his wallet, full chest of food, a well-executed interment. Sol pictured Neanderthals returning from the hunt with hearts full as theirs.

"Laisse-moi la boîte," Sol said, nodding to the cooler, to the plastic Piggly Wiggly bags overflowing with shrimpboat clothing. Too serious. Papa was always telling him to lighten up. "M'man, elle t'attends. Don't you keep her waiting," he tried teasing. He'd earned the right. Besides, Aurie didn't mind it.

Aurie glanced up, and Sol followed his gaze: the house was sturdy despite nature's attempts to knock it down every season. Most every bit of it had been replaced once or twice. Even so, his father always said it had been in the family for generations. Maybe just the idea of a house was enough; the physical thing didn't matter.

It was silent up there, no sound of dinner dishes being saved, or of Mireille singing Lutie to sleep, or Baz's constant complaints of heat or hunger or boredom.

Aurie shrugged. "Le char, yé pas ici. Mireille, I think she's out, maybe." He was right, Sol saw: Maman's old Pontiac, gray and mossy like a stone on wheels, wasn't in its usual spot by the raised road. Papa's two-tone Chevy pickup sat alone, slightly bereft.

"Peut-être," Sol repeated softly. *If you say so.*

His father shouldered the duffle bag, was on the dock and Sol handed over the cooler. It was heavy, all right. He didn't complain. His father had brought him on this job and that had been enough for Sol. You didn't complain when your father said you were a man.

There were two chairs on the dock and as Sol tipped the outboard clear of the water, cleaned the prop of weed, Aurie sat, opened the chest of iced shrimp, fished around and came out with two beer cans, dripping briny water. He passed one to Sol, then cracked his open with a satisfying *psht* before leaning back in the chair. He looked tired, Sol decided, as well he might. Hard work, what the old man did.

"Next time, Sol," Aurie said finally.

It wasn't criticism, it was encouragement. Still, Sol lifted one shoulder uncomfortably, lowered himself onto the opposite chair. A pelican softed across the jade water. "Bien sûr, Papa." The beer tasted vaguely shrimpy. It didn't matter, it was cold and it had been given to him by his father without having to ask. "Mais…" Let it rest there, an unspoken question floating across the water, just like the bird.

"Mais quoi?" his father asked, rubbing his short beard with oil-stained hands. Hands that could do so much. Sol felt utterly inadequate, suddenly, looking at them.

"But… It's nothing," Sol said, shifting his attention to the moss-choked cypress beyond the house. "Merde, Papa. I'm never gonna get it."

Aurie laughed into the mosquito-fogged air, and Sol would remember that sound in later years. The laugh was delighted. Confident. "Espère, gars. You're gonna be le traiteur after me. You got the feel for it, Beauso-leil. C'est pas facile, what we do. It'll come."

Sol snorted through his nose, took another slug of beer. "You make it look easy."

"And ma mère, she made it look easy too." He reached out a broad hand, tapped his eldest son on a sun-dealt knee. "She woulda liked you. A lot. But ghosts, especially ones dat don't want to go? They're never easy." He waved his hand in a decisive motion across the horizon. "Jamais."

The Chaisson grandfather, for sure his ghost hadn't wanted to go. The elderly man had been ailing, which was partly why Aurie had been called, to heal if he could, ease the passage if he couldn't. Later, on the margins of a huge community fish fry celebrating pépère Chaisson's life, Aurie had once again shown Sol how it was done. And he had made it look easy.

They drank in silence as the sun eased over the sketch of trees screening the gangly house from road. A vehicle hummed along the highway, but it wasn't the Pontiac, they could both tell that even from a distance. Aurie finished his beer first, slapped a biting bug from the back of his neck. Sweat stained the chest of his faded red t-shirt, made the Breaux Bridge Crawfish Festival mascot imprinted on it look like it'd been shot. Sol smiled quietly.

"I think maybe she's getting you some cake," Aurie said, popping open another beer. He offered one to Sol, but he wasn't finished his first yet, so he shook his head.

"Cake?" Like it was a foreign word.

Aurie was looking at the sky; it's what you did here, especially as hurricane season approached. Rely on the radio weather reports, sure, but the sky usually told you what was going on. Aurie chuckled, slow and lazy. Sol warmed to the sound of it, love dressed up as mockery. "Mais, your mother's always saying how hard it is to bake a cake in this goddamn heat. Didn't grow up with this climate, her." The opposite of a hothouse flower, that's what Papa called her. "Probably drove all the way up to Houma to buy you one."

"If she took Baz, that cake won't last the ride back," Sol observed, drawing another long laugh from Aurie. "Besides, she said that she was gonna read my fortune this birthday." He set the almost empty beer can on the dock, opened his hand with a grin. "She wanted to read my palm, but I asked for the tea leaves."

The laughter stilled. The chair creaked slightly as Aurie came forward. "Ça c'est d'la merde, you know, that stuff. Total bullshit."

"Papa," Sol said, turning in his seat, surprised. "I can see ghosts. So can you. Who knows what's possible."

"Écoute bien, Sol," Aurie rumbled, voice taking an edge. "What your maman does, that's not magic, hé? She makes some extra money doing her thing, but it's all guesses and being smart about people. Harmless." Sol knew his mother felt differently about it, said it was a calling as much as Papa being a traiteur, but Sol kept his mouth shut because Aurie wasn't making conversation. "A real fortuneteller, you have to watch out for her. She's using a maudit ghost, she's not doin' anyone any good, not even herself." His mouth twisted in his beard. "That ghost, it's the same as her slave. It's not what we do." Aurie looked to his son, and Sol nodded agreement.

It was getting dark now, and Sol knew his mother didn't like driving at night.

Close by, somewhere in the darkness that was not the highway, that wasn't the cemetery across the highway, Sol heard a splash, a struggle. Silence. Aurie got up, beer in hand. He gestured to the cooler. "You think you can carry that all the way up?"

Sol grinned, knew his teeth would be a gleam in the dusk, a mood-breaker. "You afraid of a few 'gators, old man?"

Then, clearly in the new silence, they heard it: a whimper, a cry. *Papa.* The in-drawn snotty breath of a frightened child. "Reste ici," his father commanded, dropping the bag, listening but still moving, putting the beer on the dock, going for the stairs. The noise had come from the house above, from the darkness.

Though his father had just told him to stay put, Sol wasn't of a mind to do it. He was days away from fourteen, was nearly as tall as his father, had earned a place in the gifted class in school, learned fast, had already seen plenty of all that was strange in this world. He'd been tapped as his father's successor and his father was a fine traiteur, the best in the parish. Sol wasn't going to be left on the dock like a child.

Taking the wooden staircase two steps at a time, Aurie looked back, once, but Sol couldn't see what was in his face, and that was probably just as well.

# DEADROADS

The house was full of ghosts.

They were scudding like clouds from room to room, drifting through doorways, seated on Maman's rocker, on the staircase, one listlessly running a hand over Papa's closed fiddle case. Sol stopped in the shadow of the front door, open to the night bugs, but Aurie had halted in his steps and the room was so cold Sol could see his breath.

One ghost, two tops, that was all he'd ever seen at the same time. Inside the big room where his mother altered Sol's outgrown clothes to fit Baz, where Lutie played with her ragtag mob of thriftstore Barbies, Sol counted seven ghosts, a ridiculous number.

They weren't paying any attention to him, or to his father. They seemed bored, depleted, waiting. One ghost that had once been a young woman, blouse stained with dark blood, hand lacerated, sat on the stairs leading to the bedrooms. As Sol watched, it knocked on the riser as though expecting an answer. A hollow booming noise, and Sol's palms were suddenly clammy; he wiped one against his chest.

Aurie dropped to his knees, hand splayed wide on the boards, ready to get rid of them, get rid of them all, asking for no help because… because…*Because he knows I can't do it,* Sol thought, standing in the doorway behind his crouching father, eyes wide.

Immediately, the ghosts seemed to know what was up, and they turned, almost in unison. Readying themselves, Sol understood, not knowing what he was seeing, never having known ghosts to work in tandem, as a team. *To do what?* But as they rushed Aurie, rushed the traiteur, their intent became evident.

Aurie was thrown hard against the wall as one of the sketchy ghosts—solid enough for tasks like this—picked him up by the throat and threw him like he was a stray cat found at the Sunday roast. Aurie's body made an enormous crash, a framed print dropping to the floor and shattering. Aurie followed it, slumped among the glass, dazed, but only for a moment.

"The cupboard!" Aurie cried, struggling to his feet and gesturing to the stairs, where the ghost of the woman waited. "Go get him, he's in the cupboard!"

The ghosts moved. Turned to Aurie, sightless and intent and *riled.* All except the ghost on the stairs, which came to a stand as Sol did as his father asked. The child's voice had cried 'Papa', but Papa was busy, so Sol would have to do.

Behind him, Aurie once again bent to the floor and the ghosts came for him. *A diversion.* Sol, intent on the cupboard, didn't see what happened next, but he heard the sound of furniture being moved, long scrapes, banging of a window in the frame, the high-toned wail of wood bending and then breaking.

Sol clutched the cupboard's knob and yanked open the door. He caught the scent of shit and urine and boy-sweat, then Baz leaped forward into his arms, sobbing. His brother was disheveled and big-eyed, all spindly legs and tanned skin, bright bluegreen eyes rimmed red.

The ghost on the stairs, the young woman covered in blood, noticed them, moonwhite eyes turned, glowing, malevolence like a cold northern wind. Sol had time to set Baz down on the threadbare rug, but that was all.

The ghost moved like stop motion film, like it wasn't attached to the regular rhythms that governed life as Sol knew it, and he supposed that made sense on some level. *Les fantômes, they're not like us.*

Even as its sharp fingers tangled in his hair, stroked his scalp like a rake, ready to snap his head back, he knelt down as he'd been taught, hand against the floorboards, finding the hum of life around him. Sol dug deep. *It's in my damn house,* he thought, anger shocking through him. He moved beyond it, couldn't feel the ghost's hand on his head, couldn't feel the cold. *It's here, in our house and it's after Baz.*

And so, for the first time in his life, he sent a ghost on its journey and though that was far from easy, he made it appear effortless. Found the rhythm of life, connected himself to it, declared his angry intention, gave it a way out. Sol's deadroad shivered in the darkness, bold silver against brutal shadow, wavering but there. The ghost's mouth parted, its hand clenched, but Sol's hair was short and the ghost did not have enough grasp on this world. It unraveled down the road soundlessly as Sol watched, astonished. He swallowed, once, lips pressed together, so scared he banged the floor loudly, no taps these, hard enough that his hand burned with the effort.

When it was done, he raised his head, too surprised to be pleased, too frightened to be proud. The ghost was gone, and he'd been responsible for that. Only a second, then he whipped around, coming to his feet, hands held wide.

Aurie stood behind him, framed by the door, Baz shivering in his arms. All the ghosts were gone; his father had seen to that. Aurie shook his head, seemingly unscathed by his run-in with the wall, with putting down six ghosts, solo. Eyes on Sol, too spent and furious and fearful to give even a nod of acknowledgment.

"I'm sorry, I'm sorry, I'm sorry," Baz was crying into Aurie's shoulder, a wail. He was held tight; Aurie's knuckles were white, clutching his youngest son's shoulder. "They're gone, I couldn't stop, I couldn't—" and Aurie said he should get him clean, but Baz started screaming, "Not upstairs! I don't wanna go! Don't make me!"

Instead, Aurie brought him into the kitchen where he stripped Baz down, washed him in the sink as though he were a baby, draped a tablecloth over his shivering body. Sol stood in the doorway, silent, a cloud of dread descending on him now that the immediate danger of the ghosts was dealt with. No time to feel any sense of accomplishment, no time for any words of congratulations. They had moved past that marker, past the time when such a distinction mattered; it was unimportant, given the now.

"Shhh," Aurie said, rubbing Baz's wet head with his wide hand. "Parles, Basile. Tell me. Slowly." But it wasn't in Baz's nature to tell anything slowly, so it all came out in a disjointed rush, French and English and Franglish, Cajun and Acadian, all those words running together.

Out of the mass of words, only one thing truly registered with Aurie: "Mireille, she left?" he questioned, voice low. "Why?"

Baz shook his head, tears tracking down his face. "It was my fault, I shoulda stopped Lutie from doing it. My fault, Papa, blâme-moi."

"Luetta?" Aurie looked perplexed, like his daughter was the last person in the world that would upset anyone. There was a lot about Lutie Papa chose not to see, Sol knew. With her seven-year-old's inflexibility and determination, with her big serious eyes, Lutie had a way of making you do stuff you didn't want to do.

Baz took an unsteady breath and told the rest, about pet ghosts and fortunetellers, about cemeteries and singing.

As he spoke, Sol noticed the last thing, the thing he would remember clearly when all the other details about this terrible day had receded into a hazy memory: a white saucer, parted from its teacup long ago, on the kitchen table. And on it, in the very center, a narrow gold band, their mother's wedding ring. Sol looked up at his father, still holding the feverish and wet Baz, who was now demanding something to eat, and made a motion to the table.

The sound that Aurie made then chilled Sol as nothing else would, ever: a keening note of despair. Aurie eased Baz to Sol's arms, and Sol took his brother to the couch in the living room, stayed with him until he slept, came back to the kitchen to find his father with a bottle of rum on the table, the ring vanished as though it had never existed.

Aurie drank mechanically, didn't acknowledge his son's presence, didn't say a word, was lost to Sol in a way new and therefore frightening. Sol walked back into the main room of the house, looked around at the mess, at insensible Baz asleep under the tablecloth-blanket.

He stepped outside into the night and watched the moonlight on the water. Today, he had sent his first ghost on its road, had fulfilled his early promise, and it didn't matter. He was alone, and he knew it.

The next morning, Aurie packed precious few belongings into the truck. Then, he burned the house to the pilings as his sons watched. They got in the truck, and only Sol looked back as they drove away.

# EIGHT

## THE FORTUNETELLER'S GHOST

They passed midnight on the road, Lutie weary of the buzzing yellow line, but Baz didn't seem to need sleep. Though she hadn't mentioned it, she thought it was probably best if they stopped soon, crashed in some cheap motel. Forward motion was its own kind of intoxication.

However, after grabbing a quick bite in Lincoln, Baz hopped into the driver's seat, extended his hand for the keys and cocked his head at an angle when Lutie hesitated. "I have a license, you know." Suspended, he'd already admitted. "It's completely safe, Lutie. And I'll get us to Denver in no time."

"We'll never make it to Denver tonight," she said.

"C'mon," Baz cajoled, eyes bright in the parking lot lights. "We can try, at least."

With pause, with caution, Lutie handed him the keys, slipped out of her down coat and wrapped it around her shoulders before sitting in the passenger seat. Baz experimented with the clutch and the stick, ground gears before throwing it into reverse, and emitted a high-pitched cackle of glee. Lutie knew this was a bad idea, but it was open highway, and all the city cops would be monitoring parties, and Baz hadn't had a drop of liquor. He seemed inordinately pleased to be driving, and it wasn't in her to deny him, which was probably part of his problem with life in general.

Something about the blur of highway and the fleeting signs made Lutie think that maybe they could leave everything behind, maybe if they went fast enough, it would be possible to outrun the past. Baz turned the music up loud, declared that he liked her taste, and Lutie felt a jolt of pride. She had impressed him, and that felt strangely good.

He didn't slow for much of anything, but an hour later he turned down the music a little, enough, and Lutie thought that maybe this would be when she'd suggest that they stop for a bit, that rest would be a good thing. There wasn't much along this stretch of highway, though, just train tracks running alongside them, and a frozen runnel of water to the north of the westward-leading highway. Every so often lights would flicker and flash along the track, and they'd be following or watching a long train of freight heading in one direction or another. Freed from the pressure of driving, Lutie wondered what the cars contained: grain, crates of electronics, powdered chemicals.

A little percussive noise, Baz clearing his throat, and he asked if she was sure.

In the lowered volume of the now-quiet car, Lutie nodded. She knew what he meant. "I'm sure. I've thought about this a lot. You don't know what it's like, Baz. How crazy it makes you feel, to have them around all the time."

Three signposts passed to the right, warning them about speeding and advising them of distances, before Baz spoke again. "I know it must be a burden, dealing with them. Dad, I think he made the best of it. He always seemed to think of it as... I don't know."

"A calling?"

Baz nodded, gaze out the windshield, attention all on her. "Yeah. That's one way of looking at it, Lutie."

"Does," she didn't want to talk about it, not like this, but there wasn't really any time that was good, and she wanted Baz to understand. "Does Beausoleil look at it like that?"

She was still trying to figure out how close Baz and her other brother were, the one she hardly remembered at all. Sometimes, she thought that they must not get along all that well, and other times, she sensed that Baz was in awe of him. At no time had she felt that her two brothers had much in common.

Baz half-shrugged, one shoulder coming up, grin pulling one corner of his mouth. "Who knows what Sol thinks about it," proving Lutie's suspicions. "He don't talk about stuff like that much, Lutie. He's real private that way. But I think," and his brows crooked together, carefully choosing his words, maybe worried about how they'd fall. "I think that he has a hard time with it. He's been on medications like you have, people thinking he was crazy, seeing things that weren't there. Dad tried to make sure no one messed with him when we were kids, but Dad, he wasn't always around."

"So, you see what I mean." Not a question. "I have to do something, Baz, because I don't want to take all those drugs. They make me stupid and slow." She lifted a hand to her head. "And the ghosts, the spirits, whatever the hell they are, they're all around."

"Do," and he paused, like this was a no-go zone. He'd just said that Sol wouldn't talk about this stuff, so maybe it was. "Do they talk to you? 'Cause Dad always said you shouldn't talk to them."

Lutie shrugged. "Maman always talked to them." Sometimes yelled at her ghost, sometimes used words that Lutie still remembered as being foul and forbidden.

It was like explaining the difference between blue and yellow to a blind person. Baz licked his lips quickly. Lutie knew she was spending a lot of time looking at him, same way he did her, seeing parallels in their similar noses, eyebrows. Maybe Baz was more like she'd have been if she hadn't had this curse of *seeing*.

When it came right down to it, Baz was happy.

And that was the explanation to offer, perhaps. "Baz, I just want to be happy. I think that if I do this, just this one thing, and make sure I take care of the ghost, then I could be. Probably like having a pit bull, right? They get a bad rap, but it's just that their owners don't treat them well. It's not the dog's fault. Same with ghosts. They're hanging around anyway, going nowhere. It scares them, it freaks them out. Sometimes, I think it makes them pissed off, and that's the only time they're dangerous. The rest of the time, they're pretty pathetic, actually."

They drove in silence for a while longer. "So," Baz said softly into the darkness, "you're doing it a favor, by bringing one in?" Like they were talking about adopting an animal from a shelter.

119

Lutie hoped that was the case; it was what she believed, anyway, so she nodded. "I think we're all doing the same thing, just a different way, you know? I think our dad," and that was the first time she'd said that, and she wondered if Baz noticed. *Papa*, she thought, *Papa, what would you think of this?* But she knew. And this was his son. This was her brother, more to the point. "I think he was looking after the ghosts, too. This is just what I know how to do."

"Okay, then," Baz breathed. He tapped his long fingers against the wheel, musical in this as well. "I know where we can find some ghosts."

Lutie tried not to laugh. "Um, Baz? Finding ghosts isn't my problem. You just open your mouth and sing. We've got ghosts."

For once, he didn't smile back, he still had a disturbed frown on his face. "Lutie, I'll help. I promise. But." He pinched his nose with two fingers and Lutie wished he'd keep both hands on the wheel. "You know. Something killed Dad. I don't know if it's a ghost or what, but I know Sol's after it, whatever it is. It's important to him, getting this thing. And," he hesitated and Lutie had the feeling he wasn't really used to saying what he said next, "it's important to *me*, Lutie. Dad didn't die in a train accident, he was murdered. In North Platte, just a few hours down this highway. No one deserves to die like he did. I'd like to help out, if I can. And maybe you can get something out of a ghost there that I can't, maybe something that Sol couldn't get out of it. So, we can all help each other with this, hé?"

He sounded so tentative, like a bright kid with a good idea scared to death of speaking in front of the class. Lutie thought that it wasn't that Baz wasn't close to his brother, it's that he wanted to be, and maybe didn't even know it.

So she nodded, understanding that. "All right, then," she agreed. "Let's go to North Platte."

As he laid lines of salt across every threshold to the townhouse, Sol realized that his logic was perhaps imperfect. It was possible that ghosts could go out windows, wasn't it? But then he noticed that the windows on both the ground and the second floor had bars on them, and guessed that the bars might have some steel in them. A little bit of iron might make a difference, like blood, something living taken from the earth's bones.

# DEADROADS

*Guessing, you're guessing, gars. Bad time to be unsure.*

His father's imagined voice, right in his head. He shrugged it off. So what if he was guessing? If the worst that happened was the ghost escaped, that would be okay. *Better than a dead fortuneteller, old man.*

It was still dark, now about five-thirty in the morning, and no one was around. Still, Sol didn't take his time. He came around to the back door, mostly because it was sheltered from other townhouse windows, and jimmied the lock with two illegal tools that everyone in the Denver Health EMS knew he had. His reputation, he supposed, was pretty suspect: a hard-drinking and possibly unstable Cajun who'd grown up in the Colorado foster-care system while his father was incarcerated for manslaughter. A legendary freak-out in New Orleans after Katrina where he'd ranted about ghosts before falling into a fever-induced coma. He also had one of the highest patient survival rates for any paramedic on the job, was extraordinarily good at what he did.

There were reasons for all of it, of course, good ones, if not all that believable. If he got busted breaking into the fortuneteller's house, he knew there would be some in the department, hell *many*, who wouldn't bat an eyelash.

Lock quietly open and he slipped in, stepping carefully over his salt-line, listening. Ghosts didn't sleep, but their hosts did, and if this fortuneteller had kept up her sealing ward, Sol might have found his first piece of luck, because that ghost would be good and *tied*. He entered into the kitchen, a sink full of dirty dishes, smell of grease and refried beans. He moved on silent feet, despite the heavy boots, clicking off his small maglight, pocketing it. He didn't know if she lived alone or not, but he didn't want to surprise anyone who might be armed. He opened the door from the kitchen into a hallway, allowing his eyes to become accustomed to the dark. The room hung with paper, the seance room, still littered with syringe casings and other detritus of a ALS visit. Maybe Madama Lopez had left; maybe this wasn't her residence, just her place of business.

Sol didn't think so. The fortuneteller was probably just exhausted, had left the dishes and the mess for the morning. Across the room, he spotted a staircase that he hadn't noticed before, hidden behind a fall of velvet curtain. He walked carefully over, peered up. There was a light on in the upstairs corridor, perhaps bedrooms beyond. Sol wished that he'd run this address through the system, found out who else might live here.

*Half-cocked, gars. You don't know what you're getting yourself into, do you?*

Under his breath, Sol told his father to shut up.

Crouching to the floor, he ran one hand across his head. Still time to duck out, nothing lost but some road salt. He knew he wouldn't. Experimentally, he stretched his hand out, could see it by the wan upstairs light spilling into the seance room, which smelled of beeswax and sulfur. And sweat. *Maybe me,* he thought, placing his hand on the hardwood.

He opened the proceedings, declared his intentions to the room: *I am here for you, spirit.*

Sol stood, waiting, hands open at his side, because ghosts didn't sleep, not ever. The room chilled. A drop of twenty degrees inside seconds. Despite himself, Sol smiled. *I know what I'm doing, Papa.*

The cold coalesced, formed, drew light against the gloom of the seance room, caught the edge of morning. A tall man, this one had been, and Sol was ready, or thought he was. In the instant that the ghost recognized Sol—saw what he was, which was one of those that could see, one of those that opened ways and paths and means—Sol dropped to the ground, hand against the floor, praying to God or his father, one of the two, that he could do this.

Binding first, deadroad later. Sol stretched his fingers again, but it was his mind that went out into the chill, chill air, seeking the knot that tied the ghost to the fortuneteller. Cut it, snap it, erode it, chew it, whatever it took. Imagine it and you could do it.

*Binding first, but don't ignore the anger, Beausoleil.*

*Fine time to tell me,* Sol thought, and was lifted, air in his throat so cold it froze, was lifted off his feet and thrown against the wall, breath knocked from him. Something shattered beside him, mirror or glass, he didn't know. His head hit the paneling with a blast of heat and fire, and he slid to the ground, his tenuous grasp of the knot fading even as he blinked away spots. He'd bitten his tongue, maybe, tasted blood in his mouth.

The ghost advanced, distressingly real and solid, no room to see behind its gray shape, and Sol was lifted again, this time by bony fingers around his throat and he knew he was in trouble, because his hand was not on the ground, and he couldn't feel anything: self, or earth, or knot.

The sun came up over the tracks in North Platte and that was a lucky thing, because it meant that Baz could find the same place he'd parked before, the same place where Sol had cut a hole in the fence. The stretch of gravel and iron rail was different by soft dawn, somehow, more commonplace. Baz knew you could see ghosts during the day but that it was more difficult, harder. Harder for Lutie, anyway, who was the one who could see them, period.

Easier for the railroad cops to see *them*, of course, so Baz advised Lutie to be quick. He had no idea what was involved with catching a ghost and moreover, didn't think that Lutie had either. In fact, he was beginning to suspect that this whole thing would result in one big fat zero. He'd then have to take Lutie into Denver, another few hours down the interstate, and explain everything to Sol.

Shit, it really didn't bear thinking about. But if they had new information, something about this place that Sol hadn't been able to figure out, screwed up as he'd been by putting their father's ghost on its road? Sol would pay attention to that, Baz was sure, and would probably not be quite as sore and angry about the fact that Baz had gone out of his way to find Lutie.

Never mind how he'd done it, which Baz *really* couldn't think about.

Like Sol had before him, Baz warned Lutie that the trains moved fast, to keep her wits about her. In her white coat, she actually blended in fairly well against the snow and the parched gravel. Trains chugged this way and that, followed by the metallic grind and scream of hard work and friction. Baz found the dip in the gravel between track and fence that he thought was the same as before.

"This is where they found his body," he said quietly, and Lutie, who had been staring westward along the line of iron heading to the horizon, turned slightly, rising sun catching her across the face, lighting her eyes green, long hair blown by the wind, lifting.

He wondered what she saw, but years had taught him not to ask. Dad had never answered, and Sol had sometimes mocked, other times berated. Baz kept quiet, waited for her to tell him what she wanted. She walked down the tracks a little, back to him, hands held away from her side, gloved fingers like the flat head of a Geiger counter.

After a moment, she stopped, tilted her head to the side.

"They're here all right."

He wanted to ask about their father, but trusted that Sol had been good at what he'd done, so he held his tongue.

Lutie answered for him. "Not Papa, though. Not him," and Baz couldn't name what was in her voice, but it chilled him. She swiveled all the way around, maybe twenty feet from him, the sun painting her pink and orange, irridescent as an exotic bird. Beautiful. "Can you sing for a bit, Baz? They're so angry. They see you, but they're...*wanting*."

He was able to identify what was in her voice then: regret.

"Is it just ghosts?" he asked, because he didn't see anything like what he'd seen that night after Sol had put his father's ghost away, that thing that had given him Lutie's address, that had allowed the rest of this to happen. That had *wanted* all this to happen, Baz realized now, with a jolt.

"What else would there be?" she asked.

He wasn't going to answer that, so he started to sing. Whatever came: a commercial jingle to start, then that seemed too trite, too facile. He found an old Hank Williams song, and it was full of being in the doghouse and somehow that fit the mood. He concentrated on that, but watched his sister.

She seemed too slight for the job, had none of their father's dark gravitas, was made of light, and he sang another Williams song, knowing all the words, learned in moving tour vans from other musicians. The sun came up behind her and Baz couldn't really see her expression, because he was dazzled by the light. Everything was all right, all of a piece. This was *good*.

He smiled, continued the song during the dawn, and he saw Lutie go to her knees like she was going to pick a flower, hand open wide against the ground and he wondered if she was talking to them, wondered if that was so wrong after all. They were to be pitied, weren't they? Lost souls; they must be so lonely. Pitied, or sent on their way to whatever awaited all of them when they crossed over.

The light was almost too bright to see, and he couldn't hear the trains anymore, could only hear his own voice, took pride in that, and it was like when they were in the church, where the light had come down and refracted and that was where Baz dedicated his voice, not to the ghosts. They could listen, sure, but he was not singing for them.

As he took a breath to continue to the chorus, all about loss and grief, Lutie gave a little cry of surprise. He kept singing, smiling, wondering if the light seemed as bright to her, as warm. He almost couldn't see her in the orange dappled sunspots.

For a moment, the air cleared, wind kicking up loose snow, which sparkled in the sun like a scatter of sequins. Lutie looked to him, eyes following fast movement, and Baz felt a brush against him, a rush of cold in the warmth, and he was buffeted, like in a stiff breeze. Startled, he stopped singing, then heard, "Don't! Keep going!" and Baz couldn't tell if she was excited, or scared.

The winds stirred more vigorously and he was immediately cold, his breath huffing out as he started again this time "You Are My Sunshine", which wasn't a happy song at all, not when you really listened to the words, but he knew he was scared. They were not alone. Another shove, and he was forced back a step, had felt a hand caress his cheek, another curl around his throat, seeking warmth or sound or life. "Lutie?" he called, uncertain.

"Don't stop!" she shouted back, still on her knees, but he heard it this time, heard the fear.

He opened his mouth again, but nothing came out for a moment, he was too frozen. A push from behind and he staggered a few feet, then felt a slicing, horrific cold go right through him, right to his heart and he thought for a moment he might pass out.

Then Lutie screamed, and Baz whirled around, reaching for her, but she was much too far away.

Oh, God, this had been a bad idea, he knew that now. Then the light that had been everywhere simply left, and in its place was cold gray, gravel and snow shards sharp as smashed glass. Once again, the cold swept though him, held onto his heart with winter's hand; Baz crashed to hands and knees, the stones unforgiving. He shook his head, and heard the rapturous gasping chuckle that he recognized from the night, recognized as something he should have known better about but that had known his needs too keenly.

"You came back," it said, and it might have been at his shoulder, or across the tracks, or in his head, Baz couldn't tell. The pain in his chest was excruciating. "And you brought such company. You're a surprising one, Basile Sarrazin. I'm sure glad we're friends."

Lutie screamed again, but the rattling voice was closer, fetid, cloying like rotting meat. "You can keep singing. They like it. I don't much care, but everyone else likes it. Pity to disappoint."

Baz gagged, spat on the ground, barely able to breathe, and instead of the ghostcold, he felt like he was on fire. "Lutie," he managed to croak, then drew a painful razor breath, and shouted, "Lutie!"

He heard her crying. He lifted his head, and she was staggering towards him, one hand held out for balance like she was on a boat at sea. "Baz!" she shouted back, then got one arm under him. "Come with me," she whispered in his ear, and his head was ringing, and the cold was back, worse than ever. Lutie kept shouting, telling things to leave Baz alone, and Baz kept feeling hands on him, stroking his face, snatching his hair, unseen fingers hooked in his belt and he whispered into Lutie's close ear: "You gotta tell them to go, chouette. I can't stand it. Tell them to go."

Lutie dropped him and he fell, no strength in him, though he knew he had to stand. Lutie stood above him, one foot on either side of his body, one hand on his chest, eyes bright in the over-bright day. "Dégagez!" she shouted, then screamed, "Dégagez!"

After a moment, the cold faded and the brightness died away, and Baz saw blue sky above, his breath coming in wispy, rasping sighs, loud to his own ears.

"Can you get up?" Lutie asked, wiping her nose on the sleeve of her coat, which was now far from pristine. "Here, let me help you up." She put one arm under his shoulders, but Baz just hugged her tight, not letting her go. After a moment, she returned the embrace.

*It isn't real*, he told himself. *I'm real, not this damn ghost.*

It was difficult to believe, of course, because the pain was so bloody real and the coffee table through which he'd just crashed was plenty real as well. The ghost though. The ghost was not, and Sol knew it. He knew it. An apparition, a slip of soul or feeling or memory, he scarcely knew which, but it was visible to him, it was merely visible, and it could only do what you believed it could.

Against his instincts—every one begging him to flee, to get the hell out of this madhouse—Sol closed his eyes. Felt the cold but ignored it, completely blocked out the sensation of being lifted by his hair, throat stretched back, exposed to whatever bit of broken glass or sharp edge that could be procured. He could die here, of course, that had always been a possibility, just not a very real one.

It felt real enough now.

Into this, Sol melded the ghost's awesome fear, which was under the anger, always. Fear of the unknown, perhaps, fear of what came next. Sol imagined what fear would drive a fortuneteller, someone gifted or cursed with seeing ghosts, to capturing one like this. Fear of being alone, fear of being useless and crazy. Sol felt all these fears tighten, and then—mind out to the room, trying to connect with ground, already intimately connected with blood and

126

iron and salt, he could imagine the line that bound the ghost and the host, or maybe the ghost showed him, who knew which? He didn't need to undo this knot, tied years ago, fretted and gnawed and tightened. He needed to sever it, and he remembered his Greek mythology and imagined his mind a knife and he cut right through the knot.

With an extended, interminable roar, the ghost dropped Sol and he bounced against the remains of the table before hitting the floor, gravity as real as anything else in that room. Self-preservation kicking in, paying close attention to instinct now, Sol shinnied back to the wall, hands sliding through a minefield of glass shards, watching the ghost circle the room at speed, looking to get out.

*Free, free, free*, it screamed, but it was not. It was trapped by thin salt lines and Sol's blood and by the iron in the windows. And now, it was up to Sol to send it to where it was supposed to go. Leaning forward from his spot on the floor, back against the wall, Sol placed his hand into the opening of his button-up shirt, onto his chest, felt his own heart beating madly, blood coursing through every bit of him. Life. *I will do no harm,* he thought, sent it out, not knowing if it would matter to the ghost, if it would care, but it mattered to Sol, that he was doing this with true aim.

The ghost turned, as though noticing Sol once more, and it blinked static, stalled. Sol held his breath, brought his hand out, brushed fingertips to his lips: intent, blood, heart, breath. And into his breath, this evidence of life, into the ghostcold, he blew a pathway, shining, though Sol himself could not see the end of it, did not know where it might go.

The ghost looked at the path, then back at Sol. It shivered, it wasn't evil or angry or scared. It was tired.

Sol watched as the ghost came into focus: a tall man, a young man, dressed in the clothes of a field hand, hands powdered with dusky soil, clothes bloodstained down one side, skin tanned a deep V at the open neck of a faded cotton shirt, a tooled leather belt circling a waist whittled by work and drought. Its exhausted eyes rested on the road that Sol had made for it, an expression of wonder and recognition on its face. It turned to Sol, and didn't acknowledge him, but the expression slowly changed to one of certitude and the ghost moved off, shimmered and disappeared.

On the floor, covered in glass, little knowing if he'd broken something within during this frantic, bizarre battle, Sol swallowed back triumph and instead settled on relief. He'd done it, and he hadn't killed anyone in the process, himself included. Delicately, gray light persistently trying to define the room, Sol tapped the ground three times, then pushed himself up with his legs, not setting his hands on the floor again for fear of cutting them on the glass. His legs, he found, held.

His head, on the other hand, rang ominously, and his browbone burned and itched. He put up a hand to feel it, and winced, fingers coming away bloody. With his other hand, he probed his side where he'd landed hard on the table. No broken ribs, he didn't think. Good.

And that's when he heard the distinctive click of a gun's hammer being pulled back, directly behind him from beyond the velvet curtain leading up to the stairs.

"You," the dark inflected voice spat. "You," like it was the dirtiest word in her language.

Slowly, he brought up both hands, circled so he could face her. The fortuneteller stood in a white nightgown, an older revolver in her hand, heavy enough to be used as a paperweight, a door stop. It was pointed right at him, and he couldn't have been more than five feet from her, close enough that there was no way she would miss, too far to make a grab for the gun.

They'd made a ton of noise and what, did he think she would be far behind? The ghost she'd bound hadn't killed her, he reminded himself. This was still a success by any measure. Unless he wasn't around to enjoy it. He wondered what Wayne would call a perk in this particular rescue.

"It's over," he said. "There's nothing for you to do now."

He was staring straight into her mad dark eyes when she pulled the trigger and proved him wrong.

# NINE

## COMES WITH THE TERRITORY

Baz weighed a ton, mostly height rather than any excess flesh, and he was faking nothing. Lutie staggered under his arm, but she'd always been strong for her size. The sun was fully up, day clear as a glass of cold water, and she couldn't see any ghosts. Not that black thing, no white light. Just Baz, panting, green, unable to keep his feet under him. They weren't home free yet, not by a long way, so she tried not to think about what she'd just seen, about what she'd just caused to happen—*he offered, he went in eyes wide open.* Getting Baz through the hole in fence was the worst, because he was all elbows and knees and when he fell, she didn't know if she'd be able to get him back up again.

As she whispered fiercely to him, "Get up, get up, or I'll leave your ass right here," she also knew she had to stop crying otherwise he'd know she didn't mean it.

To her surprise, she heard Baz laugh, "Bon Dieu, T-Lu, don't you do that. I still have your car keys."

Lutie used the moment to scan the landscape behind them through the chain link, but nothing seemed remotely alarming or dangerous. She was shaking, she who thought she'd seen every damn thing there was to be scared of. But she'd never seen a black thing like that; the mere sound of it, like a match being struck, made her think of bonfires, of things that got thrown on bonfires: the sacred books of heathen religions, effigies of evil, witches.

But that was definitely thinking about what had just happened, so she once again helped Baz to his feet where he stood, barely, waving her away before putting his gloved hands into his coat's pockets. "What the fuck, Lutie? What just happened there?" He was dropping his THs, making them into Ds. Stressed.

"Not here," she said, because if things could disappear, they could probably re-appear. "Give me the keys. Let's get out of here."

As she watched, he raised his head, eyes glowing in the slanting light. "What do you see? Right now. What's here?"

"Nothing," she said truthfully. "They're gone, all of them."

"Not for long," Baz said, but quietly, mouth turned from her, fetching her car keys from his pocket.

They had parked behind a warehouse, a dirt lot, and the dry soil made a plume of dust behind her as she spun her wheels.

Beside her, Baz shifted in his seat, hunched into his coat. "Vas-y mollo, chère." And Lutie didn't know if that was a curse, or what. She'd forgotten almost all her past and it seemed unfair that he'd retained so much when she'd been kept in the dark, lost. If only Maman hadn't left, this would have been easy. If only that hadn't been taken from her, along with all the rest.

"English," she said, finding the gear and realizing that they'd been driving all night, that she was stupid with exhaustion as much as terror.

A succession of machine-shops and auto parts distributors passed by the window; Lutie didn't really know where they were going, just away from the yards. Baz wiped his nose on his sleeve, tucked his hands under his armpits. "You okay?"

She nodded and turned up the heat so that the entire car vibrated with the noisy fan. "You?"

He laughed, shrugged and shook his head at the same time. She concentrated on the road, couldn't look at him. "You didn't catch one, eh?" he asked, after a minute.

A sign directing them to the I-80 came up on the left, looked tattered and rough from the freezes and thaws, and Lutie took the turn-off, wanting nothing more than to be moving fast in an opposite direction. She headed west, not knowing if that was right, but she owed him that, to get him home at least.

"I didn't catch a ghost, no." She hadn't even come close. The railyard ghosts had been roiling with anger—maybe they'd been murdered, or lost, or abandoned. Something that made them crazed. After the gentle ghosts in her father's church, she hadn't expected anger, she now realized. "They didn't want anything to do with me." *Say it, he deserves to know.* "They only wanted to get to you." She cleared her throat, glanced at him, then back at the road. "The white light, it held them off. After it went, the ghosts, they were…" She flipped her hand up and off the wheel, like a bird startled to flight. "They were pissed off."

A few miles went by, Baz tracing his gloved finger on the glass, head resting in the hollow between seat and window. Through the metallic vibration of the heater, his voice sounded far away, disconnected, like it was being broadcast from another time, another place. "I don't know about any light. I just felt the ghostcold." He shivered. "I'm still feeling it." He leaned forward suddenly, tried to crank the heat, but it was already as high as it could go.

Lutie wasn't really made for dodging bullets, or trains, or anything, so she looked at her brother, about to ask him about the last thing, because there had been light, which he apparently couldn't see, and there'd been ghosts, which he definitely couldn't see. And then there'd been that black thing. *He can't see any of it,* she thought.

She had seen it though, which meant that maybe it wasn't real: a black crabbed figure, more like a crustacean than a human, spiny fingers splayed on Baz's shoulder, its face, head, whatever you would call that, bent by Baz's bowed and perfect profile. It had disappeared between one blink and the next, too far away for her to catch the words, but close enough to know that it had been talking. *I can't. I can't tell him about this thing, he's done enough today. He's had enough done to him for one day.* Drugs were better than this, surely.

Baz didn't turn on the radio, didn't sing. He stared out the window as exit signs for Sutherland and Paxton fled past the car, land the same in any direction, nothing on the horizon, buff dead grass, world asphalt gray, rimmed with leaden sky. Perhaps he'd fallen asleep, he was so quiet, face angled away from her, but all of a sudden he made a muffled choking sound and said, panicked, "Stop the car!" and she hesitated, but his hand was already on the door handle ready to go, and so she came to a sliding stop, wheels churning roadside dirt behind them.

Baz was out and on his hands and knees, retching into the dead grass before Lutie even registered the cold wind slicing through the open door. After what seemed like a long time, she heard him hawk, spit. She couldn't see him through the open door, but then his hand grabbed the frame, and he appeared again, face flushed, eyes standing out like lasers.

Wordlessly, she handed him a half-empty bottle of water and he swished some in his mouth, spat it out on the roadside before getting back in. He was shivering and Lutie had no idea how to tell him it would be okay, because she had no idea if anything was going to be all right. "Is the heat turned all the way up?" His teeth clattering, face like classroom glue.

"Are we okay to go?" Lutie asked, tried to sound sympathetic, but it wasn't something she was very good at.

Baz nodded a little more vigorously than was required. They hadn't gone two miles before he made her stop again. This time, he had nothing to bring up, only the shivering, and with an apologetic grimace, Lutie felt his forehead with the back of her hand, a gesture learned from Karen. "You have a fever," she said. "We have to stop. Ogallala's coming up. We'll find something there."

Baz shook, didn't nod at all, but whispered, "Sure thing, Lutie."

There was something very young about his voice then, and it plucked a scrap of memory in Lutie, him agreeing to whatever she wanted. Instead of making her feel powerful, though, it pulled out something completely different, like she'd reached into a magician's hat not to find a bouquet of fabric flowers, but a coiled snake.

There was no more conversation and Ogallala wasn't that far away, so Lutie was able to keep from bawling until she'd found them a cheap motel room with two double beds and a bathroom door that locked. Only when Baz was asleep under the covers did she go into the bathroom and cry until there were no tears left.

Closing his eyes would stop nothing. Sol caught his breath in an involuntary gasp, and realized that the gun hadn't discharged. For whatever reason—luck, gun fault, ammunition fail—she would have to pull the trigger again, and that meant that there was opportunity now where there wasn't before.

Without thinking about it, he lunged forward, not caring if a bullet blasted through his hand, because that was better than his head, and grasped the gun in a violent twisting wrench. Madama Lopez came with it, screaming obscenities in Spanish, and with one arm, Sol curled her tight into his chest, and with the other, threw the gun as far away as he could. It landed loudly and invisibly down the kitchen corridor, and the Madama tried to dig her fingers into Sol's eyes, kick his knees with her heels, scratch the arm holding her in a vise.

Sol was ready for all that, had some experience subduing people who were freaking out for one reason or another, and he held her as close and as tight as he could. Her hair was in his mouth as he said softly, into her ear, reasonable and calm, "Shh. It's okay. It's going to be okay. It's all done now. Shh."

Over and over, and the frantic clawing slowed, the fight went out of her, and her breath came in ragged gasps. Finally, Sol deemed her ready for release, hoped she didn't have another weapon close by, and he loosened his arm. She darted away, back against the wall, eyes taking in the room, the glass, the broken picture in its frame. Her gaze circled, landed on Sol. The moment was still, and daylight had broken enough that Sol could easily read her face, the limp features fallen into despair.

"Why?" she asked in English, hollow. "I never bother you. Why you take away my work?"

The time wasn't quite right yet for Sol to relax. Adrenalin sluiced through every vein in his body, buzzed in his ears. "It's not right, Madama. They need to be at peace."

"I protect that boy," she hissed, eyes flashing.

Sol shook his head slowly. "No," he said after a moment. "No, that wasn't a boy. That was a ghost of a boy, and it needed to move on."

Her voice shook. "He was so scared."

Sol found a slight smile, brief. "The ghost wasn't scared. Not at the end." He looked around the demolished room. "Do you have a broom?"

Together, they cleaned up the glass, and then Madama Lopez poured him a small shot of dark tequila while Sol stacked the broken table into a bundle of kindling. He apologized for that, offered her what was in his wallet for replacement, then sat with her in the kitchen. She pointed to his brow, and he ducked into the bathroom to clean the cut and hold it closed with some butterfly bandages he had in the small kit in his pocket.

He studied himself in the mirror, wondering if he looked different. He had just become the kind of traiteur who could put away a fortuneteller's ghost, and he ought to be taller or appear wiser, he thought, but instead he just looked tired.

Before he left, he gave Madama Lopez his phone number, in case she needed anything. "You know," he said, finally, "you don't need a ghost to tell a fortune. Half the time, they're not telling you the truth anyway."

She stood in her doorway, salt still marking the threshold, line broken now, merely a seasoning that needed to be swept up. By daylight, she looked ragged, depleted. "But the other half?" She wasn't smiling, wasn't the sort that was made for easy company. "I can still make money. But the readings will not be as…true."

"I'm sorry," he said, drawing on one glove, and she took his bare hand, and he knew she was going to read it. He made to take it back, but she held firm and he knew this was a test for her, to see what she could tell without a ghost helping her. Relaxing as much as he could under the circumstances, he allowed her to turn his hand over, one finger running up and down his lifeline as though she was a junkie trying to find a vein.

"Bah," she said after a moment, letting the hand go.

With some regret, Sol put his other glove on. What he didn't want her doing was going out and getting another ghost, and a decent reading now might have made a ghostless path easier for the psychic. She was too old for catching ghosts; they'd make dogfood out of her. "Maybe with a little practice," he suggested.

Her gesture then was one of contempt. "Practice." Like it was a chore. "You need to treat your woman better," she accused, surprising him.

The air was warming slightly, still cold, and so dry that a hand could strike sparks from car doors. Sol huffed a chuckle, shook his head. "See? Like riding a bike, Madama."

He drove slowly back to Aurora, the streets quiet at this early hour, new year's morning, and he was half-asleep and half-wired and deep underneath it, elation wound a complicated path around his heart, warming him in a way few other things could.

The clock couldn't possibly be right. Baz shook under the covers, too cold, yet slick with sweat. It said that it was eight in the A.M. and that somehow meant that they'd been here for only an hour, and Baz knew that wasn't right, because he could have sworn he'd been here a lifetime.

He sat up, dizzy, needing something to drink. The room was tilting, a fuzzy orange, but he ignored that. Wait. This wasn't the North Platte room. This was somewhere else. Where was Sol?

Thought that and then Lutie came out of the bathroom, wiping her face with a towel. They stared at each other and Lutie put down the towel, disappeared back into the bathroom for a wet cloth, some Ibuprofen in a bottle. He nodded to her, wiped his face with the cloth, swallowed three pills with the help of a can of iced tea that had been brought from the McGregors' pantry.

"Thanks," he croaked.

"You don't look so good," she told him.

"I don't feel so good, either," he snapped, and immediately apologized. This wasn't her fault; he knew more about this than she did, should have at least tried to talk her out of it, or phoned Sol to let him do it. "Hé, T-Lu, you wanna get that cardboard box from your car? The one with Dad's stuff in it?"

She raised an eyebrow, but there was no explaining it, his need to have his father close, his father's medicines and safeties beside him now that his father was gone. Before Lutie came back, Baz stood up, went to the bathroom, and washed his face, spat into the sink, willing the medicine to stay down so it could do something for his splitting head. More than that, though, his heart felt shaky, like it had come loose within his chest cavity.

He whirled at the first rattle from the shower.

Lutie's choice of motel wasn't four star by any stretch of the imagination; it was the sort of place Baz had crashed in numerous times on an endless cycle of tours. A cheap 1960s construction on the old highway, discounts applied weekly or monthly. Of course, a bathroom here would have no bathtub, only a shower stall with a glass door rippled by hard water marks.

Behind the frosted door, Baz watched a dark mass move, sideways with a swing, like it was loose in the joints. "You know, your father was a real piece of work. Such a hard-ass." The close confines of the shower stall made its voice echo. It drew breath, rank and clogged as a sewer pipe. "But you? You're just a peach, aren't you? Think of the fun we'll have."

Without thinking about what he was doing, Baz staggered forward, grabbed the handle of the shower door, yanked it open in one movement.

He made some kind of noise as he did it, a cry, a negation, but there was nothing there, just the single-form plastic stall, streaked with black mold. Baz's breath came in painful gasps, and he sank to his haunches, then to his ass, and Lutie was at the bathroom door, hammering it hard.

"Are you okay, Baz?" She sounded concerned, scared.

Blinking rapidly, Baz cradled his head in his arms, hoping his skull wouldn't explode. "I'm okay," he forced out.

After a minute and only with the assistance of the counter, he stood again and came out. Lutie had put the box on the bed, but hadn't opened it. Baz walked carefully across the floor, like there were secret explosives hidden under the carpet. Once at the bed, he opened the box, rummaged around the plaid shirts to find the small hex bags underneath. His father had used them to secure the cardinal points of a room when he was feeling particularly paranoid, and Baz supposed it wouldn't hurt now.

He had to lie down first, though. Lutie had placed his duffle bag on Baz's bed, and he crawled gratefully under the covers, shivering again because this goddamn motel didn't have any goddamn heat. "Lutie," he said, and she came to the side, but didn't sit down. "Take those," and he waved a hand to the bags, "and figure out your north and west. You know. The compass points. Put one at each, okay?"

She turned them over in her hands. "Why?"

Baz laughed, but it was phlegmy and he ended up coughing instead. "Because I said so, Mademoiselle Je-sais-tout. Damn it, you always have to know why?"

Her eyes flashed, and Baz dissolved into laughter, which sounded mostly like coughing, loose heart banging, head sparking with pain. When it had subsided, the job was done, but Lutie didn't look too pleased about it. She stood at his bedside, arms crossed. "You should get some sleep, Baz. Let that medicine do its work. I'll get us some supplies, okay? Some food and water."

"Where are we?" Baz asked.

"Ogallala, goddamn armpit of a town, and they call this the Prairie Paradise Motel. Ha." A hard one, his sister. *She's so scared. Some people get all clingy and shrieky. She's not one of them, eh?*

"Okay. What's your number?" He tried to take his phone out from the coat he still wore, but couldn't work the zippers, and then Lutie hauled him up to a sit, took off the coat, covered him with two blankets, and retrieved the phone. She turned it on, checking the charge, maybe, and then entered in her number. "There. It's on speed dial. Just in case you need anything, okay?" She flicked a glance to him. "I'll only be a half hour. You'll be okay." More to reassure herself than him, Baz thought.

"Sure thing, Lutie," he murmured. He'd be fine if the hex bags worked the way he hoped they did, because he'd seen that weird thing in the shower, and he wasn't seeing it now. That must be a good sign. He thought about how it must have been for Lutie, growing up and seeing what she could see. Enough to make you think you were crazy.

*Well, you would. You would think you were out-of-your-mind crazy.*

Her car started up outside, and he held his breath for a few minutes before consulting his phone. With a sigh, he dropped his hand to the bed, stared at the ceiling. The wind rattled the storm windows in their aluminum frames and Baz's heart thudded along with them. Goddamn.

Sliding open his phone, the keypad glowed in dim motel light, and the windows shook, and he was scared, he'd be the first to admit it. Lutie's number was there on his speed dial, and he supposed that it signified something, that she'd wanted it in there. Women did it all the time, but never a sister. This was different. There were a bunch of numbers on his speed dial menu, some recent, some past their expiry date, some he didn't even recognize. There was the one at the top, though, the one he punched in now, knowing it was past time.

The dog barked, but Sol was prepared for that and silenced him with a few well-timed words through the door before he'd even gotten his keys out. As he opened the door, Renard tried to make an escape, of course, but Sol grabbed his collar, dragged him back inside whining before he'd had the chance to chase the birds chattering on the fence. Sol shut the door quietly behind him, murmuring to the dog, tossing his parka onto a teak and leather chair, unlacing his boots by the door. The house was warm, and smelled of whatever Robbie had last cooked there.

Their bungalow only had the one bedroom, plus an extra room they used as office-storage, no wiggle room at all, made for what miniscule post-war family Sol could only guess. It was possible to stand just inside the front door, as he was doing now, and see into every room in the house. His heart sinking, Sol realized the place was immaculate, a seething discontent running under the good housekeeping loud as the *Titanic*'s engine. With caution, he opened the bedroom door and peered in. The bed sheets were wound round Robbie, duvet pulled to her chin. She was fast asleep. Sol chanced a visit to the bathroom, shed his clothes there, and returned to the bedroom, knowing that his skin was wintery and first contact would wake her.

Every bone ground against the other, chalky with exhaustion, and he wanted nothing more than sleep, just that, no argument, no recriminations or accusations. He was fairly sure it wasn't going to happen, that Robbie would be ready for him. He parted the sheets, slid in, tried to remain contained and remote for a few minutes as his body adjusted to the temperature change, but Robbie was an inveterate tosser, extended her foot to touch his and he knew they were ice.

She moaned and turned to him, and he studied her face in the half-light, hair still suggesting some fantastic backcomb, makeup dusting her closed eyes. She'd been out, and come home too late or too drunk to put herself right before bed. She smelled boozy and smoky, as though she'd been to a good party, which he hoped she had. Despite himself, Sol grinned. Last piece of good fortune for the night: Robbie was trashed. Freckles scattered across her face, her shoulders, like some chef had sprinkled her with pepper for the oven and then forgotten to put her in. She had fallen into bed without taking off her party dress, Sol noticed as he gathered the duvet over his own shoulders. He started to laugh.

"Oh, Roberta Mack," he whispered.

With rapidly warming fingers, he reached behind her and undid the zipper of her strapless dress, rolling her gently out of it, and she was going to wake up, Sol knew it, but he couldn't leave her like that, with lace and wires sticking into her. At least she hadn't come to bed in her heels, taken out the sheets. Satisfied that nothing short of an explosion was going to wake Robbie, Sol tugged the dress from underneath her dead weight and a flurry of sparkled sequins fell like black snow onto the linens. Smiling, he draped the dress onto a 1940s overstuffed chair that Robbie prized. He continued into the bathroom to pour her a glass of water and shake out a handful of aspirin, put both on her bedside table, and then curled up against her, nose tucked into her hair, prepared to sleep for hours.

He got maybe three of them, and that was pretty much useless as far as nourishing sleeps went.

Surfacing from a dream of knots and bindings, Sol heard, "Oh, God, please kill me," and Robbie shifted ungracefully, one elbow breaking the sea of blankets like a shark's fin. Sol quickly closed his eyes, wondering if he could fake sleep long enough to go back under. Not a chance.

A long moment passed, and Sol felt Robbie's eyes on him as she pulled blankets to her, adjusting the duvet and sheets, leaving his torso uncovered and cold, maybe assessing the location of her dress, the peace offering of water and aspirin.

Then Robbie's fingers found the bruised spot on his ribs where the ghost had dropped him on the table; she pressed hard. Sol came up on one arm, gasping at the pain. "Damn it, Robbie," he wheezed, and collapsed back onto the pillow.

Beside him, he felt Robbie move to a sitting position, and the light clicked on, flooding the room with painful clarity. Sol moaned. "Rob, merde, I just worked a full shift."

She cleared her throat, and he heard her drink the water, get up, bang around the room a little. No use. Sol rubbed his face with a hand, encountered the cut and bruised brow, and winced, which made it worse. He looked up to see Robbie, a flannel housecoat now drawn around her curves like a weapon. She dropped back on the bed, a knee swung perilously close to his groin as she straddled him like a schoolyard bully, one hand to either side of his head, staring at him with mascara-smudged eyes. She reminded Sol of one of those vintage beauties from the black and white era after an exceptionally hard night at the cabaret.

"What the hell happened to you? A fight?" she barked. Under it was worry, but Sol didn't want to indulge that. Better for her to be mad at him than for her to worry about him.

"Just a call that got a little hairy. No big deal. Part of the job, chère." He reached out with one hand to smooth down her hair, smooth her down, but she jerked away.

"You don't phone, you don't say when you're going to—"

"But I *did* phone." It was futile. She was just getting started. The housecoat wasn't tied properly, and the plaid pattern moved around enough to daze him. It was possible that he had a concussion. That would have been an excellent piece of self-diagnosis to have made earlier, since he'd been driving and sleeping already. "Oh, Robbie, please," he begged, and he didn't know what he was pleading for—quiet, sleep, forgiveness—but Robbie settled on his hips and it became obvious which way she was going with this.

"You leave a stupid little message at, like, five in the morning. You don't know how to use a phone at midnight?" She held him down with her light weight and Sol sank back into the pillows.

"I was babysitting an overdose at midnight," he explained. "Ow." Because her knee had found the spot where he'd hit the floor with his hip. "You're hurting me."

"Good."

It hurt a lot more before it was over, between Robbie's inquisitive fingers and her weight on him and the movement required to turn hurt into pleasure and back again. Sol was feeling every bruise the fortuneteller's ghost had raised. But in the end, Sol, still dazed and nearly comatose with fatigue, didn't regret missing sleep, not for her. It was the flannel, he knew. Moreover, Robbie knew it, always had.

The room was bright with morning and the dog scratched at the door, whining. Sol ignored it. After subsiding, returning from glory, Robbie cautiously uncoupled from him, now heedful of his bruises, and Sol couldn't stand being even that far away from her. He wrapped his fingers through Robbie's dark hair, tipped with purple at the moment, kissed the bow of her shoulder, one arm inviting her to stay beside him, fit to his side like a puzzle piece. Only then did he fully relax, eyes closed, spent.

He'd almost drifted off again when Robbie's cold nose ran up his cheek. *I am the kind of guy who can put down a fortuneteller's ghost,* he thought.

"What are you smiling at?" Robbie asked.

"Bizarre night," he said, peering at her with one eye shut. He paused, thinking of Madama Lopez, and his hand, and her words. "Are you happy, Robbie?" A dangerous question, because he didn't really want the answer.

"Right this second?" she answered with a low chuckle.

He grimaced. "In general," he prompted, not looking at her, eyes to the ceiling.

He felt her shrug, one arm across his belly. "In general, you drive me batshit crazy, Sol."

*Comes with the territory*, he thought.

"You don't tell me what's going on up there," and she touched his temple. "And you don't tell me what's going on in here," and she touched his chest. "You could walk out that door one day, not come back, and it wouldn't really surprise me, you know?" Her voice caught on a rough edge and she stopped. Sol was sorry he'd asked. Stupid fortuneteller. "What do we have, that it wouldn't surprise me?"

Sol did look at her then, and he sighed. There was no explaining any of it without explaining all of it, and that seemed too big, too strange and dangerous. *You think she's upset now*, he thought, drawing her closer. There was only showing her how he felt, and he knew it wasn't good enough.

"I'm sorry," he whispered into the top of her head, and he was always saying that. "You deserve better," because it wasn't her fault, none of it was. She'd just set her sights on the wrong guy.

"No," she said, and Sol was surprised her voice was steady, almost re-solved. "No, I deserve exactly what I've got."

Sleep deprivation didn't help him figure that one out. The phone rang into the silence that followed. Robbie disengaged, slipped out of the bed to answer it. She came back into the bedroom, naked, hair tumbled, lovely in the light, cute as something dangling from a keychain. She had her hand over the receiver. Their eyes met.

"It's Baz," she said.

# TEN

## VITAL SIGNS

The trouble, as far as Lutie could tell, was that ghosts seemed to be following them. The small bags that they had retrieved from their father's rooming house seemed to work well enough; she saw some ghosts while she was out at the grocery store, hanging around the motel, but they fled when she came near. Shy, almost. Not wanting to be seen, but unable to keep away.

Lutie couldn't tell what they were attracted to—Baz wasn't singing, was he—but they seemed to know he could and that was enough. *Like groupies at the backstage door,* Lutie thought uncharitably. *I should have just gone back to Toronto.* She remembered that day in the cemetery, so long ago, remembered the heat of it, and remembered that her brother would protect her, no matter what. Would help her, *could* help her.

She'd taken advantage of that, and it sat in her stomach like a rich meal, badly digested.

For the next couple of hours, she watched Baz's condition worsen. Over-the-counter drugs had limited impact on his fever and she knew that the next stop would be the ER. She wondered if Ogallala was big enough to have a hospital. Probably. She retrieved her laptop from the car, but the motel didn't have WIFI and she didn't want to venture out again.

The windows rattled, but it was the wind, crossing the plains like a nomad, relentless, changing, path unknown. Baz jumped at the sound, though, and his eyes drifted open, met hers. "Hé," he whispered, voice of stone.

She gave him some Gatorade to drink, and he tried to sit up, but she told him to stay put. She wasn't a very good nurse, she knew that, but this time it covered a slow-boil of panic. She had no idea what to do. If she called her parents, they'd come, but it would take time and more explaining than Lutie was willing to offer. Besides, she hadn't called them with an emergency in years, and she didn't want to break her record now.

"You see them?" Baz asked her, the skin on his face tight and flushed, eyes at half-mast, hair dark with sweat.

"See what?" Lutie asked. "Should I turn on the TV for you?"

He shook his head. "No ghosts, right? It's too hot in here for ghosts."

Lutie sighed. "No, no ghosts." It was only a small lie; he didn't have to know about all the ones outside. That would be her worry. "Maybe I should call my parents," she suggested, almost to herself. "The Major will know what to do."

Baz smiled, but he wasn't looking at her. "Nah, it'll be okay. Don't worry." His eyes closed again, and Lutie thought his breathing sounded off, staggered.

Don't worry. A fine strategy. She needed to define what her final straw would be. What would be her signal to call 911, not CFB Shilo?

A pounding at the door startled her, but Baz didn't move. Damn it, they had the room till tomorrow morning, must be the desk manager, who had been suspicious of her Ontario plates right from the beginning. A ghost could make that noise, too, though. She knew that, knew how much more than mere apparitions they were, how solid they could get, how physical they could become when given opportunity.

She came to the door, and the loud knock—gloved hand against wood—made her startle again.

"Baz?" a voice came. "Baz, you in there?" and the sound of swearing, muffled. As she watched, the doorknob moved, and a metallic jingling in the lock caused her to back away. A ghost probably couldn't pick a lock, she thought belatedly. Probably wouldn't know Baz's name. Probably wouldn't sound so aggrieved.

The door opened with a scatter of loose snow, and a man stood there, his eyes adjusting to the relative light. He half-turned to look at something and Lutie saw it too: a ghost, materializing close by, mindful perhaps of an open door. The stranger stepped in, closed the door behind him quickly, one hand laid flat upon it, then fast, fingers to his chest, then back to the door again. "Shit," he muttered.

After a second he turned, saw her, dark eyes quickly sliding from her to Baz on the bed, and she knew who this was, who this had to be, mostly because he looked so much like the man in the photo. *Beausoleil*, she tried it in her mind, on her tongue, hadn't really thought about him much over the years because he'd been the most indistinct: Maman, she remembered clearly, Baz had been her friend and playmate, Papa she remembered as wise and present.

But this one?

He ignored her, attention fully on Baz. With one hand, he took off his knit cap and tossed it onto the table by the window, and Lutie thought he looked like he'd been in a fight—his cheek was raw and small bandages held together one eyebrow. He crossed to the bedside, ran a hand over Baz's face, and she realized he'd brought what looked like a tackle box with him. He opened it on the bed, fanned out like a kid's pop-up book, and from it he extracted a stethoscope, a digital thermometer, took Baz's temperature, listened to his chest, flipped open one eyelid and shone a penlight in there.

Lutie came closer, intrigued. Surprised.

"What happened?" her brother said, not looking at her, voice flat and uninflected. From the practiced cadence, he'd asked questions like this before.

She said they'd been down at the tracks in North Platte, and that seemed to surprise him, and he looked up quickly. "North Platte?" he repeated. "Did he...sing?" Like she'd think he was crazy. She nodded.

He held her stare, dark eyes blinking. After a moment, he turned back to Baz. "How long's he been like this?"

"This being, what?"

He sighed. "Non-responsive." Worried, but not angry.

*He doesn't know who I am.*

Lutie's hand came up, fingers splayed, a hand-shrug. "He was talking a few minutes ago. We were by the tracks at dawn. He threw up a bunch on the way from North Platte to here. He's had a fever since then."

For a few silent minutes, Beausoleil—*Sol, like the sun*—selected items from his box, started an IV with surprising efficiency, put some fluids into Baz, some medications, kept one hand on his brother's chest, checking vital signs continuously.

"Hé, gars," he finally said, but it was to Baz, who had opened glazed eyes. "You're back."

Baz tried to smile, lazy as anything. "You missed the party."

Sol used the stethoscope and cuff to check Baz's heartrate and blood pressure. Lutie hadn't asked anything about this other brother, all she knew was that he knew more about ghosts than Baz, which wasn't saying a whole lot.

"I was working," he murmured, slinging the stethoscope over his neck. "Listen, I gotta take care of something outside. These fluids will help you feel better, quick, but don't mess with the IV, okay?"

Baz nodded. "Hé, mo chagren, Sol."

Another sigh. "I know."

"No, I mean it. I'm really sorry."

With one hand, Sol reached over and ruffled Baz's hair, but he didn't stop his rise, his purposeful action. He paused at the hex bag closest to him, perched on the table by the window. Cautiously, he picked it up and examined it, then tossed it back on the table. His hand was on the knob. "I'll be back in a few minutes," he said, and Lutie thought he might be, finally, talking to her. "Keep an eye on him. You can get going when I get back. I'll take care of this." And he opened the door, slid sideways through it and if she hadn't known there were ghosts outside wanting to get in, she'd have called that strange behavior.

After he was gone, Lutie cast a sidelong look at Baz, who was staring at her. "You called him," she said, and tried not to make it sound like an accusation, but that's just what it was. She might not have done a great job at looking after Baz, but she didn't need a babysitter, either. And she'd already said she wasn't ready to meet this other brother.

"I didn't tell him," Baz whispered. "About you."

Hard laughter burbled from her lips, a choked response, bitter. "Only because you don't want him to chew you out," and she knew that was the truth. Lutie went to the window, parted the curtain to watch. "What's he doing out there?" She heard a sound behind her, Baz clearing his throat.

"He don't like to be watched, Lutie." Baz paused. "You come away from the window, chère, leave him be."

"Shh." Sol had just bent down in the parking lot, a pair of misty apparitions hanging by an old pick-up truck not twenty feet from him, and he turned his head, touched the ground, put his hand inside his coat, out again, to his mouth. And she saw what happened next: a line, a shining line opened between Sol and the ghosts, widened like a path seen at night under moonlight. She understood it was there, and that it wasn't. It simply existed for a moment, and had no beginning, no end. Sol looked to the ghosts, and she saw his lips move, and the ghosts unfolded, changed, didn't so much as take a step, but the path came to them and they disappeared along it.

Across the street at the gas station by a thicket of highway signs, where Sol didn't notice, another ghost watched, and faded away, perhaps not wanting to be caught up in such an operation, but who knew what ghosts thought?

"Lutie!" Baz hissed behind her. She turned, and Baz, eyes bright, still flushed, tried to sit up, agitated.

She came back to his side, and handed him the wet washcloth. "Sorry. I've never seen something like that before."

"You're not gonna learn anything by spying on him." He put the cloth on his forehead, something cool to wick away the heat.

Lutie raised an eyebrow. "Well, he doesn't really seem the type to just tell me."

Baz laughed. "No, you got that right."

"I could just leave," she said quietly. "Maybe that would be better." They exchanged a long look: there was a certain benefit in that plan, a certain ease. Just get in the car, drive away, pretend none of this had happened.

Sometimes, you *could* rewind the clock.

A stupid amount of ghosts. Whatever Baz had done—going down to the tracks and purposefully singing—it was because Sol hadn't warned him. Sol stopped outside the door for a minute, composing himself. Maybe Baz only suspected that his voice called ghosts to him, or maybe it was just too abstract. Ghost-sick like this, though? Well, that must make it a little more real.

Sol didn't know who the girl was, but he scarcely cared, some New Year's Eve pick-up that had gotten more than she'd bargained for with Basile Sarrazin, who had never had any problem finding company, not in any arena. Baz could pick up in a mortuary. And Sol grimaced at that, because it wasn't funny.

The hex bags, though, they meant that Baz had cleared out their dad's things in Minneapolis, just like he'd said he would. Sol was still waiting for any evidence that hex bags actually did anything, fetishes of their father's swampland upbringing. Sol would have chucked them in the nearest dumpster.

Still, if they gave Baz some sense of safety, that was something. The patient's mental state was half the battle. Belief, *faith*, never underestimate it.

His brother and the girl were staring at each other when Sol came back in, and he felt that he was interrupting something, but couldn't have said what. Maybe Baz had just told her to get the hell out.

Baz looked better, as Sol had expected. The ghosts were mostly gone now, if Baz didn't open his mouth again—what had he been thinking? And Sol knew at least part of it was on him. *Dad asks me to look out for him, and watch me screw it up.*

"So," he said to the girl, who was pretty enough, young for Baz's usual tastes, fair-haired and doe-eyed. First things first. He couldn't ask Baz what the hell he'd been trying to prove down at the tracks when there was a stranger in the room. "Do you need a drive?"

From her expression, she understood that he wasn't offering her a ride.

"What are you? Some kind of doctor?" she asked.

Questions with questions. Great. "Paramedic," he answered. "I could call you a cab," he clarified.

One of her shoulders hitched, and she looked around the room, eyes landing on a cardboard box sitting on the floor between the beds, on Baz's duffle bag. The windows. Finally, her eyes rested on Baz, and again Sol thought there was more going on than he could easily make sense of, words being exchanged in some language he didn't understand. "I call my own cabs. Besides," she said slowly. "My car's outside."

She sat on the bed next to Baz, and took his hand in hers. The box was in the way, so Sol picked it up from the floor, placed it on the decrepit desk loaded with television guides weeks out of date. On top was a fiddle case, below a few stacks of shirts. The smell was familiar, drew a sharp tug of loneliness, of unwanted memory. His dad's things, here, possibly all that Baz had saved.

*If you wanted more, you should have gone yourself.*

"You gonna go now?" Sol heard his brother say, and it was laced with something hard and fragile, both.

"It's for the best. You have my number."

*Right*, Sol thought, making a show of flipping through the shirts, his back to the bed. The list of Baz's one-night stands was like roll call in a cathouse and if she thought she was getting more of him, she'd be waiting a while.

"Yeah. I'll call. Have a good trip back," and there was a pause and Sol couldn't see what was being exchanged without turning around and disturbing it. "Stay safe."

"Don't worry about me," she said with a laugh. "And you know, Baz. You have a great voice. You do."

*Wonderful, that's just what you should say to him*, Sol thought, hand encountering a shoebox underneath the shirts. He brought it out and put it on the table, because she was leaving and they really didn't have a whole lot of time for the past and for goodbyes and for one-night stands. Baz was an exposed wound, was in need of protection and Sol didn't know quite how to give it to him, but last night he'd wrestled with the most difficult kind of ghost that there was, and so he thought he'd probably figure out a way to handle whatever came next.

She left without further word, and Sol parted the curtain to watch her reverse out the parking spot and drive away. Dammit, there was one more ghost malingering by the vacancy sign, and she slowed as she approached it, took a wide berth. Sol dropped the curtain with a sigh.

"Man, you sure know how to pick 'em," he said, and turned to find Baz wiping his eyes. Fine, he was an insensitive jerk after all. "Sorry," he muttered, shrugging out of his coat.

It didn't take long for Baz to bounce back; it never did. Besides, he had ample ammunition. "You get in a fight for New Years?" Supposing, probably, something that was a likely scenario.

Sol didn't answer. Telling him exactly how he'd received his cuts and bruises was one way to start, maybe, impress upon his brother the seriousness of messing with ghosts, especially when you couldn't even see them.

Still, he'd driven three hours straight to get here on the same amount of sleep prior, and he needed coffee in the worst way. Or sleep. He wasn't going to get sleep, he decided.

The motel was located across the street from a retro-style diner and Sol had the intention of scouting for more ghosts when he ducked out for caffeine, but the ghost that had been hanging around the vacancy sign was gone. Sol didn't know where, and the fact that so many ghosts had been outside when he'd arrived wasn't right to start with; Baz had sung hours ago and sixty miles away. Ghosts usually didn't follow you around if you hadn't bound them to you.

If this was some kind of binding, it was one that Sol had never heard of before, and a burr of suspicion wore at him in a place he couldn't quite reach.

He came back with a coffee for himself, two bottles of orange juice for Baz.

The IV had done its job and so Sol removed it, much to Baz's evident relief, and he then proceeded to slug down both juices. Then he declared that he had to go to the bathroom. While it could be true, Sol knew that Baz was avoiding conversation like it was an ex at a party. Something wasn't right about all of this, and Sol knew that he was too tired to figure it out, but he'd chosen Caffeine Road, and was committed, so he prepared himself for the specific unpleasantness of forcing the issue.

"Sit," he said as Baz came out and before he had a chance to open his mouth.

Baz took the bed. "Listen, I know what you're gonna say—" and Baz lifted both hands, resting his back on pillows propped against the headboard. He didn't finish the sentence; it just hung there, lost.

It was funny, in a way. "Ouais?" Sol asked him. "You know what I got to say on this."

Baz blinked those big eyes that had always reminded Sol of Parisienne orphans on black velvet. "Well, no," Baz admitted. "You should see what we found in Dad's room."

Diversionary tactics. In a way, going along with Baz was always easier. More pleasant and fun. Didn't always take you anywhere, though. This was deliberate bait, but Sol couldn't quite resist it. "Let me guess. A whole pile of old shirts?" Gestured to the box.

"You could use some." The brows crept up. He was going to laugh and this was serious.

"We?" Sol repeated instead, wiping the smile off his brother's face.

Baz deflated like a kid's balloon post-party. He licked his lips, almost nervous. "Jean-Guy, right?"

He was such a bad liar for someone who'd had so much practice. Sol got up, walked around and pulled the chair out from the desk. Besides, what did he care if Baz took a girl to help him clean out their dead father's stuff? *Better her than me*, he thought, looking at the shoebox that he'd put on the desk. Why had he brought her along, though, through any of this? He lifted the lid, and Baz made a weird noise that could have been 'stop' or maybe 'uh-oh'.

Inside was a French-language songbook. Sol flipped through it, saw his father's hand in the margins, assessing each song's usefulness. For what, Sol didn't know. The continuing feeling of not-rightness curled in his stomach like a beckoning finger.

Underneath, a small box, and inside that, a ring. It could have only belonged to one person, that size, a simple fiddler's gift for his bride, inscribed with the letters of poverty: 10K. Sol felt a chill, and put it back as though it burned. What the hell were they going to do with *that*? What grave could they drop it into, what bridge was high enough to throw it from, what water deep enough to drown it?

He had his back to Baz, and for that, he was glad.

The wallet was filled with the usual assortment of IDs, some old enough that Sol remembered them, others newer, made after he and his father had stopped speaking to each other—Fisheries and Forestry Warden, state police, Fire Service, even an IT service technician badge for a fictitious computer company, which was the most ludicrous disguise for their father Sol could imagine. Aurie had become stymied with anything more complicated than a calculator.

"Take what you want," Baz said from the bed. "I thought it was you in the photo, at first."

Sol had his back to his brother, but didn't miss the skip in his voice. He sighed, not knowing, as usual, how to react to Baz and his heart-patched sleeve. "I'm way better-looking." Humor might work best. The IDs spanned several years, but in every one of them Aurie Sarrazin looked beleaguered as a hound dog in hunting season.

"Where do you think it was taken?"

A strange musical sound startled Sol, like the startup tune a computer made. He couldn't identify it, wondered if there was a weird alarm clock going off in the room. Distracted, he turned over the badge in his hand. What a dumb question. "I dunno. Photo booth in a mall, for all I know."

The sound came again.

"What?" Baz asked, and Sol looked over at him and held up the ID questioningly. "Not that," Baz's eyebrows moved in ways that would make a dancer proud. "The photo. Of him and…Mom."

Sol stood very still, the weight of the wallet in his hand. "I don't know what you're talking about."

Baz made an irritated motion of his hands, almost as mobile as his eyebrows. "Would you answer your damn phone?"

"Quoi?" Then realized that the sound was coming from his parka, folded over the chair back. Robbie's present, tapping him on the shoulder. He hadn't said no to her gift this time, not after what Madama Lopez had said. What Robbie had said.

Avoid one conversation with another. He retrieved the small phone, looked at it as though it might explode, and flipped it open gingerly as a bomb squad defuser. "Hello?" and he had a momentary flash of grim humor: *who's the technophobe now, Sarrazin?*

It was Robbie, wondering if Baz was okay, and once again Sol was amazed that people paid money for these things, because what would Robbie do, one way or the other? She also passed along the message that Wayne could take his shift tonight, even though he'd been half-comatose with hangover.

Well, Sol wasn't going to make a four o'clock shift today in any case, so again, what was the point of the—

And he was just in the middle of this, irritation and exhaustion and worry coming together under the general heading of 'photo of Mom' when he realized what had felt so wrong about Baz's date, what he'd seen and not registered until now.

She had swerved to miss the ghost.

Which meant that she'd *seen* the ghost, which meant that she'd been using Baz, using Baz's ability, sketchy as it was, potentially lethal—who the hell knew what it did to Baz, what it could do—and Sol literally couldn't breathe.

Robbie was wanting to know if he was still there, and Sol found that he couldn't look at Baz. He rested one hand against the door frame to steady himself. "Look, I have to go," he said quickly into the phone, not even knowing how to fake a graceful exit. He snapped the cell shut.

"Sol?" Baz asked, and Sol knew that Baz was getting up from the bed, and he was hoping that he wouldn't come closer. Before Baz could reach him, Sol turned around, both hands held up to ward him away, the phone dropped to the floor.

"She doesn't know how to get rid of them, does she?" he said, and Baz came up short, like he'd just run into a glass door, and Sol knew he shouldn't be so pointed, but there was no one else and his fear was just on the surface, barely had to skim a hand over the side to touch it.

"What?" But this wide-eyed dumb act wasn't going to hold water, not today. "I don't—"

"She used you to get them to come, but she's not a traiteur, she's not like Dad and me, she's not sending them away, or she'd have done it." Sol was shaking like he was the one with a fever, and it had come with the speed and the force of a Japanese bullet train. Baz had been down by the tracks, and some girl at the right age for doing it had seen that he could draw the ghosts. A girl wanting to be a fortuneteller. "How," he whispered, stopped on fear all dressed up as anger. "How could you be so *stupid?*"

And he swung away from Baz, because it was either that or hit him, and they hadn't had a fist-fight since they were kids.

"I'm sorry, Sol," Baz began.

He kept his distance on the far side of the room, by the disgorged shoe box, opened like a patient on an operating table. One hand up, like that could stop anything. "I don't want to hear your apologies."

But it was unfair. Sure, Baz had been raised with the same father, but not in the same way. He hadn't been taught, he hadn't been forced to learn. If anything, Baz had been kept from it, told to shut up, but not why, and was it any wonder that some conniving tea-leaf reading bitch could waltz in and bend someone as pliable as Baz to whatever she needed?

Baz sat on the bed, his head in his hands, scrubbing his hair between long fingers. "Sol, I didn't think that it would get out of control, I thought that if I just…" He looked up, miserable. Stopped against something he wasn't going to say.

"Did you know she was a fortuneteller when you picked her up?" Because those were some long odds, Sol had already worked out, for a would-be fortuneteller to come across a guy who could call ghosts with his singing voice alone. "How'd she figure it out? Were you singing in a bar or something?"

Baz was exposed in some way that Sol didn't understand, had some kind of invisible sign taped to his back that said 'I sing for ghosts' and maybe Sol should just get used to that. All his life, this was where Baz had been going and somehow, the idea that fate had already determined this scared Sol more than anything else.

Baz probably didn't need him being such a sanctimonious jerk. Baz must be feeling sick as hell; Sol remembered how he'd felt, after the ghost in New Orleans. This probably wasn't so different.

"Well?" he asked, tried to temper his voice, sand away the hard edge of it.

The next words were muffled, because Baz still had his head in his hands. "I didn't pick her up." His head came up, and for the life of him, Sol couldn't tell what that expression meant. "Lutie." Eyes on Sol's like the word meant something, was part of their vocabulary. "That was Lutie. Our sister."

Sol blinked, because these words made no sense, weren't connected to anything he understood. He didn't move, stood there like a tree in the middle of a field, begging for lightning to come on down and make him burst into flame. It seemed just as likely as anything else.

*Sit down before you fall down.*

Sinking onto the second bed across from Baz, he kept his attention on his brother's face, because that was familiar: the ad hoc piercings, the scrappy goatee an afterthought, the way he licked his lips before speaking, especially if he didn't know the reception of his words.

"She had a right to know. About Dad. So, after I left you in North Platte," Baz said and stopped, but Sol couldn't figure out anything to say, anything at all to help him out. He needed help, Sol could see that, was floundering. Still. "I found her up in Manitoba. And so we went to Minneapolis and we—"

Sol got up, and it was probably too fast, but he couldn't stay in that room. He couldn't stay. It was like a wound somewhere deep inside had been opened and he couldn't listen to any more, couldn't take in any more, not yet.

"I need some air," he said like he was talking about running an errand to the corner store and back. His voice was completely normal. This struck him as weird. He picked up Baz's phone, held it out to him, and his hand was steady, which was also strange. *I ought to be*—but he couldn't finish that. "Tell her to turn around."

"What? I don't—" Baz said, and his voice did shake, all of him was shaking and Sol knew that should concern him, but he felt cold all over, dead.

"Call her. She doesn't walk away from this. I need to ask her a few questions. I need to find out—"

"Okay, okay," Baz demurred, one hand coming up; Sol had heard what his voice held. So had Baz. "Where are you going?"

He zipped up the parka, pulled on his cap and gloves. "Out." He remembered his father saying that, and sometimes he'd been gone for days.

"Sol—" the worry in Baz's voice stopped him cold.

*You're not him, you're not Aurie.*

He paused by the door, but didn't turn around. Waited for the room to stop circling before speaking. He was flush with prickling adrenaline, but it was going to leave him soon, and in its place would be exhaustion. "I…just outside, I'm just having a smoke. Then…" One glance over his shoulder, and Baz looked like someone had kicked him. Sol couldn't keep this up, the talking, the making decisions, any of it. "Christ, I need some sleep, Baz. Call her, and then I gotta crash."

He shut the door behind him without further word, and scanned the parking lot, hoping now for ghosts. Hoping for something to push against. *My aim is true.* Probably lucky there were none, because what was in his heart right then wasn't about making paths, or helping, or healing. The fact that earlier this same morning he'd put a fortuneteller's ghost to bed no longer made him feel invincible, because it wasn't about protecting Baz anymore. There was no protecting him: something had changed, and he'd been seen and somehow their sister had been the one to do it.

Anything else, all other feelings he might have about this, was moot, just didn't feature against this bigger backdrop. That's what he told himself. Because getting rid of a fortuneteller's ghost was one thing, a hurdle, a personal point to prove.

Preventing it from happening in the first place was another, and this was his job now.

# ELEVEN

## LE P'TIT DIABLE

Headlights traveled over the curtains as a car pulled up outside and the tinny throb of an imported engine died a muttering death. Baz cautiously went to the door and stepped outside into the brutal cold to meet Lutie. She looked at him through the dusty windshield. He came around to the passenger door and she let him in.

"He's asleep," Baz explained, dropping to the seat, but not closing the door. She hadn't answered the first time he'd called, and when he'd gotten through, Lutie was miles away. "I'm not far behind and neither are you. Let's get you a room." He smiled. Lutie was hard-eyed, unapproachable. "I think they have vacancies."

Lutie's expression didn't change; she looked out the window to the teal-colored motel-room door, peeling, number painted over, only texture now, like a prehistoric earthwork on the prairie, wayfinding for spaceships. "Well." Which was close to agreement.

In the end, she got the room next to them, agreed that they'd have dinner together once everyone had some sleep.

New Year's Day had pulled past sunset before Baz woke up, disturbed by metallic shuddering in the shower. Pipes moving on loose clamps, rush of water, then abrupt cessation. A moment, heart thudding, room dark, he belatedly realized it was only his brother. As if to prove the point, the door opened and Sol was back out, scrubbing first his hair, then his

155

newly-shaved throat with a thin towel, complaining about the water pressure, Baz's razor, the housekeeping standards, the hard soap. How broke was Baz, Sol asked, that this was the best he could do for accommodation?

Baz looked at the clock: five past seven. They'd slept away the afternoon, and that was probably for the best. For both of them.

Sol wasn't looking at him, possessed a contained solitude that kept conversation at an arm's length, was sorting through the shirts in the box. He picked one and held it to his face for a moment, maybe to catch a fleeting scent of their father before drawing the worn flannel across his shoulders, and an expression tightened his face for a moment. Baz looked away. It was too personal, whatever it was. Then Sol cleared his throat, turned to Baz, and he sat down on the bed opposite, buttoning up the shirt, fingers steady, moment gone.

He'd been in a fight, Baz saw that clearly from the bruises on his ribs, and the cuts on his temple and on his hands. He wouldn't answer any questions about that, Baz was sure. Maybe he didn't remember the fight. It wouldn't be the first time for that, either.

"Where is she?" Sol asked softly, facial hair trimmed short and neat, eyes on his fingers, then up. Calm. Most reasonable person in the universe, if Baz didn't know better.

Baz swallowed, jerked his head to the side. "Next room."

"Good," and his equanimity had a glancing resemblance to the lull before battle, somehow, the soft steadiness of it, like he'd talked himself into something that he was going to regret but couldn't avoid. Baz wished he had that knack, the ability to talk himself into the inevitable, especially in his sleep. "Let's get something to eat at that place across the street. I'm hungry."

"Should we—" and Baz gestured to the wall. To the room next door.

Sol stared at him as though he'd grown a second head. "Well, *yeah*." It was the point, after all. Couldn't accuse Sol of sidestepping anything, Baz thought.

Baz changed his shirt and, pulling on his coat, followed Sol out the room into the cold and wind, put on his hat and watched as Sol walked without apparent hesitation to Lutie's door and knocked.

She made them wait a few moments and when she pulled open the door, the first person she saw was Sol, who filled the doorway, didn't let Baz come closer. Blocking him. Protecting him, maybe, Baz thought, reconsidering. Despite this, Baz had the advantage of height; he met Lutie's eyes over Sol's shoulder.

"We're going across the street," Sol said without preamble.

"Hi," she said, and it was sharp as a blade. "I'm Lutie." Her eyes didn't move from Sol's face, and Baz had the idea that maybe he should just leave them alone, except that was a coward's way out. This, right here, was all his doing. Besides, where would he go?

Sol shifted his stance slightly, and Baz didn't know if he'd been surprised by her quick adherence to the niceties, or was simply preparing himself for the next thing.

"Sol," he introduced himself, and Baz heard a hard kernel of laughter in it. "God knows we need to talk, but I think that we should eat first. Or during. Can we do that? Can we eat?"

Lutie looked at Baz then, just for a second, with a tight smile that didn't show her teeth, the awful green light from the fluorescent above, soft yellow from behind, her voice dry as prairie air. "Like normal people, you mean?"

Sol splayed his hands: Sure thing, sweetheart. Baz didn't know how you worked sarcasm into a hand gesture, but there it was.

Lutie's head tilted. "I'll meet you there." And closed the door.

Surprised, Baz grinned, enjoying the fact that she wasn't budging in the face of Sol's considerable and practiced fraternal authority. She'd come back, but she'd done that at his request, not Sol's. This was going to be interesting. Sol didn't say a word, just turned away, head down for a second, then up, looking around the parking lot. He wasn't moving.

He wasn't going to move. He wasn't going to be told where he was meeting anyone.

"You are some piece of work," Baz said.

Sol, that slight smile on his face, the one Baz always dreaded because it meant that his brother was sticking to his guns, put his hands in the pockets of his parka, kicked at the windrow of snow laying across the parking lot. Got out a pack of cigarettes, lit one. Didn't say a word, not for the whole freezing ten minutes it took Lutie to get ready and come out.

When she did, she pulled up in surprise at the sight of the two of them waiting for her, and Baz hoped that Sol was satisfied. Baz was merely frozen.

Wordlessly, they crossed the empty road, the old highway. These motels and restaurants and gas bars were leftovers of an earlier era of travel, were witness to a once-steady stream of Studebakers and Bel-Airs, were now succumbing to a slow decay, and Baz wondered if places had their own kind of ghosts, separate from the humanity that came and went so quickly.

The diner's neon sign lit up a full skirt of striped awning and Baz smiled wide as they entered because the whole place was red vinyl booths and chrome and pictures of 50s-era cars. The owners had pinned 45 rpm records to the walls as though they were exotic butterflies. The diner screamed 'road trip' and Baz felt immediately at ease, warmed up and ready to go. It was a faux construction, but it wasn't a bad one.

They sat in a booth away from the cold window, tri-fold menus offering a mind-numbing assortment of burger platters and shakes and sandwiches. In the background, Elvis warbled about fools rushing in, and though Baz thought he might soon crawl out of his own skin, neither Sol nor Lutie looked anything but utterly calm.

"You're in Ontario now," Sol stated, ordering a beer from the hovering waitress while giving the menu more consideration than he was giving Lutie. Baz hoped she saw through this, but there was no way to know. "So why did Baz find you in Manitoba?"

Across the table from Sol, next to Baz, Lutie's eyes flicked up, down, and Baz's stomach flipped uncertainly.

"My folks are there. I live in Toronto." Curious, but not asking how he knew. Easy enough, though. Sol must have seen her plates. She snapped the menu shut; Sol still studied his as though someone had written a novel in the margins. "I'm at U of T."

Sol made some sound, but didn't look up until their waitress brought their drinks, pen and pad ready for their food order.

"What's your major?" Sol asked, ignoring the larger bait—mention of her 'folks'. He must be wondering, but he wasn't asking.

Lutie's mouth turned around her straw. "Second-year psych."

"Useful," Sol murmured, and Baz remembered that Sol had started at the state university, done a year, then transferred to the community college. It had been a difficult year, that one, in a lot of ways. Money had been one part of it; time looking after Baz had been another. Sol didn't show his bitterness often, and it startled Baz now. The waitress was waiting for Baz and he smiled up at her, ordered a burger and fries.

"She grew up in foster care," Baz said after the waitress left, broaching the topic, since Sol was dancing around it and Lutie seemed to be willing herself into the next county. He elbowed her, raised his eyebrows. Sol needed to know about what had happened to their mother. "Like us."

Sol's eyes were as opaque as a shark's. Alert, roaming. "Not like us, Baz."

"Our mother's dead," Lutie fired across his bow, or maybe she was going for the direct hit, and Baz knew what she was doing, because he'd been on the receiving end of it in the McGregors' kitchen. "When I was nine. She committed suicide and left…"

Baz had no idea what this news would do to Sol, who never talked about Maman. Baz couldn't remember a single time when his brother had mentioned her name. At least their father had given Baz the one photograph, had cursed her when he'd been drinking, had acknowledged her existence with his misery. Had every once in a while, and only when very drunk, played lullabies on the fiddle and told Baz they were hers.

Beside Baz, Lutie stiffened, seeing the look Sol gave her. Refraining from touching her, comforting her, Baz cleared his throat. She didn't need his protection, he reminded himself. "Sol. I'm sorry, but—"

Lutie interrupted. "Don't, Baz."

Baz's attention bounced between them. He opened his mouth, and then shut it. Sol hadn't moved, was watching Lutie with interest, finally.

"Do you know what I did this morning?" One hand turned his bottle around, and his voice was terse, controlled. Baz didn't want to know, couldn't predict anything that Sol might have done that morning.

Lutie's hand came up. Go on, it gestured.

But Sol always made you ask. "What?" Baz said, going through the formality, wanting things to be different, for Sol to be different. *I want her to like him*, he thought, fleetingly. With despair. *I want her to stick around. I want her to want to stick around, Sol.*

With one thumb, Sol scratched his eyebrow, where the butterfly bandages must be itching. "I got rid of a fortuneteller's ghost," he said, kept his voice low. "She'd trapped it against its will and it was making her crazy. You know about that part, right? The part where a bound ghost turns you insane?" He looked directly at Lutie and Baz might as well not have been there.

159

Baz heard the pride, the warning. There had been the whole Katrina business, when Aurie had specifically broken the frosty impasse with his eldest and told Sol not to go, and Sol had ignored him, and had come back broken. Something overcome, this morning, some notch carved wherever Sol kept track of how well or poorly he was doing.

Again, still, Lutie did not move, held herself rigid as a dressmaker's form. "M'man did okay with it." Words as weapons, childhood name a bullet to the heart.

And Sol smiled, dimples disappearing into what was now formally a beard, not an afterthought, everything deliberate. "Right up till the bathtub, hé, chère?" Another swig of beer, and Baz saw that his brother wasn't indifferent, wasn't cold. He was so far from that, and all the words flying across the table were sharp because of it. "You don't need to cover up the truth for her, she's long gone. That ghost she had was company enough, I guess. Better company than her husband. Than her kids. She left us all, Luetta. Just you last."

The food came and maybe the waitress sensed what was going on, because she dropped the plates and ran.

No one touched anything. And then Lutie said, "I didn't say she did it in a bathtub. So you tell me. Who's covering up the truth?"

Slow, slow smile, recognition of a hit, of kinship, who knew, and then Sol said, "I thought we were gonna eat like normal people." He pulled his plate toward him, but his words knocked on Baz's heart like a door-to-door solicitor making the rounds and Baz understood what hadn't been said so much as revealed.

"You *knew*?" Baz said, unbelieving, and for the first time, Sol's impassive front faltered.

Reaching for the pepper, Sol rolled a shoulder like he was taking a punch, looked briefly at Baz, but his words were for Lutie. "Happy?"

"No," she shook her head. She hadn't made a single move yet. Not for food, not for anything. "I'm not." She turned, maybe to make sure Baz understood, because Baz knew how he came across, knew what people tended to think of him. "He's known all along, that she was dead. Knew it and didn't tell you."

Baz wondered if the fever was back, because the diner was orange and too hot for him, and he felt a chill come over him. He wanted her to like

160

Sol. Hell, *Baz* wanted to like Sol. He wasn't making it easy, not by a long shot.

Across the table, Sol took a forkful of slaw into his mouth, followed it with the tail end of his drink. His eyes cut sideways, uncomfortable. Finally, his attention rested on Baz and Baz had no idea how to make sense of that look. He swallowed, adjusted his voice. "No. I didn't tell you."

"How…" Baz couldn't even finish it, couldn't ask. He didn't know how to ask Sol this, and it was unfair for Sol to demand it with his silence. So he waited. Lutie did too and Baz wondered that he'd just learned this, that he didn't have to fill all of Sol's silences.

After a moment, Sol put the fork down, met Baz's stare. "When I started work for Denver Health. I was able to access records. It was the first thing I did."

Baz made a quick calculation. "Four years?" It was incredible. "You've known for four years?"

"Ouais, gars." He sighed. "Mo chagren. Mais," and his brows came up a little and he picked at the pale tomato in his clubhouse, teased a piece out the side. Choosing words, setting them up like a screen. "What good would it have done? Eh? She was," and he lifted a hand in Lutie's direction as though she was an abstraction, and then caught himself. "You were with a family, and you had been for years, the court records said, and the social worker I spoke to said you were doing good there. What? I was gonna phone you up? 'Hé, T-Lu, laissez les bon temps roulez?'" His best and most effective Cajun accent and Baz felt more than his heart in his mouth, because he heard it, everything that Sol hated about where they came from, who they were. Sol turned to Baz, clear-eyed. "She finally had it good. Let it lie, eh? It was done."

"You called my social worker?" Lutie demanded, the first real reaction Baz had heard from her. Outrage, because that was easier than anything else.

Sol ignored it, stared at his plate.

"Did Dad know?" Baz asked, and he shouldn't have, because he wasn't sure he could cope with the answer.

Slowly, Sol shook his head. "Nah." His smile was a fiddle string; his words the peg, turning. "I don't think so, anyway. We weren't really talking to each other by then, were we?"

"Why?" Lutie asked. "Why didn't you tell anyone?"

Sol licked his lips and looked away. Without looking back, he lifted his shoulders. Up. Down. Baz knew this gesture: he wasn't going to say. Maybe he didn't know himself, or didn't want to share, but they'd never hear about it. Instead, Sol picked up one of his sandwich triangles, gestured to the waitress and asked for more water.

And that was as much as Baz could take.

Lutie watched Baz leave; he was out the door in seconds and Sol let him go. Lutie made to stand and Sol lifted his chin, looked her in the eye. "Leave it alone."

He seemed on the verge of telling her she'd done enough, and that was true, was more than true, but Baz had been the one to seek her out, hadn't he? He'd been the one to turn the key, get all this in motion. So what if he was unprepared for consequences, that wasn't her fault. Whatever lay between these two, that wasn't her fault either. She stayed seated while Sol slowly picked apart his sandwich.

"You didn't talk to your father for four years?" He didn't volunteer anything, this one, and she wanted to keep him off-guard, not ask the obvious. It seemed safer.

Sol looked at her before answering. "We didn't agree on a lot of things." Like that was an explanation.

"Why was he in jail?" Her eyes narrowed. "Was that why you cut him off?"

His eyelids flickered, and a smile crossed his face briefly. "What makes you think the not-talking was my idea?"

"You're joking, right?"

A full smile, a real one, bitter as the bottom of a staff room coffeepot. But no response. She waited, finally chose a fry from her plate. They were stone cold. After a while, he called the waitress over and asked for the check. The waitress wondered if everything was all right, when any idiot could see it wasn't, and then she asked if she should package Baz's meal to go and Sol smiled in a way that Lutie was coming to realize meant its opposite. The answer was no, but he said yes to both things.

"It's a long story, and Baz shouldn't be alone." He stared at her, empty-eyed, unreadable. "He doesn't know what he can do, he doesn't believe it." He paused, was very still. "At least, not before today. You put him in a lot of danger."

"And you know what he can do?" she asked, pointedly. "You've worked that out and decided not to let him know? You let him loose, and he calls up what he calls up—"

Sol let out a huff, maybe of shock, maybe anger. She could take whatever he dished out, though. "Calls up? Like, lining up a bunch of cooperative ghosts to be your own special lapdog? You *used* him."

It stung, sure, but it was beside the point. "He sings, and more than ghosts come. You know that." She shook her head slowly, like a disappointed school teacher. "I'm not the one putting him in danger."

He considered her, and she didn't know what was going on behind the calm eyes and the beard, and the pressed-together lips, all his masks. He paid and she let him, then grabbed the white plastic bag that contained a Styrofoam box filled with food that no one in their right mind was going to eat, and stood. Lutie followed him down the aisle, past the stupid records and the goofy prints of old cars, pulling on her coat and finding her tuque in the side pocket.

Outside, the wind came in from the west, swept down the street, swinging traffic lights on their clamps. Lutie looked across to the parking lot, but she couldn't see Baz anywhere. He'd probably gone to the room; it was too cold for just wandering around.

Sol wasn't crossing the street. His hands were searching his pockets and he eventually found and lit a cigarette, and they stood there while he smoked, Lutie cold but not freezing, not wanting to be there, particularly, but angry enough to stay.

"What do you mean, 'more than ghosts'?" he finally asked, picking a fleck of tobacco from his lip. The streetlight illuminated half his face and it wasn't enough to read him properly, even if Lutie knew how to do that. He was waiting for an answer, though, was apparently good at doing that.

The pompom on her tuque rolled to the side as she bent her head. Not a shrug, really, because whatever Sol could do with ghosts was way beyond her experience, so why was he evading now, with this? "I can see ghosts, right?" He nodded in agreement, and it felt strange, to say that straight, without fearing a medical assessment.

"Yeah, I know that." Hurried, impatient, old ground.

"And that other stuff, I can see it too." The pavement was cracked, long lines leading nowhere, no sense to them.

Sol, so apparently practiced at waiting for it, looked hard at her, and she could see that his calm had worn thin. "What other stuff?"

Lutie didn't like to be questioned. Especially, she didn't like that he was asking her to explain what she didn't know about, when he knew perfectly well what it was. "Screw you," she said, hands up. "I don't owe you anything."

His teeth gleamed white in the night as he laughed, turned from her, streaming smoke as he circled away. One hand up to touch his temple, then another drag before facing her again. "Hey, this wasn't my idea."

"You've made that really clear, thanks." And she heard what lay underneath her words, hoped he didn't.

He flinched, though, and she knew he had. Another long moment as he looked into the night, but she didn't see anything in the shadows. His voice, though, was softer when he looked back to her. "What else are you seeing, Luetta?" Then shifted, eyes narrowing, almost like he was remembering something. "You seeing something—dark?" He'd been considering another word, and Lutie wondered if it was French, if he only knew how to describe this stuff in his first language, in their parents' language.

She nodded once. "It came when Baz was singing. It wasn't a ghost. It…" She had his attention now, all right. Her brother ground out the cigarette on the pavement, came closer, hands in pockets, Baz's cold dinner swinging from a loop on his wrist. She took a breath and said it all at once. "I think it knew Baz. It didn't act like the ghosts, they were all grabbing him, wanting a piece of him. This was black, like a crab or a huge spider, and it was talking to Baz."

The upside to Sol's reticence, to his bull headed calm, was that she could talk about this and he wasn't telling her she was crazy, he wasn't freaking out. There was something to be said for that. "You hear any of that conversation, Lutie?" She shook her head. "You think Baz did? You think Baz could see it?"

She shrugged, but Sol didn't look pissed off any more. He looked worried.

"It disappeared, not like a ghost does. You know?" And Sol nodded. It was weird, being able to talk about this, weird and so good. "I have a lot of questions," she admitted quietly.

Sol nodded, but his expression had changed again, this time to resignation. "I'm sorry. He should have just left you alone. You should go back to school, take your medication, forget all about this."

"I'm here now, though." It was the truth, and he couldn't wish her away. "So talk to me."

He blinked, face held stiffly, maybe a response to emotion. "What can I say to you?"

"Well, first off, what was that black thing? Why's it after Baz?" It was cold, and she wished they'd go inside, either to the diner or to the motel, but she knew Sol wasn't going to talk about this in front of Baz.

"I think it's the same thing that killed our father," he said, point blank, and Lutie suddenly knew what it was like, getting hit this way. He wasn't even trying to use it as a weapon, either. "I don't know what to call it. Like a demon, a devil, un p'tit mauvais. A small bad thing."

"It wasn't cute, you know."

Wordlessly, he handed her the restaurant bag, then lit another cigarette. "I know." He turned, started walking across the street. "I don't know much about them." A door had shut within him, and Lutie didn't quite know what to say. He'd been Aurie's boy, she remembered Maman saying. He'd been taught, sort of, but not enough, had cut their father off, cut off the teaching, rejected it. Guessing now, just like her. A little better at hiding it, maybe.

"Don't you want to kill it?" she shouted after him.

He turned in the middle of the street, empty of traffic, held out his arms, a question. "What do you want me to do?" He kept walking, heading toward the motel, and Lutie caught up with him. Before she could ask again, he said, "You don't kill those things. You try to avoid them. Better that they don't know you're there."

"Well, Baz has this one's attention, and if it killed Aurie, too? I don't know about you, but I think we're past trying to get out this thing's way."

He stopped outside the door, and strobing television-light spilled from between the curtains, a sign that Baz was inside. Sol scrutinized her, weighed her worth, and Lutie felt uncomfortable under this gaze, shifted from foot to foot, cold among other things.

"I'm looking into it." He hesitated, hands on his hips, breath pluming into the night as he sighed. "There's a ghost working this part of the track.

It has a thing against people who are about to catch out. You know,"
and he smiled slightly, bemused maybe, "railroad slang. Catching out,
getting on the road, leaving the past behind you. Those lucky assholes
who've thrown in the towel, kissing boring goodbye, looking to follow
their bliss." He stared knowingly at her, quoting Joseph Campbell, trusting her to get the reference. Not some bayou hick, make no mistake.
"I'm pretty sure it's the ghost of a railroad cop that was murdered near
here about thirty years ago, according to the drifters along the tracks. I
talked to someone at the historical society in Brule, which is where the
murder happened, but they wouldn't give me any more than that. At first,
I thought this ghost killed our dad, but I don't think so anymore. Maybe
the devil you saw is controlling the ghost, maybe le diable just likes all
the confusion a big méchant ghost causes, I don't know. The murders first
showed up on my radar a few weeks ago. Dad came here, looking into it,
same as me, and it got him killed."

"How do you know that?" She kept her voice down, but a deep fear had
sprung up in her, because it had been unreal before, just on her own, but
this was different, was so real. "That he was killed by something different
from a ghost?"

With one hand, the one not holding the cigarette, he made a gesture,
folded a couple of fingers down. "He was making that sign when he died.
It's a ward, but not against ghosts. Against evil. He wouldn't have made
that for a ghost." His eyes were turned away from her. "He came to my
place in Denver, after." Voice rough, now. He'd been visited by their father's ghost, and how weird would that be? "He said that he'd been killed
by un diable." He looked at her, direct, and he was calm again, collected,
distant. "It's dangerous for you guys even being here. Why..." and he
looked away, fighting for it, because he wasn't the sort of guy that liked
asking for what he didn't know. "Why did Baz go down there, to Bailey
Yard?"

Common sense told her to lie, to say that she hadn't been trying to
catch a ghost, but he already knew so much, and he probably couldn't like
her less than he already did. Still. "Baz wanted to. We'd been talking about
ghosts and I was saying how hard it was, seeing them all the time around
you, and—" She remembered Baz's words, what he'd wanted out of it. Sol
hadn't asked her why she'd gone down there; he'd asked why Baz had. "He

wanted to help you. He thought that maybe I could find out stuff from the ghosts about Aurie's murder that you couldn't."

He'd been smiling in that sardonic way he had, but he wasn't smiling any more. Brows crooked, puckering the bandages, and he shook his head, attention to the ground. He went to a beat-up Jeep, worn black paint, missing a few faux wood side panels, and unlocked the back. After a minute, he returned with a bag of road salt. The corner was cut and he poured a line across the doorway to the motel room, more on the windowsills.

Then he gave her the salt bag, heavy as a baby, and unlocked the room.

Inside, it was warm, and Baz lay on the bed, watching TV, a mournful expression on his face. He looked up as Lutie came in, then back to the noisy program. Pissed off, but not at her, at Sol. The door was held open for her, and Sol dipped his head beside her ear and she smelled night and smoke and salt. "Make a line at every window, every door. Get him to eat something. Don't let him out of your sight, don't let him sing one damn note."

And he shut the door behind him as he went out into the night.

One drink wasn't enough, but a whole bottle would be far too much. He had another shot, then one more. At the bar, elbows on the counter, on a mission, none of this remotely to do with pleasure. Drinking was work, right now, necessary armor. No, its opposite: a necessary opening. *Like a shaman downing peyote to talk to the gods,* he thought.

*I have no idea what I'm doing.* Not his father's voice, his own. By the glass-end of Beam number four, Sol thought he'd had enough. Available to things, not so tightly wound, able to see crap, hear things clearly. Hear more than ghosts, probably, because ghosts, merde, he could always see those. Hell, half the time he made it to the bottom of a bottle was an effort to wipe them out.

This wasn't about that.

*Papa never talked about les diables,* Sol thought. *Not to me.* But sometimes, his buddies would come through town, usually on tour, musicians most of them—T-Jean, and T-Lou, the Thibodeaux brothers, and all those other guys whose last names ended in x like the marks of illiterates—and the rum would flow and the neighbors would bang on the wall in complaint. Sometimes, they took the party out and Baz and Sol wouldn't see Aurie for days. These were the times before the manslaughter trial, before the botched exorcism, a time when Aurie had friends.

They traded ghost stories like cigarettes, like laundry-day gossip, like new lyrics to old songs. Sol had been the young one, and Baz the younger one, Sol handy with ghosts, Baz a prodigy with a fiddle, allowed at the knees of the masters, around to refill glasses and fetch bags of cheap potato chips from the store. These rough guys with ball caps and overalls sometimes needled Aurie about his apparent way with devils and angels and Aurie had smiled, ducked his head, embarrassed, Sol had thought at the time, bashful at such praise.

He'd been proud of his father, then.

After prison, the friends had been fewer, the reckonings in the dark with a bottle more intense. The talk had not curled tight circles around double stops and swamp pop anymore, but spoke increasingly of devils, and things that moved freely in the night. Sol had been done with Aurie by then, and hadn't listened, not to any of it.

He wished he had now, because what he knew about les diables currently amounted to this: unlike ghosts, they were not, and never had been, human. They were something else, a flip side of a foreign coin. Good on one side, evil on the other. That was how humans thought of them, Sol supposed. What did words like 'good' and 'evil' matter to such creatures? When he was a boy, he'd thought of them as something out of folktales—their kind of mischief dragged unwary children off docks, curdled milk, caused girls to sleep through their wedding day. After his incarceration, Aurie had ranted about les diables, and descriptions of them had become more deadly, painted a portent of dread, unravelers of dreams. More than a nuisance, not a full-blown Apocalypse, maybe, but bad enough.

Sol turned his glass around, refracting bronze light, wishing for more, edges numbed, able to blank out the gibbering anxiety, the nattering of negativity. *I can do this*, he thought. *I have to do this*, more to the point. Those shamans probably got stoned for a reason: if their supernatural correspondent ripped them apart, they could at least die happy. Not quite enough Beam for that, unfortunately.

Rising from his seat, he nodded to the bartender, who had begun with questions, then been wise and experienced enough to back off. Payment was on the bar, under the empty glass. Sol pulled on his warm coat, felt the nearby presence of the railroad tracks like a magnet, siren song. *God, I'm too drunk for this.* But not really, because once outside, remarkably close to the tracks, a whistle blew and he jumped the fence, windmilled down the graveled incline to the rails, and a train smashed the night, roared by and if Sol had thrown himself under it, he wouldn't have died happy, not at all.

He had a half-bottle of rum resting in his inside pocket, just in case he hadn't gotten the balance right between sober and drunk, awake and dreaming. Everything he'd ever done, everything he'd been taught to do, was anchored in the earth and he didn't think that devils cared much about the earth. *I don't need a fight, not tonight.* This was a fact-finding mission, he had no illusions about trying to rid the world of any evil tonight. He didn't give a damn, really, about any of it as long as they left his family alone.

It had talked to Baz, had marked him, somehow. And Sol? Well, Sol was about to mark it in return.

The moon was a thin scrape of silver, a skater's incision on a frozen lake, rimed the tracks following the departing westbound, and Sol smiled in spite of the cold and what he was there to do. If he'd been at a bend, the train would have had slowed enough to catch out; he could have been home by midnight, warm in his own bed, tracing the patterns of constellations on Robbie's freckled back as she dreamed. He thought of his cell phone in the motel room, maybe on the floor. He hadn't picked it up again. It was pointless. He always came home, and Robbie must know it by now, didn't need some tag and release program to tell her that.

The rum flask rubbed a warm groove against his bruised ribs and he thirsted for it. Ignoring that want, he wandered westward, away from the light, away from the agitated rumble of the nearby interstate, only the lonely sound of coyote and the occasional whoop of owl to disturb the night, not even the blast of a train in the distance. He made sure he was nowhere near Claude and Tomson's shantyville; they didn't need the kind of trouble he was borrowing tonight. After a while, he slowed, took his bearings, not wanting to become another rail death statistic. He didn't know how to call these things. Maybe there was no calling them.

Ghosts came, if you did it right, if you offered incentive. Earth, blood, breath, life, afterlife. It worked, to a point. But ghosts had once been people, had some vestige of human emotion—fear, anger, hate, love. Mais, les diables? Who knew? Probably best not to know, because that meant you'd gotten too close, offered too much.

The rails scarred the prairie, bound on either side by a bank of rough grass and battered snowfence. The sky above was clear, which was why it was so cold: a massive blush of star, covering from rim to rim, gorgeous and too big for the heart to embrace. Sol withdrew the rum, took a slug, felt it hit his belly and rush to every extremity. The cap didn't screw on easily, like it wanted to be open in his hand, but Sol argued it back on, slid the flask into his inside pocket, cold against warm, sky huge above him, iron running in two directions at the same time, going home and heading out.

He crouched down, drew off his glove with trepidation and shoved it into his pocket. He lit a cigarette and considered the night. No ghosts, nothing but wind and snow and the trailing wail of train, now long gone. Inhuman sky above. *I don't want to do this*, he thought, knowing that kind of attitude would get him nowhere. *I've already done my impossible deed for today*. He buried his hand into the gravel, finding the hard-packed earth below, firmament of the ages, traces left for those who could see: the grooved crescent imprint of buffalo hoof, tears of exile. Licking his lips, he took a drag of his smoke with his other hand.

He thought powerfully of Baz, not as he appeared now with the markers of fashion piercing his face and ears, not the careful way he handled Sol, same as he'd handled their father. Instead, Sol thought of his brother as he'd been at nine, ten years old, when he could sing as loud as he pleased under bent cypress wooly with moss, sun and heat making him brown like some sort of wild creature more at home on a boat than on land. Sol concentrated on Baz's voice as it had been, soft and sliding from English to French and back again, not even knowing there was a difference, just whole in his skin, so bright he could break your heart.

Sol sent that out, from heart to hand to earth.

Crouched low, cigarette done, hand so cold he couldn't feel the pain anymore, holding on to this memory, and behind him, gravel moved, shifted in the night. Where the devil could not see him, Sol smiled. Blinked, then ran a tongue over lips chapped and split from dry cold, knowing that he was open enough, that he would be able to see it, and it could see him. He would be at its mercy. So be it.

Its chuckle sounded more like stone rattling on stone, a wash of flood-water over a beach littered with bodies. Sol smelled swamp rot and engine oil in the air, a thousand miles from the nearest bayou. It stirred fear in him, stirred failure, opened a void vast as an ocean. He felt like that shoe box back at the motel, open to the world, secrets bared.

*Gotta be open enough for this*, he counseled himself. *Leave yourself open just enough.*

He turned. The rails glowed in the wan moonlight, and some yards away, a dark mark against the frost-burnt grass, was a creature, big as a Harley. Loose-jointed, close to the ground, eyes catching moonlight when its head swayed side-to-side like a slow conductor's baton. Another chuckle, and every hair on Sol's body rose in response.

The devil was twelve feet away from him, maybe less, and it was solid, present, ruinously so. Arms hung from its spider body; Sol couldn't tell how many, it seemed to change as he watched. It approached raggedly, reorganized itself, became more man-like, as though on a whim.

"Hey, good-lookin'," it rasped like it was going to burst into song. It laughed again, coughed, as though the air strangled it. "Whatcha got cookin'?" And it scraped one talon-like finger over its obscured face, striking sparks. Sol smelled sulfur, the inside of a furnace, creosote.

"We haven't met," Sol said, mouth dry, wanting the rum, dead weight in his inside pocket. "But you know me."

Its head turned, and Sol knew this because of the moonlight glinting pale green from its eyes. "You guys all look the same. I thought you were gone, thought we were even. So fuckin' tricky, you people."

A minute, Sol looking at it, ungloved hand like a block of ice hanging at his side. Against the soles of his boots, he could feel the thrum of earth. He paid attention to that, because he knew it, trusted earth like nothing else. Waited for this thing to understand the situation. Finally, it chuckled again. "Hey, you ain't him!" It slithered and scratched closer, every step drawing sparks from the stones. Came close, and circled behind and Sol turned, following it, hands held out, no weapon to go against it. *I'm not giving it my back*, he thought, and didn't know if that was wise. It was like bear attack advice: look bigger than you were, play dead, climb a tree, run, back away, whistle.

"No. I'm not him. He's dead. You killed him."

It had a spider's silent rush, pic-pic-pic'ed to the side, collected itself. Stroked its flank with one clawed hand, head draped in fine hair, Sol could now see. Maw open, black teeth row upon row, breathing ragged against the poison air. "Yeah, I killed him all right. You're the other one, I guess, hé, gars?"

So sly, remembering Aurie's cadences, or picking up Sol's fast. It wasn't human, but it sure as hell sounded like one. A wave of pure adrenalin surged up Sol, toe to head, flashing like fever and he wanted to run so badly he had to concentrate on keeping his feet planted firm. "The other one?" He didn't sound stupid, he sounded cold, thank God.

"The other guy. You Sarrazins." Clicking forward, pause, step again. Closer. Sol didn't budge. "You need something, Beausoleil?" The more time in its company, the more it seemed to figure out about him, the more it took from him.

Needing something from things such as this was probably a bad idea, but still. He licked his lips. "I need you to keep the fuck away from us."

Clickclickclick, scuttle of stone, scrape against chitinous shell, spark and spark. "Sorry," it said. "No can do."

Sol kept his hands out, fingers frostbite cold. "Why d'you kill him?" Still surprisingly calm. That was the Beam talking, he thought. Steady as she goes, just enough to override the adrenaline.

The thing swayed back and forth, same movement as a mother lulling a newborn to sleep, now not more than a body-length from him, reeking of a shrimpboat hold in August, of the submerged Ninth Ward, bloated bodies wedged under attic rafters. Sol took a step back, remembering that, and it laughed. "Why not?" it asked, huddling next to a fringe of hoary prairie grass. It gathered itself, became less human again, more like an insect, hard-bodied. "He was tiresome, your papa. We hated him. Oh, how we hated him. Always so damn contrary. But he got old, worn out." It sighed. "He fucked up."

Contrary. That was one word for Aurie. The thing was talking in the plural, though, and that meant there was more than one of them. Sol blinked, filing information for later, not assessing it yet, because that took his attention away from what was right in front of him. "You…knew him for a long time?"

It waved a claw, a hand, a talon. "Too long." It hustled to one side, teeth gleaming, maybe a smile, maybe a threat, and Sol's insides froze. "Too damn long. So I get to move onto the next thing."

*Oh God*, Sol thought. "Leave Baz alone."

"That's what you're here to tell me? 'Leave Baz alone?'" Repeated it like he was doing a bad DeNiro impersonation.

"Yeah, that's what I'm here to tell you."

"Make me." A thrill of laughter. "What a wonder he was hiding, your old man." It shuffled away, laughing still, like something was funny. "Aurie Sarrazin, always trying to work it out, trying to get the best of us, but he never did. Didn't in the end, anyway. But," voice carried away, thin stranglehold on what could only be jealousy. "You shoulda seen him when he was young. What an arrogant asshole. Never knew what she saw in him, but then I never could figure you guys out." You guys. Humans, maybe.

*Don't try to work it out. You don't have time to work it out right now.*

The devil scurried back to Sol, amazingly fast, sleek green eyes shining in the moonlight. "Who knew that Aurie woulda come up with a kid like that? Well, not Aurie, really. Maybe in spite of him, hé? Had me hoodwinked. You have *no idea*." Closer, and Sol backed up so he was between the thin lines of iron and he hoped it was enough protection. "This little light of mine—" it sang, awful coarse retching, untuned catgut stroked by horsehair.

Sol's stomach ached, the ground shook and he felt a rush behind him, like the sudden suck of enormous wings. He was protected, was between iron, and he heard a laugh, but only barely, because of the noise and the grinding and the light from behind.

And he realized, right then, that he was standing on the tracks of the Union Pacific Railway's major east-west corridor, making small talk with something that wanted to kill him. This was exactly how his father had died. Without thinking, he leapt to one side, away from the devil, and an eastbound freight train roared past, all lights and oil and sparks and steel, eight thousand tons of steel and freight going seventy miles per hour, Sol rolling ass over shoulder, bones singing, blood pounding hard in head and chest, the flask breaking inside his coat, jagged glass sliding down his side as he bounced and rolled out of the way.

A train, a goddamn train and he'd been conversing with that thing like an amateur, an idiot. *You don't negotiate.* Car after car rushed past, too fast to read tags, ascertain cargo. Sol came to his hands and knees, breathing hard, head down, a few minutes now, le p'tit diable wouldn't cross, he didn't think, but who the hell knew, really?

To his knees, then his feet, staggered to the side, one foot crossing another, down to one knee again, back up, breath coming in gasps, one hand inside his parka to his side, wet with rum certainly and blood probably, he didn't know. The train kept coming, car and car and car, finally the end, Sol standing straight, ready for it, whatever came next.

The train passed, last car flashing red into the night, and Sol leveled his attention across the tracks, every instinct brought to bear. Beyond the iron rails, before the snowfence, was only emptiness, a hollow lack. The devil was gone and the train swept to the east, away from places Sol called home, to industrial, populated parts. Sol stepped back, but there was no danger here, not anymore. The danger had moved, and he could not say to where.

# TWELVE

## CATCHING OUT

Lutie had fallen asleep in front of the TV. The noise of it was considerable: a mobile-mouthed man was instructing viewers to phone immediately, get two kitchen choppers for the price of one and he'd throw in a free garlic peeler. Act now, he didn't have all night. The sense of urgency wasn't what had wakened her, it was the doorknob rattling. She checked the clock beside the bed where Baz lay sprawled, restlessly sleeping. Past midnight.

Sol came in, met her eyes, and the smell of hard liquor wafted in on the cold behind him like he'd brought half the bar for a party. One hand was bloody, she noticed as he stepped carefully over the saltline and closed the door behind him. He unzipped his parka and the sound of smashed glass accompanied the movement required to toss it on the floor. Alcohol or blood, his shirt was soaked through. Without hurry, Sol crossed the room to the bathroom, flicked on a light, leaving smears of blood on the door jamb and switch. He half-shut the door, and after a moment, she heard water running.

Lutie stood up. She'd been dreaming of something bad, but she couldn't catch the tail end of it now, just fleeting dread. She stood by the doorway, not looking in, staring at Baz sleeping, momentarily striped with acid light escaping from the bathroom. "You okay?" she asked Sol through the crack, even though it was pretty obvious he wasn't.

175

"Yeah," he said in response. "Just a cut." A pause. "You wanna bring me the first aid box? It's by the bed."

The box was heavy, industrial-sized, and he turned as she stood hesitating at the doorway, kit in hand, but only briefly. One hand held a bloodied towel to his side. She tried not to look. It was her brother and it was a half-naked stranger in a motel bathroom a long way from home. Just another weirdness, she supposed, in a day full of it.

"Save it there," and he motioned with his nose to the counter beside the sink. "Can you open it up? See if I got gauze in there and find some antiseptic." The instructions that followed were to the point, accurate but unrushed, no sense of alarm. He'd done this before.

At his request, she looked for shards of glass still embedded in a series of shallow gashes across his ribs, and used sterilized tweezers to pluck them out when she found them. Then, with her help, he cleaned it all out, packed it with gauze, taped it up. Under his clinical eye, it didn't seem so much about compassion and sympathy as straightforward housekeeping. He hardly winced at all, but that might have been the booze helping out, killing whatever pain he was in. "Did he eat?" Sol asked as she crumpled paper wrappings into the garbage.

"A little. He's pretty upset."

Baz had apologized for Sol's behavior, over and over, before ranting about Sol's apparent need to keep everything and everyone at a calculated distance. The anger was short and sharp and Baz hadn't seemed to enjoy it one bit. He'd cut off abruptly, claimed the bed, fallen asleep more or less immediately.

Sol nodded. "Yeah, I guess he would be."

"Your girlfriend called." About four times, though she didn't tell him that either. Three times before Lutie worked up the nerve to answer the phone under the chair, tossed or lost, she didn't know which. Sol's eyelid flickered, and his lips clamped shut. In the stark bathroom light, he was easier to read. Either that, or he wasn't putting up the same kind of front.

"Any message?"

Lutie shook her head. "Just wanted to know if everything was all right. I said yes."

Sol laughed, low, not really amused. "So, you lied." She was standing closest to the kit; he handed her the antiseptic spray to put away.

"Sorry. Maybe I shouldn't have answered, but Baz was asleep and I didn't want the phone to wake him. I didn't tell her who I was." She felt Sol's eyes watching her close the case, snap it shut. "What happened tonight? Where did you go?"

Baz stirred in the next room, a garbled mumble. Sol followed the sound, then he looked at Lutie, lowered his voice. "We'll talk in the morning. You should get some sleep. What time is it?"

She told him, and then he surprised her by saying, "Some birthday, hey?" because she'd actually forgotten. Not the first day of the year anymore, but the next, and it was, indeed, her twentieth birthday. Her brother leaned against the vanity, looked terrible in the green light, bruised torso, now a bandage taped under his left side. Compact, well-made, none of Baz's willowy grace. She didn't see anything familiar, familial, in him, not like with Baz, except maybe in the way he could hold her stare.

"Yeah," she agreed, hand falling to her side.

He paused just enough so she noticed. "I remember… I mean—" and he petered out. She held her tongue, her questions. She waited tables week-ends, had for almost a year, and she could tell when people were drunk, when they were too far gone to hit edit. Not him; he'd had a few, sure, but just enough to loosen up. He was still careful, while other things moved underneath. "I guess I was eight? You were born at home, M'man didn't make it to the hospital. Scared the shit out of me. I thought she was dying."

It happened to be one of the few stories that Maman had told her about life before. That Lutie had come early and fast. Boys, they were lazy, Maman had said, took their time, gave you the opportunity to plan things out.

Sol fiddled with the clasp of the first aid box, though it was already closed. "Dad was there, made me help. First time I'd seen anyone being born. Baz, he sent outside. He wanted to stay." A small smile accompanied that. "God, I'm so sorry, Lutie. This is so messed up."

Understatement of the year, but Lutie wasn't going to argue. "You tried to find that thing, didn't you?"

He lifted the box, winced, switched hands. "In the morning. Get some sleep." He accompanied her to the door, gestured to the bag of salt—did she want it? She shook her head. She'd slept without saltlines across her door for her whole life; she wasn't about to start worrying now. The devil, or whatever it was, wasn't after her anyway.

177

In her own shabby room, she slept for a few hours, awoke mid-morning, cursed the lumpy mattress, and stared at the water-marked ceiling until she could put off going to the bathroom no longer. She showered, but there was no hair dryer, so she dressed quickly, slapped on some makeup. *Happy birthday*, she thought.

Somewhere in the depths of all the things piled on the chair by the door—bag, pajamas, yesterday's clothes, coat—her phone rang. Diving in, she answered it by the third ring, heard a rousing rendition of "Happy Birthday to You", sung badly. Marshall, and Bree, Karen and the Major in the background. One by one they wished her well, until only the Major was left, and Lutie sat down on the bed, near tears at the calm sound of his voice, made for the pulpit, for the confession box.

"Whereabouts are you now?" he asked.

"Ogallala, Nebraska. I decided to drive Baz back to Denver. I might be a little late starting classes, I guess."

A pause, because the Major usually heard it when she was lying, or unsure. He didn't always point it out, though. "That so. How are you doing?" Because that was the important part, of course. To him, anyway.

"I don't know," and that was the truth. "Baz got sick, so we stopped and now Beausoleil's here." It all came out in a rush.

"You don't sound happy about that," the Major commented dryly.

She didn't know how she felt about it. He'd been there when she'd been born, remembered things about her that she'd never known. "He's a hard-ass," she said instead. "Really pissed off that Baz went out and found me. Reckoned I was better off not knowing, I guess." She didn't tell her father about the other part, how Sol had known where she was, known about the Major and Karen and all the rest, and never come knocking. How would the Major feel about *that*, she wondered.

"And how are you doing?" A repeat question. He wasn't going to take 'I don't know' for an answer.

This time, "The usual. You know." He did know, of course, had experienced it first hand and for many years, how she was when her expectations were high and unmet.

"You giving him a hard time?"

She clenched her hand on her lap, hair dripping. "Maybe. About the same as he's giving me."

That brought a chuckle. "Should I be worried about you, birthday girl?"

Her heart ached and she wished she was in that stupid kitchen at CFB Shilo, not down here where the money was all the same color and crazy people spoke with lazy accents about things that doctors told her she should take strong drugs for.

"Hey, hey, hey," the Major cajoled. "I didn't mean to make you cry." He held on for as long as it took.

Finally, Lutie wiped her eyes with the back of her hand, knew she'd just smeared her mascara to shit. "Yeah, I'm good, I'm okay." She sniffed. "It's all just. Weird."

"Birthdays were always hard for you," he said and that surprised her. She remembered cakes and parties and friends with those pointy hats. In photographs. That's what she remembered, the photographs of those things. Not really the other stuff, not like it had actually happened to her.

"They were?"

He chuckled. "Yeah. You'd always get sick, usually some kind of stomach cramps. You never wanted us to make a big deal about your birthday, but then if we didn't, you'd get all mad." He made it sound like she was cute when she was mad, when she knew she was anything but. "I always thought that it was when you thought about your Sarrazin family the most, and wondered if they were thinking of you."

Why was he always so right? A hard guy to be around, sometimes, because of that. "I don't know," she said, equivocating. He didn't have to know how right he was.

He did though. A laugh. "When are you going back to Toronto?"

If she said 'I don't know' one more time, he would get into the car and drive down, so she took a deep breath and tried to sound reasonable. "Soon. A day or two, I promise. I just want to make sure Baz is okay."

"Take it easy," the Major said. "Don't be so hard on yourself. Or on them."

Not all their phone calls ended in her telling him that she loved him, but this one did.

It wasn't that he was weak-willed, he was just tired. Staying mad took too much effort and that had always been a problem for Baz; he couldn't hold a grudge to save his life. He stirred as Sol came in the door, cold blast of winter cutting through the room, shaft of precise prairie sunshine slashing the bed like a laser beam. Baz groaned, pulled a pillow over his head. Sol didn't tell him to get up, he didn't have to. Instead, he moved around the room like the Tasmanian Devil, opening drawers, sorting through God-knew-what on the table, emptying broken glass into the metal garbage can. Shit, he could even make the reading of a newspaper sound like a full orchestra tuning up. Reluctantly, Baz came up on his elbows, watched his brother study the city section of some paper he'd retrieved from a bus shelter or restaurant. Sol never paid for anything he didn't have to, a vestige of their upbringing.

No anger, no matter how hard Baz tried.

Sol was all about keeping things close, and it wasn't surprising at all, now Baz thought about it, that he'd done what he had. Was it really fair to be pissed at Sol for just being himself? *He should have told me, even if it was the wrong thing to do*. It was true, that thought, and it didn't matter.

This morning, Baz felt more himself, less shaky and hot. After Baz had dressed, Sol insisted on taking his temperature, being all doctorly and Baz let him, knowing it was Sol's way of apologizing.

"So," Baz said as Sol flashed a light in his eyes, "am I okay?"

Sol's mouth twitched an almost smile, making things worth it. "Honest answer?" A practiced basilisk stare beyond the light beaming in his eye. Inherently funny, because Baz had received the look a million times and it never did anything but make him want to bug Sol more.

Baz giggled, dipped his head away from his brother's penlight. Sighing, Sol tossed it into the medical box. Baz wanted to say something, to let him know what he'd done, but Sol already knew. *More important to me to say it than for him to hear it*. But nothing came out, and Sol moved off to the desk under the window, picked up the book of songs, flipped it open with one hand.

Then Baz's phone rang, still that bayou jangle, and Sol looked up from the book, same level stare that would give a WWF wrestler pause, but not Baz. Sol's mouth twitched again, trying not to laugh, and Baz realized that he wasn't going to change that ringtone, not for a long time. Sol turned the chair around so he could sit in it while balancing the book on his bent knee. "It's her birthday," he said before Baz had a chance to answer.

"I know that," Baz lied. God, the stuff that rolled around in Sol's head, only to pop out like one of those nickel gumball dispensers. "Might not be her. Might be a gig. I'm in demand, you know."

"It's her," he thought he heard Sol say, but he was already answering and he knew it was her as well.

She said she'd come over in a minute and Baz used the time to tune up his father's fiddle. It was a beauty, beat up and mellow, the bridge slightly flattened so that double stops were easier. Baz experimented with a few notes, and Sol's eyebrows twitched. Strange, but Baz had never been able to figure out whether or not Sol even liked music, let alone music that would remind him of the swamps. Sol certainly gave no evidence of inheriting their father's musical talent. *He inherited other things*, Baz thought, but sadly, because who the hell wanted to be a ghost buster when you could be a musician?

"Okay," Baz said. "What'll it be?" And experimented with "Happy Birthday to You".

Sol flinched. "God, please, no. That'd mean we'd have to sing." He got up from the chair, the book still in his hand. "You know any of these?" he asked.

"Nah, I looked through them. They're all Acadian, or straight from France, maybe. Not anything Dad would have played."

"Yeah, but the notes are all in his handwriting," Sol mused, scowling at the book.

"Did you phone Robbie?" Baz asked and Sol didn't answer, but there was a knock at the door, and Lutie was there, effectively changing the conversation.

Lutie, after accepting Baz's birthday greetings, immediately turned to Sol and said, "How's your side?" gesturing with one hand and Sol held her stare a long time before shrugging.

"It's okay."

"Did you change the bandage? Has the bleeding stopped?"

Sol got up, eyes glancing sideways at Baz first. He offered Lutie the chair and wandered to the bed, sitting as far away from the both of them as he could. "I'm fine." The garbage had been taken out, Baz realized with a jolt, incriminating bloody evidence gone, something that his brother had done before Baz had wakened instead of taking a shower.

"So, what'd you do last night?" Another fight wouldn't have surprised him.

Sol leaned against the wall, legs stretched out, a hole in one dirty sock, right on the ball of his foot, like he'd been spending his time grinding out things against rough pavement: cigarettes, bugs. He hadn't come to Ogallala with a change of clothes, had probably expected to scoop Baz's sorry ass, haul him back to Denver, and let Robbie nurse him back to health. He'd only come because Baz had called.

"Yeah," Lutie said. "You said that we'd talk in the morning. Well," she paused, dry low voice betraying no humor. "It's morning."

Sol stared at her, head cocked to the side. He looked both tired and amused.

*She's better with him than I am,* Baz thought, a little wondrous, a little sad. Maybe even a little jealous.

"I wanted to see if I could find that thing last night. It's a devil, for sure." One hand held to his side, tucked under an elbow, protecting a hurt, avoiding Baz's open stare of surprise. New. This was new, this was Sol sharing and Baz had the distinct feeling he wasn't going to like it one bit.

"A devil?" Baz asked, like Sol had just explained that he'd gone down to the tracks looking for the Easter Bunny.

The shrug. "Un petit diable. C'mon. You remember Dad and his buddies. You remember them talking about this shit."

The fiddle was still in Baz's hands, and he remembered it in his father's hands, circle of porchlight, summer on the prairies, smoke and rum and laughter. Devil in the kitchen and in the woodpile, songs of crossroads. Music, not reality. "Not a ghost?" He heard the uncertainty in his own voice. "It's like a ghost, right?" He stared at Lutie, who shrugged.

"I saw it down at the tracks, when you were singing. It was talking to you."

Sol cleared his throat and Baz had the sudden swooping sensation of ambush, that these two were working together. "Whaddit say, cher?"

Baz kept his fingers on the strings, plucked out softly, adjusted the tuning a little. He'd thought Lutie was on his side. "It knows my name," he said, after a long moment. "And it's been coming around. Not just then, at the tracks."

"Since when?" His brother's voice was uncommonly gentle, and somehow that scared Baz worse than anger or accusation. "How long's this thing been hanging round?"

Baz looked up at Lutie, smiled a little, but it came out wrong. It had been hanging around a long time, he knew, longer than he was willing to admit, to them or to himself.

Back to his tuning, which was easier, finding the pitch. "How do you think I found you, T-Lu? I made a deal," and his fingers stilled, understanding. "I made a deal." Softer, this time looking at Sol.

"What kind of deal?" Sol's voice was strained, despite obvious efforts otherwise.

Baz took a breath, and it came out in a rush. "It gave me Lutie's address. It said we'd settle up later." Like a draft choice traded; could be nothing. Could be everything. "It knows my name, knows Dad's name…"

Sol interrupted. "It knows names, it takes things from you. That's what it does. But it can't touch you, Baz. It can make you be in the wrong place at the wrong time," and he smiled, winced at the same time. "But it can't lay a hand on you. Doesn't mean it's not dangerous. But don't give it more credit than it's owed."

They shared a long stare and then Baz nodded. "It says that it don't really care about the singing, that it cares more about the company the singing brings." Then he looked at Lutie. "I think that thing's after you, Lutie, and I brought you right to it."

Sol shook his head. "It didn't say that last night. It's not after Lutie. It was pretty obvious it was after you, Basile." He sat up, but slowly, like an old man, tenuous, as though he didn't trust his body to do what he asked of it. "Luetta," he said as he swung his legs over the side of the bed.

Lutie's chin came up. "No," she said.

"Luetta," he repeated, coming to a stand. "Please. Take Baz to my place in Denver. Then get the hell away from us. This is dangerous."

"No," Baz echoed, and Sol didn't seem remotely concerned that both of them were not backing down. "I'm not going anywhere, not until we get rid of this thing." Rattling in the shower, the ability it had, just to appear. Baz didn't want to be more than a dozen yards from Sol. "You think I want it showing up in Denver? Hell no."

"It's not going to be showing up anywhere," Sol assured him, and Baz remembered this voice from his whole life, Sol taking care of things. It was so easy, it would be so easy to believe him, except—

"No." Not a question, not a refusal. Just Lutie, being firm. "I mean, yeah, I'll drive Baz wherever he wants to go, but not before we figure this out." She seemed on the verge of saying something else, but shut her mouth, pulled weird dimples to either side of her mouth as she frowned.

Sol shook his head like she was six and arguing bedtime. "I can handle this. Baz," and he looked at him, at the fiddle on his lap, "this thing's after you. I don't think it wants you dead," and that hung strangely, and Baz knew that the devil sure as hell wanted Sol dead, and that a devil's murderous intentions didn't scare his brother, "but that don't mean it wants you happy."

"So, what are you going to do?" Lutie asked.

It took him by surprise, that question. Baz could see it. Maybe their father had asked him these kind of questions, but Aurie had been out of Sol's life for a long time. "Dad was hunting a ghost when le diable killed him. These two, they're connected. There's a drifter living on the tracks near Brule I gotta talk with. He might know more about the ghost. Railroad bull named Jack Lewis. I know what to do with a ghost. So I start there, push the same buttons Dad pushed." He opened his hands wide. "I piss off le diable, it shows up. I deal with it." He stared at Baz, and Baz felt the hit before Sol delivered it. "I don't *make* a deal with it."

"Have you done this before?" Baz demanded. Sol sounded like he knew what he was talking about, but experience told Baz that wasn't always the case. Sol was good at faking things—excuses to teachers, lies to probation officers, dodging social workers.

But Sol had said as much as he was going to on the subject of devils, apparently. He rooted around by the desk and found his phone, opened it, and had a conversation that was all about work, and trading shifts. Behind where Sol was conducting his business, Lutie stared at Baz, who stared back.

It was pointless to argue, but she looked like she was ready for the next bell, so Baz shook his head. She scowled and Baz thought that maybe this was the best birthday present they could give her, getting her out of this.

So they packed. Nothing for it. Lutie returned to her room, and Baz could hear her through the thin walls, banging things, around, outside to the car, trunk slamming.

"Hey," Baz asked, his duffle bag on the bed, the box they'd retrieved from Aurie's room still on the desk: it was for Sol, after all. Baz wondered if his brother had seen the photograph of their parents, but he wasn't going to bring it up, not now. "What should I tell Robbie?"

Sol opened the door; he had on his parka already, which smelled like a Havana distillery, lit a cigarette and leaned against the worn aluminum siding in the brazen light of noon. They'd let Lutie's room go, but Sol had taken theirs for another night.

Their eyes met. As usual, Baz had no idea what Sol was thinking. "I'm just looking into Dad's death." It would be worth Baz's life to open it up more than that.

"C'mon," Lutie said as she brushed past. "Daylight's wasting." But she turned and looked at Sol, same steady stare.

"Take care, Lutie," Sol said to her. He licked his lips, unsure for once. "Don't be a stranger, now you know where we are."

"You too," Lutie replied, hesitated, then got into the car. Baz stood for a moment longer, but Sol didn't say anything else.

"I'll see you when?"

"J'sais pas, gars. A day? One week? Whatever it takes. I work the case." Eyes up. "I work the case. This thing thinks it has a deal. It has no deal. This can't drag on. The trou d'cul knew Papa for a long, long time before it killed him. It don't get to do that with us. Not with us."

And Sol meant all three of them, of that Baz was sure.

Sol drove a few miles west, past the tiny outpost of Brule itself, saw that the open sign on the Coffee Caboose Museum was on, thought about stopping by, but knew that was a distraction. He wasn't really hunting a ghost and Bart wasn't going to be able to tell him anything he didn't already know. Lewis had died at the Megeath crossing, burned alive in his own house. What Bart didn't know was that Lewis's ghost was coming in this direction, would get stronger the closer it came. Might be made stronger by the presence of a devil, for all Sol knew, and that was the only thing he cared about, that the devil seemed to be wherever the ghost was.

He didn't know where the Megeath crossing was; not much seemed to be between Brule and Big Springs. Some abandoned homestead, a dirt road. He'd have to check all of them. He parked by a rise in the road just west of Brule, slowly made his way down to the tracks. He bent down, bare hand to the ground. He tried to call the devil just like he had last night, used his memories of Baz singing as a lure. Nothing came. *Maybe these assholes don't like coming out in the daytime.*

Somehow, Sol didn't think that would matter.

He hadn't been drinking, maybe that was it, he wasn't loose enough to be seeing devils. He didn't see any ghosts, either. All he accomplished was to freeze the crap out of his hand. It would just come when it wanted, Sol presumed, was operating on its own perverse timetable.

The westbound from Lincoln slowed coming through Brule, and Sol checked over his shoulder as it approached; it hadn't picked up a whole lot of speed yet, and it fished something out of him like a worm on a hook. He stared up-rail, feet on the gravel, stopped walking, watching the train come, one moment of indecision, almost instantly shifting down, abandoning the leap of his heart. It would be so easy to catch out, to haul himself up on that train as it slowed coming round the corner, get the hell out of this town, leave it all behind.

Instead, the train blasted by him, and he had only a brief spasm of regret, watching it go. He had work here, and Baz was in danger and his father had told him not to negotiate with the damn things. If he knew how to kill it, he would. But last night, he'd been *talking* with it, and no good would come of that—it would just run circles around him, or trick him into a senseless death. He had to find another way.

His shadow fell short as he strolled in the track's ditch, sun high and bright and cold in the endless blue sky, the prairie silence only interrupted by the sound of the wind through grass. Sol hunched into his collar, cold now, gloveless, mais, he had not thought this through, had left his gloves in the Wagoneer, parked some distance away. He kept walking for something to do. To keep warm. Collect his thoughts.

The bank beside the tracks rose, and Sol could see the Brule watertower in the distance, saw that there was an access road a few hundred yards to the east. Immediately before that, though, he spotted a huddle of garbage, pallets and boards piled up in a loose interpretation of walls, an old blue tarp frayed and ragged, held down with coarse yellow rope. He could see a thin trail of smoke now; he'd thought it only a dump, someone's bright idea to avoid removal fees, but now he could see that it was a dwelling, a small fire spluttering in a makeshift ring of stones to one side.

Sol paused, took two steps towards the hovel.

"Man, what's the matter with you? Lost your balls? Can't catch out anymore?" The mocking voice surprised him, because it was close. Sol stopped, peered into the darkness of the tent flap. It didn't sound like the voice from last night, but who the hell knew what these things were capable of? He was level with the scrap heap, the embankment a shadow overhead.

The darkness of the shelter was impenetrable. Sol took a step towards it. Slowly, details emerged from the pit beyond a fall of tattered blue tarp covering the hut's entrance: a soft fold of worn army surplus jacket, a cap pulled low. A light-colored beard, hands gnarled around a bottle. The man came halfway out, stared at Sol.

Not a devil, but that was okay. More than okay, because Sol didn't know what to do with a devil, not really. In fact, it felt like this ought to happen, that this was the reason he'd come down here in the first place. Not for a devil, but for this. *You're not ready for a devil, gars.*

"It's been a while," he explained. "And I'm getting a little old for it."

The man pulled over a plastic tub that had once held mayonnaise and sat on it, eyes never leaving Sol, bright and light beneath seams of scarred skin and grime. "You're either old enough to do it, or dead."

Sol held the stare. "You're DJ. Claude told me to come lookin'."

DJ's eyes narrowed, then he gestured with the bottle to a crate. "Have a seat if you want."

Sol took the bottle when it was passed to him. It was rum, or something like it, and it burned going down, hit his stomach with a pleasant bang. He made a face though, because DJ laughed, brittle and hard and so like a crow Sol grinned back.

"Then I still must be the right age," Sol sighed, feeling his side with his fingers. "'Cause I don't think I'm dead yet."

The grin didn't leave the man's face. "Don't leave it too long. Man can get stuck in one place." The bottle came back again, and Sol drank with ease this time.

DJ wasn't much older than Sol, turned out. He'd be here for the winter, goddamn Nebraska, because his dog was sick and it was probably going to die and it couldn't take much more travel. The others had left, had gone to where the wind was mild and the skies sunny, but DJ was okay, was doing okay.

Although the rum-alcohol was warming Sol's stomach, he stretched his legs out toward the fire, trying to get what little heat he could. He heard a whimper from the hut, and DJ turned his head sharply. "You be quiet there, love."

DJ was from out east, he said, from Maine of all places, but that had been a long time ago. He'd lost what French he'd had, and Sol commiserated without sharing beyond having a Cajun father.

"This stretch okay?" Sol asked, exchanging a smoke for another slug of booze.

DJ checked on his dog, shuffled back to the fire. His face was superbly creased, like a sculpture in wet slab clay. It bore the signs of every day lived like this. So too did his eyes, which never rested, which traveled over Sol's face like it was a map to somewhere interesting. "Nah, it's garbage. Shitty to be stuck here, but what can you do?" And he shrugged, looking back at the dog, a small black speck huddling in the shadows. "Weird stretch of track. Bad. Bad stuff here."

*No kidding,* Sol thought. "What bad stuff?"

DJ's mouth twisted. "You should talk to the suits. Suits think they know the story. Fuckin' bulls. Deserve what they get." Bright eyes that missed little. Crazy or not, DJ was observant. "You don't look like a suit."

Sol smiled. "That's what Claude said."

DJ chuckled. "How's that old bastard doin' anyways? Haven't seen him for awhile. He got spooked a while back, don't come up this way no more."

Sol told DJ what he knew of the old-timer, which was apparently the same as ever. "Claude don't look like he spooks easy," Sol finished, returning the conversation to where he wanted it, practiced at talking with ramblers and drunks and the unhinged. "But he's no liar, either."

DJ took a long swig of the bottle. His pants were tied up with a length of rope, and his heavy boots were laceless, two or three pairs of socks peeled down from pants too short. He ignored Sol so hard it was the same as staring at him.

Sol shifted on his crate. "What scares someone like Claude?" That was a direct question, which were the worst kind with guys like DJ, who never liked the feel of an interrogation, of being penned in. And asking questions of crazy drifters sometimes took you in circles, and sometimes it gave you all the truth you needed. Often, both.

DJ looked away, removed his soft-brimmed cap and scrubbed a hand over his matted hair. "Shit."

Sol gave him room.

"Shit," DJ repeated. "You see ashes flying, you see that coming, the blackness, you run. Inside it," and he took another slug from his bottle. Sol looked at the fire, waited for him to continue. "Inside it, that's some nasty shit. Crazy stuff." He coughed. "You run, man, you see something like that."

After a minute or two, Sol asked, "Only on this stretch of track?"

"Why you need to know so bad?" DJ fiddled with his rolling papers like he couldn't decide if he wanted another cigarette.

Another train whistle came on the incisive wind, and the question hung there right along with it. DJ decided another smoke was the thing to do, and Sol realized that the drifter was giving Sol time now. *Gotta love the nutcases, crazy like foxes. He probably sees ghosts, same as me, but no one's telling him it's normal.* Sol stared out across the prairie and touched his side with one hand, not pressing hard, small comfort to the hurt he'd taken the night before. Finally he said, "It's what I do, cher. Chase down the crazy shit." He shook his head, almost in disbelief. "Took over my dad's business."

"That's some shitty business your old man left you." DJ considered him, lit the smoke with an ember.

Sol took a long breath, released it, watched his breath cloud the air, then dissipate. "This ash cloud. Did it start up in the fall?" He wasn't really guessing. He knew.

DJ spat, wiped his teeth with one grubby finger. "Yeah, maybe. Voices in the middle, batshit nuts. Something burning, flying around in the air like—" but he didn't know what it was like. "Laugh like it wants you dead. Scared Claude down the line. Scared off some others. I got the damn dog." His breath rattled a little, phlegm a permanent resident in his lungs. "But it kicks up sometimes. Don't matter time of day, place. Nothing to say it's comin', or who it's coming for." His eyes were darting everywhere, he was getting agitated. If he'd been a patient, Sol would have changed the subject. "Regular folks don't seem to notice it. But us, down here?" He stared at Sol, eyes a hard and broken blue. This was what happened when you were born with talent and had neither instruction nor meds. "You shoulda taken that train clear out of this place."

He stood, threw the dead soldier way over the track and it caught the sunlight. "I'd be out of here myself, weren't for the dog." DJ hawked, spat on the ground. "Goddamn pets." He didn't sound like he meant it. Sol knew exactly how he felt.

"What do you know about Lewis? The bull that got killed?"

DJ's face screwed up. "How old do you think I am? Shit," shaking his head. Then, "Yeah, Claude told me. Some guys had had enough, he was the meanest bull in Bailey Yard. They killed him just up this track a bit," he waved his hand to the west, "in Megeath. Not much left, there. Burned him alive in his own place, Claude said. Probably deserved it."

Sol got up and thanked DJ for the liquor and the talk. DJ told him to come back anytime.

"Except you won't be here," Sol smiled. "You'll be in California."

"That's right, man, I'll be gone. You should be outta here too, if you know what's good for you." DJ stretched. "I'm in need of some coffee." He stared at Sol, and Sol grinned back, reaching into his pocket and pulling out some bills.

"It's a cold enough day for it."

"You're going to check out the Megeath crossing, aren't you? You really don't know what's good for you."

Sol stared up track, to the west, away from DJ's camp, away from Brule. He supposed he was, and turned to tell DJ as much, but the drifter was already walking purposefully down the tracks away from him, and so Sol sighed, started up the track in the opposite direction toward his vehicle.

The Megeath crossing wasn't on any map, but it couldn't be very far. There would be a burnt-out house, its foundations at the very least, maybe some other signs of habitation. It wouldn't be the sort of place anyone would clean up, not in this part of the country. Rain and snow and wind would do the slow demolition; thirty years was nothing to Mother Nature.

He wondered how far Baz and Lutie had gotten by now. Wondered what story Baz would feed Robbie once they got to Denver, and couldn't even entertain the thought of them standing in his kitchen, dog barking its head off, talking about him when he wasn't there.

Finally, he stopped, tired, side aching. The Wagoneer was some distance away. He had no idea where the Megeath crossing was. Walking around pointlessly was a fool's game, especially when it was this cold. And that was the moment that he saw the clouds roiling in the sky, between himself and the village of Brule, down by the tracks, too close to the ground to be cloud, too horizontal to be a tornado, a moving entity, muddy unnatural gray. One moment only, then he was running for the rise, still in the distance, where he'd parked the Wagoneer. The cloud blossomed across the horizon like blood in water, and it wasn't a cloud at all.

It was something worse.

# CHAPTER 13

## HOW FAR THEY GOT

Baz knew right away, right from when they pulled out onto the old highway west instead of heading for the interstate, that Lutie wasn't going to be ordered out of town. If Sol had been thinking straight, he'd have known it too because it didn't take a goddamn genius.

They continued along the two-lane highway for a few miles before Baz spotted a watertower that said 'Brule' and Baz didn't know if that was a company or a place. In French, he knew it meant 'burnt', and that didn't sound inviting no matter which way you looked at it.

A highway sign told them the speed limit was changing, and she slowed. "Sol said he'd hit a dead end with the Brule historical society," she finally explained.

*Bingo,* Baz thought. *Reason enough, T-Lu. Go right ahead and see if you can beat Sol at his own game.* "So, what are we here for?"

She dropped below the speed limit on the empty road, her narrowed eyes sweeping to the left of the cracked asphalt, pulled in suddenly to a set of tall silos, seeing something that Baz hadn't: a parked railcar decorated with a collection of signs. The Coffee Caboose Museum & Platte River Historical Society. She swung the car to the left and tucked in behind a large truck. She didn't answer him, it was almost as though he hadn't spoken, and that felt familiar as a paper cut.

He watched her mount the steps to the caboose as he got out the car, rubbed his chin, knew he should have shaved, but had drawn the line after Sol had commandeered his razor yesterday. He knew what he looked like, with his silly haircut and provocations of piercings. *Maybe I should stay out here*, but it would be warm inside. More than that, he wanted to see what she'd do, how his sister did things differently from his brother. He caught the door before it slammed, ducked in out of the bright day. An older guy with a newspaper sat at the counter, turned as they came in.

"If you're looking for something hot to drink, your waiter Bart's trying his hand with the sump pump out back. Froze up, the boy said. Tricky pump, he said." The old-timer's mouth twitched, amused. "Sump pumps. They're some tricky." He lifted his coffee cup. "I got the last of it, sorry."

Lutie hesitated, but didn't look to Baz for any guidance. Instead she turned and they went back outside and around the corner of the caboose, headed towards the track. A tall young man was fiddling with the door of the pump house, and he looked up as they approached, pushed back the brim of his green and white ball cap. It advertised a feed company in Paxton.

"Hey," Lutie said, hands in her pockets, smiling broad enough to draw dimples. "You're working hard."

The young man grinned, face pink, speckled with small blemishes.

"You must be Bart," she continued, and Baz knew what was coming. She was twenty years old, and blonde, and new to town. "The guy inside said."

"I am. You must be looking for coffee." He gestured to the pump house. "It's seized up, old piece of junk. Might be awhile before I can make another pot."

"Sump pumps. They're some tricky," Baz said, and Bart gave him a sharp stare.

Lutie stepped in front and away from Baz. "That's okay. We're not really here for coffee anyway. I'm actually a history major. From Canada? I always stop by any museum I see." She smiled wide. "My name's Lutie. This is my brother Baz Sarrazin."

"History? That's my major, too. In Lincoln." He removed his work gloves and stuck them in his belt, smiling at her the whole time. "Bart

Andersen." He cocked his head, glanced at Baz. "You any relation to that writer who was by last week, asking about the fire? He was a Sarrazin too."

Lutie answered, a quick nod. "Yeah. Sol said we should stop by."

"So what did he tell you?" Bart asked, half smile still playing at the corner of his lips. Hard to tell if he was suspicious or not.

*Okay.* Baz shrugged. "Not much," and that was the truth.

Lutie cleared her throat. "He said there'd been a murder down here, a railroad bull named Lewis, a long time ago."

Bart's gaze flicked away before returning to Lutie. She blushed a little. A fetching little creature, playing it, playing this boy like a violin.

"History, eh? Well, you look pretty much at home here."

Bart laughed. "It's the hat, right? Yeah, I'm from here." He shook his head. "But that don't mean I'm sticking around."

Lutie glanced at Baz, trying to include him maybe. He raised his eyebrows a little, but didn't say anything.

Bart leaned back against the pump house, hands reddened from the work and the cold. "Reporters aren't usually all that interested in the kind of history that comes from this part of the country. Your brother was more interested in the murder, for sure, but it happened before I was born. So, after he was here asking about it, I made a few phone calls. No one really wanted to talk about the fire. Most of the old guys I asked said the drifters that came through here were okay. The fire, they were just trying to scare Lewis."

"What else did they say?" Lutie asked.

Bart laughed, stretched his hands out. "One guy's story was different from his buddy's and the buddy's story was different from the next guy's." He grinned, ducked his head, back up to Lutie's pretty face. "Plurality of oral narrative." Now he was just trying to impress her, Baz thought, wondering on what planet this would be considered impressive. Bart flicked a glance at Baz, eyes narrowed. "What do you study?"

Baz smiled wide. "Music."

Shaking his head, Bart looked away. "Well, in history, you know that the truth is never, ever, out there." He straightened, gestured to the ground beneath his feet, then back up to Lutie. "The story is there, in the ground, waiting to be dug up. And here, waiting to be told." Pointed to his own chest, then looked away, embarrassed maybe.

They were performing some kind of mating dance and Baz didn't recognize the steps. But Lutie did, evidently. She shifted her weight so that she faced him fully, one hand in her pocket, the other playing with a strand of blonde hair. "Material culture and oral history? You *must* be a grad student."

Bart shrugged, but didn't look at Lutie anymore, pink all over. Christ, it must be boring here if these were pick-up lines. "I like a good story. And that fire is a good story, turns out. Your brother was right."

Bart paused, gathering his words, but finally just kicked a hard divot of displaced sod, at a loss. Thirty years was a long time to pass around the truth, hand-me-down information worn and creased and missing bits, even Baz knew that. It was the same with music, it changed each time it was passed along, that was the nature of the thing.

"What did they say, the seniors you talked with?"

*Trying to bring down the big game Sol couldn't,* Baz realized, even as he admired her style.

Bart looked away again. He sighed. "As far as I can tell, the fire was started by a group of homeless guys that had been harassed by Lewis over the years. Lewis sounds like he was a mean bastard. The hobos probably meant to just warn him, maybe give him a taste of his own medicine, but it got out of hand. The cops tried to find them, of course, especially as Lewis was police just like them, but the murderers must have all shipped out right away. Came down hard on all those drifters that were still around, but no one I talked to thought that the cops caught any of the guys that actually did it."

"So, has there been anything since? At the murder site? Did Lewis have a widow, or does anyone, I don't know, lay flowers or anything?"

Bart shook his head. "Nah, he lived alone in a trailer, apparently, across from the old fairgrounds. Right down by the river. Died in springtime, so the river would have been running high. This whole place changes," and he ran his hand across the field, flat like he was tamping down what might grow and swell. "Can you imagine that, staring out your window at water when you burned alive in your own tin can? One of the old timers said that the police hauled the trailer away, afterwards. Nothing left out at Megeath now, nothing but a broken down barn. Rickety old thing, two more winters and it'll be gone." He seemed suddenly self-conscious,

saying all this, but he then grinned at her. "Me too." He glanced at the caboose and maybe he had to say it because he wouldn't believe it otherwise.
"I'm starting doctoral studies out in California," like that was a come-on
and maybe it was, but not in Baz's world.

Lutie changed her pose again, seemed at once both older and younger.
"Yeah, I have to get back to school too. Promised my dad." Baz knew she'd
wring every last bit of information out of this kid, and it was definitely
more than Sol had been able to get.

A few minutes later, they stood on either side of her Toyota and Lutie flattened the piece of paper Bart had given her across its cold top. The paper
was worn, folded, perhaps worried, fetched from the depths of Bart's pocket,
blue ballpoint pen, series of numbers just needing dots for her to connect
so she could see the full picture, numbers leading her to Bart's cell phone if
she wanted it. Wanted him. She already saw the picture made whole. She'd
said she hadn't had a pen, but a good student always had one, even when he
was fixing a sump pump. Sure, he might have had a pen, but he didn't have
a clue. She sighed, balled the note, but couldn't throw it away. She put it in
her pocket, took some bit of him with her, out of this place.

Baz leaned his elbows on the roof of her car, staring at her. His eyes gave
him away, even as he said, "What was *that* about?"

His eyes were the same shade as the seas around some tropical island
with shallow waters. Lutie's fingers drummed the roof as she watched him
wind up for some jabs. "Bad student habit. Just doing the research. Who
knows, might come in useful."

"You gonna call him?" Baz asked, couldn't seem to keep a smile from
his face.

"What?" Baz was laughing at her, not with her. "That guy? Not my type.
Besides, he won't be here next week and neither will I."

Which made Baz grin harder, his bright eyes almost disappearing,
scruffy and wind-battered, like a dog-mauled chew toy. Waiting for her
to get whatever joke he was making. She felt the gotcha before she understood it, as was often the case.

*Right.* She shrugged like it didn't matter, like her foster family hadn't
learned early that she wasn't the kind of girl you teased. "Oh. Fine. You

don't mean Bart." She had no snappy come-back, only the matter at hand. "You really think Sol's going to pick up if I call him?"

That laugh again, starting high and dropping, climbing. Sheer delight. "Chère, I don't think he knows where the 'on' button is with his phone." His eyes weren't on her, though, they were following something on the horizon behind her. She almost turned, but his attention snapped back to her, intent and resigned. "We're going back to Ogallala us, hé?"

The wind, and his laugh. A devil, and ghosts. It was all so weird. "Yeah, we're going back. Sol should know about the Megeath crossing. Might be some help."

Baz was staring off behind her again, and so Lutie turned to look.

She swallowed, following his long stare. They called this weather a chinook, she remembered from when they'd lived in Calgary, the warm wind off the mountains. It blew steadily, mixing with the colder morning air. To the west, near the tracks across several fields, the sky was green, the color someone went before they threw up. Lower to the ground, the cloud front was black. Lutie stared at it, then back at Baz. "A storm, maybe? It's nowhere near us." She opened the door. "Get in."

The bank of clouds was moving to the south, the edge dark like eggs left too long on the griddle. She eased into the car. Mild still, but it would still be snow, not rain, if it fell now. The clouds moved strangely, were too low to the ground, near the river to the west. Their motion was slow-quick-quick-slow, elegant as ballroom dancers crossing the boards, but unnatural in weather.

Unnatural.

"Though, gotta say, T-Lu, I think Bart *liked* you." Baz was going to laugh then, Lutie could hear it burbling up, so she accelerated out the lot, skidding wide and she sawed the steering wheel to the right, chirped rubber off tires, and floored it. Like one of those G-force tests that astronauts endured, the acceleration slammed Baz back into the carseat and the Toyota shot down the side road.

She looked out across the flat prairie grass, past fence posts flying by in a gray blur, was staring down the storm front.

"What the hell, Lutie?" Baz demanded, one hand grabbing the door handle.

The car picked up speed, going west, following the storm. She had no plan, only a burn to get to the root of this, because there were ghosts, and she knew about ghosts. She knew what was unnatural.

The bulk of the cloud scudded close to the ground, brushed up against prairie some distance away, closer to the river. She pulled down a side road, veered right into the haze and had to stop immediately. She couldn't see five feet in front of the car. She might drive right onto the tracks, over them, into the river for all she could see. Specks of dirt collided with the windshield.

Stones pinged against the car, hard, a brief tattoo, and then something else entered the conversation: Laughter. It came from outside the car, was so low it was almost one with the wind. It had that big encompassing sound that some ghosts had when they were up, when they had the run of a place, when they weren't scared of anything.

"Stay here," she shouted to Baz.

Lutie wrenched up the door handle. She'd only heard the one boom of laughter, cold like the wind, dark and deep, but nothing more. On the other side of the car, Baz was getting out, had either not heard her, or had decided that he was going to ignore her. He ducked low, only a gray moving shadow against pitiful light. Lutie slid on a moment of breathless panic that Baz was going to become lost in this dusty day-for-night, that he'd fade out of sight and wouldn't come back. That she'd lose him.

Thinking that, she lurched forward, came around the front of the Toyota, hand stretched out to Baz's shoulder, but the wind suddenly shifted and a howl of ash curled up, suffocating her. Eyes streaming, she tried to lift her head, tried to find her feet. She couldn't see anything now, all a watery gray tinged with black flecks.

She heard laughter again, farther away and the wind receded. Now the air smelled sweet like a candy factory was in nearby operation. Could be the scent of corn mash, what they fed the cattle, but Lutie knew it wasn't that. It was the scent of flesh in decay, and every hair on the back of her neck stood up.

The shifting cloud hung in the sky in a wide curtain, reducing the sun to a dull lamp in the heavens. Wordlessly, Lutie stood, drawing Baz with her. Though she could not see it, she sensed that the prairie was still there beyond the ash, as endless and timeless as always, gray and bereft, underfoot, and the wind—the wind that never stopped—blew from the north, had traveled thousands of miles without encountering anything more significant than a jackrabbit. They were inside it now, whatever this ash cloud was.

Her brother walked a few feet, eyes squinting, trying to see beyond the ash. "Baz," Lutie called, afraid.

Baz grimaced, halted, hands wide: What?

"Don't sing," she advised, the only thing she could think to say. It was better than what was really on her mind, which was *I'm scared*. She gestured Baz back and Baz came. "And stay close," she warned.

With those words, the smile left his excitable face.

"What the hell is this?" He turned in place. *He can see it*, she thought. *He can see the ash. Does that make it more or less real?* This wasn't a place designed to support human life. Sounds were sharp, the air so dry it was tinder, ignitable, like gas was in the air.

He coughed, the ash getting to both of them. He bent over, hacking, then straightened. "Hey, Lutie," he called. Lutie sidled close to Baz's shoulder, could feel the warmth from him in this cold place, the two of them the only colors in a bleak landscape. Baz cocked his head to one side, eyes set at a hundred miles. *Shhh*, he mimed. *Listen*.

Something was coming.

Sol had seen more than his fair share of strange things in his life, but this took the cake.

He hadn't made it as far as the Wagoneer, had been between the tracks and his vehicle when the cloud had come to him, had rolled over him as a wave might, fast and unavoidable. Now, he could see nothing but filtered gray light and dirt and drifting ash. A screaming wind robbed breath from lungs, robbed the will to keep breathing.

Then, from far away, a crash, and the wind calmed and the ash swirled to mere drift. The sudden cessation of wind-noise was followed by a murmur of voices and Sol froze, had no weapon, nothing with which to protect himself. Unprepared in the extreme.

Just then a barking cough echoed through the haze, words on the wind, a snatched conversation. He recognized the voice and held very still. *Bon Dieu, non*, he thought, fought down surprise only to find anger. *Not here, what are they doing here?* But denial had never done him much good, so he took a deep breath and moved. Two steps, three and then he was out of the ash and into the cloud's hollow center. He saw them before they noticed him, which suited Sol just fine.

"You're coughing to wake the dead, Baz," he said.

Sol concentrated on his sister, leveled a stare at her, because he was certain coming out here, going to Brule instead of Denver, hadn't been Baz's idea. "Did you get lost?" he asked her, and knew she didn't take teasing well, took pride in being right, reacted badly to surprises, couldn't muster an apology to save her life. He knew all that, had known all that from the word go. In some ways she hadn't changed from when she was little.

"We're not lost," she said, chin coming up.

"Okay," Sol agreed slowly, not smiling, fighting a smile. It wouldn't have been a pretty one. "So, where are we, then?" Softly, recognizing his own need to be right.

"Guys?" Baz lifted his hand to touch Lutie's shoulder, and Sol didn't know if he was keeping close for Lutie's sake or his own. His one word was a warning: the crashing again. Crackling of flames, very far away. The ash around them began to glow.

Baz raised both eyebrows. "Shit," he said, for all of them. "What's happening?"

"Hell if I know," Sol replied, knew he sounded surly and he wished that it was different, that he could offer Baz some explanation. "What do you see?"

Baz cocked his head, shrugged. "I'm not seeing anything. Cloud? Ashes? You?"

Sol shrugged back. Same-same, for all it mattered.

"Do we have a plan?" Lutie asked after a minute of silence, and Sol had no plan. She said 'we' but Sol knew she meant 'you'. She was, what? Twenty today. Too young for this. *You were laying spirits when you were twenty. You were doing a lot of things by the time you were twenty.*

Behind the glow and nearing crackle of fire, the wind picked up again, came round as though it had merely been on an errand elsewhere. On it came the scent of blood, metal, carrion. Sweet smell, cloying, choking. *Death.*

That last smell landed like a punch and just as Sol thought that, the wind came on fast, roaring like a freight train, and Lutie staggered back, blown hard as though she'd been shoved. Baz grabbed at her, keeping her upright. Lutie's sudden shout was one of surprise, not pain. Then whatever it was coalesced, turned, came for him.

Sol landed on his back and he hit his head on something hard and edged, a field stone, maybe. He lay still for moment, hating the sensation of falling. No, not falling. *Landing.* No further thoughts on that, then he was lifted by his shirt front and hit so hard on the face that blood burst in his mouth like the liquid center of gift-wrapped chocolate, burst and sprayed and, *Goddammit, Sarrazin, open your eyes.*

Sol got his hands up, met rotting cloth and bone, unyielding for all it was falling apart, and pushed hard. A ghost, not a manifestation that resembled the living, but a spirit sustained by its hate, pared down to bone and sinew and malice. They rolled down an incline, embraced, then came apart and Sol scrambled to his feet. Their struggle had led them right down to the tracks. He couldn't see Lutie or Baz through the ash haze. Only this: big damn ghost, rails and ties dim shadows beneath the ash.

The ghost wasn't a gauzy apparition, either, it was a brick shithouse. Some ghosts were barely there, couldn't really harm anything in a physical sense. Not this one. This one was different, more vital and dangerous than even the fortuneteller's ghost. Sure, its hate made it strong, but it was more than that. Something to do with le diable, no doubt. But Sol had no time to think about it, because in its skeletal hand was a dark club. A police baton, and Sol knew this was Lewis's ghost, a man who had killed with a bat, had made sport of clubbing hobos brainless.

Sol ducked low to avoid the ghost's sudden lunge. It was big, closer to seven feet than six, a monster, and as Sol twisted out of its way, it adjusted its swing, made contact with his shoulder and Sol yelled, partly in pain, mostly in surprise. *Merde, it's fast*, he thought, tracking the club in the thing's hand, and saw the movement, felt the movement, as it swung again.

He rolled out of the way, rolled towards it, inside its reach and into its feet, or where its feet should be, planning to knock it to the ground, but Lewis sure as hell knew what to do with a body at its feet.

Instead of toppling, the ghost slammed a boot into Sol's curling body, connected with hip and Sol was moving too fast to really register it on a conscious level. The ghost swung again, missed, and Sol shot to his feet, hands scrabbling in the gravel to find upright, panting, hip now a block of radiating pain.

The thing was relentless, not allowing Sol the opportunity to do anything, to establish his connection with the ground, to find where its bindings were, to sever things between the ghost and whatever was holding it here. Sol backed up against the rails, four sets running along out of sight.

Risk. Opportunity. Despite everything, he grinned, spat blood to the side. A situation he could rise to, could cope with, and alone with being in a moving ambulance rig, this was the one place where he knew exactly what to do. He'd been here on the tracks before, the devil had tried this trick last night. Sol wasn't stupid; he knew to use iron for protection, and he had time enough, he hoped. He peered around, trying to see beyond the ghost, but that wasn't possible. In fact, it wasn't *advisable*.

The ghost came on again, bat swinging. Laughing, power beyond imagining. Sol backed up, feet finding purchase on the icy wooden ties between the tracks. Then over the tracks, iron between him and the ghost. He didn't say anything, just dropped to a crouch and his hip registered that fact. Unbelievable, astonishing pain on top of ghostcold so shattering he couldn't feel his fingers. Speed was essential, everything was pointless without it. Not the best circumstances to find an opening, send this méchant thing on its way.

It was no regular ghost, beyond being merely old and tough. Old and tough, Sol had dealt with. No, more than that, it was present in a way most ghosts weren't, was *allied*. No other word for it. This one was bound to chaos, to evil, just in a different league altogether. Sol wiped his bloody mouth on the back of his hand, put it on the ground again, prepared.

"You think that's gonna help you, cher?"

He hadn't heard the devil coming this time, and he wasn't drunk, but it was here anyway, picking its time and its place. It was dark with ash, cloying, choking. There: the devil skitched and scratched, and was barely visible across the tracks, hovering behind the skeletal spirit of Lewis, one claw around the ghost's arm like it was holding the ghost back.

Sol didn't say anything to it: what was there to say?

Fingers against ground, intent absolutely clear: *You are going away from here, you.* The ghost was laughing and the devil inched closer, but would not cross the iron rails.

The ghost wasn't coming either, had pulled up short on the other side of the tracks. Fine, Sol didn't need for it to come to him, he could swing the road to it. Intent, pure, form the line, open the path—but worse than not coming forward, the ghost wasn't sticking around. As Sol watched, as he sought out the tentative connective knot, the thing dissipated, faded into the ash, whirled skywards, leaving only the devil.

"You're not gonna get rid of my pet like that, Beausoleil Sarrazin, it ain't that easy. Your papa sure thought so, and lookit where that got him. But my ghost needs some fun, always on the hunt for that. Wonder where he'll find it?" It chuckled and it coughed and Sol's surprise fell into leaden fear. "It's on you, this next one, Sarrazin."

The ground shook and the train's lights were suddenly everywhere, and even though Sol had left himself enough room, didn't think he was in danger, he was closer to the rails than he'd thought. No time for forming any thoughts, let alone a connection, an opening, *shit*, he didn't even know where the devil was anymore.

The train rushed past and Sol swore, daylight upon him now, no ash, no cloud, no darkness. Daylight and steel and the sweeping train wind buffeting him back on his ass, no hand on the ground, no connection, just a Nebraska winter's day, too close to a train, not close enough to a devil or a ghost. Not close enough to those he loved, those he cared about. A train between him and Lutie and Baz. Between him and a devil.

He had to wait for the cars to pass, of course, and the waiting wasn't easy, but by the time the last had rumbled by, he was on his feet, anxious. Last car, line of cottonwoods near the frozen river to the south, and there were Baz and Lutie waiting for him on the other side, the Wagoneer behind them, a little distance from Lutie's parked car. A moment, and Sol saw it on both their faces: fear, followed by relief.

They were both alive, though, and the devil wasn't anywhere to be seen, nor the ghost, and Sol knew that his own almost incomprehensible relief would look like anger, but he had no control over that, none at all.

# FOURTEEN

## IRON RAILS, IRON BARS

Sol wasn't happy to see them, not at all. He was livid and Lutie recognized it immediately. She could see his scowl from across the tracks as he placed one unsteady foot in front of the other like walking was a new activity. As he neared, Baz stepped out in front. "Don't get mad. It's her birthday." Pre-emptive words, an answer to the scowl, an excuse, a get-out-of-jail-free card. What did her birthday matter in this? Not at all and Lutie knew it.

Baz's words brought a quick smile to Sol's face, but his teeth were bloody, the cut above his eye bleeding again. The smile was no better than the scowl. "Her birthday," Sol repeated softly, almost to himself. "That's *great.*"

The bright sun disguised nothing about going a round with a giant ghost. Baz lifted one hand to his brother, who flinched, but Baz wasn't taking that, was shaking his head as he tried again. "Where'd it get you?" He gestured vaguely, voice low but no-nonsense, as though sympathy would be turned away and he was probably right.

"What did you see?" More than simple deflection, that question: it was an easy way to separate the normal from the supernatural, asking Baz what was visible and what was not.

"You, too damn close to the track. You were fighting something, getting thrown around some," Baz said, but Lutie talked over him.

"The ghost, burned to the bone. Big bastard, too." She hesitated, unexpectedly wanting to protect Baz, as though not naming the obvious would do it. She took a breath. Shielding Baz wasn't an option. "And the devil. They're connected, for sure."

Sol's eyes were still bright with anger, but he seemed unable rather than unwilling to agree with her. Baz asked him if he was okay, no longer no-nonsense. Sol licked his blood-flecked lips, about to say that he was fine, Lutie could tell, but instead he looked at Baz, and the anger shifted and fled, leaving something much more difficult.

His chin dropped and he stood very still, his bare hands tucked under either elbow, all his weight on his right leg, the other bent, toe barely touching the ground. Beside him, Baz reached out to take Sol's arm, and Sol's hand twitched in return: *Give me a minute.*

The Wagoneer was unlocked, thank God. Lutie left them alone and pulled down the tailgate. It gave an arthritic whine, and she crawled into the back where the massive medical kit was held fast behind the bench seats. She dragged it across a threadbare and dog-haired carpet through a maze of man-debris: shovel, toolbox, cordless drill, sleeping bag, baseball mitt, box of ropes, carton of spare car parts. Sol limped over and sat heavily on the tailgate; Baz tried to unzip his brother's parka and was quietly berated in French. Finally, Sol pushed his help away.

Baz held up both hands, giving up, allowing Sol to do it himself. Questioningly, Lutie gestured to the kit. Sol nodded to her. She opened it up, found where he'd put the packs of gauze and handed him one.

He touched the back of his head, wincing, as he tore open one of the packs with his teeth, pressed the square of gauze to his bloody mouth. "There's some water bottles rolling under the back seat. Can you find one for me, birthday girl?"

Sol sounded calmer than either of them, gave them curt instructions for cleaning the cuts he couldn't reach or see and pulling them closed with tape and cotton and butterfly bandages. Although Sol told them repeatedly that he was okay, he still needed Baz's help to get his left arm out of his parka. With the chinook, it wasn't too cold, and as soon as Sol got his arm free of the sleeve, he stretched it out, flexed his hand, rotated his wrist, then his elbow, face screwing up as he tried to roll his shoulder.

"That's enough, Superman," Baz protested, evidently fed up with Sol's self-diagnostics. Pearl-button snaps were easy enough to undo, and they discovered that the earlier bandages along Sol's left ribcage were soaked through with new blood. Lutie changed the bandage, but Sol seemed more concerned with his shoulder, a huge club-shaped bruise coming up like a Polaroid picture, black and red and purple.

Lutie had found a bottle of frozen water in the back seat. Sol scowled as she held it out, probably thirsty. Lutie wrapped the bottle in a stray t-shirt, told him to hold it against his shoulder, watched him as he scowled harder.

"There's Tylenol 3s in there," and he gestured to the medicine box with a finger. He swallowed the tablets dry, made a face as he did so.

After a minute, Sol slid from the tailgate to take most of his weight on his right foot. His breath escaped between clenched teeth and he closed his eyes for a moment, mouth fixed on the thin edge of profanity. With his right hand, he undid the top button of his fly, inched down his jeans and his boxers, revealing a spectacular bruise on his hipbone. He took one long shuddering breath as he pressed fingers to either side, assessing for internal damage, Lutie assumed. He transferred the wrapped bottle of ice to his other hand, held it against his hip with a hiss.

"I'm driving," Baz said. Then he gestured beyond the tailgate, into the territory of rope and car parts. "Lay down in the back. Keep that ice on the bruises."

Sol gave him a look, and Lutie just about burst out laughing. He wasn't going to say what was on his mind, probably deemed it pointless, and instead shook his head, tossed the water bottle in the back and eased up his jeans. With difficulty, he put on his parka, not allowing Baz's help with it. He pushed off from the Wagoneer, stood in the clear prairie light, face turned away from them, staring out at the horizon.

Lutie closed the tailgate, taking his hint. He shouldn't be driving, but he was stubborn, and it was hard to argue with a brick wall.

Sol came around slowly, stiffly, and opened the driver's door before turning to Lutie and gruffly informing her that they'd meet back at the motel. Baz moved then: he got between Sol and the driver's seat, slender body inserting himself right in the middle, and Lutie recognized that screwing up courage sometimes meant allowing yourself anger.

Baz held out his hand. "The keys." Long moment, eyes locked. "Don't be an asshole." Sol seemed close to pushing Baz out the way when Baz lowered his voice, pitched same as the wind. "You never let anyone help. You're so damn selfish."

*Wow, way to kick someone when they're down,* Lutie thought, and then, amazed, watched as Sol withdrew his hand from his parka's pocket, handed over his keys. Without a word, he walked slowly around the truck, one hand touching the vehicle at all times like it was home base and he'd be tagged out if he let go.

Baz stared at Lutie, shock on his face. He didn't seem to call Sol on his behavior often; it was probably the first time Sol had backed down.

Once behind the wheel of her car, Lutie led them out of the field and they hadn't gone a half-mile down the road towards Brule when she noticed lights flashing across the long stretch of prairie. Police, nestled right in around the silos by the track. She slowed the car and pulled to the side of the road, Baz following in the Wagoneer. As the truck eased up beside her, Sol rolled down his window.

"Well?" she asked.

Sol had one hand out the window, eyes intent on the far silos, on the emergency vehicles. Two ambulances, a fire truck. Three police cars. Baz said something beside him from the driver's seat and Sol said something back, Lutie couldn't tell what had been exchanged, but then Baz's voice rose.

"No!" Baz exploded and the Wagoneer inched forward a little.

"Hey!" Lutie called back, and Sol turned in his seat. His eyes were unreadable, dark, tired and in pain and he looked like he didn't want to deal with any of it, but that he was going to anyway. "I'll go find out what's going on, I'll meet you back at the motel," she said, heart thudding. She didn't know how any of this worked, how to talk to cops. She couldn't let her brothers know that. "The way you look, any cop sees you, Sol, they're going to haul you into the station."

Sol's smile disappeared. She had a point and he knew it. He tried a different tack. "We can read about it in the papers, or make a phone call from the motel. You don't have to go there."

"I have to go there," she replied, and rolled up her window, leaving Sol speechless. Baz gunned the engine and pulled ahead of her, heading back to Ogallala before Sol could jump out to argue.

Two cops leaning against a cruiser gave her a good look as she pulled into the parking lot beside the Coffee Caboose Museum, and one came off the car just like a dog would that had caught a nose-full of rabbit. She didn't cut the engine, tried to look like a lost tourist, which wasn't too difficult. Except tourists didn't really come along here.

"Not a good day for a coffee, miss," the cop said, a highway patrolman by the patch on his uniform. Lutie glanced behind him, but whatever was happening, or had happened, was blocked by the caboose itself.

A smile might work wonders. She'd put on makeup today. It was her birthday. All good reasons to think she'd be cut some slack. "I was just here not an hour ago. Bart said to come back, that he'd have a pot on."

The cop exchanged a look with his buddy. Too much information? Lutie's smile faltered a little.

"Bart's not going to be making coffee today." He paused, bent down to give her a good look, one gloved hand on her door. Then he asked her to get out of her car.

Once back at the Prairie Paradise Motel, they tried to avoid each other in the room, which was impossible. Baz bit his tongue half a dozen times, watching Sol wrap a bag of ice from the motel's machine, alternating shoulder and hip, not staying still, edged. He downed some more pain-killers from his box, but didn't say a word or give any other indication about how he was feeling.

After an hour or so, Baz sat outside with Sol as his brother killed cigarettes one after the other. Baz told him that they'd been to the Coffee Caboose Museum before the ash storm, told him what he and Lutie had learned about the railroad bull. Sol asked few questions, remote, which told Baz that his brother already knew all about Lewis and how he'd died. Back to his usual self, back to square one.

The sun was lowering beyond the roof line of the tatty motel before Lutie's car pulled in, Sol leaning against the cinderblock wall, Baz laying flat out on the Wagoneer's hood, hands in pockets, staring at the sky. He sat up, recognizing the thin hum of the foreign motor, running on cheap gas, gerbils, a twisted rubber band. She sat in her car for a minute before turning off the engine, sun coming at such an angle that Baz couldn't see her face. Sol didn't move, wasn't even looking in her direction. Finally, when Baz thought he could stand it no longer, Lutie got out. Baz could see right away that she'd been crying and he didn't know if she'd want him to point that out, so he didn't.

In a voice flat and firm as a hospital bed, she told them that Bart was dead, head bashed in, the police claiming that a dust storm had covered the field all the way down to the river, and then Bart had been found behind the caboose, by the pump house. Inside the caboose, the guy who'd gotten the last cup of coffee provided witness to the whole thing: Bart had been stooped over the broken pump, then suddenly fallen like he'd been hit, probably clipped his head on the housing as he'd gone over. A freak accident.

After considering the pavement for a long time, Sol met her eyes, glanced over at Baz, accusation there. "Stupid idea, going there when you and this maudit bioque had been seen talking to the dead kid same day. Way to cover your damn tracks." Amateurs, that's what he was calling them.

"He was leaving in a couple of days, heading to grad school in California." Getting the hell out of town, she was saying, doing something that his ancestors had never done.

"I know that. You think I don't know that?" Sol barked back at her. Baz couldn't say what roughened his brother's voice, because it was too surprising, too fast. "How hard did they look at you?"

Lutie was crying again, silently, angrily. Her mouth quirked into a half-smile. "Not very. Buddy in the coffee shop knew I wasn't there when Bart died." She glared at Sol. "He was twenty-four. His mother drove up just as I was leaving." She shook her head and Baz wanted to reach out to her, wanted to put an arm around her, but he didn't know how to do it without losing a limb. "The cops took in some drifter instead. Some guy that was coming up from the tracks just at the wrong time. Poor guy was screaming from the back of the paddy wagon."

Baz watched Sol stiffen with those words.

"It's cold. We should get inside," he mumbled, and Baz slid from the hood, dropped to the pavement.

"I think Sol's got a cake waiting for you," he said, because Lutie was too pale and seeing the body of a boy who'd been flirting with you was no birthday present.

Sol glanced back over his shoulder. "I don't have any cake," he explained unnecessarily. All his attention had gone inside, gone deep, running like a German submarine in Allied waters.

"Shouldn't you go to the ER or something?" Lutie asked, closing the door behind them and taking off her coat.

Sol glanced at her, perplexed. "Nothing's broken."

Lutie gave up on that front. "Shit. I'm going to have to get my room back, aren't I?"

Sol moved silently around the room, restless. Lutie took the chair by the desk and Baz sat on the edge of his bed. "Listen," Sol started, but Lutie had had enough.

"I'm tired of listening to you," she retorted. "What did that thing say to you, down by the tracks?"

Sol didn't hesitate so much as take his time. Enough time to make Baz wonder if what they'd hear next was the truth. "It told me that this one, this next death, it was because of me," Sol said, finally coming to a stop, and leaning against the door. "Instead of me." The truth, all right.

"This isn't your fault, Sol," Baz said. "It's been killing for a long time, it didn't start because of you."

"Well, I sure as hell didn't stop it." He gathered himself. "The devil said that the ghost belonged to it and that I wasn't going to get rid of it easy." He sighed, turned to Lutie. "We know from two different sources that Lewis was killed down by the river, near the Megeath grade crossing." He didn't wait for her nod. "Ghosts hang around where they die, usually. Lewis worked in North Platte, that's where he swung that bat. His ghost is on its way home, that's what it's doing. All the guys that murdered Lewis are dead; that's what the drifters told me. By all rights, that ghost ought to be long gone. Only one thing's keeping it here—that goddamn devil."

Baz interrupted. "The ghost, it's not coming after you unless you go after it, right?" Sol didn't move, wasn't gracing that dangled carrot with a response.

"I'm more worried about le diable." Short, to the point. He picked up the book again, by Lutie's elbow, slim blue volume, cloth bound, edges worn to pale beige. He hesitated a moment, took in both of them with his stare. "I was looking at this last night, trying to figure out what Dad was doing with it."

210

Baz inched forward to the edge of the bed, and Lutie slowly got up from the chair. Finally, Sol wandered to the bed between them, and lowered himself to it, wincing. He flipped the book open, turned a couple of pages. "You know Dad was a musician," he said to Lutie, who sat gingerly beside him. She didn't say anything. "He played the fiddle. He gigged with Cajun bands that came north needing a bow. But these," and his finger wandered the book's margins, "these songs are from Acadie, where Mireille was from. Not his kind of music."

"But," she stopped, uncertain. "But he must have used them. Those are his notes, Baz said."

Sol nodded. "Yeah, he was using them, but not for entertainment, I don't think." Sol looked at Baz. "You think it makes a difference *what* you sing, when the ghosts come?"

What had he been singing? "Amazing Grace", old Hank Williams, "You Are My Sunshine". "It's better when I'm singing stuff that's...hopeful? The sad stuff, that's when it got weird."

"Place matters, too, maybe," Lutie added. "When you sang in the church, it was okay. The ghosts there, they were happy to hear you. But down at the tracks? They were different ghosts, those ones. Angry. Upset."

Sol was paying attention, but was trying to find something in the book as well. "Okay." He stopped at a page. "This one, 'Les trois hommes noirs'." The book was passed to Lutie, whose brow furrowed, trying to read the once-familiar language. "The three men in black. Dad's written 'never again' beside it. It's like he tried it and it worked so badly that he's warning himself not to do it again."

"Worked so badly with what?" Baz asked. "Dad...he couldn't call up ghosts by singing, could he?"

Sol actually laughed. "With his voice? God, I don't think so. He never said anything about it to me. Never said much. Never said enough."

Said too much, Baz thought, but he kept it to himself.

"What's the song about?" Lutie asked, book still in hand.

Sol licked his lips, concentrating. "I can't work it all out, but I think it's about this couple. They get married, and on their wedding night, three devils come to the party. They steal away the bride. The husband talks to Lucifer, who takes him to his wife in Hell. As long as she wears his wedding ring, she'll be able to come back."

"She takes it off," Baz said, so low he didn't know he'd spoken out loud.

Beside him, Sol nodded. "Lucifer threatens her husband." He shrugged, and his hand came up to his injured shoulder. "So, yeah. She takes off the ring."

Baz shuddered involuntarily, but said nothing.

Lutie closed the book, small and slender in her hands. "What are you thinking?"

Sol wiped his swollen mouth with one hand, and then sighed: "I don't know what I'm thinking. But this devil was after Dad, said it knew him, had known him a long time. Said that it didn't know what our mother had seen in him. And, Basile," Sol raised his eyes, stared long and hard at Baz, who felt chilled all over. "Baz, it wants something from you. I can't—" He stopped, voice catching, and he wasn't going to show them that. Baz watched him fight for it. "That ghost's bound to the rails somehow. I don't know if this devil can move far from the tracks, I don't know—" as though he should know, didn't want to talk about it until he did, like it was some kind of sin, not knowing everything. "But I don't want you near it. I don't want you caught up in this shit."

Lutie snorted. "Too late. What? You're just going to take care of it? Alone?"

Sol nodded. "If I have to." He rubbed his knee with one hand. Maybe that hurt too. "Or maybe we just walk away from this one."

They weren't words Baz had ever heard from Sol before.

"Just leave this ghost to murder people up and down the track?" Lutie asked incredulously. "So the thing that killed Aurie can tell you that it's all your fault? You've got some martyr complex, Beausoleil."

Sol stood up, resumed his slow painful pacing. "If you got a better idea, Lutie, I'm all ears."

"And the white light? What about that? In the church. By the tracks with just me and Baz. Down there, the devil only came after the light faded, after Baz stopped singing. But not this time. I didn't see it this time."

Sol blinked. "I don't know what you're talking about."

Lutie took a breath. "The white light, when Baz sings."

It was like she'd hit him. "A light? Like, from above?" And Lutie nodded.

Baz cleared his throat. "All around," and his hand lifted, almost of its own accord, trying to describe it. "Like full-on summer, man. It was—" The word that came was stupid, was inadequate. It was all he had. "Nice."

Sol steadied himself with one hand on the desk. He looked at Lutie, mute, hollow; some recognition passed between them that Baz couldn't name.

Lutie drew unsteady breath to say, "You don't want angels to notice you." But it was soft, something remembered from a long time ago.

Sol shook his head. "No, you don't." He looked at Baz. "Congratulations."

*Better that they don't watch over you,* Baz remembered their father saying. "Angels?" His voice was tiny, faint.

"Not like you see on Christmas cards," Sol clarified.

*He'll know what to do,* Baz thought, glad he was sitting down. "Like what, then?"

Sol kept his hand on the desk, perhaps needing to. "I don't know." He lifted his head, and Baz had never seen him look so unsure. "Aucune idée, gars."

"It was white light, it wasn't a…an…*angel*." Lutie interrupted, drawing herself up, willing a reasonable answer.

"If you say so, T-Lu," Sol said quietly. "But don't go depending on them for anything. They aren't there to look after you, they don't care about us. If it came when you sang—" His voice dropped and he caught Baz's eye. "What did that mauvaise chose say to you again?"

Baz thought about it, what the devil had said. "It said it liked the company I brought."

Sol closed his eyes and swore in French. "You two get the hell out of here. Just—" and Baz thought maybe he should sit down, he was so pale. "I don't know about the devil, I don't know how those guys work, but I can get rid of this ghost. You're right, I have to get rid of it. Maybe I can figure out the devil if I get rid of its ghost. Maybe if those two are gone, maybe the angels will leave us alone." He grimaced. "Leave you alone."

"How long?" Lutie asked, timetable fast. "How long will this take?"

Sol's face clouded. "It takes me as long as it takes. But you? For you, it only takes thirty seconds, exact same as the walk to your car." He stopped. "I'm not taking responsibility for you getting mixed up in this. I already explained that."

Lutie stood as well, vibrating with anger, shivering with it. "I'm already mixed up in this, in case you haven't noticed. I'm not going back to the Thorazine. I'm not nuts. For once in my life, I'm perfectly fine."

Sol shook his head. "You're not. No way do I phone your nice church family in Canada and tell them you were killed by some kind of devil. You get back in your car, you go to Toronto. You get back on your meds and forget about this."

"'Cause you're so good at doing that."

She didn't know, she had no way of knowing, how little effect arguing with Sol had. Anger colored their words, sure, but also fear, and under that Baz recognized something deeper and it hurt. He spoke up, trying to cut through, distract them. "So, is there just one devil? Three devils? Trois hommes noirs? Has this got something to do with Maman, and her ring and Dad? What are you trying to say, Sol?"

Sol looked like he might answer that, and then a phone rang, Baz's Cajun tune, and Baz reluctantly scooped the phone from his coat pocket, looked at the number, back up at Sol. "Where is your phone?"

Sol shrugged: I don't know, I don't care.

"Well, it's Robbie calling me. She asked me last week if you were stepping out on her. You know, you say you're protecting people, Sol, you say you're doing good and it's a calling and whatever, but you're not." He held out the still-ringing phone, and after a moment's hesitation, Sol took it.

The conversation wasn't a short one. Sol went outside for some privacy, but the door was so thin they heard everything anyway, every false start Sol made, voice low and pained, and the long silences as he listened to Robbie, or where they both endured an interminable impasse, impossible to tell. Through the window, Baz watched his brother lean against the wall, smoke trailing against the glass like words floating away from him.

Baz looked up at Lutie, who had resumed Sol's pacing. Following in his footsteps, literally. "If only Sol had told me where you were, that you were safe," Baz said, thinking of his first encounter with the devil. That wasn't fair, he knew it wasn't, but still. "None of this would have happened."

Lutie sat on the bed beside him. "It's not his fault," she admitted. "It's no one's fault."

Through the door, they heard Sol say *I'm sorry*, over and over and he meant it, anyone could tell he meant it. Baz closed his eyes. "What do they want? What do they want with us?"

Lutie put a hand on Baz's shoulder and he leaned against her. "I don't know that they are the sorts of things that have wants like us. The angel likes your singing. Everyone does. It's a gift."

"Well," Baz said, rubbing his head with one hand, the other arm around her. "It's not. I wish…I wish…" And she hushed him. Outside, Sol was quiet, and Baz took a shaky breath after a minute. "The devils don't just want chaos, I think. Those assholes, they make it, they dream it up."

"Well, if it's chaos they want, they've got it." Lutie got up. "I should go get my room back. I'm not going to drive you anywhere today." She peered at him, eyes narrowing, chin coming up slightly. "Are you okay?"

Baz nodded. "Yeah. I'm okay." Anything else wasn't possible. He had to be okay, if just for her. So she could be okay.

Her eyes cut to Sol's silhouette, shoulders and back pressed against the window, head bent, his hand holding the phone to his ear. "How about him? Is he going to be okay?" They couldn't make out what Sol was saying now, low murmur of soft talk, stop and start, stop and start.

Baz smiled, wan. "Who knows?" He stopped, stared at Lutie. "You should ask him, tell him to show you how he does it. I don't think the meds do you any good. All this is crazy, but it's real, and you should know how it works." He paused. "It's what I would do."

She didn't say anything else, and Baz wondered that he'd had such a stellar life to be offering her advice. Lutie agreed to have dinner at the diner across the street again. Baz even suggested that maybe they'd find a bar in town, that surely there had to be music. It was her birthday after all.

She left to see about the room, and passed Sol, who walked in through the open door. She pointed to the room next door, and he nodded agreement, pale and distracted. The cold slashed through the room and he watched her go, but Baz had the feeling he wasn't seeing anything. He shut the door gently, tossing the phone back to Baz, and went slowly to the window, leaned against the desk, sunlight bright behind him. Baz waited.

"Listen," Sol said, finally. "There's something I have to do." It was not coming naturally, having to explain himself. "I'm going back to Brule."

Baz made a noise: of all the things in the world his brother wanted to do.

Sol turned, face composed, held a hand up to Baz's protest. "I've been doing this awhile, Baz. Give me some credit, okay?" He waited for Baz's nod. "I'm going to the crime scene, see if there's anything they missed. Then the station house, find out if I can talk to the drifter the cops locked up."

"*What?*" Baz exploded, voice raised, hands raised and Sol looked genuinely surprised, obviously wasn't used to Baz questioning his every move. "You can't," Baz said. "Look at you."

Sol blinked, brows crooked. "I have my EMS badge with me, they'll tell me what I want to know. The drifter's name is DJ. He's half-crazy and he warned me about Lewis's ghost already, so he sure as hell knows what's up. He's a bright guy, might have seen something this time, maybe the devil, or something like it. Besides—" He paused, but not so Baz would have to ask for it. Baz realized that now, that Sol wasn't trying to be difficult on purpose.

Finishing his thought was the only way Baz could help him, otherwise the words got stuck. "You want to see if you can get him out. You know he had nothing to do with that kid getting killed."

Sol nodded, now flushed, embarrassed. Another new expression. "Ouais, gars. C'est ça. He's a drifter. He don't belong in a cage."

"You're up for this?" Baz asked, gesturing to Sol's bruises. "I can come with you." Sol stared at him. "I'll be fine, and you said it yourself—the ghost wants you dead, not me. Angels love me, devils think I'm okay too. I'd be worrying about yourself, cher."

It made Sol laugh, as intended. "You look after Lutie. She's trouble."

"She's not trouble. She's *in* trouble." Point blank, and Baz didn't mean to ambush Sol, but sometimes his mouth just ran out ahead of him. "You should teach her how to handle ghosts, man. She don't know and it's gonna get her messed up if you don't. Telling her to take her meds," disparagingly, "like that worked for you."

"Works to a point," Sol said. "Some days, I think everything would be better if I just popped a bunch of anti-psychotics." He looked so sad and defeated Baz didn't know what to say. "I'll think about it, okay?"

It was more than Baz had expected, frankly, and more than he'd bargained for, and he heard the Wagoneer start up and leave before he had a chance to say what was on his mind, which was 'be careful'.

It took Sol a while to spot DJ's encampment. Police may have gone through the hovel or not. It was hard to tell, because it was in such crappy shape to begin with. The tarp had blown away, though, and was now caught in the branches of a cottonwood across the tracks. In the midst of it, improbably pristine, was the white plastic tub DJ had used as a chair.

No cops, no police tape. Sol walked a little way up the track, looking for anything that suggested the ghost had been here, or the devil, but those guys didn't leave evidence. He hadn't found anything at Bart's murder site, either.

Without a human to inhabit it, DJ's home looked like garbage. Without DJ, it *was* garbage. Sol lifted the edge of a piece of plywood, thinking that he'd stack it against a broken pallet, maybe stick the tarp under it, so that things weren't quite so messed up when DJ came back.

Night was nearing, and Sol looked around, mindful there were things that wanted him dead haunting the tracks. Last night's cold, though, was hard to imagine in this freaky warm chinook, always Sol's favorite thing about living close to the Rockies. He picked up a sheet of plywood and it slewed to the side. Sol looked down at the mish-mash of articles trapped underneath—canned goods, a few magazines, a collection of bottles, a blanket in tatters. Garbage, right enough.

A ball of black hair the same size as a throw cushion.

Sol bent down, one hand to the side, taking weight off his battered hip. He tilted his head, trying to figure out what it was, then prodded the fur with two fingers, ridiculously squeamish given his day job. Given his night job. *What's it gonna do, Sarrazin? Jump up and bite you?* He could see now it was a small dog, muzzle gray, little stick legs stiff, nose tucked under curl of tail. It wasn't warm; it had been dead for hours.

Sol swallowed. The one thing the drifter had loved, the only thing that had loved him back.

Loved or not, the dog was fresh meat no matter which way Sol looked at it, and something needed to be done about that. He fetched the white tub and walked stiffly with it down to the tracks, bent awkwardly and with no little effort, filled the tub with gravel and loose stones. A train passed, long on the whistle, this one heading west, over the mountains, snagging Sol's heart.

The dog was so small, it only took two trips to cover it with rocks. Sol placed the last stone on top of the cairn and rested his hand there, knew a determined coyote would make short work of his makeshift crypt, and coyotes, mais, they were all determined. His shoulder ached; he'd need to get it seen to, probably. *I should be icing it instead of doing this.* Still, this had been the right thing to do, for himself as much as the dog, or DJ.

Same as what he'd do next.

\* \* \*

The jail in Ogallala served three counties and it still only held sixteen prisoners at a time. Sol pulled up to the nondescript brick building, checked the address, hoped for the best. The best turned out to be an exclusively female staff who looked half-starved for something to happen. Sol was unsure if his entrance qualified, and wished for one split second that he'd brought Baz, who was a one-man happening under any circumstance.

Still, a stranger with an EMS badge? It ought to be enough.

A deputy came in behind him, threw a joke to the women, referring to them by their first names, and it knocked Sol off balance; he suddenly realized he was a mess. A bunch of butterfly bandages tacked across his brow like bows on a cartoon kite. His lip was fat and broken, his gait impaired with limp and wince. His parka alone made him look indigent, a loopy Gulf War vet. Merde, he should have taken Baz's advice, cleaned himself up a little, but he'd been in a hurry, thinking of DJ, of how they'd talked about jumping on a train and heading west and how a jail cell in Ogallala, Nebraska was the very opposite of that.

The deputy, who seemed to be dropping off paperwork, eyed Sol even as he flirted with the jailer taking the stapled forms, and the fluorescent lights were unforgiving, lethal. The whole front reception desk area was stark, sterile, made to be easily cleaned if someone bled or puked all over it. Sol had been in places like this for his whole working life, had a role here. Hell, in some ways he belonged here.

Only one way to play it.

He smiled as one of the jailers came over. She wasn't returning his smile and she didn't call him 'sir'. "Can I help you?"

Sol nodded. "Yeah. I'm an EMS worker from Denver," and he fetched out his ID from his pocket and slapped it on the desk, aiming for unconcerned. Belonging here. "I've got a friend who's been riding the rails around here for the last few years, and I'm trying to find him."

The deputy, perched on the side of a desk, was beef-cattle big, had probably been the running back in his high school days, had that easy way with the women behind the counter, was used to being heard and seen and obeyed. "Well, what are you doing here? You oughta be talking to the railway police, then, right?"

"Yeah, I been to Bailey Yard and talked to some of their bulls." Sol paused. He'd come here for a reason, no point in backing down now. "I heard that you picked up a guy this afternoon." He met the deputy's eyes and he knew that he wasn't being deferential enough, that this guy would hand him his ass just for looking at him funny, but Sol didn't have it in him right this second to look at the deputy any other way. "DJ? His name's DJ. He's from Maine."

The deputy's eyes narrowed. "He's a friend of yours? Homeless guy with an arrest record from here to Arkansas?" He came off the desk, glanced at Sol's ID, handed it back to him with a jaded expression: so this was what a Denver paramedic looked like. He led Sol forward, past reception, and Sol cast a look to the women there, smiled for something to do. One smiled back; long odds to begin with.

Smiling Jailer came closer, but it was only to unlock the sliding metal door. The sound of it set Sol's teeth on edge, and he fought a momentary flutter of panic. The smell, the sounds, the oppressive fluorescent lights. It was coming back to him. Not merely recalling work, hospitals and uniforms. What he was feeling now, it went back further than that.

Sol nodded to her, forced himself to. "He's probably worried about his dog."

She returned the nod as though pleased that someone recognized the particular stresses of her job. "He's awful upset about it. Hours now, shouting about it. The other prisoners, they complained."

"Gave you trouble, did he?" the deputy said. "A dead body spitting distance from that squat of his, and he's getting worked up about a dog?"

Smiling Jailer smiled again. "Not much trouble. But you know these guys, they hate being under lock and key, even if it's for their own good."

Sol bit the inside of his mouth, had a moment of dread passing through the doors, a shrill klaxon ringing in his head as the lock was slid behind him. The deputy took him to a small waiting room, antiseptic as the rest, hallways a battered white along the way, narrow, dim shouts coming from further along the row. The skin on the back of Sol's neck began to crawl, and he had to counsel himself to breathe normally—*just a room, it's just a room*—while the deputy gestured to a metal chair behind a nasty table, marked up with ink and chipped beyond easy fixing.

"We'll see if DJ's up for a visit, Mr. Sarrazin," the deputy said. "You want a coffee?" Yessir, he wanted a coffee, wanted it bad, but his heart rate was already up, he knew that, and he knew it wasn't because he was nervous about the cop, or being questioned.

"Thanks, no," he said.

The deputy hesitated. "You all right, son?"

Sol realized that while he'd been in plenty of police stations, worked with cops all the time, liked them, hell, partied with them, there were cops and there were jailers. Though this was just a county jail, it felt like waiting for his old man to come out in the orange jumpsuit, make sudden and intense conversation, a whole week concentrated into sixty minutes. Sol would tell Aurie lies about how everything was all right, that he and Baz were doing just fine, that nothing was wrong.

Sol quirked a smile. "Yeah, you know. I'm okay. Just had a call that went wild a couple of nights ago." He motioned to his face. They shared a look, and Sol sincerely hoped they were actually sharing more than a look—that they were swapping experience, war stories.

The deputy paused. "No kidding." Maybe reassessing him.

Sol swallowed. Only a matter of minutes before some part of this facade cracked. It was always better to be quiet than to yak your fool head off, though, so Sol waited, wondered if there was some paperwork he'd have to fill out. Sol had long known that there were certain kinds of people who became cops: those that wanted to do good and to protect the innocent. And those that liked to exercise power, those that thrived on the automatic respect. Sol hadn't quite figured out this one yet.

There had been a lot of the latter type in his dad's joint, and Sol had seen the way they'd looked at him during his first weekly, then monthly, visits. They were seeing a criminal in the making, some scared seventeen-year-old kid with a spotty psychiatric history and a no-good father, haphazard attendance at school or employment on highrise construction sites when he wasn't getting picked up for public disorderlies. Sometimes Sol had brought the barely-teen Baz, and that had lightened the whole visit, but Baz had acted out so badly afterwards that Sol didn't ever think a trip to see Aurie was worth the subsequent fights and the drugs and the running away. It had been a long four years.

The deputy wasn't moving. Maybe Smiling Jailer was getting DJ. "Any chance you might cut him loose?" Sol asked. "He's not gonna like being in a cell." He shrugged a little, surprised at how quiet his voice was, how low. The accent. His heart going like a triphammer. The deputy had one hand on the door, which was still open. For that Sol was profoundly grateful. He knew that beneath his father's plaid shirt, he'd sweated right through at armpit and back.

"A boy died and DJ's a witness," the deputy explained. "And it's cold out."

Sol nodded; one night in a cell, at least. He'd probably be able to calm DJ down, though, at least. His own sharp fear was strong in his nostrils: fear of places like this, fear of getting stuck in a place like this. "Okay. I'll see if I can't set him at ease about the dog."

"Suzie's getting him now. You're right. He's damn twitchy." Not the only one, Sol thought.

It had been voluntary, his stay in the psych ward that one time, almost nineteen and out of his mind with worry and ghosts and Baz's constant truancy, trying to fix what was all around him, not being able to control anything, his father flying into dark rages at every visit: *You just send them away. Don't talk to them, don't monkey around. I showed you everything, and you learned nothing!*

Then someone ran down the corridor outside, calling for a medic.

The deputy told Sol to stay put, stuck his head out into the corridor. Sol didn't stay put, it wasn't really in him to do that, he stood at the deputy's shoulder as Suzie the Smiling Jailer—now near tears, not composed, not smiling at all—quickly relayed the news.

Somehow, the prisoner had used the rope holding up his trousers to effect. No one had thought he was suicidal. No one had checked. Hell, after the ranting, the complaints from the other prisoners, it's a wonder that another inmate hadn't beaten him to death. The deputy saw Sol at his shoulder and told him again to sit back down.

Sol wasn't of a mind to sit back down. He pushed past the deputy, down the corridor, just going, not really thinking about what he was doing, a shiver starting up in him like shock but not, a deep fear, a hole in him that went straight down all the way to despair. *You can't die in a cell, DJ.*

He came to a locked door, the push bar unyielding and that's when the deputy caught up with him. The deputy pushed him aside, and Sol knew that he must look crazed, some mix between psycho and vagrant. A long look passed between them. Sol knew all about jurisdictional issues, about what out-of-state certification meant or did not mean. Both of them knew what minutes might mean, as well.

"I'm a paramedic." It came out strangely, mostly because Sol's throat had constricted at the thought of DJ knotting a rope. He couldn't have said why; he dealt with stuff like this all the time. "Please."

The jailer pulled out her set of keys, looking to the deputy for guidance. The deputy nodded. And even though Sol didn't want to do it, didn't want to go into the lock-up, he was going to.

One look, though, told him that there was nothing to be done. DJ was still hanging, and the best that Sol could do was help the deputy untie him, lower him to the floor, and by that time, the local guys were at the jail and Sol wasn't needed, definitely wasn't wanted.

He watched them work, knew the drill, could do nothing, not with any of the equipment, not with Colorado certification. Not by putting a hand on DJ's chest, because his ghost was long gone. Out of this place, and Sol would have to take slim comfort in that. He watched the whole dance; the strip being run, the beginnings of the report. No heroic measures, nothing heroic about this.

The deputy finally noticed Sol again, and gently but firmly guided him by the arm, took him into the front where he was sat at a desk, the deputy opposite, pad of paper out now. He was asked questions about next of kin and date of birth and anything else he might know about DJ. Sol answered best he could, monosyllabic. He was thinking of the dog, of the cairn of stones. Finally, he was told to stay in touch, but he couldn't remember his cell phone number so he made something up. Finally, he walked back out through the front doors, where a drift of snow still lingered in the shadows next to the brick wall, a line of trucks and police vehicles breaking the constant wind. The sun was only a glow beyond the far horizon. He couldn't remember when he'd last eaten.

*This is no way to live your life*, he thought.

Sol had been here before, or a few places just like it, standing in front of police lock-ups, empty-bellied, beat up, in trouble and alone. It had been a bad stretch, that time when Aurie was first in prison, and Sol remembered little of it but anger, just months and months of it. There had been cops and fights and no keeping of noses clean, not until it became obvious that social services was going to separate them, would put Baz in a group home and Sol in juvie or worse.

Their social worker landlady had stepped in, convinced Sol the only way to end it was with help, if you could call the antipsychotics and the brief hospitalization help. Sol's trip to the psych ward had scared both brothers. Baz had settled down, settled in. The meds had given Sol a couple months reprieve from all the ghosts, had slowed down the craziness. Drugged silence had been a gift.

After, their father hadn't looked at Sol the same way, and that had been the end of their trust. The drinking, the fighting, it had mostly stopped, like Sol had sealed it away, cemented over a well. Grow up, he'd told himself, and it had been what was necessary. The only way to get rid of the anger was to not care, and that's what he'd done.

*I am nothing like you, Papa*, Sol thought, fumbling for his truck keys. And he knew he was exactly like his father in every way that mattered.

# FIFTEEN

## BIRTHDAY PLUS ONE

The Old Roadside wasn't much of a place, not for a birthday celebration. Not for a funeral, either, really, or a getting divorced party, or even just a beer after work. It was probably adequate for descending to a certain level of intoxication and certainly for getting into a Friday night fight, but not much more. Baz eyed what passed for a band in Ogallala the night after New Year's Eve and despaired.

Across a table only kept from tilting by a folded cigarette pack under one leg, Baz watched Sol shift from beer to bourbon. That likely meant that they would get thrown out before too long, but Baz didn't want to ruin what was left of Lutie's big day by pointing it out.

Sol hadn't joined them for dinner, had met them afterwards and hadn't demurred when Baz suggested a birthday outing, had merely nodded without comment, and that ought to have been Baz's first clue that things hadn't gone well.

Between bourbons three and four, Sol told them he'd buried DJ's dead dog at the tracks and unstrung the suicidal drifter at the jail, two stark notions tied together with an inadequate 'then', followed by silence.

That was that, and Lutie stared, and it was not exactly happy birthday with a candle on it. The next round came and Sol took his fast, and Lutie took hers thoughtfully, and Baz just took his because he didn't want to think of much else.

"Well, I've had worse birthdays," Lutie stated loudly and Baz thought, *The night is still young.*

Sol's tattered eyebrow lifted and he'd had one too many drinks to wince. Feeling no pain stage. Hold him here, and they might be okay. "Me too," he murmured so only Baz could hear, turning his glass as though he was trying refract enough light to set the table on fire.

They sat in silence as the band finished murdering the song, and Sol's eyes glittered, maybe looking for a fight. Baz paid attention, didn't want to be Sol's keeper, but roles got switched at a certain point on nights like this, and it was usually a good idea to pay attention to when that happened.

"I always hated my birthday," Lutie shouted above the next musical catastrophe, which Baz couldn't even identify. "Next round's on me," and she made to rise, but the waitress was already there, too quick for Baz's liking.

Lutie continued. "Last year, all my friends forgot and I ended up in the ER, talking to the walls." Her nose was in her purse, looking for her wallet. Without breaking any kind of rhythm, Sol passed some folded bills to the returning waitress, and Lutie glanced up, but Sol wasn't looking at her.

"They dope you up?" Baz asked, bending his head forward so they could hear each other over the thump of bass.

She shrugged. "Some. It was better for a while. The ghosts were, anyway. I wasn't better."

The band abruptly stopped: break time, like they were on a clock. Only a lone dancer complained, weaving between the risers and a brass pole that Baz guessed had a more pragmatic use during the 'buffet lunch for businessmen'.

Sol leaned back suddenly, voice low. "Worst birthday, though?" Sol eyed Baz darkly and Baz didn't know which one he'd name, because there were so many to choose from. "Gotta be that one in '98. I turned seventeen and you were—" He waved his hand vaguely. "I think I ended up in the drunk tank. Something about a car."

"A cop car," Baz nodded, smiled wanly and sideways at Lutie. There had been some social workers in addition to the police. It had been a scary few weeks, mostly due to Aurie's reaction when he'd found out his eldest son had stolen and demolished a police car. His youngest hadn't been involved, but only because Baz had been two weeks on the streets, incommunicado. It was the first time Baz had been glad his father was behind bars. It was not the last.

"When's your birthday?" Lutie asked, and such a question coming from a family member was indelicate, but so many things about her were.

Sol smiled, and it disappeared into his beard. "Tintamarre. M'man always said it was lucky."

Lutie nodded. "She would. Acadian national day. August 15th?" Baz saw Sol's smile deepen, a tidbit of knowledge shared like a joint at a party. She'd remembered something of their past. *Tintamarre*. "I bet that's when they met. The big Acadian festival at Caraquet, it's usually around Tintamarre. Aurie must have gone up there to play." Baz thought of the photo they'd found. "So, what'd you do after you got out of lock-up? When you were seventeen?"

"He came and hauled my ass off the corner," Baz interjected. "I'd been hanging out, making money anyway I could." He laughed, and it wasn't funny. "See? The Old Roadside is better than that. Almost."

They sat in silence after that, Sol's attention a million miles away. He had that stare, the one that was really easy to misinterpret. Or totally easy to interpret, which was part of the problem. Suddenly he repeated, out of nowhere and with heat: "I hauled your ass off a street corner, stupid shit. That's when I decided." Turned the glass around and around. "I'd had it. I caught out."

Baz couldn't say anything to that, thought he'd misheard, or that Sol was just going to start saying things that no one could understand. Lutie, though, she didn't mishear, or second guess.

"What do you mean, you caught out?" Not belligerently, but maybe a little annoyed that he'd used jargon she didn't understand.

The gaze didn't come back to them. "Denver's a good city for it, big yard, railroad hub. Catch east, get to Chicago, west, you're in San Francisco before you know it." He downed the bourbon in one gulp, nursing grudges, not alcohol. "North. Time it right, you can ride the rails north."

It was bottle talk, because Sol had always been there, as far as Baz could remember, had sometimes been drunk, had sometimes been so surly with fatigue or stressed by exams that he was the single biggest pain in the ass that a teenager could inherit from an incarcerated father, but he had been there. Baz had always counted that as one of his problems, that his brother kept such a close eye.

"You?" Lutie's voice was low and thick. "You hopped trains?"

Unbelievable, maybe, to her as well. Hard ass, feet on the ground, first to judge and to order, Sol wasn't built for flights of fancy, for midnight runs. For catching out.

"Where'd you go?" Baz asked, but the moment was gone, Sol had pulled down the shades, had spun his empty glass across the table, was looking for the waitress, a thirst in him that not much was going to quench.

Lutie looked over to Baz, lifted her hands questioningly.

"We should get going before the band starts up," Baz suggested, but he knew that Sol was in no mood for taking hints.

"Yeah," Lutie said. "I'm too tired to work out a plan." She was wary now, Baz guessed, about ordering Sol around. She was giving Sol room to agree with them, giving him room to come with them.

Sometimes, though, it wasn't good to give Sol room, because that meant that Sol was going to take room, would stay, would find the waitress and tell her to line 'em up same as a firing squad. "You coming?" Baz asked for the sake of doing so. Someone had to walk with Lutie. He didn't have the luxury of babysitting Sol tonight. *Not my job*, he told himself, but it *was* his job and he knew it.

Sol sighed, stretched cautiously, his head tilted back against the padded bench. "Maybe one more," like it was code. "You go ahead."

"No," Lutie said. "We go together. I don't want anyone running into that thing tonight."

Sol's eyebrows came up and he laughed. "Vraiment, chère? That thing?" Sounds of language mixing, no sharp edges, just blur.

"Really," and she already had on her coat, handed him his. "You're going to feel like shit in the morning, no matter what."

"I'm gonna feel like shit?"

She put her hands on her hips. "Don't just repeat everything I say."

She'd been raised an eldest child and it showed. To Baz's amazement, Sol slowly got up, took his abused and stained parka. "You are just like her," Baz thought he said but Lutie didn't react to it.

Out into the cold and Sol missed the first step. Baz caught his elbow before he went down. "Easy," he said, feeling suddenly like his brother was a badly put together marionette, that he would fall apart at the least provocation. Sol straightened, withdrew his elbow, righting himself. Trying to right himself.

Lutie was on his other side, and Baz was glad of that, just in case Sol needed some help. After her first question, though, he was less happy about it.

"You say Aurie's ghost came to you in Denver, and that's how you knew he was dead. Did M'man do the same thing? Did she come to you?"

Sol, patting his pockets for cigarettes, snorted like their mother's ghost was a television show he'd heard of but never watched. "If she had, then I'd have known she was dead, right from the start, no?" He found his pack, then started looking for his lighter. "I don't know, chère, she didn't show up to me. She never looked back."

They walked and Sol found his lighter, lit his cigarette, and they walked some more. The night air was cold like the inside of a meat locker, and Baz tucked his chin down. "When?" he asked when neither of them said anything else. It was unfair, that they knew and he didn't. "When did she die?"

Lutie didn't answer, just looked straight ahead. Sol turned to her, and then he took a long drag and he said to Baz. "November."

"Things would have been a lot different if she hadn't done it," Lutie said softly from the other side. "If you had found us before that."

Sol let out a bark, not quite laughter. "If she hadn't left in the first place." He flicked the butt away and it sailed across the parking lot, trail of sparks like a miniature comet. "I don't know where she is now. Heaven, Hell, some other place. You get fucked up, you die with a ghost tied to you. Tied to a ghost." Sol's voice dropped to match the wind whistling over the broken asphalt. "She can stay between worlds for all I care."

They didn't say anything else because the motel was right there, or at least Baz thought that was the reason. Lutie said goodnight in that northern voice, and Baz responded with his flat Midwestern one, and Sol just hummed under his breath as he tried the key in the lock, sounding like a southern washboard, spare and lean and hard.

First light, Lutie bought muffins and coffee. Balancing a cardboard tray in mittened hands, she crossed the parking lot from the retro diner, eyes on her brothers' room. The curtains were still drawn; she was up before them. Coffee was a peace offering. Muffins, an opening salvo.

Maybe she knocked louder than was necessary, but if they were both asleep, she had to, right? Coffees balanced on the tray, temperature still chinook mild, and Lutie knew she needed to leave today. The whole situation was ridiculous by daylight. She was in the middle of her second year, getting great grades, had a room in a student house, a job waiting for her. And here she was in the worst motel in Nebraska, about to nurse one of her long-lost brothers through a hangover, work out why the other could charm angels. Not even taking into account hunting the devil that had killed the father she could barely remember, or the violent ghost working in tandem with it.

Her hand came up to knock again, but Sol pulled open the door and he looked pretty much as Lutie expected he would, given the last twenty-four hours. He glanced at her, then at the coffee, leaned against the doorframe and smiled.

"Âllo, ma chouette," he murmured, plucking a coffee from the tray as she brushed past him into the room.

"I have something for you to eat, too." She shook the bag at him, grease blossoming translucent stains on the paper.

Sol made a face, opened the lid of the coffee and inhaled. "Thanks." He didn't look twice at the bag.

She heard the shower in the bathroom, and Sol tapped the door, told Baz that Lutie had brought coffee and if he didn't hurry, he'd drink it all.

They sat opposite each other and in the morning light, Sol looked like he'd been left at the curb on trash day, ripped and stuffingless. "Bon Dieu," he said to the floor. "I shouldn't have drunk so much last night." If it was an apology, it was a poor one. His head came up. "We got a lot to do today."

Not an apology. Self-castigation. "Like what?" Lutie asked. Trust Sol to have come up with an agenda on little sleep and much alcohol.

He wouldn't look at her. With his splattered pants and battered unshaven face, he looked like he lived by the tracks. He looked just like she imagined her father had looked, how she remembered him. She saw the swallow he took. "I'm gonna show you what I do. See if I can teach you."

"God, why should I learn that?" Before she even thought it through, thought about what she wanted or didn't want, the words were out.

That seemed to amuse him, which only served to piss her off. He leaned elbows onto both knees, kneaded his shoulder with one bruised hand. "I'm not saying you go look for them. Just...you should know how to do it." Then he did look at her and he didn't look like anyone who lived by the tracks or under a bridge, someone who pushed around a beat-up shopping cart. Lutie straightened up, seeing it. He continued, "You're gonna go back today and I don't want to send you away without knowing how to get rid of them. If you're not gonna take meds, you should know."

Before she could say anything, Baz came out from the shower, hair flopping wet into his eyes, t-shirt announcing his unlikely affiliation with an ironworker's union, smile widening his face, pleased to see her, always that and it lit her inside, being greeted with such affection.

"Good morning, birthday plus one." He tossed a towel to the bed where it wilted among the turbulence of the disarrayed sheets. "Sol's got a surprise for you."

"She's not surprised." Sol provided the update, passing Baz a coffee. "She says she don't want to know."

Baz popped the lid, opened the bag, looking for creamers, maybe. He took out a muffin, eyed it before cramming half into his mouth. Around it, he said, "She seemed curious enough before. Spied on you through the curtains." He smiled through the crumbs, turned to her. "You are so full of shit."

Lutie turned up a hand, a sort of shrug, a capitulation. "Okay, so show me."

Baz sat on the desk, long legs tangled. "So, how are you gonna do this without calling up that devil? Unless you want it to come around?" He paused and Sol shook his head, possibly in disbelief. "And Lewis? You call that one out, you got a fight on your hands. Look how good that worked for you yesterday. You want nice friendly ghosts for her to practice on, cher."

Sol had finished his coffee, and now he put both hands on his knees, levered himself to a stand. "No such thing as friendly ghosts. First lesson," and he turned to her, catching both of them in his glance. "If they're hanging around, they're confused. And if they been around for a while? They're pissed off and that's not good."

Hopefulness warred with apprehension in Baz's face, and Lutie saw it perhaps a moment before Sol. "So, you want me to...you know. Sing some up for you?" Baz asked.

"Not a chance," Sol said. "Lutie, can he use your laptop? I want him to find out more about those songs in the book, see if he can find the music to go along with them." That non-smile again, attention to his brother. "You know about Google, right?"

Sol drove, but not far, only to a diner immediately adjacent to an Ogallala park on the other side of an old folks home, a five-minute drive. Hell, everything was a five-minute drive, either that or it was out of town. The diner had WIFI, another sign that Sol had scouted things out in advance. Baz ordered a big Saturday breakfast before Lutie and Sol went out into the cold, had Lutie's earbuds to plug into the computer, the blue book beside him.

Once in the park, Lutie looked back and could see Baz in the window of the diner, and he lifted a hand to her, Sol still walking resolutely to a park bench in the gray landscape. A screen of leafless shrub protected them from the road, paths leading from the sidewalk to behind the two-story brick seniors facility. Sol could keep an eye on both of them from here, Baz protected inside.

Was *she* protected, though? Lutie didn't feel like she was, and at the same time, didn't think Sol would deliberately put her into danger. That wasn't his style, as far as she could tell. But what did she know? Under twenty-four hours, she'd known him, that and a lifetime.

*He never teased me*, she remembered, *not like Baz did. He kept an eye out; he saw me.*

She turned and followed him, knowing that small-town cops would be interested in the tableau: two strangers, one particularly worse for wear, hanging around in the park waiting for something to happen. She sat down on the bench next to Sol and for one moment wished she had some stale bread to feed the birds, just to look normal.

Shifting a little, cold enough in spite of the warm mountain wind, Sol scowled beneath his tuque. "Usually, people die in hospitals and old folks homes," he said. He would know. "This one," and he gestured to the building behind them, "is as good as any." His eyes were on Baz in the diner's window: head bent, for all appearances researching Acadian lyrics.

"Ghosts haunt where they die," she offered, stating one of the few things she knew, one of the few things she remembered.

"Usually," Sol said, face calm and expectant. She shivered. "You cold?"

"No, I'm scared," she said fast, dripping with faux dread.

Sol looked sideways at her. "You're some kind of funny, hé?"

A man with a dog walked the far edge of the park. No kids, no play equipment: which came first? She frowned. "Yeah, I guess I think I am." It was like teasing a bear, and Lutie couldn't help herself. He took himself so seriously and there was only room for one of them to do that at a time. A long moment passed before Lutie asked, "Did you mean what you said, last night?"

She didn't look, so she couldn't tell what was in his face, but he moved slightly before sighing. "What did I say?"

These things were easier said when you weren't looking at someone. "You drink too much."

A dry chuckle. "Too much? Maybe not enough. You?"

That drew her round and his eyes were hard, glittering. She'd made him mad. Good. "I'm not the one with a drinking problem," she said.

He nodded, marking the hit. "So, what'd I say that's got you so upset?" Taunting her right back in a way that disallowed a flippant remark, the kind she would have served up to any of her other family.

She looked away. "What you said about M'man. How you don't care where she is now." Then, she raised her hand to him. "You don't have to answer that. I can guess."

She couldn't, not really, but he didn't have to know that.

He didn't laugh this time, and she knew she'd won. It didn't feel good, though. Her tongue was too quick, had always been too fast, too sharp.

"So," she said after a while, when it became clear that Sol wasn't going to talk anymore, that she'd shut him down. "How does this work?" She looked over at him, and his attention was on the far line of bare cottonwoods marking the edge of the park.

It took him a moment to answer. "You need to go in with a pure heart," he said and that sounded so unlikely she almost laughed. Go in with a fifth of bourbon, maybe, or go in with a shotgun, go in with the intent to kill. Sol sounded slightly embarrassed to be saying it. "You concentrate, here," he tapped his temple, "and here," and his hand moved to his heart.

"Like…meditation?"

He shrugged: How would I know? "You clear your thoughts, concentrate on the one thing, until nothing else matters. You connect, and then you can open a road for them." He pointed to a bare oak, the lone large tree in the park. "Tell me that you can't feel that tree, how it reaches down into the ground, how the roots grab the earth, hold onto it. You can feel that, right?"

And she could, she always had been able to grasp that, so she nodded.

Sol cleared his throat, came off the bench and walked a few steps on the winter-burned grass. He bent down, took off his gloves and shoved them in his pocket, spread one hand. "I usually use my right hand, but it don't matter. Dad used his left, said it was closer to his heart." His dark gaze shifted to her, then back to what he was doing. "You lay your hand down as close as you can get, and you feel..." He stopped, suddenly self-aware that he was on his heels, hand on park lawn beside a bench, like he was looking for a four-leaf clover out of season. "Come here."

She crouched beside him, hand exposed to the cold. He took her right hand in his left, covered it, held it to the ground. His hand was warm on hers, and through it she felt a tremor. "Maybe you shut your eyes, chère, maybe that's easiest." She did and his voice, divorced from image, wasn't so hard, or remote. It was like a humid day in August.

On top, his warm living hand, below, the stirrings of the earth, the humus of leaf and worm and bacteria, teeming life, all connected. A flash, a moment of that, and then her brother's slow voice, lazy almost. "You got it? You keep that, that's what ties you here, 'cause next you gotta send it out. You look," and she opened her eyes and he took his right hand, placed it to his chest, under his shirt, skin to skin, nearest to his heart. "One hand to the ground, make the connection, keep it here inside you. Then send it out, from your heart, to your mouth, your breath is life, right? You take it, all that life, and you send it out..."

And he moved his right hand from his heart, made a circle with his fingers to his lips, breathed out and uncurled his fingers, and she saw the distortion in the air like gas fumes disrupting light's straight lines. He'd made something that hung in the air for a moment, then he took his hand again, cut glance to her—*do you see?*—and tapped the ground three times. The distortion, the malfunction of light, sparkled, fled, disappeared.

"When you make that, and there's a ghost near, you try to slide it their way. They see it, or sense it, or whatever they do, and that's where they want to be if they're just the confused kind, the ones looking for a road home. It comes to them, like..." he let her hand go, pushed his fingers together, apart, "...like magnets, hé? Like that."

Lutie cleared her throat. "So, where do they go, this road home? Is it a good place, where they go?"

Sol put one hand down, then reached for the bench to pull himself up and Lutie remembered the horrific bruise on his hip where the ghost had kicked him yesterday. She took his elbow, but then he made a stuttering hiss and it was his damaged shoulder and side, and Lutie just backed off so he could do it himself.

He stood, one hand to his ribs, then he said, "I don't know where they end up. But it's gotta be better than sticking around here. Even those guys who were good people when they were alive, they go crazy after hanging around between for too long."

"Have you seen a lot of people die, in your work?"

That earned her a laugh, under his breath as he scanned the park, as he looked over to the diner, but Baz was still working away. "I try not to let them die, that's kinda the point of my line of work." Lutie scowled, and that made him laugh again. "Yeah, I seen my share."

"Is it why you chose it?" He stared at her. "To be a paramedic? So you could make sure ghosts got to where they were supposed to go? Doesn't it drive you mental?"

Too many questions all together. He grinned, ducked his head. "Well, yeah. It makes you nuts. But what's the choice?"

Maybe it wasn't a curse, something to be overcome, to fight. For the first time in a very long time, Lutie allowed that thought. "Do most of them just go?"

He nodded, and he didn't offer more because you had to come to him and maybe that wasn't such a bad thing, sometimes. He only gave you what you asked for, no more, didn't cram you with unnecessary words.

"So maybe she did, right? Maybe she just went." There was no keeping it from her voice, the thin thread of doubt, of fear. Of hope.

"Probably." Sol nodded, took a couple of steps, no nearer, no further, just circled her like the slow orbit of a far moon. "Most of them do."

"What difference would it make, having a ghost tied to you?" She didn't know how much he knew about this, but it had to be more than anyone else she'd ever met. *I am leaving and this might be my only chance to ask.*

The pacing stopped. His attention was fully on her. "Don't you do it, Luetta. Don't even think of it. You think you'll get some kind of power, and you do, it's true. But there's a cost." His words faltered, and she didn't know what he was thinking about that it pinched his face like that. "It wears you down, takes away that feeling you just had, where you can feel the trees. It takes away how you feel about your friends, and your family. It takes everything you got just to keep that ghost close. It's like that saying about having a wolf by the throat, that you can't let go cause it'll eat you whole. It's like that."

She looked away first, over at the diner, and Baz was no longer there.

Sol gyred away from her again. Sighed. "There's no damn ghosts here," he said, but he didn't sound disappointed.

"I know," she agreed. "I don't think I can do that, what you just did." She sat down again, knew that Baz would be joining them shortly. He'd gotten bored, sitting alone in the diner, watching them in their strange dance. "How long did it take you to learn?"

He stopped his movement, came back to her, but he didn't sit down. "A while," he admitted. "I don't remember, I was just a kid. It gets easier, the more you do it. Faster. It's not hard now. Usually." His back was to the diner and so he didn't see Baz walking towards them, Lutie's knapsack over one shoulder. "Harder when they're tossing you around. They gotta be big and mean for me to have much trouble. I was hoping for a nice old lady for you."

He laughed, and then sensed or heard Baz behind him and turned. "You give up already?"

Baz spread his hands. "I didn't give up, man. I got what I needed." He flung himself down on the bench. "So, are we surrounded by ghosts? Is this like, ghost central?" He winked at Lutie. "I just sat down on a ghost, didn't I? Squashed him." Big stupid shining grin and Lutie couldn't help but smile back.

"Nah, there's nothing here. Beausoleil was hoping for a bunch of blue-haired seniors with tricky hearts who were still waiting for the next pinochle tourney, but we're out of luck. The dead are all happy in Ogallala."

Baz let out a little sigh of laughter, and eyed Sol, who stood a few feet away. "Well, you look ridiculous out here, on your hands and knees in this dogshit park."

"What'd you find out?" Sol countered, an easy rhythm to them, Lutie realized now, Sol ignoring Baz the more outrageous he became.

Lutie watched Baz straighten up, some levity knocked out of him. "Trois hommes noirs, haven't found it yet. Dad didn't want to touch it, and I don't really want to, either. But there's another one, he wrote 'works like a hot damn' beside it. You imagine him writing that? I got no idea what it's about. Or, I think it's about an old mill, and something about a chicken. Or a bird or something. What's duck in French? It's got a good tune, though, some kind of reel. Dancing music. I found three different versions of it, so I downloaded a couple to your hard drive, chère. That's legal in Canada, right?" The bag sat between them on the bench, and Baz buried his hands into his pockets. Laughed, and then looked up at Sol. "We could use a hot damn right about now."

Sol scrubbed his beard with one hand, found his gloves, drew them on. "Yeah, we could at that."

Baz didn't move. "It's a happy song. I could sing it, get some practice ghosts for you." He smiled at Sol's black expression. "Just a few bars. I'll shut up before anything too weird happens."

"Because singing for ghosts isn't weird," Lutie muttered.

Sol shook his head. "No way," he said, ignoring whatever Lutie might have to say on the subject, and that didn't sit right with her.

"How am I supposed to practice without some ghosts?" If Sol could learn, then she could too. And setting ghosts on a path was next to tying them to you, and she'd thought she'd been able to do that, too.

Sol stared long and hard at the both of them. He took a couple of steps from them, hands in his pockets. "The tracks. We can try the tracks," he suggested. "More ghosts there, but no little old ladies. Hard core." He raised his eyebrows to her: You game? And of course she nodded. He didn't smile, instead he turned to his brother. "You go back to the motel and wait for us there, Baz."

Baz laughed, high-pitched, eyes glinting in the wan sunshine. "I don't think so. That devil's got a bad habit of appearing out of nowhere, and I don't want to be alone waiting for the damn thing."

He had a point, even Sol could see it. Finally, Sol dipped his shoulder. "Fine. You wait in the truck, though. You keep your mouth shut." Said that while walking away, jabbing a finger in their general direction.

They headed west past Brule, past the now-closed Coffee Caboose, past the place where they'd last faced Lewis, far from inquisitive eyes, parked on the south side of a grade crossing near the fairgrounds, nothing on the landscape except for some bare trees behind a torn-up snowfence, a broken down barn falling in on itself. Miles and miles of grayed out grasslands.

Getting out of the truck first, Sol nailed Baz with a look. He acquiesced with a sigh, leaning back into the passenger seat, eyes to the roof of the truck, epitome of boredom within seconds. With one last warning glance to his brother—*stay put*—Sol led Lutie across the tracks to the river, which was an icy runnel cutting the landscape, defining the territory, a meek boundary.

"Running water," Sol pointed at it, then jerked his thumb to the tracks behind them. "Iron."

"Does that matter?" Lutie asked.

Sol paused, unsure and showing it. "Water isn't reliable, not always. Sometimes it's like a safety net, especially when it's moving. Ghosts have trouble crossing it. But standing still, like swampwater? Not so predictable. Rivers are usually good." He grinned. "Aqueducts are even better. Iron is a safer bet, and salt is the best of all."

"What about fire?" Lutie said, watching the Wagoneer, where she could see Baz's dim outline against the gray plains.

After a second, Sol shook his head. "Couldn't say. It cleans things, I guess. Sometimes. Didn't help with Lewis, though, burning up like that. I know iron and salt. Water and fire, they're not so easy."

"Sounds like a cooking show," Lutie said, scowling. The landscape was bleak and ghostless. "You think it happened here?" she asked, finally. "I mean, I guess this is where it happened. Maybe this isn't such a great idea, so close to where Lewis died."

Sol shook his head, spoke lowly, not even looking at her. "The Megeath crossing is west of here. There'd be a granary, and a house, or what's left of it." He looked over his shoulder at the broken barn. "Not this."

Her brows crooked. "He died in a mobile home, across from the fairgrounds. There isn't anything left. Except the barn, Bart said."

A whistle sounded, far away. Sol was shifting his weight, one foot to the other, eyes scanning the terrain. He'd been barely listening to her, at first, looking for ghosts, back to her. Now he blinked, then his eyes widened a little. Lutie lifted her hands. "I'm sorry. I thought you knew."

"Come on," he said, shortly. "Let's get out of here." He turned momentarily to the river, as though the devil was sneaking up on them from behind. Lutie glanced over at the Wagoneer, couldn't really see Baz through the spattered windshield. She splayed her hands wide, giving up, not knowing if he was watching her.

As it happened, he was.

Then the train blasted between them, cutting off Lutie's sight-line of Baz sitting alone in the Wagoneer.

Prior to Lutie's silent plea for help, Baz had been flipping through his father's stolen library book, trying to figure out which one he'd try first, if his ghost-busting siblings ever changed their damn minds about his usefulness.

He knew one or the other of them would ask for his help. Eventually. Of course it was Lutie. Sol wouldn't have known how to ask for help if his head was on fire. And besides, she had that cute little pissed off shrug and Sol's back was turned. As if either of them would know, anyway, if he just sang here, in the truck.

If Aurie had been able to call ghosts himself, call angels, Baz had never heard about it. But obviously, Aurie had some kind of experience with it, had some kind of ability or luck or help. Open across Baz's lap, the book was slowly revealing its secrets, the songs were becoming real, taking on rhythms, melodies. It might have taken an internet-less Aurie half a lifetime to collect melodies for these songs; for Baz, it was a couple of afternoons.

According to Aurie's scrawl, happy songs correlated with good results— *très bonne! Excellent!*—sad ones with darker outcomes.

But none of the Acadian songs seemed quite happy enough, and so he grinned widely to the windshield, wished Lutie could hear him. The train was coming through; he could barely hear himself sing. He'd rustle up some ghosts for them, for sure. He belted out 'Feelin' Groovy' like he was conjuring sunshine, launched into it without hesitation.

It was halfway normal, singing in the car. Hell, he'd always been allowed to sing in the car, hadn't he? But he wasn't moving, and the car wasn't moving, and that meant that he wasn't safe, that he could be found.

\* \* \*

Immediately, Lutie felt a deep cold seep into her bones, ghostcold, and realized what was happening. She shook her head. "Oh, Baz, no," she said to no one in particular.

Behind her, Sol turned sharply, looked at her, came to her side, followed her attention. The train wasn't a long one, but it was plenty long enough. They waited thirty seconds, a minute, the sky bright and heartless. The train passed, a blur, too close for comfort. It was a stupid place for anyone's home, really, even someone used to trains.

The final train fled, leaving an odd silence and they both stared at the Wagoneer. Baz wasn't really all that far away although the sun was at a bad angle so neither of them could see through the dirty windshield. The air was cold, ghostcold, and both Sol and Lutie knew that Baz was sitting in the Wagoneer, singing.

Sol marched across the tracks to his truck, Lutie right behind him and to Baz's credit, he didn't stop singing even after Sol wrenched open the door. It would be easy to get caught up in the song as Baz was singing it, the dappled and drowsy, the loving of life, the wide smile. Instead, Lutie kept watch across the wide hood of the Wagoneer, scanned the strip of land between them and the rails, the ruined barn providing cover for what might come.

Nothing, not yet. But it was cold.

Beside her, Sol wasn't paying attention to anything except Baz. "What the *fuck* did I tell you?" he asked, but it was no question. It wasn't anger in his voice. It was something much different. Still, his hand curled into Baz's collar and he hauled him out of the truck, or maybe Baz wanted to be out anyway.

Lutie sidled closer to Sol, and Baz looked past them to the barn. Surprisingly, he seemed totally unconcerned. "Anything yet?" Disengaging Sol's grip, Baz took maybe five steps away from his brother—*getting braver all the time*—his voice laughter incarnate. He took a deep breath, didn't look at Sol. *This is something he can do. The one thing he thinks he can do to help.*

One more verse, but softly, under his breath, with laughter, ignoring Sol's pleading eyes. They were in the middle of a murder site, Lutie reminded herself, and then noticed movement by a clump of buffaloberry. Motioning with one hand, she glanced at Sol, who nodded, and then

239

she followed his eyes to a further movement, nearer to the stand of cottonwoods by the barn. Two ghosts.

He fanned out, holding one hand out to Lutie, telling her to stay put. "Baz," he called softly. "Shut up. Now."

The nearest ghost appeared to be a young man, clothes nondescript, and it looked hollow-eyed, as though the boy had died of starvation or sickness. Who knew where it had come from, what its story was, why this young man had become stuck. Further away, the other ghost had a long tunic that flapped in an unseen wind. Chinese, from the coolie hat resting on its back when it turned, old-fashioned, as though it had stepped out from a sepia-toned daguerreotype.

*Glad they like Simon and Garfunkel,* Lutie thought, as Baz stopped singing. The silence was enormous.

"Get back in the truck," Sol said, but Baz didn't move. Fine time for him to find backbone. Sol sighed. He couldn't just leave the ghosts. Lutie understood that about him now. Sol couldn't leave things alone when he could do something about it.

Then she paid all her attention to what Sol was doing. He bent down, and she saw him clench his jaw as he did it—*too fast, you gotta make the morning last*—and put one hand to the hard cold ground, closed his eyes, head bent for a moment.

Finding his connection, feeling the threads of underground water, the vibration of the land.

One moment, then pushed his hand inside his shirt, and Lutie bent down too, put her hand out against the ground, tried to feel something of what her brother was feeling. Hand to heart, declaring his intention, and his eyes slid to hers—*understand?*—and then he brought fingers to lips, opened the road and it shimmered in the cold air for a long moment before it settled along the ground, swung over toward the boy, Sol guiding it, fingers of his right hand twitching. Lutie watched as the boy looked back, but only once, then stepped onto the road Sol had made, followed it, not noticing them, eyes half closed in acceptance or ecstasy, it was hard to tell.

Three taps on the ground, then Sol looked over at Lutie, and he said, softly, "The other one, see what you can do, T-Lu."

Her hand was cold against the ground, but she'd found the hum of the earth already, so she looked up at the Chinese rail worker, *who knows how*

240

*long it's been walking this half-life*, and she was well aware Sol was hovering close by, waiting to intervene if necessary. For once, his implied control wasn't an annoyance; it was a relief.

Hand to heart. *C'mon, mister, you need to get going.* Hand shaking. *I really don't want to screw this up.* Up to lips, blowing out, imagining the road shining from her.

Nothing.

Sol was right beside her, crouched. The ghost looked confused. It had come for the singing, and that had quieted, and Baz had taken a few steps toward them, his eyes straining, but seeing nothing, face a blank.

"It's okay," Sol allayed her flash of disappointment. "That one's not going anywhere. Been around a long time, just wants out. Try it again."

She tried again—connection to earth, hand to heart, declaration of intent, open the road—and again the path failed to appear.

Deliberately, Sol took Lutie's left hand, pulled it to the ground, covered it with his own. He met her eyes, but said nothing.

A shiver ran through their combined hands, a *connection*, and Lutie could feel the slow rumble of Sol's heartbeat loud in her own ribcage. Deliberately, he brought her hand to his chest, through the opening in his denim shirt, skin warm, almost hot, too intimate, and his head dropped for a moment before she felt it, so strong it was like a voice in her head, but there were no words, just a declaration of hope, of release, pure as sunlight. Pure as fire, and it was strange, that Sol had said fire was unpredictable, because here it was, intent and dedicated, within him to direct.

Then he brought her hand to his lips, dry and featherlight, scratch of beard—like Papa, remembered goodnight kisses—and breath of life across her fingertips. *He's making this seem so easy.* Like a current of water or the air out an open highway window, miles flashing by in mid-summer, the road opened right across her hand, and she felt Sol bend it to his will: *this way, the exit.*

The road opened and the ghost melded with it like two pieces of quicksilver joining on a flat surface, and then Sol took Lutie's hand, bent down all her fingers except for forefinger and middle which he held together, the ghost gone now, and he tapped her fingers three times against the ground. *Done. Closed. Goodbye.*

The road melted into the ground with an almost imperceptible sound of flow, too low for human ears to hear.

Lutie stared at Sol for a long minute, and he seemed to realize that he was holding her hand, and he let it go. Then all the color drained from his face, and Lutie found herself grabbing a handful of his coat, just to keep him from falling over backwards. He put one hand out to steady himself, rocked onto his knees, the other hand to his head.

Baz crouched beside them, but he didn't touch, didn't ask questions, seemed to know better, or know that questions were pointless.

"Okay," Sol said after a minute, muffled, still in a ball. "Maybe next time." He raised his head, motioned up, and Lutie helped him to his feet. His lips were bone white. Baz seemed about to say something, but Sol's attention was on their sister. "You good to go?"

That wasn't the real question and it was the only question, so Lutie nodded. She was so far from being able to do what Sol had just shown her. Might as well watch the sun to learn how to hang in the sky. They should get out of here, because there was no way she could face off against a ghost, let alone a ghost like Lewis.

They both had momentarily forgotten about Baz, and that was the second mistake.

Perhaps he saw opportunity, or misinterpreted Sol's words, thinking that Lutie needed a little back-up, some way to lull the ghosts enough so she could easily guide one on its path. In any case, Baz picked another song, happy again, something daffy that might have been by Donovan or Arlo Guthrie, Lutie didn't know which.

Lutie had her arm on Sol's, steadying him because although he wasn't admitting it, would never admit it, he was sore and beat up and shouldn't have been doing this, not today. With the first note out Baz's mouth, Sol tensed, took one step but Lutie was in the way and he had to take a second to get around her. No imprecation was going to stop Baz, because once started, Lutie suddenly remembered, Baz was extraordinarily difficult to stop.

When the light came, no one was expecting it, not for some lame hippy song.

Baz didn't notice it, not at the same time as Lutie did. It had no epicenter, no point of origin, it just was. The light nominally came from the vague area of 'above', but was without heat, without source. It filled the whole, was everywhere, and Lutie grabbed Sol's sleeve in fright, but he was already moving to Baz, was finding his way in the washed out landscape. For the first time that she'd witnessed since meeting him, Lutie saw fear naked in Sol's face, and it was all for their brother, no one else.

The light played havoc with sound as well, because Lutie watched Sol pull Baz to his knees, instinctual, go to ground, and maybe Baz stopped singing immediately, the song fading out, but the light stayed. She couldn't tell, because she couldn't hear. Sol covered Baz like there was a blast, shielding him—*hiding him*—and there was no doing that, it was hopeless.

Lutie, only a few steps away, crept to their side, hunched over, one arm across Baz's back, and Sol took the opportunity to look up, eyes trained beyond the wash of light, letting Lutie protect Baz a little.

He put his hand down on the ground and Lutie knew that when the light left, as it would now that Baz had stopped singing, there would be ghosts. There would be a lot of ghosts.

# SIXTEEN

## GANG'S ALL HERE

He'd always been told not to let Baz sing, that it was bad, that for whatever reason it was bad. It called notice to them. It called notice to *Baz*, and what was the very last thing that his father had said to Sol, but to look out for him. Keep him safe. Don't negotiate.

The light was neither good nor bad, it just *was*, and it bathed them in warmth on a cold winter's day, which most people would interpret as 'good'. Sol didn't. Sol couldn't. The light fell under the heading 'attention', it was like a searchlight picking out an escaping prisoner, and there was no way he could hide Baz from it.

Not when Baz had invited it.

"Ta gueule, ta gueule, ta gueule," he whispered into Baz's ear, pressing him to the earth. Baz's hands were clamped over his ears, his face screwed up in pain or alarm, hard to tell which. Then Lutie was there, and she sensed enough to know what was in need of hiding, and she covered Baz with her coat, her arms, her long blonde hair.

It left Sol with enough time to prepare for what would come next, because Lutie had said last time that the ghosts had come on the heels of the white light. With them, a devil, and Sol should have known that it was a stupid idea, bringing Baz with them.

He did not know how to best a devil, did not know how it was done, but he sure as hell knew what to do with a bunch of ghosts. First things first.

It would have helped if he'd had a decent sleep, if he'd had something to eat, if he hadn't been so beat up, if he hadn't had a raging hangover, but there was nothing to help any of that, nothing of remedy in the offing, so he would just have to go forward.

He was sure the ghosts would swarm Baz, as Lutie said they'd done last time, and so he stayed close, would not be able to draw them away, a pitiful distraction, given that Baz was right there. Not a distraction, then, but a weapon. Hand on the ground, making a connection, rumble of water, thrum of earth, matched to his beating heart.

Life.

He imagined floodwaters, and the need to divert them, and he touched his heart before he saw his first ghost, opened the path, held it while the fickle light played over the ground, and Sol wanted to believe that the light was benevolent, that it had an interest in keeping them safe, but that was the way to disappointment at best, madness at worst.

When the light left, the cold was brutal, and Sol held the path even as Lutie cried warning, his name, once. Then he saw them, legion, so many at once, as it had been that night with Aurie's ghost, when his father had once again demonstrated how dangerous it was to have Baz sing.

Sol was ready but not prepared, and many of the ghosts rushed past him, missing or avoiding the path even as others found it. The path was necessary, but also a drain. To hold it, he had to attend to it, which meant he couldn't deal with the ones that got past him.

"Lutie!" he shouted, hand trembling against the ground, frayed handhold to life, to what moved under the skin of the earth. "Lutie!" Voice hoarse in juxtaposition to his brother's, hoping she'd know, that she'd understand.

Hoping that she'd know to protect Baz, to keep him safe while Sol was occupied by the ghosts. But what could she do? What had he shown her that had any practical use right now?

Keeping his hand on the ground, Sol crabbed backwards until he felt Lutie and Baz against his back. The strain of keeping the path open was tremendous, was like holding a live wire fallen on the ground. His bones sang, black spots danced in his vision.

Then the ghosts were gone. Some down Sol's road, still shining in the dust and the cold, but others blinking out, not fully gone, but away again.

Last conscious act: he closed his road, three taps. Behind him, Lutie's arm snaked across his chest, keeping him close. He collapsed into her, unable to keep upright anymore. The three of them, in a huddle on the prairie grass, embraced by a thread of iron, and one of water.

Lutie's breathing was ragged, catching, but Sol couldn't hear Baz at all, which was worse. He turned, tried to turn, but his bruised hip protested, and his breath caught through teeth suddenly clenched in pain.

There, to Sol's right, just beyond where they lay, black against the silvered wood of the sagging barn, a rickety form, legs and burr-pocked body, like something dragging itself out of an oil spill. Its eyes glowed acid from the mass, but it came no closer.

Thirty feet away, that was all.

A creaking noise, haunted house rusty hinge, fork on stoneware, and Sol recognized its laughter. Despite his fire-lanced hip, Sol came up onto one knee, used his hands to push all the way up so he was on his feet, put himself between that which was loved, and that which was despised.

"Oh, my," it said.

"Lutie," Sol called softly over his shoulder. "You okay?"

A moment, and the thing scuttled sideways a few feet. Sol moved with it, knowing it was faster than he was, even if he'd been having a good day. *Toying with me.*

"Yeah." Her voice was hushed; she saw what he saw.

"Baz?"

Cloth against cloth, then, "I'm okay," and Sol closed his eyes, relief radiating through him.

It didn't last.

"Gang's all here," the devil said. "Bonjour, tout le monde!" It sounded like a French-language kid's show presenter. "We have some accounts to settle."

"So we do." Sol's voice dropped and he took a step forward, hadn't the first idea of how he was going to fight this thing.

"Sol," Baz said from behind, "I can—"

"Not a chance," Sol said. "Don't you try it, we can take our time with this one," and that seemed the most absurd thing he'd said thus far. He trusted Baz to know what he meant. Singing was what had gotten them into trouble in the first place.

Then Sol understood what the devil had implied with its greeting. It grinned as though Sol had subtitles, rows of gray teeth like a shark's, angled inwards. *Gang's all here.*

A crashing from far away, scent of ash now in the air, the threat. They were at the Megeath crossing, where Lewis had died and the ghost would be more powerful here than anywhere else on earth. Maybe the devil couldn't physically harm them, but other things could. "What do you want?" Sol asked, but he knew, finally. He'd literally seen the light, and he would have laughed, had it been in him.

"I want to touch God," the devil bowed its head piously.

"Fuck you." Coming from behind, Lutie's voice was bone hard. She knew God from God, apparently. Sol had never had religion, not in the usual sense, but she had. This would be hitting her in ways he couldn't quite wrap his head around, not given the when and the where.

One thing was obvious, though: she'd get in the middle of it if he didn't do something.

"Get to the truck, both of you." As if they'd do it, they wouldn't, neither of them were listening to him anymore.

The devil tsked, skitched and clattered to the side, circling them. The sky darkened. Ash cloud, and Sol approached the thing, held his hand out behind him to ward off anything Lutie might try. There was silence behind, no sound of Baz nor Lutie moving, getting into the truck, nothing.

"He don't sing for you, p'tit diable."

It sighed. "How many times do I have to say it? I don't care about the singing. I'm probably the only one that doesn't give a damn about the singing." It laughed, a saw cutting through metal, all hot oil and spark. "Me, give a damn. That's a good one."

The crashing was close now, and Sol was sure if he turned around, the ash would be thick enough that he wouldn't be able to see Baz and Lutie. *It don't care about the singing, it cares about the company the singing brings and that would be—*

Considering the scope of what the devil was after opened far too much in Sol, something too big for them, for any of them, a cosmic chess board laid out in all directions. *I want to touch God.* He, and Baz, and Lutie, they were of the firmament, not sky, not fire. They were not angels. But Baz could call them, and that had been enough.

Sol dropped to his knees, hand out, knowing he'd have to stop the ghost first. A ghost bound not to a fortuneteller, but to a devil, and Sol was certain this would be what would kill him.

Hand splayed against the hard dirt, nourishing generations of wheat, sun and water and buffalo. Usually, it worked. Any other day, it would have worked. But he was depleted, was out of balance. Everything was out of balance and Sol needed his hand on the ground not to start any process, but to keep himself from falling flat on his face.

*Fuck it, I'm tapped.*

The devil laughed, clattered forward like a handful of cutlery thrown at a wall and Sol's eyes widened as he realized he'd left himself too apart. It was like one of those appalling nature shows where the wolves cut the sick caribou from the herd and brought it down. Thinking this, Sol's head came up, finding what he needed from the earth, just as the ash shadow covered them all: Sol, devil, ghost, brother, sister.

*No time to be the weak one in the field,* he told himself. The devil winked and disappeared in a burst of soft charcoal, like iron filings released from some magnetic hold. Lewis's ghost blew through the shimmer of black powder, flattened Sol with one swing of its wooden club, caught him on his upraised arm instead of his head, which is where it had been aiming. Sol rocketed backwards with the blow, and it was no time to be on his back, in this ghost's way.

The ash swirled, and enormous heat rose behind Sol—fire, and that made sense. It wasn't cleansing, not with Lewis, not for his ghost. It was payback, was part of Lewis's strength.

Sol would have to rely on his feet to find his ground, not his hands. His primal connection with the earth, with life, was still there, and he tried to concentrate, but that bat of Lewis's was a lethal distraction. This thing had created bodies from North Platte to Brule, was in the thrall of a devil, was ten times as strong as anything he'd ever faced before. But if he could get rid of the ghost, he would undermine le p'tit diable. He could hope, anyway.

One small problem: the ghost was enormous, had Ted Williams's swing, and they were standing in the very place it had died.

*Time. I need time.* Enough time to make his ghost road, just a few seconds. The abandoned barn, some shelter. *Five seconds, that's all I need.* He got there before the ghost, sliding between door and frame, and skidding into the darkness, knowing that the opening wasn't wide enough to let Lewis pass without some negotiation; ghosts tended to forget they were ghosts, followed the same rules they did when they were humans. They didn't pass through walls, which Sol hoped would allow him enough time. He did not doubt for a second that Lewis would follow him.

Murderous ghosts usually wanted to follow him. A talent, of sorts.

The ash floated in the air still, the glow of the ghostly fire through the missing boards, that and the ghastly sound of Lewis's dragging walk, and Sol backed further into the darkness of the barn.

He stood breathing hard for a moment, then bent down, sucked air as his hip flared with pain, one hand to the earthen floor, no foundation to this structure, built straight on the prairie. He found his connection, brought his shaking hand to his chest, heart hammering so hard it caused the medic in him concern. *Fait attention. Concentrate.* The light coming in from the outside, house-fire bright, flickered and died, and the barn pitched into blackness.

Lewis's ghost might be big and lethal, but it was also noisy, which was about the only advantage Sol had. So he heard the ghost when it shoved open the barn door, using its massive strength, blotting what little light there was. In the darkness, Sol had a sense of its mass in front of him, a presence rising higher than his head, close enough to touch.

Abandoning all efforts to aim anything true or otherwise, Sol tackled the giant around the waist, getting a firm grip on the moldering cloth, the sinews in his hands ropy and taut like a stringed instrument. The blows it could administer from that close were negligible, so Sol kept pushing, knew he could get it down if he angled and turned. There was nothing to it, really, and then the ghost stepped back with Sol, and Sol lost his footing and they crashed backwards into an ancient stall, Sol headfirst, bearing the brunt of it.

Dazed, he rolled to the side as he fell, out of the way, far enough so that even with its orangutan's reach, Lewis wouldn't get him on the first swing of that bat. Nothing came. Silence. Sol came up on his elbows, scrambled back, listening. Still nothing. Gone. Again. Sol swore.

*It's gone, goddamn, fucking merde trou d'cul—* and he still couldn't make out anything, only soft darkness, no fire, no ash, no nothing. Not daylight either. *En garde.* Silence. Then he was picked up from behind and thrown across the dark expanse, a moment of giddy flight. Being tossed across a room wasn't a novel activity for Sol; based on his trajectory, he had a brief moment to appreciate how hard the landing was going to be.

He was wrong, though, because he fell into moldy hay, and it was marginally better than smacking his head against a wall, or any of those other hard landings he'd had in his years of putting angry ghosts and drunks and psych patients to bed. Even so, he tumbled immediately, breath knocked from his chest, heard the gutteral rattle of the ghost.

He dug deep, centered, hand to earth, hand to heart, bringing fingers to his mouth, just taking breath—

He had time to do that, and then saw a blur of black on black, moving so fast, and then bony claws were on his chest, smell of gasoline and burnt rubber in his nostrils, and he was picked up again, slammed so hard against the wall he wondered for a second if he'd go through. Sol had time to get a foot up and tried to break one of the thing's femurs—*must be like dry sticks*—but the sole of his boot slid uselessly down the length of bone.

*Lutie*, he thought, no air left at all.

The ash covered Sol just as she heard the devil's laughter fade away to nothing, but Lutie didn't dare leave Baz, not when she understood it was her role, that it was what Sol wanted her to do. Even though Sol needed help, anyone could see that: Sol wasn't in the position to put up much of a fight, and if he couldn't create his deadroad for Lewis, then he was lost. He wouldn't last more than five minutes one-on-one with a ghost like that.

She coughed and hacked in the ash storm, and Baz's head came, up, face the same color as cafeteria coleslaw, and she thought he looked like he was going to be sick. Instead, eyes streaming, he asked, "Where's Sol?" and Lutie didn't know how to answer that.

*He's led the ghost away from us*, she wanted to say, but the words caught in her throat. Baz grabbed her hands, held them down, crouched on the freezing prairie, wind so high it made its own sort of music. "Where is he?" Baz demanded, his grip tight, eyes wild.

Against the wind, Lutie struggled to her feet. The devil had disappeared, but Sol and Lewis had gone into the barn, and the ash was laced with the glow of fire. Could ghosts light fires, she wondered. Would Lewis burn Sol alive in the barn? Would that be the revenge exacted?

Sol was the threat: the ghost and the devil wanted him out of the way, same way they'd wanted Aurie out of the way. To get to Baz.

*Well, they don't know about me. Sleeper cell, you assholes.*

She heard a crash from inside the barn, knew there was no room for error, no time for practice. Practice was a luxury for students, for dilettantes. She was going to send this ghost away. That was her only choice, her only avenue. Sol's only chance. Hand to the prairie. Find the connection, all of it was there for her to reach out and use. All of it, spread before, a wash of color. Not a line, not for her, but broader, vaster.

Her aim was true, all right. Her heart: *Come on, you useless bastard.* Her head: *I am smarter than you are, and I say it's time to get the hell away from my brother.* Her mouth: *Here it comes.*

Blew on it, and instead of a road, it was a net, and it shimmered out, thrown and dripping.

It did not lead away from her, and why wouldn't how she did it be different than Sol, didn't that make sense? Hadn't she always found her own way?

The net went out, flashed against the earth like a sheet flung over an unmade bed. It blocked the ash and the fire, washed darkness across the sky. It was huge. What Lutie let loose on the day flashed and faded, and then left them alone between the river and the tracks.

Far away, a train whistle sounded, and Lutie turned a slow circle, hands held wide. No ghosts. No ash. No sign of the devil. Midday, the year an infant, cold wind caressing winter grasses, buffeting the branches of the cottonwoods.

She had done *something*, all right.

Arms clutching the other, Baz stood beside her, face still an uncomfortable color, wind and glare causing his eyes to squint below drawn brows. "Lutie," he whispered.

And then she was running to the barn, because that's where he'd been, that's where the crashing had come from, the noise of a fight and now there was no sound whatsoever, only the wind battering barn boards.

Baz was right behind her, and they entered the barn, roof sagging inwards, open to the sky, letting in more than enough light to see what had happened. What Lutie had made happen.

The barn was empty.

No ghost, of course, and Lutie had been certain of that: she knew it was gone. But no Sol either. A small owl flew from a corner as Baz shouted Sol's name, but his voice was the only sound, the owl the only living thing on the move. It circled over to the trees, disappeared into the tangle of dark branches.

She hadn't made a road. She hadn't sent the ghost to wherever it was supposed to be. She hadn't taken anything in, either, made Mirielle's binding. Lutie had done something else. *Like dirt swept under a rug,* she thought. *It's still there, I just can't see it.*

It. The ghost. Lewis.

And Sol, her brother.

*Oh God,* she thought. *What have I done?*

Baz was scanning the perimeter of the barn, walking over collapsed walls, lifting up pieces of board like Sol might be trapped underneath. For a moment, his progress looked methodical, but then he grew more frantic, tossed the boards to the side, and his hands kept going, kept trying to lift things too heavy, and a thin keen noise escaped him.

"What have I done?" she asked aloud, barely, coming up to Baz's shoulder, leaning against him, and he whirled around, grabbed her by her shoulders, looked like he wanted to shake her, only stopped himself through mica-thin control.

His eyes searched her face. Slowly, she shook her head. "I don't know," she whispered. "I don't know where he is."

With a jerk of his head, Baz let her go, one hand coming up to cover his mouth, and Lutie's throat tightened so hard and fast it hurt.

"Is he—" and he couldn't finish it. Ash, and the sound of the devil, both these things had been present, before. That and light, and it was beyond anything Lutie knew how to deal with. Baz opened his mouth, looked past her, and his expression was empty as blue-skied prairie.

Lutie didn't have the necessary words, didn't even know what those might be.

Most of the afternoon crept by, and Baz refused to leave the ruined barn. He knew his reticence worried Lutie, maybe even annoyed her, but he was past caring what might rub his sister the wrong way.

When it was just Sol acting on his own, things were calm. Sol in the driver's seat looked like job done, no fuss, no drama. With Dad, it had been theatrics, all the time, and it had been fun, Baz could admit it now, ghostbusters and music and hairy midnight boozecans. But this, Lutie's dealings with ghosts, this was big and frightening and out of control.

Baz realized he was being childish. Ghosts were scary, were the definition of goddamn scary, underneath Aurie's funhouse and Sol's competent silence. *Sol, and Dad, they kept me from it. In their different ways, they kept me out of it.* He'd never known, had never been shown, what they did and aside from two times—when the fortuneteller had died, and when Sol had been sent back from New Orleans—neither had ever screwed up so profoundly that Baz had noticed.

Finally, after Baz had rightly concluded there were no more hiding spots to find, he walked to the doorframe, leaving Lutie in the middle of the barn, in the middle of her debacle. Baz wished he could leave her, wished that she would just go. Wished he could leave this scene, that things could go back to how they'd been, before.

Finally, he heard a rustle from behind him and then Lutie settled in, sat on the transom, took his hand and dragged him down to a sit. He was brittle as spring ice, as cold.

"What now?" he asked, even though he knew she had no answers. Yet he still had to ask. *I have to get out of this habit, expecting other people to have answers.* That felt a lot like telling himself to grow up, and he shook his head like water had lodged in his ears.

She shrugged, and he studied her profile a moment before staring out at the prairie, looking for similarities in the terrain and finding none. "I really need something to eat. I can't think." She said it, terse. She was so mad, so mad at herself. Baz didn't have it in him to be nice about it. The breakfast seemed a long time ago, watching Lutie and Sol on their hands and knees in the winter-blasted park. He'd eaten, then. They hadn't.

The sky was turning orange, sun close to the western horizon, making it hours since Sol had disappeared. Truthfully, he was hungry too. Leaving seemed like an admission of guilt, though, a point of no return.

"So, what do we do?" And his voice sounded small, lost, and he hated that.

"Something to eat first," Lutie said emphatically, hand stretching out, inviting him. "I don't think they'll deliver pizza out here." Making a joke, trying it out. She waited for him to smile, but he didn't have that in him either. She sighed. "We'll take a look at the book, I'll figure it out." Talking to herself, not him. Right. She was going to figure it out.

But a thread of certainty was growing in Baz, a hot dreadful line through the bleak landscape: he knew what he had to do. He'd done it before, had that conversation, which he would describe as bone-rattling. He deserved to have his bones rattled. He deserved worse. Sol would kill him, but he'd have to be here to do it, which suited Baz just fine.

"I'm not going anywhere," he said, ignoring her proffered hand. "You can leave if you want." He gestured to the Wagoneer, silently waiting by the crossing. "You have a key?" She could walk. For all he cared.

"He left the keys in the truck." Her eyes were as empty as her voice, water and white sand, surf, blue and green in equal measure. She took a careful breath, wouldn't look at him. "Don't do it."

"Don't what?" He stood then, wondered where his heart was, and knew. "What do you not want me to do now?"

Her mouth twisted. She ignored his question. "I need your help with the songbook, Baz. Please. Whatever I did, it wasn't the same as what Sol showed me. I don't think I sent them away for good. With the right song, maybe we can call back Lewis's ghost. And maybe Sol." She nodded once, for emphasis, a period at the end of a declaration.

"Maybe? Maybe you can do that." He almost laughed, but his throat closed up. "It'd be a whole lot better if you could just *un*do it."

She had a temper. Baz knew it. He was hoping for it. "You're not helping, Baz." Standing, the both of them, now. He was a lot taller than her, which just seemed to make her madder, having to look up at him. "You're not helping!" and she was shouting, she was crying. A shaky breath, then another. "We have to do this together." Drop of a register at least, low, afraid, sun slanting sideways. "So, don't go off alone. Don't talk to that thing. No deals."

And that was what she didn't want him doing. She had seen his plans on his face, and he cursed himself for being a transparent fool.

"No *more* deals, you mean," he said. Petty, that's what he'd resorted to, and his own anger cut him, hurt from the inside. He couldn't hold it, it slipped sideways within him. "I'm sorry." He wasn't made for holding grudges, not with anyone. "I'm just…"

It hung there, what he was now.

She shook her head, and the dying light caught filaments of copper and bronze in her hair. The temperature was falling as quickly as the sun. Her mouth was a hard line. "If I say I'm sorry, it's done," she explained. "And this can't be over, not yet."

Those words ought to have caused him cheer, but they felt flat, unauthorized, pitiful, even. *I have to do something*, he thought. *I have to be able to do something.* But he remembered being young, and alone in their bayou house, when everyone had gone: Sol, and their dad, but mostly Maman and Lutie. He hadn't stopped anything from happening then.

*You're not going to stop anything now.* They got in the Wagoneer, and Lutie drove, had to adjust the seat to reach the pedals and for the first time, Baz felt tears well up in him. He looked out the window and it passed.

Back in an Ogallala truck stop, Lutie consumed a western omelette with all the dispassion of a remote military campaign while Baz ignored a plate of pale fries. Over cans of soda, they studied the blue book their father had left them, but it revealed no clues. They found three more songs on the internet, including one beside which his father had written *très dangereuse*. A site dedicated to the Acadian festival circuit of the seventies, words similar enough that Baz could impose the melody to the lyrics in the book. Baz forced himself to listen intently, memorizing. It was slow, and sad. He recognized the tune, deep down, stirred. He'd always been a quick study when it came to music.

Nothing else came easily, just music and charm. They were probably related.

Nerves were fried. Lutie went to bed early, but Baz knew she wouldn't sleep. He knew he wouldn't sleep. It was all pretend, all of it, except for the bits that were shockingly real.

The room he shared with Sol felt empty and damp, earlier shower mist still clinging to everything, a slick of cold moisture, the inside of a cave. Baz sat on the edge of the bed, knowing that tomorrow he'd sing for ghosts, would sing for one ghost in particular. His father had told him singing was dangerous, had said it to his face when he was a kid, had written it in a book in case his son forgot the obvious, but Baz had no idea yet what the song would do. It might grow flowers for all he knew, make his nose lengthen. They had nothing else.

Lutie had nothing else.

He, however, had one other card to play, and it didn't matter what Lutie wanted or didn't want, how much guilt had backed up on her. He, Basile Sarrazin, he had a devil. Or the devil had him. Baz knew which it was, but he didn't want to think about it.

He drew on his canvas coat, needed his goofy hat for a night this cold. He didn't have to drive anywhere, he could walk to the tracks. Besides which, Lutie would hear the Wagoneer, it sounded like a space shuttle launching. He left quietly, pulled the door shut, left the television still blaring because the walls were thin. He'd become expert at leaving quietly, so a woman wouldn't suspect.

A staggeringly good set of tricks. Charm, musical blood, the ability to lie to women, to leave at midnight. A couple of other talents that didn't bear thinking about just now, at night, meeting up with a devil.

He didn't have to call it: le p'tit diable was waiting for him in the parking lot. Baz wasn't expecting it of course, and nearly jumped out of his skin when the death-rattle chortle came from behind an abused Ford Escort, laughing like Baz was a bad joke.

Baz couldn't see it and he wondered if that was better or worse. He stopped, hands still in his pockets, head ducked down. It wouldn't hurt him. Not physically. The wind whirled round, nipped his ears, made his jewelry cold on his skin.

He swallowed. "You know why I'm here," he said, cutting right to it.

Tonight, it sounded like old dried leaves skittering across pavement, almost insubstantial. *It's a trick, don't let it fool you, like a bird pretending to have a broken wing.* Laughter, but tired. "I need you to sing for me," it responded.

Baz shook his head, not a 'no', precisely, more confusion. Disbelief. "I thought you didn't care about music."

It coughed. "I don't."

"Then why?" Baz asked.

"I don't have to tell you. You just need to do it."

Baz's eyes narrowed, trying to follow the sound of it as it circled. "When? Now?" Alone in the parking lot with white light, the noise of it. The attention. Still, Baz nodded. "And you'll bring him back here, you'll bring Sol back?"

The thing made a noise, swore in French, in some other language. After that, English. "I don't bring anybody back, that's not my job. You owe me, Basile Sarrazin. Don't forget. For the address. When I say sing, you sing. Understand?"

Baz was shaking, body and voice. "But you have to bring him back."

Though Baz couldn't see it, not clearly, he heard the thing patter closer, and he felt it brush against his leg, like moving gorse, the size of a large dog, or a deluxe baby carriage. Baz jumped back, electrified.

"I don't have to do nothing, kid. Your sister was the one that got all fancy. Get her to fix it for you. She has options. That's right. Tell her that she has options. And tell her to give me back my goddamn ghost while you're at it."

And the diable rustled so close that Baz collided against the car, one hand flung out to save himself from falling, from being on the ground with the thing. He grabbed the sideview mirror of the Escort and kept upright, but only silence met his frantic gaze, heart going like a rabbit on a road.

It was silent and once the fear and fright had subsided, Baz realized that he was alone. That he had accomplished nothing. That the devil was gone, and with it, any chance of bringing Sol back.

# BAZ, BEFORE

After M'man sent the ghosts away, Baz didn't stick around for the tongue-lashing. He'd suffered that often enough to recite it by heart. Instead, he went upstairs, avoiding his mother as best as he could. Luckily, she seemed more concerned with yelling at Lutie in the kitchen.

Baz was bored within ten minutes. Before he'd left, Sol had hidden away most of his best stuff and Baz still hadn't figured out where the cache was. Their bedroom was boring in the extreme: too known, too hot, too much a place of exile. The sun crept across the sky, and Baz eventually understood that lunch was not forthcoming, despite the fact that his mother had been in the middle of baking when she'd come out to the cemetery, flour on her shaking hands. She hated baking in this heat, Baz knew, which was probably why she was so pissed off.

She was *really* pissed off, though, judging from the banging downstairs, the rapid footsteps as she rushed up the staircase, searching for something in the room across the hall, then back out again, down the steps, bump-a-bump-a-bump. A door slammed, and then the Pontiac's trunk, and then she was back in again.

It was stupidly hot under the roof and the house had nothing remotely like air conditioning, only an old fan Sol had rescued from storm-wreckage and repaired. When turned on, it drowsily stirred the sweating air around the room like soup. The two screened bedroom windows faced out onto the bayou, opposite the highway and the cemetery, and Baz killed some time squinting through Sol's binoculars, trying to spot the pelican's nest and tracking the slow pass of alligators.

He tried to ignore the muffled sounds of his mother's temper made manifest.

Once, he heard Lutie's cry of complaint and then M'man hushing her. *Petite misère, she gets away with murder*, he thought, carefully re-positioning the binoculars on the desk, aware of where he was putting them because there was no end to the tortures Sol would devise if he found out Baz had touched his things, even those he'd left out in the open.

No sign of his brother and father, of course. Baz thought they'd been gone for a couple of days already, maybe more, but it was hard to keep track in this heat when he had better things to do. Papa had given a curt nod to Sol as he was packing the boat, and Sol had hopped in, *readyready-ready*, sharing their secret traiteur code in the identical grins, signaling adventure, excitement. The work of men, not boys, and Baz had been left on the dock.

Sol had said, in a voice that had changed perceptibly over the summer, a voice that reeked of condescension, that they'd be gone for a week. *Back in time for mon anniversaire, maudit bioque, j'ai espoir de something good.* Then rubbed knuckles hard on the top of Baz's head, laughed when Baz had tried to hit back, thin arms too short for Sol's suddenly huge reach.

Baz wasn't planning on giving the asshole *anything* for his damn birthday.

Despite this, Baz wished Sol was here now, that Papa was, even. There had been ghosts in the cemetery, not too difficult to figure that out from the temperature alone. Maman's reaction had simply iced the cake. No use in pretending that Maman's freak-out was due to baking in extreme heat, because it hadn't been. No, the massive meltdown had been in response to what Lutie had been doing, what Lutie wanted — *un fantôme, comme toi, M'man*. Whatever the hell that meant.

Bump-a-bump-a-bump up the stairs, soft chatter, intense and angry. Maybe Maman had forgotten him. Baz crept by the door, ready to make a noise, but not brave enough to test her temper by opening the door when he'd been told to stay put.

A mutter, a soft sob. Was Maman…crying? Baz's brow furrowed, and he scratched his side, shirtless now in the oppressive heat of late afternoon. A mosquito had found its way in, came out of the shadows, and Baz silently slapped it away, listening by the door.

"Non. Jamais!" And then, louder, calling to Lutie, "Anweille! Bouge-toi, Luetta! Now!" More scurrying, Maman talking to herself so softly Baz couldn't hear, all the words running together, didn't matter what language it was, Baz understood exactly what she was saying, if not the meaning. "I'm not doing it, I can't." Silence, like she was on the phone, but the phone was attached to the wall downstairs in the kitchen. "Chtedi," she said, her French different from Papa's, nasal, full of drawl, "I tell you, I'm not doing it." More rustling in the bedroom. "That's not fair. I *can't*. Tabarnac, t'es un p'tit câlisse." And Baz had never heard his mother swear like this, the language of the church, the sacred made profane.

*Who is she talking to?*

She was definitely crying and all of it was so wrong—the day, her tears, the fractured crazy one-sided conversation. "Pas lui. Ne le blesse pas." Baz leaned against the door, knew he couldn't open it without her losing it completely. He didn't want to be responsible for that. He'd already done enough, hadn't he?

*I shoulda stopped Lutie.*

It had been such a beautiful moment, before the ghosts had come. The day full of bright sky, and so warm, smell of salt and oil and dust and rot. Home. The light. Bathed in light softer than forge-like August ever brought, touch on his skin, one with the day, his voice and the light, the light, the light.

Followed by ghostcold, and Maman. Lutie wanting a pet and that was that. "Women," Baz said softly, one hand touching the door, listening to the mad chatter of his mother on the other side.

An hour later, Baz opened the door as quietly as he could manage, and it swung into the hallway a foot or so, wide enough that he could see the bare boards, the hall landing. He darted a look, then dared to step out. He stood at the top of the stairs, listening. Downstairs, the sound of Maman's voice, constant, angrily gathering things, banging doors. Below that, white noise, Lutie grousing about some infraction. He had to pee, so he ducked into the bathroom, bent wire holding a roll of single-ply, a basket of doll parts by an enameled tub dotted with chips and decorated with Lutie's bath crayon artwork.

He stood to relieve himself, glanced out the window beyond the faded curtain lace.

Maman walked to the car with a large cardboard box in her arms. She balanced it on one hip, opened the huge trunk and Baz realized it was full of boxes. Their father's green suitcase that he used when gigging up north during festival season rested among them. She slammed the trunk, big as a queen-sized mattress, turned, gestured to something that Baz couldn't see, and Lutie reluctantly crossed the worn track between house and dirt lot next to the highway. As Baz watched, she got into the car and Maman shut the passenger door.

"Best zip up, son. You're the man of the house, now." The sighing voice was so close Baz sprayed piss against the beadboard as he jerked around. His hands grappled with his fly, backed against the window, suddenly without air in his lungs. C'est quoi-là? What the *fuck* was that?

Towels and linens were kept in the angle between eaves and roof behind a door with squares of canvas for hinges and an old wooden spool for a knob. The cupboard door was open a crack and inside, something moved. Baz's breath came in thin gasps.

"Comment? Cat got your tongue?" And whatever it was, it thought it was funny and it laughed.

Baz didn't wait for more.

He thundered down the stairs, missed two, slid, hit the wall at the bottom and kept moving. Shirtless, slick with sweat, so hot, and the mosquitoes were thick in the shade of the cypress as Baz burst through the door, across the planks that joined the house to the land, but the Pontiac was gone, dust still hanging in the air along with the bugs.

Baz didn't stop, bare feet tough as hobnail boots, across the lot past his father's truck, onto the cracked highway where he came to a halt, breathing hard. The Pontiac had already taken the bend to the north, was out of sight, the throb of its engine fading into the stir of crickets and bird. The sun hit him sideways, an orange, magic light, still so hot his feet felt that they might fry on the old pavement.

He stood for a moment, hands hanging loosely at his side, breath coming hard, disbelief providing a last armor against the evident truth. Stay in your room until your father gets home, she'd said. And then had packed the car, taken Lutie, and driven away.

Maybe they needed groceries, he thought, a kind of last-ditch attempt at reason. Then he felt a tendril of cool breeze, as though respite. Colder than respite, in fact. This was not a safe place at all. He was standing not twenty feet from the cemetery, almost exactly in the place where Old Robichaux had bought it a few days ago, and Baz's breath came off-kilter again.

Unnatural cold, in the middle of the highway, no Maman, no Papa. Merde, not even Sol. None of the neighbors were walking distance, and Papa had the boat. Baz thought he might be able to drive the truck if he could find the keys, but to where?

He'd never had a ghost talk to him before, but maybe that wasn't bad. *Stupid tout-emmerdé, it's bad. We all know I'm the one who don't see ghosts, so what the hell was that thing in the closet? Maybe I'm making stuff up, maybe it's the heat.* Still, he was standing beside a cemetery and night was falling fast. Making up his mind, he turned, headed back to the house. *Maybe they'll be home soon*, he thought, last sandbag against the flood.

Night one alone was spent on the couch, listening to the scratching upstairs, footsteps passing back and forth as though waiting for something, banging and the occasional sigh. Baz didn't get hardly any sleep. He padded to the kitchen on whispering feet, ate the remainder of a loaf of bread with peanut butter straight from the jar.

Dawn painted the main room pink; Baz didn't dare go back upstairs, but it was cold outside and he didn't know if that was ghostcold or just morning cold, so he pissed in the kitchen sink. "M'man, elle explosera if she finds out, her." He said it out loud, words hanging in the cold air, and didn't feel anything but fear.

On the table, in the middle of a saucer, rested her wedding ring. Baz stared at it, buttoning his fly, eyes darting around the room, felt a slice of cold. "Bon Dieu," he whispered. He had no idea what it meant, the ring, what his mother meant by leaving it, that's what he told himself. What had she said? Pas lui, ne le blesse pas.

*Not him, don't hurt him.*

The sun rose, and the house grew gradually colder. To keep himself company, he sporadically hummed a tune under his breath, sang a little. By noon, Baz had been touched a dozen times, cold fingers prodding him, one pulled his hair, ran cool contact down his spine. Into the kitchen again, found a bag of salt in the baking cupboard, ignored the wedding ring, knowing somewhere deep inside what his mother had done, what she was saying by leaving it. He retreated to the cupboard under the stairs, sprinkled salt around him, whimpering.

Night two was sheer misery and everlasting.

# DEADROADS

Dark like the inside of a baseball mitt, and so airless and hot Baz thought he might pass out. He wrapped his bare arms around his bent knees, bathed in sweat, stinging his eyes, feverish. Over his head, where the treads of the stairs made an uneven ceiling to his hideout—his prison—he heard the scratching again, long and thin, fingernails torn perhaps. Talons, maybe, like an osprey. There was no way he would know, could know.

He wondered what time it was, could only see gray seeping from around the door's thin outline. Dawn. Dusk. A dense cloudy day, maybe, though he couldn't hear rain. He tried not to hear much of anything; he'd heard plenty already. The scratching. The moans, the screams. Mostly, the pacing, slow and stately, ominous as a clock ticking down, weighted, shifting footfalls against the floorboards where he sat. Something substantial was out there, circling him.

The cupboard stank. He stank. He'd lost track of time. Once or twice he'd tried to get some food, get out into the kitchen, use the toilet, but it had been so cold once outside the cupboard that he'd been able to see his breath. Inside, here, it was warm. *It's warm because it's fucking August.* Ghostcold outside, though. Warm meant safe.

Without Maman, without Papa, he wasn't going out. *I'll starve,* he thought, huddling closer, dropping his forehead to his knees. He was so thirsty. Past the point of hunger where your stomach growled. *I'll have to leave soon. She's not coming back, she's gone.*

He knew that now. His teachers hadn't come right out and called him slow, but it was hard, following Sol in school. *Oh, you're Sol's brother,* because Sol was good at everything, and all Baz could do was sing and where did that get you with teachers? But he wasn't stupid, not really, despite the report cards. And he'd had a lot of time to think about it, trapped below the stairs in the cupboard where Maman stored toys and games and a much-abused pink Barbie penthouse.

His sister had called up ghosts and somehow he'd helped her. She'd wanted one for a pet, though Baz couldn't fathom why anyone would want that. Why Maman would want that. His mother had told the ghosts to leave and they had, as long as she was there.

*Elle partait. Elle n'est pas ici.* Like the song, one that Papa had sung not so long ago, as he'd burned some scraps in an oil drum, black smoke rising in the night. *She's gone, she's not here.*

## Robin Riopelle

*Le soir des noces après souper*
*Trois hommes noirs sont arrivés*
*Trois hommes noirs sont arrivés*
*En demandant la mariée.*
*Elle n'est pas ici.*

Baz could almost remember the tune, only heard once. Almost.

A chuckle, close-by, on the stairs above his head. No point in crying. *They don't care about tears.*

And then, finally, the sound of an outboard motor, the faint burr of his father's voice on the dock, and it was going to be over. Baz could almost believe that it would be over.

# SEVENTEEN

## HOPE IS A PRONOUN

Nothing was open, not this early on a Sunday morning, not even the gas station. Technically, it was still night, the sky hung with stars, soon fading, soon gone. Birthday plus two, but Lutie didn't think Baz would be making any jokes about it today. Her hands were frozen, even deep in the pockets of her Canadian winter-certified parka, tuque secure on her head, pulled down over her ears, colder than cold at this time of dawn, this time of year, this part of the prairies.

Nothing was familiar and everything was the same. She kept walking.

Whatever anyone wanted to say about it, this whole mess rode on her. It wasn't fair, she hadn't asked for any of this, had been dragged into the middle of it. But none of that factored, if she was honest. It was still all on her. Sol was gone, and Baz would probably try to cut a deal with the diable, had maybe already tried last night. A small comfort, then: Lutie knew he'd be rejected because the devil had no incentive to change anything. This was what the goddamn thing had wanted, wasn't it? For Sol to go away. Evil already had a marker on Baz, hardly needed anything else from him. That was sort of on her as well, because it had been her address he'd bargained for.

*This isn't useful*, she told herself. *Blame isn't going to fix anything. Blame means that it's beyond repair, and it's not. It can't be.*

She hadn't stuck around just so she could screw things up, she wasn't in the habit of screwing things up. Walking purposefully, she crossed the park, still unoccupied by the ghosts of old people. He'd made it look easy, Sol, so damn easy, and it hadn't been. It wasn't. Nevertheless, she'd gotten rid of the *one* ghost, all right. She'd done it almost first try.

Baz had been so angry with her in the barn, and she deserved it. Sure, she didn't know what she was doing, sure she hadn't had any training, other than what Sol had shown her. But Sol was *gone*, she'd done that, and Sol was all Baz had. She'd sweet-talked Baz into finding her ghosts, into singing when he knew it was dangerous, and this was what grew from that seed. She wouldn't be surprised if Baz didn't want anything to do with her.

A story unfolded every time Baz opened his mouth, and she couldn't imagine not knowing what those stories were going to be. Angels, devils, ghosts, brothers. Estranged from her for all these years, returned in a way that made their absence suddenly impossible, intolerable.

Her thoughts wandered back to Sol, the dark brother, unknowable, a distance in him that invited nothing. Had he always been like this? A dim childhood presence, a shadow against the light that had been Baz. But there, always there. She remembered him scolding her, lodging calm complaint to their parents against her. Catching her eye at the table when she was doing something in defiance of her parents, marking her. In many ways, he had seen her in a way no one else had, had seen the truth of her.

She stared at the low-rise buildings, wanting open prairie, wanting big sky and endless nothing.

*I have to do something.* But there was nothing that she knew to do, no knowledge that would help. Only what her mother had shown her over two mad years of constant motion. Two years that Lutie had tried to erase from her past, lock away. *M'man was nuts, she had nothing to teach me.*

The diable would have no interest and perhaps no ability to bring Sol back—*whatifhesdead?*—and Lutie bit hard on her lip, keeping back tears. What if she had killed him, sent him off to wherever ghosts went, swept up in the wash that Lutie had un-dammed, not a road, but a flood. *No. He's alive. Whatever I did, it wasn't the same as what Sol did. If Baz can get Lewis back, maybe Sol comes with him.* She didn't want to think about what might be happening to Sol, wherever he was, because all her hope rested on him being with Lewis, and that hadn't been going very well in the barn.

She covered a kilometer, then two. North of town, out to the hospital, and she saw one ghost, fleeting, in the distance, but it didn't hang around and was gone by the time she got close. The sort of brief sighting that would, when articulated to the parental units, prompt an upping of her meds. *Am I crazy?* Traffic was starting to move along the roads, interstate truckers rousing from their slumber before the rest of the world.

*I am not crazy. Think, Lutie.* She'd always been smart, could figure out puzzles and knots, and this was no different. Find Lewis's ghost, find Sol. They'd deal with the consequences once Sol was back. It would, however, mean that Baz would have to sing again, because calling back Lewis's ghost wouldn't be a matter of getting lucky, it was a matter of talent. And once Lewis was in the ring, it would be a matter of power.

Somewhere between talent and power, Lutie was hoping for a bit of grace, that someone, something, would smile upon them. That was different than luck, she told herself.

No ghosts now, just prairie, and she stopped, looked eastward, dawn streaking the sky, another day. Another chance maybe. Not just for Baz, or Sol, but for herself. Sol was the only one who really saw her, who could cast eyes on her and understand what was underneath. Scary as that attention was, Lutie realized it was rare and she wasn't ready to let that go, not yet.

The Megeath grade crossing was eight miles west of Brule, marked only by a broken barn, across the feeble highway from a fairground that had last seen a fair sometime during the Carter administration. They knew exactly where the crossing was now, when it was much too late. Lutie drove fast, which was fine by Baz. *Let's get this over with.* Baz clutched his father's blue book, and that was all the ammunition they had: an old musical recipe book, Lutie's unproven ability, and a thirty-year-old crime scene.

And his voice. That, always.

He wasn't stupid, he knew what he could do was dangerous and strange, even for *his* family. Apparently, his father had some talent or knowledge in this regard and it hadn't made any difference in the end. *And I can't even see what I call up.* Wielding this trick was like being an idiot savant, able to calculate distances and dates with no ability to apply it to the real world, a freak with talent but no purpose.

For his part, Aurie had at least indicated what songs worked well, but not with *what*; Baz thought that happy songs tended to result in happier ghosts and the occasional angel. An angel, however, attracted devils and how much did anyone want them around?

*I don't feel like singing a fucking happy song, anyway.*

There was a time when he'd been allowed to sing; he could remember it. A long, long time ago, under a canopy of cypress and oak, voice carrying across land so water-logged it had the same viscosity as chocolate pudding. His songs hadn't called anything back then, it had just been singing. *He gave me a fiddle,* Baz thought, watching the optical blur of wire fencing beside the highway rise and fall like a line of music. *He gave me a fiddle to stop me singing. Wonder when he figured it out, what I could do.*

"How about this one?" he asked, pointing to the book, and he sung a snippet of song, the tune memorized earlier in the day. Not really in his range, what he'd heard, so he transposed the key, brought it down. It still sounded off, not right. He might attract howling dogs.

Beside him, Lutie made a face. "I thought happy songs were what we wanted. You know. Lull ghosts into submission?" A question. They were still unsure how the singing worked. It was not the time to be unsure, and there was no other time. "That doesn't sound real happy."

"Well," Baz reasoned, "we hook Lewis with the heartbreakers, reel him in, then sing him a happy one. Lull him like a baby." His gaze cut to her, then back to the fenceline. Reading in the car always made him feel like throwing up. "Do you think the words matter?"

After a moment, Lutie shook her head. "I think it's the sentiment that counts. If the melody is happy, then the sentiment is happy. You could be singing about dog food for all the ghosts will care."

"Yeah, but I'll care if I'm singing about Alpo," he pointed out.

She grimaced: point made. "See? So it matters to *you*, and if you don't believe what you're singing, then the ghosts won't either. If you think it's happy, it's happy."

Right. Baz slouched down in the car seat a little more, pissed off that she seemed so sure about something she knew nothing about. Pissed off that he was listening to her.

"'Cause I don't have a fuckin' clue what this one's about," pointing to the words, Aurie's pencil mark: *works like a hot damn.* "I put it through one of those online translation programs, but it said that it was about a chicken and a windmill, and they're all dancing. Which doesn't really sound, you know. Happy. Sounds demented."

"Then don't sing that one. Find the saddest one in the book, because Lewis isn't coming for happy, he's coming for the ones that are sad."

They'd grabbed breakfast early; Baz guessed that his sister had been up for hours, was economical in her sleep. Economical in most everything, actually. Over eggs and toast Baz had hesitated, then admitted to his conversation last night with the devil in the parking lot. The devil was cutting no deals, he explained to her. The thing had wanted its ghost back, and expected Lutie to do it. *It's paying attention to us, to me and to her. It couldn't care less about Sol.* Still, it was encouraging, thinking that they could bring back something, that Lutie would be able to accomplish something.

"Do your best, Baz," Lutie replied, eyes on the road. "That's all we can do now." More to herself than to Baz.

Lutie dropped down a gear, and Baz thought it was for the slow curve in the road and the conditions were right for black ice, but instead he spotted the collapsed barn as she turned into the dirt road leading to a grade crossing, two crossbucks warning that a train might smash through at any time at all and it would not stop for a stupid little import car with foreign plates.

The Megeath crossing. Some little village had once existed here, or a homestead, a house. Little trace of it now, except for the barn. The trailer that Lewis had died in had been erased from existence, seized as evidence, Bart had said. That kid was dead, and Baz hoped that his ghost had found its way to where it needed to go. *The truth is here, in the ground. And here, in your heart.*

With an indecipherable glance, Lutie eased down the dirt road, cautiously crossed so they were between iron rails and the meandering Platte River. She drove the car down to the bank, the river lacy with ice, lashed with dead rush, further than they'd come yesterday. The engine sighed to a close, the silence enormous, the task ahead larger still.

Baz nodded to her. "Okay, so this is the game plan, Lutie. I'll sing a sad song first, get Lewis back in the here and now, then hit him with lullaby. Rock him to sleep, and you see if you can make a deadroad, because he's gonna be one pissed off ghost. We don't want him helping that devil anymore. And Sol will...will..." He cracked a grin, all he could do to cover his fear. "Show up." He would not be doing a very good job of putting a brave face on anything.

"Lewis isn't a 'him'," Lutie murmured, and Baz remembered the lesson, his father impressing it on Sol, Baz overhearing as you did when you lived on top of each other. "A ghost is an 'it'. They aren't like us, there's no predicting what they might do."

"Sol's a 'him'," Baz returned with a bit of heat, male object pronoun a declaration of rebellious hope, a talisman, lucky charm.

She laughed, bitter. "Do you think Sol's going to be placated? That he's going to be happy you're singing for ghosts? That he's going to be pleased?" Lutie's face screwed up as though she was thinking of more unlikely emotional states Sol might eventually manifest.

No. Sol would be *pissed*. But thinking of a pissed Sol was better than thinking of a dead Sol. The door handle was cold beneath his hand, easy to open, outside would be freezing, sun making no dent in the temperature today. Clear meant cold; cloud cover was just that, a blanket. Nothing comforting about the weather today; the chinook had passed.

"Can you handle this?" he asked like he was wondering about her ability to get a pizza order right. "I mean...are you gonna...?" Too much to say, too much said, not enough, choose one. "We don't have a choice." Ready or not ready, enough knowledge, pitifully little, none of it mattered. There was just now, and trying something desperate, the two of them, because they had nothing else and Sol was gone.

"No," she said after a minute, pulling open the door, wind creasing a line across the car, thin air crystalline. "No, we don't." Which meant she didn't think high-tailing it back to Canada and forgetting about the Sarrazin boys was a viable option.

The area between the grade crossing and the river was mostly flat, a stand of cottonwoods describing the line of river as the land dropped down to meet it, ubiquitous snowfence leaning precariously, silvered by cold and sun and wind. They could see anything coming for miles, which was a potential problem: they didn't want anyone stopping—you got a flat tire, need some help? It must have occurred to Lutie as well, because she had parked near the river where the land dipped, just below the sightline of anyone driving along the cracked highway, nestled by the rushes.

Flames from Lewis's trailer would have lit the night, would have been a beacon for miles around. Baz tried not to think about what it would be like to be burned alive in your own tin can. No one deserved that, not even an asshole railway cop. And here they were, about to ask his ghost to come back to this place, where soul had been ripped from flesh, unfinished business like the smell of ash in the air. *We all have unfinished business, why should this méchant trou d'cul get another chance?*

He didn't want anything to do with ghosts. Never had. All he'd ever wanted to do was make music; it lay in him like an aquifer. The desire hadn't dried up, it still came out, it had to. The only time he ever felt whole was when he was on stage. As Baz unbent from the car, he ran a hand across the roof of it, remembering Sol's hand doing the same thing to the Wagoneer only the day before yesterday, knuckles bloody, keeping hold of some kind of reality. They were tenuous, the Sarrazins, Baz concluded, not well-stitched to this world, could come unraveled with the wrong snip, a strong tug.

It wasn't a particularly comforting thought, that one, so Baz retrieved a smile from his arsenal, put it on and followed Lutie to the edge of the frozen river. A tree had fallen into it some time ago, its roots exposed and gray, a dark scorch running up it. Maybe hit by lightning. Maybe burned by something else: A murder had happened here, long ago now, and things like trees didn't forget.

"Not much of a river," she said. Looking up, the harsh sunlight caught her eyes and they reflected green. "Bart said that the trailer was close enough that Lewis would have been looking at water as he burned."

*Nice touch*, Baz remembered, *no wonder his damn ghost's pissed off.* He didn't say anything, because he knew Lutie was thinking it too. He wanted to ask again if she could manage this, but that was dumb and pathetic, so he sighed a little, held up the songbook to declare his intent, and opened it to the marked page.

He'd never sung this song before, and *très dangereuse* surely meant it brought something nasty. In this case, nasty was exactly what they were going for. Closing his eyes, he pinched his nose once, found his key, and began to sing.

Head up, and he kept his eyes on Lutie, because he might not know what he was calling up, but she would be able to see it when it came. The other times with Lewis's ghost, he'd smelled ash, and he could always feel ghostcold. But the day was frigid enough that ghostcold might not make much of a dent. His voice caught a little and he faltered, but then cleared his throat and settled into it.

After one verse, Lutie's eyes narrowed, but he didn't stop singing; their agreed-upon signal for that was her raising her hand. His breath plumed white in the air, verses gathered like soldiers. He paused before the last chorus and Lutie shook her head in frustration.

"Five of them, keeping their distance, but no Lewis. Be careful." She knelt, one hand out, ready for whatever might come too close. Waiting in the shark cage for Jaws, surrounded by smaller but no-less-deadly predators. Waiting for a bite, waiting to be bitten. Sharks made Baz think of alligators, the swirl of their unseen tails as they moved through murky waters, eyes above water, so much danger down below.

Heat of bayou, Great Plains cold, polar opposites, and yet together, here. The withered grass bent, movement by the dead tree that had fallen in the river. Among the exposed rootball, gnarled as old hands, something moved. Baz's voice faltered. He couldn't see ghosts, he knew that. The only thing he'd ever been able to almost-perceive was un diable.

A coarse chuckle confirmed it. Lutie's hand came up, the one that wasn't on the ground.

"That's it, girlie," the thing said, cat-tongue rough. "You bring m'boy back for me. Useful, that one."

His boy. That damn ferocious ghost. The devil wasn't going to let them bring Sol back, Baz knew it then and he couldn't speak, couldn't do a damn thing, because this meant that Sol was gone, was dead to them, and whether or not a body was there for them to bury or burn, it didn't matter.

*Unfettered access to me, a direct line to an angel, that's what the fucking thing wants.*

Baz had run up a tab with this devil and it would collect. Maybe today. Maybe later, and Baz knew this was just what his father had fought all his life to avoid, his son being in debt to a devil with the talent he had.

*Papa loved me.* He knew that in the deepest part of him.

"Oh, I'll bring him back, all right," he heard Lutie say, and she deployed the beloved pronoun, edged like a weapon. Like knowledge of love, the word spun and settled. For the first time in a long time, hope unfolded, hands held out in adoration. Baz believed her, had to. "Keep singing," Lutie continued, not sparing Baz a look.

*Try to stop me, chère,* Baz thought, already opening his mouth, moving to the third verse, slow sad song, full of longing, a song of the Grand Dérangement, families ripped apart, sent from Nova Scotia to different parts of the globe, mothers and fathers and children on separate ships, the French Acadian deportation, names like Breaux and Arceneaux and LeBlanc and Richard arriving in Louisiana and Boston and the Caribbean. A song of farewell and loss. He might not truly understand having a particular connectedness to place, he who'd been birthed in a drowned land to a family as restless as Cheyenne nomads. But he knew about knots picked apart, about becoming unstitched from those you loved. He knew about that.

These were not things he thought about often, and weren't easy thoughts to begin with, so he meshed the multiple Sarrazin-Cyr losses into the song, closed his eyes, wove the disappearing throb of his mother's Pontiac as a bass note, heavy, tolling same as a church bell. *C'mon.* At the end of this chorus the song would be over, and he didn't know what he'd sing next, because this one was the best he could find, the saddest, the one that ached for the way things had been. If it didn't call ghosts, he didn't know what would. *C'mon, Sol.* The words, all Acadian French, staggered off his tongue clumsy as closing-time drunks and he hoped pronunciation didn't count for much.

Another chuckle, and Baz opened his eyes only to see the shadowy devil hunker down among the roots, eyes gleaming green, a smoky-gray blur among the parched tangle of dead roots. He was glad he could only see it obliquely, because the thing was horrific. Lutie still crouched on the ground, fingers out as though the earth itself was radiating heat. Her hand was small and white, delicate, and Baz remembered his father's hands, large, capable, hard. How was she to do what she had to with hands like hers?

Then the sky buzzed, washed clear white, a dazzle of brightness beyond mere sunlight, and Baz knew what this meant, but there was no way to warn an angel that a devil lay in wait. *Besides, the angel can look after its own damn self. It's Lewis I want.* But that wasn't true. That wasn't what he wanted at all, the ghost was merely a means to an end. *C'mon, Sol, you gotta come back.*

He kept singing, thought that he could repeat the chorus, but then he would have to end it, because even he couldn't keep a steady grasp on such a sad song. There were limits. The light brightened, and it hovered near, above, filled the sky, soon filled all of Baz's senses, enveloped the day like a nuclear blast. Baz could close his eyes, but it made no difference, open or shut.

The landscape disappeared. The light was all, that and Baz's voice carrying an ancient tune with truth in his heart. This time, inside the light, it was mild, not warm, not cold, it just was. No body, no being, only voice and loss. No awareness of anything beyond that. One thing, though. One thing tied him to the earth, one thing filled the longing with meaning, otherwise it was just sentiment, which was fleeting.

The light, the angel, whatever it was, paused, listening, perhaps waiting, but Baz couldn't guess how angels worked. They were fashioned from light, unlike the devils, which were made of baser things. *As are we.* Himself, and his sister, and his missing brother, tied together not just by blood, which held its own dark turbulence of moving iron and oxygen, but by something much stronger and more true.

Finally, not caring about anything but those ties, Baz put all his love, his sense of kinship, into the final line of the song. The light folded him into itself, burned away everything but the bonds that held, that had held for years over histories bleak and unexplained. Love was the gift Baz offered, and one was given in exchange.

# EIGHTEEN

## THE DEADROAD

After making himself perfectly clear about his expectations concerning homework completion, Sol left Baz to it and escaped their tired apartment by way of the back staircase. Once on his own on East Colfax, he acquired a flask of Beam with a doctored ID card and headed to the park. The sun disappeared behind the tops of broken buildings and Sol dropped the hit of acid he'd sandwiched between his student bus pass and suspended driver's license.

A couple of hours later, cold to the bone, epically misjudging the season, he smoked a lot of speed-laced dope with the sketchy older brother of an ex-girlfriend's best friend, shared the last of the Beam, and then wandered alone down to Denver Yards. This all took the better part of the night and he didn't really worry too much about whether or not Baz had finished his homework because it was a lost cause whatever way you looked at it.

He couldn't have said when, precisely, he'd decided to catch out: near dawn, thirty seconds prior, two months ago, all were probably true. Now, coasting through prairie, the deed done, he told himself that he'd only caught out because he'd been so high he hadn't actually thought it through, but that had nothing to do with it, if he was honest.

At this moment, all that mattered was the strength of the train as it pulled away from Omaha. The train had slowed then stalled its run in Omaha and Sol wasn't ready to stop, was nowhere near ready to stop, needed a new train like a drug, one that would take him away from home, away from what was left behind, prairie now flashing by like a moving ocean of grassland out the side of the open boxcar, autumn tipping everything gold, harvest time. Sol knew nothing about farming, so he couldn't tell by looking if these crops represented a good year or a bad one. All he knew, really, was that he was having one of the most fucked-up years of his life, and that his harvest was going to be pitiful, painful even.

*I can't go on like this,* he thought, but even as the thought came to him, he realized he wasn't going to have to go on like anything; he was already moving, literally in a different direction. To Canada, magnetic north, like he had a string tied to him. Strings behind and strings ahead and him being pulled, maybe apart. It felt that way, like one of those medieval death sentences. Drawn and quartered. Halved, more like it.

With one hand, he took out a pack of smokes from his jean jacket, shook one out, cupped it against the wind so the match would light. He leaned against the doorframe, one hand tucked under the other elbow in an effort to stay warm, eyes on the horizon. The first drag was heaven, blew away from him as all things were blowing away from him. *Maybe I have no ties*, he thought. *I have no ties*. Take out the maybe, reinvent himself.

The after-effects of the drugs slid messily around, and his head was fuzzy and achy, enveloped in a blanket of haze, acid still floating in his system, making everything more interesting, more tenuous, more apt to develop a life of its own. Better this way, a necessary distance from reality. Geography was an indistinct subject, terre inconnue once beyond Denver, knowledge of place rooted in asphalt, not paper and ink. Had they crossed the border yet? He had no idea. Destinations were beads on a string: Denver, Omaha, who knew what came next?

The train had left Denver at dawn; Sol hadn't slept in the more than sixteen hours since he'd dropped the acid, had watched the landscape slide by, mind wandering mile after mile after mile. It was a sunny day coming up, redolent of the summer past, now late October, two months into his seventeenth year. He'd gone hungry for the last week, no child welfare check coming. He'd mistimed the sequence of payments, not able to easily predict how much an almost thirteen-year-old kid could eat when left alone—in two days Baz had gone through what Sol had estimated was a week's worth of groceries. Rent was three months past due, but the landlady was cool with it. He hoped she was cool with it. He'd been avoiding her, so he didn't really know her relative state of coolness.

Blew out more smoke, and it trailed behind, gone.

He hoped they'd be in Canada soon. The border was a place of magic, liminal space. One moment, all laws known to him—so well-known by now—the next transformed, another place, where the language sounded different and the currency colored like origami paper. Laws were made and broken and he would never be able to tell the difference. Up north, their mother's country, the land itself a construction of songs and stories. Canada could be anything he wanted it to be.

He lay back on the open boxcar, the rumble and noise blotting out his sense of corporal being, and he floated, drugged and at peace with it, smoking away his past. The train was moving so quickly, he couldn't feel any connection to the ground, to the earth and that was fine. Connections meant rootedness, meant all the lessons his father had taught, all the ghosts and the responsibilities his father said were his. Connection was spurned. Instead, he wanted to float, to not-be.

*Like Hamlet,* and he smiled at that thought, eyes closed against the anvil sun, so much noise and vibration he almost didn't exist at all.

When he sat up to stub out the last ember, to flick the cigarette out the open door, he suddenly remembered having a beard, the feel of it against his fingers. He lipped another cigarette to his mouth, feeling his smooth chin, puzzled. This cigarette, he didn't light, he held it there, remembering whiskers. The drugs, that was all, that was it. He stretched back, feeling the boards of the boxcar against his bare hand, recalled belatedly that his hip would hurt if he stretched too far, he should really ice it some more. *Lucky I didn't break anything.*

He sat up straight, one hand running down his left side, whole and so gaunt he'd be able to count ribs if he cared to. Hand to face, taking out the cigarette from his mouth, running fingers through hair long past its last cut because barbers cost money and he sure as hell wasn't giving Baz a pair of scissors.

*Robbie always sings when she cuts my hair and she can't carry a tune to save her life.*

For a moment, he thought he might pass out. *Just the drugs*, he kept telling himself, but it wasn't that, it was something else and damned if he could remember what. Two selves, sliding together, apart, together again. His breath came ragged, and he looked at his hands and they weren't right either. His left pinky had been broken in a house call, caught in a stretcher's undercarriage so it was crooked like an old cat's tail. Except it was straight as he held it out, blocking the rising sun, light leaking through the gaps. *Je vais aller au nord. Enough of this shit, I'm going north and I'm not coming back. Jamais, jamais, ever.*

"Hey, buddy, you gonna smoke that one?" How he hadn't noticed the other drifter in the car was beyond him, and Sol thought he'd jump out of his own skin. *If it is my skin.*

He stared, wide-eyed, able to hear his own heart, even above the train. In the corner of the car, dark against the bright light of the prairie outside, a shape moved, resolved itself into arms and legs, a scraggly beard, army surplus pants held up by string. As Sol's eyes adjusted, the man shuffled forward on his ass, disturbing the small dog by his side. The dog whined and the drifter hushed it with a movement of his hand. "Well?"

Sol handed the cigarette over, got out another one and lit it, passed the drifter his book of matches. Together, they sat on the edge of the car, pant legs whipping in the wind. In exchange, the drifter, who said his name was DJ, tried to give Sol half a squished peanut butter sandwich, but Sol refused with a frown, used to being hungry, used to refusing food when someone else needed to eat.

But that wasn't quite it, and he knew it. *You don't just take food in these places, gars. Mon Dieu, what kind of maudit bioque did I raise?* Almost under his breath, but not quite, Sol told his father that he wasn't making the rules anymore. Still, he knew better than to take food from strangers. To take food in strange places, in this place. Here. Not here.

"You talk to yourself, but not to me. That's okay," DJ said, eyes an alarming blue in the sunlight. The little black dog nuzzled Sol's hand and he patted it, chucking it under its ears so it groaned in pleasure, broad head pushing back against his hand, wanting more. *Renard*, Sol thought, because that was a dog's name, wasn't it? It meant 'fox' in French, and that was a stupid name for a beagle, but Robbie had laughed and laughed at his suggestion for the puppy. Her hair dark in his hands, sliding away as she smiled, freckles on her nose, her shoulders. She had such a great laugh, it started something inside him, like she'd turned on the ignition.

*Fuck, what is wrong with me?*

"So, where you headed?" DJ asked.

It wasn't the sort of question drifters asked, Sol knew it, and he shook his head. Still, it wasn't the weirdest thing he could be asked, or that he could ask himself.

"Nord," he said. "J'cherche ma mère, et je pense qu'elle est du nord. Maman, elle est canadienne."

"Always with the mother. Why d'you need her so much?" Eyes like the sky, might as well be the sky.

"C'est mon frère, Basile. Il a besoin d'elle. Pas moi." He didn't need her, not like Baz did. *I don't need anything, me. I'm telling M'man that Baz is all alone and that's it, I keep going and I don't look back.*

"You sure about that?" The drifter looked away with a smile. "What's wrong with the phone?"

The dog was now nudging his elbow with its nose, trying to get his attention. Sol stared at the drifter, a thread of recognition tugging at him. "Where are we?" he asked, suddenly, the English strange in his mouth, realized now he'd been speaking French, that there were differences between the languages.

The drifter laughed, low chuckle like broken glass. *He's dead*, Sol thought, more confused than scared. Most dead things didn't scare him, not lately. *He hanged himself in a jail cell.* "You don't know?"

After a minute, Sol shrugged with one shoulder. "Halfway to Winnipeg, probably." He seemed to remember going through Omaha, changing to a Canadian National car in the yards there, but it was a long, long time ago. It had happened years ago.

The drifter shook his head. "East-west corridor. The only thing that moves north-south goes down to New Orleans. That where you want to go?" One blue eye hard on Sol, who struggled to keep himself calm. "Yeah. I didn't think so." With a smooth motion, as though they weren't going a million miles an hour, DJ stretched his hands out, precariously balancing, legs swinging out into the open spaces between steel and grassland. "We're going east. Chicago first, then Detroit if you're lucky. From there, Toronto. But your mom, she's up in Nouveau-Brunswick, eh? My stomping grounds. We still have a way to go." DJ eyed him, then stared out at the prairie. "You should eat."

Sol stayed silent, one hand on the dog, trying to stay inside his skin, inside his skull. He sensed danger, but remotely, like he was reading about it happening elsewhere, to someone else. "Am I dead?" he asked suddenly. As he said it, he heard his own voice deepen, crack, emerge from youth into realization.

Lean, drugged up, hungry—all these bodily concerns changed as the sun lit the darkest corners of his haze, coming in obliquely as the train took a slow curve, engine noise changing, coming through some outpost on the prairie. A discordant clang of warning: here comes the train. The train responded with a loon's mating call: two longs, a short and a long—*lookout, here I come!* Sol's hand clutched the frame of the open door and he looked at his knuckles, bruised, and had to lower his arm because his side rippled with sudden and ghastly pain. He leaned back from the open door, hip throbbing, shoulder screwed, scooted back a foot or so, reeling from sudden vertigo.

"You're not dead, my friend, not yet," DJ answered, but it wasn't DJ, it wasn't human at all. It wore a DJ suit, maybe Sol himself had clad the thing in such attire looking for answers. Hard to know, here.

"You killed my father," he said, and the thing laughed, liquid, slow, full of seaweed and salt.

"That wasn't me." Sunlight hit it, and it threw no shadow. Slowly, it started to shift, darken, hair became black, hematite eyes. "Wish it was, I always hated Aurèle. You still have a way to go, I said, before you get to me." It chuckled. "Et toi, bougre? You still have to find your M'man."

Sol stared at the thing that wasn't DJ for a long moment, and it smiled crookedly, head dropped to an unnatural angle, skin smooth and beluga white before blackening as though it was burning in front of him, no flame, only smooth flesh like polished coal and raven-blue hair, clothed in ash. Then not a man at all, something else dark and armored, eyes glittering like embers in an inferno, calm, deadly.

Sol blinked, too shocked to be scared. The dog had crawled under his jacket and was shivering. *Les trois hommes noirs*, he thought, in this dreaming between-place. *There's three of them. And that other one, it couldn't hurt me.* This one, here, this one, it could draw blood if it wanted to, it could rip him apart.

The train had slowed considerably as it came through the crossing, which was the only reason he did it, could do it. With the silence of a bitten-back curse, Sol swung out of the moving car as it chugged past the empty grain depot, slowslowslow the train called to the residents, and the dog flew from him, a blur and a whine. Sol dropped to the ground, a ball of rolling pain, over before he'd even properly registered he was going to do it.

He spent a long time staring at the sky before trying to move, hearing the train fade into the sunlight, no sound of a devil following him, no scurry of gravel or hiss of clogged lungs. No sign of the dog. The day was still sunny, still some memory of summer, some town past Omaha, a long way from Denver, a long way from Baz, who would be wondering where Sol had gone, or happy that Sol wasn't there berating him for not having done his homework. *Non, il n'y est pas, Baz, he's not there doing homework. He's with Lutie, wondering where the hell I am.* Bearded chin and cheeks, hair still short from Robbie's last buzz cut, body not as whip thin, grown into its bones, padded with muscle, flawed with injury. A million miles from anything he recognized as home.

*Where the hell am I?* he asked again, but under his breath, to the wind. He'd made this trip when he was seventeen years old. This was memory, not fabrication. Back in the broken Nebraska barn, by the side of the frozen Platte River, a ghost had been killing him, he'd been dying. And then…then, but recollection was slippery, the memory moving, almost unable to be seen. Somehow, Lutie had gotten rid of Lewis's ghost, he'd felt it, a wave, all wrong, nothing like what he'd tried to teach her, and he'd been caught up in it. And now he was here, in a remembered landscape on a remembered trip.

*C'est moi,* he thought. *This is me, back here. Lutie didn't make me a proper deadroad.* The devil had said that he wasn't dead, not yet. *In between.* Cold came over him. *That devil's full of crap; Lewis must have killed me. I'm one of those guys who just won't go when their time's up.*

Last time he'd been here, all those years ago, a limit had been reached, a bare toe dipped into a pool too cold. *I was so out of it that first leg, it's a wonder I didn't get hit by a train or beaten by a bull.* Denver to Omaha, high as a kite, then changed to a CN car heading out of Omaha, the company name—Canadian National—enough for him, like it would take him directly to her. To Maman.

*I turned back. After Omaha, I turned back.*

Sol remembered. The drugs had eventually worn off. He'd had no food, no money. The task—find one woman in the second-largest country on the planet—had slowly revealed itself for what it was: impossible. Despite his many absences and run-ins with the cops and the school psychologist, he'd been an exceptional student, able, resourceful; he'd been an even better apprentice to le traiteur. And it had been easier to catch a train back to Denver, to shoulder the responsibility of raising a wild teenaged brother, to being a man among wastrels and criminals, than to find his mother. Truth, then: easier to do all these things than to face her, after what she'd done. After what she'd left behind when she'd gone away.

Shield, and block, and parry: *She kills herself, soon. Couple of weeks. I still could make it, if I just keep going.* Present tense, past tense. *I could have stopped it, then. I could have stopped her, changed everything.*

But not now.

Sol lay on his back, staring at sky, indeterminate time, blue and mid-temperature, unknown month. *I made it this far that October. This is as much rope as I took.* After the worst of the pain had subsided, he stood shakily, glad that the effects of the drugs had moved off him, had receded into memory, into the memory of that day. Only his present set of bangs and bruises impeded him, that and memory, which was a different sort of impairment.

He placed his hand on the ground, cold, dusty, grit and pebbles and thin strands of grass, trying to find a connection in the bones of the earth. He'd wanted none of it at seventeen, no connections whatsoever. He'd wanted out. *I left them all behind.* But now…now… He bowed his head, realizing what he'd lost, then and now. Discovered that what he'd pushed away still resided deep within.

*It's all I ever wanted.* Sol's head jerked up, eyes burning, sore, feeling nothing against his fingers. Aching. His need was a weight, deep inside and he'd carried it for years, his whole life maybe, longer than he could remember.

# NINETEEN

## COMING THROUGH

S he had screwed up again.

This time, she cried in frustration, her hands balled at her side, thin keen sound like a garrote, strangling her. The noise escaped her throat and she didn't recognize it, had never made such a sound before, had never been as scared perhaps, as full of self-loathing.

She was alone by the river bank, which was the problem. One minute, Baz had been there, singing so as to break your heart, and she'd felt it, she'd felt her heart break. The next, that damned white light, so fast and her too far away to cover him—as though that would have helped—and the angel had found Baz. Found him, taken him, and now she was alone, not even the devil hiding in the roots of the dead tree. Not quite alone, though: there were at least five ghosts, no six, and they milled about as though they were starstruck by the promise of a celebrity on the red car-pet.

Angry, Lutie walked toward one, open, connected, and the ghost seemed to see her coming. It turned, terror in its eyes, blank only a moment before, and fled. She'd seen this before, approached ghosts with anger, and they would leave, maybe thought she was going to shred them to pieces. *Maybe I am. Maybe I will.*

It was cold enough to freeze the tears on her face, and so she swiped at them, but more came. The ghosts disappeared in her vision's swim, and she wiped again, wiped until no more came. The ghosts, now down to three, hung well away from her, but they didn't leave. *Fine, that's fine.*

"Baz?" but it came out small, pathetic. *I'm not going to cry again.* She straightened her shoulders, looked around to be sure of the number. When Sol declared his intentions to ghosts, when he crouched down and opened a road for them, the ghosts came at him. It was like hitting a wasp's nest with a stick. She didn't care. Maybe she deserved this. Far away, she heard a bleat of train, and she kept an eye on the track.

The nearest ghost, just on the other side of Lutie's Toyota, was that of a woman, shaggy haired, looked like an inmate escaped from the asylum. Lutie stared dispassionately, maybe twenty feet and the car between them. The ghost's hair was matted, eyes downcast, mouth slack. It wore a loose white robe, dried blood on its wrists. *A suicide*, Lutie thought. *Goddamn suicide nut-jobs.*

"Okay, sweetheart," she whispered under her breath, her anger not surprising her, it was so constant, but the sheer depth of her reservoir was astonishing. Every hurt catalogued, saved here, hoarded like gold, like injury and anger were currency, could make an over-the-counter purchase. The ghost blinked, walked quietly around the car, one hand stretched out as though touching the heads of the winter grass, nodding in the wind. Its feet were bare, and Lutie shuddered.

*They don't feel the cold.*

Maman had said that one winter, the one before she died. They'd been in New Brunswick by then, living in a back room let to them by a man with awful breath and a dog that humped Lutie whenever she wasn't vigilant. The place had smelled of rotting newspapers in the fall, and kerosene in winter. Mireille hadn't spent much time there, Lutie remembered. Instead, like this ghost, she had circled the local churches slowly, looking at their entrances, looking for a way in, a way out. Maman had held her hand like that sometimes, feeling for that which wasn't there. She cried in her sleep, but never when awake.

*T-Lu, you show 'em. You show 'em who's boss. They're scared, that's all they are, big scaredy cats. All they want is someone to protect them, and they'll do whatever you want.*

*Pourquoi, M'man? Pourquoi ils ont peur?*

*Because they don't know what happens next, and everyone wants a mother.*

# DEADROADS

It was quiet on the prairie, just the low vibration of a train miles away, coming closer, but not too quickly. Lutie didn't want to bind this ghost. She'd had enough of madwomen. They weren't strong. They were needy, sucked you dry. Lutie had had enough of that to last a lifetime. Unlike Sol, she didn't care where this ghost went, had no desire to put anything to rest. *It's not my damn business.*

Both of them. She'd lost both her brothers now.

She wasn't going to catch this ghost. She wasn't going to send it to a better place.

She was going to destroy it.

With both feet planted firmly apart, she connected with the ground, felt the shiver of grass and microbe, the running of water, the firm line of warm iron and the speeding of the engine, hot, appearing to her internal vision as red. Red for heat, for all that was purposeful mechanics, designed and manufactured. The rest was humming green or white, made according to no plan known to her or any other human. Faith was required here, and it happened to be the one thing that Lutie possessed.

It was real, all of it, the red metal, the ghosts, God's unfathomable will.

Ghosts were tied to place of death, and this madwoman's ghost had wandered away, called by Baz's song, lured by it. It was vulnerable, an easy thread to cut. She didn't know how to open a road for the dead, didn't think she probably could. But she could sever things, of that she was sure. She was good at cutting things off, had learned from her mother. This ghost, far from its remains, from the memory of where it had been, would wither and disappear. Would be lost. Surely this is what it deserved? Surely this was what it had wanted when it had been a woman and taken its own life?

*It's what M'man had wanted.*

She was concentrating so closely on finding the ghost's tenuous string that held it to this earth that she didn't smell the ash, didn't notice how the day darkened. The train crept closer, and the noise of it, the diesel wafting along the breeze, blocked out any threat she might have otherwise perceived.

Of all things, it was the madwoman's ghost that warned her. Maybe the ghost really wanted oblivion; maybe it saw a kindred spirit in Lutie; maybe it was just crazed from God-alone knew how many years spent between existences, but it pointed behind Lutie, and Lutie turned just in time to avoid the club.

She didn't have time to think. No natural athlete, no talent for fighting, she simply got out of Lewis's way, was able to move quickly, if not purposefully. The madwoman's ghost scattered like blown leaves, or Lutie might have gone right through it as she fell. Lewis loomed over her, covered in ash, char flaking off it, shedding skin and clothing, bare bones curved with heat, cracking with the sound of gunshots. The train was loud in her ears, and it passed by as she lay on the ground, rolling steel rattling her bones in unison.

The bull's ghost stilled, sunken red eyes fixed on the train, something of longing in its steady distracted gaze. The long line of cars bound for elsewhere, out of this place, not stuck. Able to leave, able to find rest at the end of the trip, everything a ghost was not permitted to do.

It passed, the train, but Lewis was still there. The moment held.

"You can't go home," Lutie said, pointedly. She talked to ghosts. She'd always talked to ghosts. She didn't give a rat's ass what her father had said, what Sol had said. There was a note of triumph in her voice.

Lewis's ghost stood for a heartbeat longer, not looking at her, looking at the tracks. It had come, eventually, or had been sent, perhaps to kill her. It was in thrall to the devil that had been plaguing them, and that would make a difference in what happened next.

*Ma petite, it's like calling over a cat,* she had said. *You want to offer them something, and then you wrap them around your finger comme ça.*

Finally, Lewis's ghost turned to her, red eyes glowing, burning like embers, hot on her. She remembered what she'd heard about Lewis, how he'd taken pleasure in beating hobos to death, had despised their impermanence, envied their freedom. *Maybe he knows where Sol is. Maybe he can show me.*

"You need someplace to stay, Lewis?"

The club held slackly at its side, the ghost hovered a moment. *Don't go, don't go,* Lutie pleaded, still on the ground, but daring to come up on her elbows, and then her arms, all the way to a sit. The thing was huge, deadly, ugly. Bound to a devil, but Lutie knew about cutting things off, and she wasn't going to stop now.

Whatever village the engine had slowed for—a huddle of graying houses, the empty granary—it had disappeared with the train. Sol was left on the high prairie, grassland rolling away from the lines of rail, waves of bronze and gold soft as fur, as though one stroke would make it purr. *It shouldn't surprise me*, he thought, looking for the missing village, one hand pressed to his bandaged side, fingers spread as though he could contain the hurt. *Nothing about this should surprise me.*

Last time, when he'd abandoned this journey, he'd hitchhiked back. He'd gone this far on the rails, stopped at a nameless hamlet, begged a cup of coffee and bummed a ride from a trucker on his way to Denver. Turning around was easier than catching out.

Sol scanned the tracks, not seeing even a road, much less signs of human habitation. A spray of birds chattered to flight, and he sighed. It was a long walk back. Either start walking, or stay here, and he wasn't willing to be a target, wasn't going to wait for something else to make the next move. He took a few steps, able to read east and west easily enough, the sun helping him. A point in the afternoon, land flat as far as the eye could see, no mountains to hem, to cradle, to assert the land's permanence, to state that it wasn't going anywhere. *A mother's steady hand.* But not like Louisiana either, where the land was tentative, unwilling to give any support, indifferent to notions of safety and duration.

He swallowed hard, not wanting to think about sinking land, about drowned houses, bodies piled on overpasses, confused ghosts unable to find their way out, their terrain turned toxic, unknown and unknowable. Instead, he remembered Baz on Robbie's couch, that stupid haircut, and her careful laughter, not knowing what Sol's reaction would be, thinking him some kind of fragile glass, breakable. *Or maybe I pave her way with eggshells, make her guess what my breaking point will be, when I won't come back through that door.*

It was ridiculous, thinking that here, but he knew Robbie as well as he knew anyone, better than he knew himself, and then he thought, *I am such an asshole.* The rails to Denver were littered with shards of glass, things that he'd smashed along the way. *Break them myself and at least it's predictable.* He stopped walking after a few steps, hip aching, and he put a hand to it, eyes to the rail ties, binding slender filaments of iron to the land, gathering together a nation, allowing for people to leave at will.

Allowing them to go back home, he realized.

Looking up, Sol experienced yet another revelation in this day, already full: it was indeed still possible to take him by surprise. The ash cloud blocked the sky to the west immediately in front of him. Sol smelled it at the same time he saw it, rolling like a dust storm toward him right on the rails and he knew that trains also could come along here, and he wasn't falling for that again. He stepped to the side of the tracks, unprotected between the iron lines, but also out of the way of any train. The cloud rolled over him, choking him, ash in his eyes, down his throat, everything constricting, a cough coming immediately, fire along his slashed side as he gasped for air.

The day became instantly gray, swirling with flakes like snow in nuclear winter, everything soft haze, diffusing whatever light tried to penetrate, a pall, a gloom.

Only a moment, he knew, before Lewis would appear and he was bent over, exposed, not ready. Despite the effort it took, he dropped to his knees, hand out, needed to send this thing on its way not because it belonged elsewhere—though it certainly did—but because he wasn't going to be able to fight it. The first landed blow would finish him.

The trouble was, Lewis's ghost was so damn quick. It appeared out of the ash just as Sol's coughing subsided, just as he felt the vague tendril of connection tremble along his hand, ready for him to pluck it out of the earth like a spreading root system of an invasive plant. Blackened rags hung from Lewis's spare frame, tattered like plastic bags caught on a tangle of wire fence, and the ghost swung his murderous bat, eyes burning from beneath the brim of his charred ball cap. Sol scrambled backwards, the connection lost, and he knew if he didn't find it again, he was dead.

*Aren't I already dead? Maybe this is Hell, missing Robbie and all the things I've screwed up, and having to fight this trou d'cul over and over.* He rolled away over gravel, into grass, the day turning to night, swirl of gray becoming blacker, and he smelled not just ash, but burning. Flesh burning.

He knew this smell, had worked enough car accidents and house fires to recognize it, and his stomach curled up on itself. Roll and roll, on his feet, trying to ignore his side and hip, but his leg gave under him as he tried to stand, gave out entirely as though tendons had been severed. The pain coincided with a flash of light, which Sol thought meant that he'd been hit by the bat, and just hadn't seen it coming.

He fell, pain exploding like a rocket, the light gone, everything so dark he couldn't see a damn thing. Except. Except the red glow of the ghost's eyes, silent, never saying anything. Some ghosts talked to you, and Sol knew better than to answer, but this one, this one wanted no connection to the living. This one wasn't making conversation; it wanted Sol dead, had been told to kill him. It was reaping the harvest and Sol's hip wouldn't allow him to stand, so he looked up at the dark form, black against black, beyond any kind of usual pain. Looked up, in the end waiting for the damn thing to make the next move, because Sol Sarrazin was out of moves.

Wind, screaming, that was the only sound, and it swept through Lewis as though he wasn't there, took him apart like a thumb smudging wet ink, a smear, indistinguishable from the sudden unnatural night. Sol stared, trying to make sense of it, but Lewis suddenly wasn't there, just the night, and the wind. The song of the wind, which became a different song, keening, a melody of loss.

*Baz.* Not his road-voice, the one permitted in the car, singing along like a happy kid at Scout Camp, but his true voice, the one that their father had feared so much he'd forbidden it. Feared this voice not because it called ghosts, Sol realized, as his father must have realized at some point, but because it called something else, something bigger and unknowable and untouchable. *You don't want them to notice you.* Not because they'd hurt you, or because they'd snatch you away, or anything else imagined or awful. But because an angel noticing you meant that a devil would too, and that put you in middle of whatever went on between them, neither caring who got caught, who got killed. Angels and devils weren't made for humans to understand. *That devil, the one that killed Papa, it's using Baz,* Sol thought, heart sinking. *Oh, Jesus, merde, Baz, cher. Stop your singing.*

He struggled to his feet, looking for the source. This time, his hip held, but only if he put all his weight on the other leg. He wished, briefly, for a cane or a crutch. Even as his eyes adjusted, he could make out nothing in the gloom. Just the voice, singing in French, mispronouncing badly, and then that came to an end, soft as a Bible being shut on a pulpit. He looked down, and between his worn leather boots, a broken line of cracked yellow paint snaked past him, running along shattered asphalt. A road. Something, better than nothing.

A form moved in the dark ahead of him, another black huddle of mass, near his feet, moved and dodged and Sol knew what it was. Again, surprise. He couldn't reach down without going all the way to his knees, and he didn't want to try to get back up again now that he was upright, so Sol whistled under his breath, short and sharp.

The dog came.

Last time he'd seen this thing in life, he had been stacking rocks onto its frozen body. The dog had also been on the train with a devil wearing DJ's form, and Sol wondered if that meant that the devil was nearby. But no. He didn't think the dog was in league, it had just been swept along. *Kinda like me.* In its short life, the dog had been loved by a drifter and Sol had taken care of its last journey. By tending to that, had he some kind of favor owed to him?

*It's my job. I don't do it for the thanks.*

The little dog sat by his leg, gave a short ruff of acknowledgment. Said 'hi'. Sol didn't feel too ridiculous saying hi back. In response, the dog put one paw on Sol's foot, then trotted off a few yards, just on the edge of the blackness. It looked back.

*They don't let you down*, Sol thought, but he was thinking of his own dog, how Renard never came when called. How happy the damn thing was to see him when he'd paid the fifty bucks and was allowed to take him home from the pound. *Good to see you, too.*

Ignoring the fact that it was like a lost Halloween episode of *Lassie*, Sol followed the drifter's dead dog along the road. Seeing that he was falling in behind him, the dog led on, stopping to let Sol catch up, not letting him lose track. Sol went slowly, not able to see the road, hopeful that a semi wasn't going to come barreling out of the gloom to run him over.

Without the sun, time was difficult to gauge, but eventually the black became a bad bruise, and then a rain cloud and then soft as an old dog's muzzle. The sun came through, and Sol was on an indeterminate road, surrounded by nothing but rolling prairie and sun-burned grass, yellow passing lines faded but present. Encouraging, in a way, indications that there might be things to pass, or things that might pass you, or things coming in the opposite direction. Like that. In the distance, very far away, a figure walked toward him, and Sol recognized the bounce, the way Baz's center of balance was somewhere high in his chest, like he'd topple in a stiff breeze. Like he'd take off in flight.

In his own center, where his balance sometimes secretly faltered, the weight, the need, tightened and he couldn't stop a grin from splitting his face. His hip gave a sharp lancing pain, and the muscle there shivered in anticipation of folding. Sol couldn't walk any further, and so he slowly sank to the road, the dog licking his face enthusiastically before Sol pushed it down. As his brother inched across the landscape toward him, Sol kept one hand on the dog, grateful.

The angel could have been a little more precise, could have saved him a walk, but Baz wasn't going to complain. Not much, anyway, not when he could see his brother in the distance, sitting on the empty road, gray bowl of sky arcing above, nothing but grass and hill and hollow as far as the eye could see.

Baz walked faster, worried that Sol would disappear, maybe, or that he was badly hurt, because Sol didn't usually just stop walking and sit down in the middle of a road. He hadn't been moving quickly before that, had favored one side, nothing graceful about him. A small, dark shape darted around Sol, just in his shadow.

Twenty yards separated them before Baz figured out the shadow was a dog, and only then because the damn thing barked at him. He couldn't help smiling, big and genuine, opened his arms as though he and Sol had run into each other on some exotic shore. *Can you believe it?* the gesture meant, and Baz didn't really care where the angel had dropped him off, as long as it meant that Sol wasn't dead.

The little dog wagged its tail, and Sol looked at it, one hand coming up as though to call it. Even as he did, the dog ran off into the grasslands, its bark fading as it went until the whole landscape was silent, not even birdsong or wind. Sol didn't attempt to stand, looked up at Baz, and then away. Baz knelt down to his level, the indeterminate sun somewhere above. They didn't say anything for a long time, Sol's attention on the horizon, eyes squinting, stained parka open to the mild day.

"Where the hell are we, cher?" Baz asked him.

Sol didn't answer for a moment, head tilted, listening for some sound that maybe Baz couldn't hear. Baz stayed steady, waiting for his brother to return. Finally, Sol sighed and shook his head.

"A road has to cut through somewhere, even a deadroad." Voice soft, tentative and therefore unfamiliar. "Did that damn ghost kill me?"

Baz raised his eyebrows, wishing that Sol would look at him. "I don't think so. Lutie somehow…I don't know what she did."

Sol was nodding, a brief smile pulling aside his mouth, and he still wasn't looking at him, was looking everywhere but at him. "Yeah. I don't either. She send you?"

Something was strange about his voice. Baz shook his head. "No, I don't think so. The angel did that."

Baz watched as his brother bit the inside of his mouth, lips pulling in, chin down. Everything pulled in, held too tight. "L'ange, hé? Oh, God, Baz…" and his voice dropped, fell away. One hand came up, knuckles red and cut, and he covered his mouth. "You," he began, words muffled against his hand, as though they were seeping out, bleeding from him. "You're scaring the shit out of me, Baz."

His face must have been something, because Sol laughed, finally stared at him, dark eyes full, reflecting the blue day.

"This, coming from the guy that sees ghosts, the guy that fights devils?" Baz wanted to touch Sol, wanted contact in this strange place, but he knew Sol wouldn't allow it.

Sol nodded. "Ouais, cher. T'as raison. Mais," and there was always a 'mais' with Sol, "mais, them angels, Basile, they don't care about us. They don't care about you. I don't know what they want with you. Or what les diables want with you. It scares me, not knowing."

It was a speech, for Sol. Baz nodded, swallowed, knowing that Sol wouldn't like what he was going to say next. "I think the devil, the one I made the deal with, I think it has business with the angel. It wants me to sing, because that calls up the angel. I don't think it can do it on its own." He shrugged. "I think that it's what it wanted from Dad, and when he wouldn't do it, the thing killed him."

Sol took that, hand coming up to cover his mouth again, eyes away. The dog hadn't come back. The dog was gone. The sun hadn't moved in all the time they'd been here. With a sigh, Sol dropped one shoulder, rolled it, wincing. *He looks so damn tired*, Baz thought.

"It's been around longer than that. And it wants more than an angel, no matter what it says. Man, it hates us."

Baz stared. "How do you know that?"

Far stare, mind away, back through time maybe. "It knew Dad. It knew Mom." The word didn't stick in Sol's mouth. "I don't know. There's more to it than that." Another pause, picking his way to even more difficult territory. "Same angel, each time you do this?"

It wasn't like that. Baz didn't know how to explain it. "I don't think there's more than one. Or, it's a whole lot of angels at the same time. It's not the kind of thing you can count." Like water, he wanted to say, like an ocean. Like air or sunlight, as elemental as that.

"There's more than one devil," Sol said, voice still strained, as though he was trying to say something else, was speaking in code, hoping that Baz would understand. "I saw one here, but it wasn't your devil, the one that killed Dad."

"You saw one?" Convinced that no cars were coming, Baz sat on the road opposite Sol, who didn't appear to want to move just yet. "What's been happening, in this place? You seen Lewis?"

Sol nodded, and now the opposite was happening—he wasn't taking his eyes off Baz, and Baz didn't know which one made him more uncomfortable, stare or avoidance. "Okay, so I was in the barn, and Lewis was there. And then?" He lifted one hand, unable to explain. "I was here, except it wasn't now. It was fall, 1998. Everything the same as then, I was the same. Younger. I went through it all again, Baz. I got wasted, caught out, exactly the same." He shook his head, eyes wide. "You were twelve years old and I left you." Steady gaze, right on him, inescapable. "Like I didn't know what that was like, what getting left was like. What you getting left alone in a house was like. After everything you been through, I was gonna do that." He faltered, collected himself, voice breaking. "I did that."

Baz kept his eyes on his hands. "Why?" he asked the ground. Then had to look up, to see what Sol made of the question, to figure out what Sol wasn't going to tell him. "Why did you have to go?"

Sol didn't look away, didn't dodge. It was like a penance, maybe, having to answer. "I didn't have to. I wanted to. I couldn't handle—" and the voice was too tight, finally, and he had to stop. Baz reached out, put one hand on Sol's ankle, just to let him know that he was there, soft, as though Sol might shake it off. "I was trying to find M'man. I was trying to—"

Baz just wanted him to shut up, to stop him, but it was like trying to stop a flood, an open wound, the wind. "Shh," he said, some murmuring sound, but Sol shook his head, vehemently.

"No, just let me finish," he said, and now Baz couldn't take his eyes from Sol's; he was stuck. "I wanted her to come back, take care of things, take care of you, because I'd had enough. That's what I told myself."

"You were seventeen, cher. You remember me at that age? Shit, I couldn't look after a house plant let alone—"

Sol held up his hand. "Ta gueule, Baz. I was trying to find every way to ditch what I'd been saddled with. But," he stopped again. Baz didn't interrupt him. "I wasn't looking for her to look after you. That's what I thought I was doing, but that wasn't it." He took a breath. "I never stopped looking, not really. Not until I found her."

Still air, no birds, no wind. Silence. First thing Sol had done, when he'd started work at Denver Health, he'd told Baz and Lutie. He'd found her, dead. He hadn't given up, not like the rest of them had. Sol looked away, across the prairie again, eyes bright.

"It's not a sin, Sol," Baz whispered, barely audible, finally deciphering Sol's coded words. "It's not a sin to miss her."

Sol smiled, teeth white against his scruffy beard. "She left. I was so pissed."

"I think it's okay, Sol. To miss her, to hate her." Baz swallowed. "To love her."

Sol took those words, seemed to hold them close, and Baz couldn't tell if they cut or burned or soldered. Finally, his brother breathed out, tears tracking like rain on a window. "I'm gonna miss him, too. Papa."

"You and me both," Baz said softly.

Sol nodded, and they sat there for a long time, Baz with one hand on Sol's foot. Finally, Sol rubbed his face, lifted his hand to Baz. "Help me up. You got any ideas about how to get out of here?"

Baz stretched, grabbed his brother's elbow and hauled him to his feet, but Sol didn't let go. Wordlessly, he got one shoulder under Sol, who permitted it. One glance told him that Sol was more at ease, now, in this weird half-world, had let go of some poison kept close.

"Yeah," Baz said, "I got an idea. But you're not gonna like it."

Baz told Sol that he was going to sing, call back the angel, see if his ticket here included return passage. Sol's mouth tensed, but he didn't say anything, which meant he didn't have a better idea. Sol had already admitted that he was scared for Baz, that he was worried. The next step was why that would matter, but Baz already knew why his brother worried. Some things Sol didn't have to say for Baz to know.

Baz slipped the blue book out of his pocket, picked out the one song that their father had said worked like a hot damn, the song that Sol had forbidden in the motley park, back when Sol had been in control. They were a bit beyond that now. They had passed the invisible point where Sol called the shots. They were into new territory, where Baz could take up the slack a little, carry his share of the load and Sol would let him.

With much of Sol's weight—figurative and literal—resting on his shoulders, Baz smiled at his brother, the bright sunny smile that always had caused their father to grin in return, unable to deny him. Sol stared back, close enough that Baz felt his shallow breathing, caught every flicker of eyelid. Not able to deny him, no, but neither able to smile about it. Different than their father, and Baz should remember it.

Baz's smile faded, and he took a deep breath. Then, he started to sing.

The ghost cocked its awful head, but Lutie didn't scare easy, didn't scare hardly at all. *Screw this deadroads crap,* and instead, she did something almost the reverse. She didn't know how to make a deadroad, that was obvious. Who knew what would happen if she tried that again? She had to keep Lewis close, not send him away. *Luetta—ce n'est pas une rue, ma poussinette, c'est une porte.* Not a path, but a door. Mireille's ghost had resided within her mother, wasn't bound by a string, it was tucked inside, like a letter in an envelope. Lutie didn't need to make a road leading away from her; she needed to open a door within. *You need someplace to stay, Lewis?*

First though? First, she had to do what Sol had claimed to have done, what her father had royally screwed up: she had to cut a binding, because she sure as hell didn't want a ghost inside her that was also bound to a damn devil.

So. Feet apart, heartbeat of earth on the soles of her feet, reaching out, understanding the grip on Lewis, the wear of binding against its anger, raw wound from the shackles. This thing was bound and it was in pain— *you look after them, Luetta, that's all they want. Someone to look after them.* Lutie could do something about that, because the devil wasn't looking after Lewis, it was torturing the ghost. *M'boy,* like Lewis was its slave and maybe the ghost was, for all Lutie knew.

Lewis's ghost stared at her, unmoving, maybe not knowing what she was going to do. Not coming after her with that bat, anyway.

Lutie suddenly grinned. She wasn't the sort that Lewis in life had hated. Those had been men like Bart, or those other dead guys along the tracks from here to North Platte: they had been leaving, had been getting ready to catch out, and that had driven the ghost crazy. Easy to kill them. The ghost had gone for her brother Sol, who could not keep his eyes from following the trains, even now. Sol seemed steady, and was anything but. No wonder this ghost hated him, hardly even needed the devil to tell it as much.

"Hey, Lewis," she said to it, "I'm going to do you a favor." And the ghost looked surprised for a second, less charred, suddenly more whole.

Wound round him, felt with the same sense that connected her with the earth, Lutie found not a knot, but a growth, tendrils wrapped around the ghost's very bones, a living, sinuous binding of hate and pain. *No wonder it does the devil's bidding, bound like this.* Her anger was sharp and hot, and both things were needed to sever this bond.

It wouldn't take long, she didn't think, for the devil to notice.

One strike, her mind a laser, both burning and cutting, cauterizing, one slice, then—

Lewis turned, roared, in pain, in anger, hard to tell, and Lutie screamed as the club came down on her, missing her head, catching her shoulder. The ghost writhed like it burned, and maybe it did, but Lutie didn't stop. The bones of her left shoulder felt undone, in a state of not speaking to each other, simply screaming. But the binding between ghost and devil was frayed, and she had no time to consider what condition her shoulder was in. She had to do two things at the same time now: cut the last of it, and open a door, because a loose ghost wasn't going to bring back Sol, or Baz, but a bound ghost might. She didn't want the ghost, she didn't want *this* ghost, but Lewis had been to wherever Sol had gone, and it had come back. Maybe Baz had called it, maybe not, but if it knew where her brothers were, Lutie wasn't letting it go anywhere.

So: ignore the pain, cut the binding, unravel the last of the sticky threads. And then it was gone.

Howling, an inhuman, awful noise, lamb-gutting, rabbit-strangling, deer-dying sound—the devil's cry came from far-away, beyond usual senses, too distant to do anything, severed from its boy. The pain in her shoulder was just this side of bearable, and her job was unfinished still, but Lutie did it anyway: she smiled. She hated that thing, its black legs and its green poisonous gaze. The way it knew them, the way it had bargained with Baz, who didn't know any better, using his love against him. It had been instrumental in her father's death. It had hated him, and Lutie returned the favor on her father's behalf now.

The devil wasn't here, it had left the ghost to do its killing for it. The devil had strayed too far, and they were standing on the spot where Lewis had burned to death: it was a place of power. She hadn't killed the devil, but by severing its hold, she'd hurt it, anyone could tell, the sound it was making.

Lutie held very still, offering a way out, a path away from the pain the ghost had endured when it wore flesh, the burning hold that had been the devil's. The ghost didn't hesitate. Instead, it shook, a tremble of light and fog, and its form became more what it had been: a tall, tall man, full of anger and longing, a bat, an insatiable desire to crush masking a need for shelter. The ghost took the open door, passed through it and into her, banging around like a rat in an empty barrel. Breathless, Lutie shut the door behind it, locking it in, keeping it tight, safe.

She shuddered, once, as the ghost filled inside, buzzed along her nerves, swift as any intravenous drug given in a psych ward. Gasping, Lutie fell forward onto her hands and knees, retching, invasive foreign poison in her now. *Get a grip,* she told herself. *Get a grip, steady, it's yours, you don't belong to it.* She couldn't let Lewis take over, because she needed the ghost. She needed what it knew.

*I am stronger than Lewis. In every way.*

And she was. She was stronger. She had been raised with love, and with madness, and she needed both now. Deep breath, then she came to a queasy stand, arms wrapped around her middle. "Lewis," she whispered. "Lewis." She wasn't ready to give the ghost any free rein. She kept it close, and she could feel it turning within her. "Lewis, you tell me what I want to know, and I'll get my brother to sing for you. The good stuff, none of that lame sad shit."

It was enough, that promise. She felt Lewis still, go quiet, thoughtful. She didn't hear what it said, she felt it.

*Wait,* Lewis told her. *Wait.*

\* \* \*

*If I did what I'm supposed to, what Papa told me to do, I'd never let him.* But Sol was too gone, too wrung out, barely keeping it together in this between place. There was a certain appeal in letting go, in surrender. In letting Baz and Lutie handle things, for once. Baz was consulting the book in his hand, and Sol tilted his head so he could read the words, because he sure as hell didn't understand them the way Baz was butchering them.

A song about a bird, and a mill. Dancing. Anything with dancing, and the only thing that Sol knew his brother liked almost as well as singing was dancing. A fool for it, and good at it, of course, rhythm like he had. Sol remembered, so clearly he could almost smell warm cornbread cooling in the kitchen, their mother with arms around Baz, heads bent, eyes to their feet like they'd dropped something between them, Mireille teaching Baz steps.

A line to their past, to his past, to her. Here.

One verse, French murdered, but Sol didn't think it would matter. Their father had sung this song in his worn voice, and it had done something for him, called ghosts maybe. *He didn't call no angels with a voice like that.* The devil had to up the ante, needed Baz, not Aurie, to get an angel in the ring.

Which was his first clue about what would happen next, and what would happen after that: angel, then devil.

Baz swallowed, paused, started on the second verse. *I should stop him. This is too dangerous.* Visceral, his instinct to protect Baz, to get him out of harm's way, because that's exactly what the terrain between an angel and a devil would become, a killing ground.

It was too late, though, because the sky lightened to a washed-out yellow, pale as baby hair, and under his battered shoulder, Sol felt Baz shiver as though he'd caught a sudden chill.

"Stop," Sol said, amazed that his voice was no more than a whisper, considering he'd never meant anything so much in his life. "Please stop, Baz," but Baz couldn't hear him, Sol didn't even know if he'd managed to say it out loud.

All around, the landscape bloomed with light. Sol had the feeling that if he'd looked at his brother, he wouldn't see anything, couldn't see anything. He squinted, the light too bright, too much. As he took another scorched breath, ready to tell Baz to shut up, that he didn't care if they stayed here forever, his brother suddenly let go of Sol, and Sol dropped like a stone.

He came up on his arms almost immediately, white all around him. Shaking his head, he looked frantically around, could see nothing but glare. In the arms of an angel and who knew where they would set down next, or when. "Baz!" he shouted, panicking, trying to find his feet, get them under him, but there was nothing to push with, no strength in him. "Baz!" he called again, voice cracking, reverberating hollowly, the light swallowing his every sound. Gray lines crossed his vision like a hyped-up Etch-a-sketch, describing horizon line, up and up and over, down: tree. Line, and line, moving more quickly now—railway tracks. All strangely two-dimensional, all stripped of color and form, only monotone shape.

Almost home, almost back.

Sol opened his mouth to shout again, then heard it: skitchskitchraasp. Dragging of crustacean limbs over ground, smell of carbon heavy in his nostrils, clogging his lungs so that a denied cough punched his sternum like a physical blow. Sol covered his mouth, shivery breath against what was coming, because he could now feel cold earth beneath his prone body. Hip and shoulder and side were one solid scream of pain.

He'd have to deny that, too, for the moment, because the devil hadn't noticed him, and by the sound it was making—low groan, drag of body across gravel—it wasn't in great shape, either. Sol didn't try to guess why this might be, only that it was coming for the angel, and the angel had Baz, had his brother somewhere in its embrace, and that the only way to protect Baz was to protect the angel, which meant he had to get rid of the damn diable, le p'tit mauvais.

Hand to ground, wanting to find the beat of life, wanting connection. He ached with it. It came immediately, had been waiting, maybe years, for him to want it this badly. Now he dragged himself quietly to a kneel, ignoring everything that movement cost him. Fingers under his shirt, against his bare skin, heart loud against his trembling touch: *I open this road for you, devil, wherever it may take you.* His hand was shaking and he hoped it wouldn't matter. Up to his mouth and he closed his eyes, felt all the life around him, everything that ghosts and devils and angels were not. This was his; it was not for them, or of them. Life rushed through him, he merely a conduit for it as it changed, altered into an arrow, a direction made manifest. It burned and throbbed and he held it for one moment, full, then it came out, across his fingers, into the haze of light, lifting, lifting, shimmer brighter than even what the angel had brought, Baz's song lingering in the air like perfume, like oxygen.

The devil was suddenly right there, caught in shimmer, and it turned its head to Sol, close enough to touch, each scale and dripping gelatinous external organ lit by what the angel had caused to come. By what Sol had opened for it. It was half-dead already, Sol could tell, and with a twitch of his fingers, he brought the road around to the devil as the thing lunged toward him.

There was no sound, none at all, as the devil disappeared along Sol's road, its multiple legs folding in, cilia waving to no purpose at all. It was not looking at Sol, it was moved and moving too fast for that. Sol held his road, wanted to make sure the devil wouldn't fight its way back, claw along the pathway, shredding as it went.

Silence, no slither or rasp or scratch.

Then Sol felt his connection, the one he was holding, pull hard, as though the deadroad wanted him on it, too. He braced himself against the ground, shouting his pain, denying it and falling headfirst into it, white fading to dark gray, the landscape indistinguishable from soft dust, barely a horizon. *End it, end it, you moron*, and he straightened two fingers of his right hand, touched the ground, where he hoped the ground was, and tapped three times, releasing his hold as he did so—on the road he'd made, on the earth and all its life.

Like the rebound of a bungee jump, recoil of a powerful rifle, Sol was thrown back, slammed against something unforgivably hard, vision going crimson, fading to black. Then someone or something grabbed him by his coat, shook him, only a roaring in his ears, and he struggled against the hold, colder than he'd felt in years.

"Sol, Sol, *goddamn* it!" She sounded frantic, whoever she was, and Sol opened his eyes, but vision was too much, too much color, too much movement. He felt sick.

He tried to tell her to back off, not so close, then he thought: *Baz*.

Forcing open his eyes, he saw Lutie, near enough he could barely focus on her. He was sitting upright on the cold ground, leaning against—he turned his head in an effort to get his bearings. God, he was dizzy. Lutie's car. He was slumped against Lutie's car, his sister on her knees beside him, both fists in the shoulder of his parka.

"Stop shaking me, chère," he said, but it came out so quiet he didn't know if she heard it.

Apparently, yes, because she froze, hands still on him. Then she drew him against her, wrapped him in her arms, and he wished she would stop it, because he wasn't sure if he was going to throw up or not, but moving him around like that wasn't making him feel any better.

He got his hands up, finally, gently pushed her back a little so he could see her. Her face was pale, tear-streaked. "Where's Baz?" he asked, then he lifted a hand to the door handle, pulling himself up, holding onto the car, looking over the hood to the river, where he saw his brother, lying among the dead rushes, unmoving.

Only three steps before Lutie got Sol's arm over her shoulders, holding him up before he fell, and they staggered over to the riverside, where he stumbled to Baz's side, one hand going out like he was finding a connection. And he was, he realized, this was exactly what he was doing. One hand on Baz's chest, hoping to find life, and it was there, pressing up against his hand, making to leave, to vacate.

"No," Sol whispered, looking to Lutie, then back to Baz's still white face, eyes closed, no response. "No, you don't. J'te laisse pas faire ça, Basile. I don't let you do this," but so low, a murmur, nothing wrong with Baz, not physically, nothing for Sol to do but prevent him from dying.

Across Baz's body, Lutie laid her hand on top of Sol's. She was crying, Sol knew it, heard it, and one tear dropped on the back of her hand as she bent to kiss Baz on the forehead, fair hair covering his face.

Then the pressure subsided, as though it had changed its mind, and maybe it had, maybe Baz had. *Maybe he knows we're waiting on him,* Sol thought, as Baz took a shaky breath, eyes fluttering open, the color of sky and water combined. He coughed, Lutie clutching him as though he might jump up and run away. Sol fell back on elbows, then all the way down on frozen ground, staring at the Nebraska winter sky, blue.

Far in the distance, a train's whistle blew, two longs, short and a long. *Look out, coming through,* Sol thought, and started to laugh.

# TWENTY

## IMAGINING HOME

Lutie's Toyota rolled to a halt in the motel parking lot. Nobody moved, not for a long time, so long in fact that Baz thought maybe Sol had fallen asleep in the back seat. Better that they get inside the room before resting, but that would mean moving. He heard Sol clear his throat, heavy with what had set up shop there, and then the liquid sound of a dry tongue forming the first words Baz had heard from him. "It's gone. The devil."

Lutie set eyes straight ahead through the windshield, acted like she hadn't heard.

After a bit, Baz shifted in his seat, looked over his shoulder at Sol. Something lying dead at the roadside was in better shape. "Well. Excellent."

Sol started laughing, a little thin, too close to some edge. He soon stopped, catching his breath, knuckles caked with dried blood as he raised one hand to the Toyota's door handle. It lay there for a moment and Sol's mouth tensed as he pulled up, the door swinging out against his weight. Twisting round, he strained to see in the hard noon light, light that hid nothing, disguised none of what had happened to him. Finally, Lutie loosened her grip on the wheel, took a deep breath. "I took care of Lewis." She turned, stared at Sol. He wasn't smiling, he was concentrating on trying to move, Baz could see that. "That's one ghost gone."

302

She sounded very sure of herself.

Sol raised his head. "That's good. That's good, Lutie." Pride, maybe, was in there. Sadness, definitely. Baz didn't want to figure it out. Sol swallowed, and Baz looked away. "I'm gonna need a hand, getting out of the car."

Goddamn. Asking for help, so weird and surprising Baz hadn't seen it coming. *I should have seen it coming.* Without another word, Baz jumped out the passenger door, felt fine, felt good, like he was shiny from the inside. He could do this. Lutie was catatonic and Sol looked like he'd seen the business end of a wood chipper. That left Baz to take care of things, finally.

Lutie lurched out her door and together they got Sol into the room, deposited him on the bed. He asked for the medical kit and so Baz got it. First thing, Sol downed a glass of water. Another. Then one more, slowly, to swallow a bunch of pills from a variety of containers. Baz got ice from the gas station across the street. Sol checked Lutie's shoulder, made her hold out her arm, wiggle fingers, rotate like a pitcher. She didn't cry, even with the bruise. Ice pack. Painkillers. Then Sol saw to himself, but they were out of gauze, and out of tape, and out of butterfly bandages. Sol tossed paper onto the floor, sorting through empty wrappers for enough to suffice. The kit was almost as depleted as they were. Sol said as much.

Baz started laughing, slowly, and then Sol joined in and Lutie looked at them like they were both nuts. "You," she said, pointing at Sol, "You get to bed." Sol's laughter faded. She turned to Baz, "You make sure he gets to bed—"

"I heard you, Lutie." Sol chided, but softly.

"Put him to bed," like her radio wasn't tuned to Sol's station. She was crying now. "He needs to—"

"I know," Baz said quietly, putting an arm around her. "I know."

The numbers flashed by, calculating cost upwards, and Lutie was so tired she thought she could just lie down over the hood of her car, let the tank overflow, gasoline everywhere. Instead, she shook her head, kept her hand steady on the nozzle. Beside her, Baz unlatched the hood and lifted it, cocked his head, searching for the dipstick.

*Make him sing. Just one fuckin' song, just one song for me, girlie.*

The ghost wasn't great company, for starters, that hadn't helped her sleep. The fact that Lewis had smashed her shoulder hadn't made things easier either. Sol had slept for more than thirty-six hours, right around the clock and into the next day. Her? She'd had Lewis in residence for a day and a half, and she was scared to go to sleep: catnaps, dozing fitfully, waking, afraid. *Maybe I'll never sleep again.* The ghost was belligerent, which Lutie could have predicted, but also reticent, which she hadn't counted on. *What the hell was I expecting? An imaginary friend? A buddy to keep me company?* At the moment, and ever since she'd bound the ghost, she'd had to put up with its murmurings, musings, the muttered comments of a middle-aged man not well-versed in social graces, angry and unwilling to answer her questions, to interact with her on any level. Other than to swear at her.

Sol couldn't know. She'd decided that, driving back from the Megeath crossing. He'd warned her, it was the one thing he'd implored her not to do, and she'd done it. Caught a ghost. Not because she wanted to read fortunes, or to keep other ghosts away, but because she'd wanted her brothers back. Lewis had been her only lead, her only chance at redeeming the mess she'd made. Binding his spirit hadn't made a difference in the end; the angel and Baz's singing had gotten Sol back. Still, no regrets. Severing the devil's hold on Lewis had allowed Sol to put the devil on a deadroad, and that was one less thing to worry about. For Sol to worry about.

No way was she going to ask Sol to take care of this for her. Lewis had tried to kill her brother, more than once. It had almost succeeded. Lutie would handle Lewis herself. She would find a way.

*You got more than you bargained for, girlie, didn't ya?*

Lutie pressed the gas nozzle more securely, ignoring Lewis. The ghost twisted in her, suddenly thumped at her interior, rushed up her spine, trying to wrest control. Lutie concentrated on the dazzle of sunlight against her car's roof, stared so long and hard her eyes watered. Finally, she pushed the ghost down, like keeping the contents of her stomach in place. "Please tell me this gets easier," she whispered, not to herself, not to her dead mother. To Lewis, but the ghost did not answer.

"What's that?" Baz called, wiping the dipstick against a piece of torn paper towel, then lowering the hood, satisfied.

She shook her head, tried for a smile. "Nothing."

*Just one song, he can do it, just one.*

Baz edged closer, bent down, eyes sparkling in the midday light. Ants in his pants. "You sure about this?"

God, of course not. Of course she wasn't sure. How could she be? But she nodded anyway. "Yeah, it'll be good. I'll like having the company." Whether he would like her company was another matter. "Are *you* sure?" He glanced involuntarily at the Prairie Paradise Motel, across the intersection from the gas station. Lutie followed his gaze: the back of the Wagoneer was open, and Sol carried a box out of the room, placed it on the tailgate, his limp evident even from a distance. "He could probably use your help."

After a moment, Baz shook his head. "Nah. Some things I just can't fix." He hadn't said much about what had happened, after the white light. Neither had Sol. They'd been together, Baz had admitted that much, licking his lips nervously. Sol hadn't said anything, but then, he wouldn't. Now, Baz looked like he might say more, but then Lewis started nattering again, and Lutie brought her hand to her mouth, turned away. Collected herself. She heard Baz crumple the paper towel, and he brushed by her to put it in the bin. "Anyway. Toronto's gonna be fun. I have Dad's fiddle, a few hundred bucks, nothing keeping me here, that's for sure."

"Well, you can pay for the next fill up." Her voice was terse, trying to hold down Lewis, trying to have a conversation. "And if you're planning on staying in Toronto, you'll have to get dual citizenship. But that shouldn't be too hard."

He grinned, and a fierce burn started in Lutie, that he wanted to come with her, wanted to see where she lived, who her friends were, where she hung out. "Citizenship? I'm not planning on getting a job or anything." Just in case she'd gotten the wrong idea.

She nodded. "Yeah, I didn't think so."

"I'll get my things ready. See you back at the motel." She watched him go, his bouncing walk, running across the street, stopping a car with one hand and a tip of his fur-trimmed hat. *God, he's going to drive me nuts.* But he wasn't. She knew it.

She finished gassing up, noted the price, and went to the counter inside the station to pay the spotty attendant. There was awkward flirting on the kid's part, and Lewis hissed with covert amusement. She handed over her credit card and stared blankly at the boy behind the counter as he commented on the Canadian bank account, her accent, why was she here anyway. He wasn't even really looking her in the face, eyes roaming all over, checking her out, searching for a pen. She signed quickly, tried to ignore Lewis's filthy suggestions about the kid, about what they could do in a locked roadside bathroom.

If the attendant noticed she was odd, was shaking, it didn't deter his enthusiasm for the chase. Even his parting words, "Come again," sounded grotesque to her. She turned on the ignition, jammed the car into gear, and crossed the intersection back to the motel.

"I am getting rid of you, first chance," she said out loud, firm as she could manage. A raw chuckle reverberated in her ears.

*You can try. I'd like to see you try.* Cut the ghost away, and it would turn on her. She knew that. Sol had told her. She parked the car, slid out, wished she could leave Lewis behind as easily.

At the moment, Sol was too beat up to notice the ghost. He had woken earlier that morning, swallowed a bunch of painkillers with juice that Lutie had brought, ate a stale muffin, then another. He was at the motel room doorway now, in shadow, but she felt his eyes on her, a smile slowly coming over him as she slammed the Toyota's door. Sol had made it his mission to sever fortunetellers from their spirits. *Does harboring this jerk make me a fortuneteller?* Maman had read tarot cards, tea leaves. Lutie didn't know how all that worked, it wasn't something that Mireille had ever showed her. *Isn't psychology just modern fortunetelling?*

"You got enough gas to get you out of this one-horse town?" he asked as she approached. Lewis was quiet within her, wary. The ghost knew what Sol could do, Lutie guessed, wasn't looking for a fight, or to get severed.

She nodded. "Yep, fill up costs less than a case of beer." Met his curious gaze, but only for a moment. "Value for money in this country." She came around the back and opened the trunk of her Toyota for Baz's gear, came back around. She leaned against the car, Sol still watching her. *Over to you, Mr. Inquisitive.* "Sure we can't talk you into seeing a doctor?"

He looked away with a short strangled laugh. He was wearing a dark hoodie with a firefighter's fun run logo on the front, fetched from some-where in the back of the Wagoneer, covered in dog hair. Out of laundry, time to go home, he'd joked. Past check-out time now, the manager would be coming by any minute, looking to collect another night if they weren't careful. Sol checked over his shoulder, and moved out of the way to let Baz through.

It was too early to know exactly what had changed between them, but Lutie saw that Baz was less deferential, more forthright about what he was thinking, what he was wanting. For example, this morning Baz hadn't backed down when he'd told Sol he was going to Toronto, even though Sol had tilted his head, put one hand on his hip and sighed mightily. Baz hadn't tried to razzle-dazzle with explanation, he hadn't bent under Sol's understated 'hasn't she had enough of us?' stare. Finally, Sol had simply shrugged.

Not quite giving up, but letting things go when a fight wasn't necessary, wasn't winnable.

Sol had finished packing, but would see them off like it was his duty and maybe it was. He wasn't the one who did the leaving, Lutie realized. A point, with him. Baz passed by her on the way to the trunk, swinging his duffle bag, hip checking her into the car, grinning, promising trouble. He slammed the back, just one bag and the fiddle, not taking the box, giving that to Sol to take care of. He walked slowly back to the motel doorway, empty-armed, and stood in front of Sol.

Baz cleared his throat. "We could come with you."

Sol scratched his chin. "Jesus, Baz, I don't need you to come with me. I'm not made of sugar." He flexed his hand, rolled his shoulder slightly. "Besides, the chief is gonna take one look at me and it'll be the desk for the rest of the week. Sit on my ass and drink coffee, that's about it."

She heard Baz chuckle. "Think you can manage that?"

Sol didn't quite smile, but his glance slid past Baz's shoulder and met Lutie's eyes. "You don't let him behind the wheel, T-Lu. He's an accident waiting to happen. And he don't have a license, either."

Baz's eyebrows shot up. "Merde, Sol. I can't let la p'tite soeur drive me everyplace."

Lutie sighed. "Sure you can. It's my car, and I know the way." She smiled, hard. Despite her hurt shoulder and the bound ghost, it *would* be fun, everything would be an adventure now. Baz's very existence seemed to promise that. And when he sang, Lewis calmed right down. She could do this.

The brothers didn't hug, it wasn't like that. Baz laid a hand on Sol's shoulder, softly, told him to drive safe, say hi to Robbie for him, that he'd phone, he'd be back to pick up the rest of his stuff soon. Sol had a careworn expression that told Lutie he'd heard it all before. Same. Different, because he didn't even make an effort to open his mouth in argument, in disagreement.

Sol did move slightly to see around Lutie as Baz retreated into the white car, nodding to him as though Baz had made some face, then attention back to Lutie as the door slammed shut, sub-compact tinny. He considered her without speaking. Waiting was okay, really. Lewis was so still, Lutie couldn't feel the ghost within her, could only feel the great weight of not wanting to leave. "It's a long drive," she said.

"You should get going then, chère."

She couldn't look at him. Instead, she dug in her large purse, pulled out what she'd removed from the cardboard box back in Minneapolis the week before, when she thought she'd never see these guys again. She'd stolen from her brothers, from her father, when she still thought of them as the enemy. Baz hadn't been looking. It was easy to take advantage of Baz, and it felt cheap now.

She handed the photograph to Sol, who took it, glanced down quickly, would have glanced back up, but he checked himself, kept his eyes on the picture. Their mother, their father. The Caraquet Festival, 1980. When things had started, wheel in motion.

Lutie cleared her throat, tried to explain. "Aurie had it at Jean-Guy's place. I think you should keep it." He already had most of their father's other things—his clothes, his fake IDs. The ring, the blue songbook. Why not this too?

Sol turned it over, looked at the inscription, ran one finger over his mother's handwriting as though that brought her closer, like he was touching her, this vestige of her. Finally, he looked back up. He was still too unknown for Lutie to name what was moving in his dark eyes, but it wasn't anger. His lips parted like he wanted to say something, give some kind of explanation or ask a question. Closed. Open, shut. He dropped his attention to the photo again, overcome. He held their parents in his hands, together.

After a long moment, he said, "You look like her," like he was noticing it for the first time. He nodded as though confirming it. "You're like her." Said it because he wanted her to know it.

Lutie raised both eyebrows. "That's a good thing?"

And then Sol did the unthinkable: voluntarily, he stepped forward and put his arms around her, not tightly, but enough that she knew he meant it. One arm high, the hurt one low, keeping in mind her own injured shoulder. He smelled of engine oil, and dog, and ash. Into her hair, he whispered, "Yeah, that's a good thing."

Lutie pulled away first, didn't look behind her at the car, rubbed her nose with a gloved hand, wished that she hadn't a ghost in tow, because she didn't want to hurt Sol. *I don't want to disappoint him.* But Sol, now smiling quietly, not so widely that his teeth showed, wasn't going to find out, she reminded herself. She was going to ditch this ghost, she just had to figure out how.

He was still leaning against the open door as she pulled out of the motel's parking lot, framed by darkness, and he lifted his hand as they went, waving when he must have thought she wouldn't see.


The radio remained off for the entire trip back, sun in his eyes the whole damn way, visor down, sunglasses on, flatlands mounding into hills eventually, every mile taken on the interstate, making good time. He exited the main highway at the airport, heading into Aurora just in time for rush hour.

Sol had avoided stopping along the way, mostly because he wanted to get back in time to have a decent sleep before his morning shift, but also because it was Tuesday, by his reckoning, and Robbie has just had a long weekend without him, no explanation. He'd found his phone under the motel room's desk, but the battery was drained and damned if he'd brought any kind of recharger with him. He could have stopped somewhere, grabbed a coffee and used a pay phone, but he could barely walk and didn't want to tempt fate. *I could have phoned her.* He'd be home soon enough, so what was the point?

*The point? I'm chickenshit and I don't want to be chewed out once over the phone, then when I get home. That's the point.*

The evening commute was complicated by a pile-up on the I-70, and as Sol inched past the clean-up crew, ambulances long gone, troopers directing traffic, he checked for ghosts, force of habit. Most days, he wasn't above pulling over, asking the crew if they needed any further help, just so he could send some new ghosts on their way before they got too stuck.

This time, though, there was nothing. Either no one had died or they'd died and gone. Nothing for him to do and he was glad for it, because no way would he have been able to make a deadroad, not today.

*Jesus, I should just mind my own business.*

He knew that Baz would probably sing all the way to Toronto and that Lutie would be regretting her decision to bring him right about the time they hit Chicago, but he figured that they'd work that out between them. It didn't wear at him, the decision to do nothing. *See*, he told himself, *I'm learning.* Since traffic was bumper to bumper, wasn't even inching forward at this point, Sol glanced at the photo Lutie had given him.

Aurie looked so young. They both did. They were. They had been. *Younger than me now, there*, Sol thought. *I wonder if you knew what you were getting yourself into, old man?* But he couldn't ask questions like that and not drive himself crazy. Maman was so serious, grave. He remembered that about her, that it had been like pulling teeth to get her to laugh. Baz could do it. Baz had always been able to do it. *At least one of us could.* He put the photograph back on the passenger seat, tapped the steering wheel, imagining the feel of the doorknob in his hand, the shape of it.

Imagined coming home.

Once past the accident, traffic moved a little better, and he was going against the main stream of it anyway. He turned south again, sun now coming obliquely from the side window, orange over the Front Range, and he wound through the bungalow-lined streets, some garbage cans already at the curb for morning collection. He'd have to remember to bring out the trash, a physical chore that he'd be hard pressed to manage in his condition. *Let it slide, Sarrazin. Some things you can let go.* How he was going to function at work tomorrow was beyond him, and he had no idea what his shifts were past the next one, but he had the feeling that he'd agreed to a whole bunch in a row, maybe even a double shift to make up for the time off this last weekend. A desk for the next few days sounded pretty damn good, but not as good as his own bed.

The streetlights came on as he found parking and killed the engine. He sat for a moment, road vibration buzzing through his system like a drug. *Move*, he coached himself. *Move and don't seem all beat up, 'cause Robbie'll have a fit.* He looked at his house: post-war bungalow, nothing special, buff clapboard, front door with three small rectangular windows descending like they were coming down a staircase. Patchy snow on the ground and the place had never seemed so precious and welcoming. The curtains were all drawn and the chainlink gate was ajar.

He opened his door and levered himself out, went to the back of the truck and retrieved the cardboard box of his father's things, placed the photo on top. He shut and locked the Wagoneer, willed himself to walk—slowly, stiffly—up the path. Steps one by one and she would hear him now if she hadn't before.

He held the storm door open with his body, key in hand, trying to figure out how to balance the box and turn the key at the same time. He wondered if he should ring the bell, get Robbie to open up, but that would be admitting his state, and he wasn't quite ready to do that, to himself or to her. Necessity was the mother of invention: he pinned the box against the storm door with his hip, and got the key in the lock.

The knob was as he'd imagined it, felt good and right in his hand.

Just at the same time as he turned the knob and hefted the box back into his grasp, a small internal voice, distant and vaguely childlike, asked, *Where's the dog, Sol?*

Where's the dog, and the door swung open into darkness.

Carefully putting the cardboard box on the floor, Sol couldn't disguise the moan of pain that caused him, but he knew he didn't need to worry about being stoic for Robbie, because she wasn't home. He clicked on the living room light. *She's taking him for a walk*, he told himself in response. Not bothering with his boots, he took off his parka, made to throw it on the chair. He stopped himself mid-motion, because the chair wasn't there. Robbie's mid-century Danish armchair that she'd bought at a yard sale last year was gone.

He didn't panic.

Instead, he dropped the parka on top of the box, shut the door behind him and collected himself, but his heart was going fast, too fast for this to be reasonable, for this to be normal. He could see the whole house from where he was, light from the living room illuminating the things missing, like he was looking at one of those kid's puzzles in a magazine: Can you spot five differences between the two pictures?

There were more than five changes between what Sol had left and what he'd come back to. Gone: the Danish chair, Renard's bowls, the vintage toaster that didn't work but that looked fantastic, photos of her nieces and nephews on the mantelpiece. Slowly, he surveyed the rest of the house, looking for that which was not there. From the closet in their bedroom: all her clothes, all her shoes. The kitchen: a bag of dog food, the fancy muesli she liked for breakfast, a half-empty box of chocolates a friend had given her for Christmas and that he'd been forbidden from touching. The bathroom: her perfume, the box of cotton balls, her toothbrush, a package of tampons, the contents of two drawers where she kept her hairclips, hairspray, brushes, makeup. All of it.

After a half hour, Sol came back to the living room. He'd found evidence of her—a sweater that she'd missed, huddled in with his, a stocking in the dirty laundry basket. He didn't bother disguising his limp now, but before he sank into the chair at the kitchen table—he'd bought that on his own, he remembered, twenty bucks from a firefighter moving out of state—he grabbed the bottle of rum from the top shelf, took down a chipped mug from the cupboard. Three mugs, neatly divided because there had been six and Sol couldn't remember when they'd come into the house and maybe Robbie hadn't been able to remember either.

He poured himself half a mug, took an enormous mouthful. On the table was a folded piece of paper, her hand naming him on the outside fold, loop and loop of the 'S' curved like a river going nowhere. He didn't touch her note, left it exactly where it was. The only reason the letter wasn't a ring was because he hadn't given her a ring. The only ring he had made was around her, circling without landing.

He had come home, in the end, and it was nothing like he'd imagined.

# ACKNOWLEDGEMENTS

Fittingly enough, this all started in a bar. I first heard Barde's version of the traditional folksong *Les trois hommes noirs* at the University of Victoria's pub; the tune haunted me and haunts this story.

It's impossible to write about heading west and catching out without tipping my hat to Kerouac's *On the Road,* Jon Krakauer's *Into the Wild* and Richard Grant's *American Nomads,* all of which shine a light about what it means to belong and the need to get lost.

Huge *bisous* to Marilou Gosselin for minding my wayward Franglais and to Suzanne Hicks in Lafayette for sharing with me the finer points of modern Cajun. Gillian Cross guided me through stab wounds, cardiac arrests and EMT party tricks. Christina Pilz became my eyes on the ground in Denver and Nebraska. Sandi and Dennis Jones made me feel like I was a writer. Joy Temple gave me beer and an ear when I needed it. Celine Kiernan set the bar higher. But mostly, my Eeyore and my Tigger, Janice Morrison and Elizabeth Sisson, who cheer, weep and berate. All that is right is theirs; all mistakes are mine.

My agent Sandy Lu kept spirits from flagging and believed in *Deadroads* even when I thought it was officially a lost cause. Ross E. Lockhart and Cory Allyn guided the manuscript down the messy corridors of publication with humor and aplomb.

I keep a foot in two worlds, and without my wonderful families on both sides of the adoption divide, I couldn't have written of familial fractures and delicate rapprochements with any sense of veracity. I thank them for their openess.

Finally and always, Genevieve, Charlie, and beloved Aaron never doubted I could.

Photo credit: Lizz Sisson

# ABOUT THE AUTHOR

Born in Ottawa and raised on Canada's west coast, Robin Riopelle's life has been marked by adoption, separation, and reunion. Like many of her characters, she has a muddy past, and a foot in (at least) two different worlds. She's always had interesting work in museums and social service agencies. Some things she has done while collecting a paycheck:

- told unsuspecting people the whereabouts of a long-lost family member,
- go-go danced in front of 700 people,
- traipsed across a wind-whipped hospital rooftop with a nun,
- lost a frozen beaver head under a parked car.

Robin Riopelle is the author's birthname. She currently lives on the border between French and English Canada with her criminologist husband, two seemingly delightful children, and an obstreperous spaniel.

In addition to writing fiction for adults, Riopelle also illustrates children's books. *Deadroads* is her first novel.